DISCIPLES OF DREAD

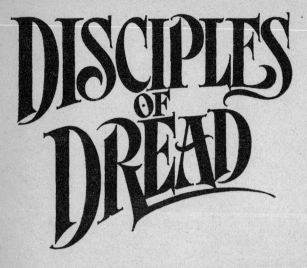

HUGH B. CAVE

A TOM DOHERTY ASSOCIATES BOOK
NEW YORK

DISCIPLES OF DREAD

Copyright © 1988 by Hugh B. Cave

A TOR Book
Published by Tom Doherty Associates, Inc.
49 West 24 Street
New York, NY 10010

Cover art by Lee MacLeod

ISBN: 0-812-51648-6   Can. ISBN: 0-812-51649-4

Library of Congress Catalog Card Number: 88-19231

First edition: September 1988
First mass market edition: August 1989

Printed in the United States of America

0 9 8 7 6 5 4 3 2 1

For Peggie, with love

Prologue

The restaurant was crowded. Probably all the nice ones in the city were busy at this hour, Maria told herself. Her escort smiled as they were led to a table close to the salad bar.

He had not requested such a table. All he had done, so far as Maria knew, was stare into the eyes of the hostess when she greeted them.

He was not Mexican. With his lithe figure and handsome olive-hued face, he could have been a movie star from some exotic land in the Middle East. Amazing. Because she was only a manicurist. In fact, she had done his nails that morning at the hotel where she worked and he was a guest.

She still did not understand why she had said yes that morning when Kalim invited her to dinner. She had a boyfriend. She loved her boyfriend. She and Juan had even set the date on which to be married.

1

But this man now smiling at her across their restaurant table, this Kalim with the last name she found all but unpronounceable, had somehow made her forget Juan.

Now he was doing it again—with his eyes, his hypnotic smile, with something that reached into her mind and commanded her to stop thinking about anything or anyone but himself.

All right. She would worry about it later. "Yes," she said, looking around the restaurant crowded with elite Mexicans and well-dressed tourists. "Yes, yes, it's lovely."

He hadn't said a word, yet she had answered him.

A waiter in glistening black pants and a red silk shirt stopped beside their table and handed them red-velvet-covered menus. "You would like something from the bar, perhaps?"

With the penetrating gaze of her companion fixed on her, Maria quickly said, *Gracias, no.* Now, why, without even thinking, had she done that? She and Juan always had margaritas when they dined out, if only to bring back the joyous memory of their first evening together.

Her companion smiled at her.

"You wish to order, then?" the waiter asked.

Kalim ordered. As if able to read her mind, he ordered *chimichanga* for both of them. Her favorite dish, though she and Juan could seldom afford it. "And," he said to the waiter, "we'll go to the salad bar also, of course." He spoke what Maria thought of as "Mexican" fluently.

The waiter thanked them and went away.

"Come." Kalim extended a smooth, long-fingered

hand across the white cloth. "I'm famished!" At the salad bar he handed her a plate and motioned her to go ahead of him.

It was a very long salad bar. The longest in the city, perhaps. No, if it were that, the menu would surely boast about it. But still it was long, with a lineup of bowls and trays that caused her to turn to her companion with an exclamation of delight.

Strange. She hadn't noticed before that he was left-handed. But he rather awkwardly held his plate in his right hand between thumb and forefinger, with the rest of his hand cupped under it, and was spooning peppers onto it with his left. And as he did so, a white powder dribbled from the fingers curled under the plate into a bowl of guacamole.

Preoccupied with what he was doing, he bumped into her and glanced up. "Go on!" he said sharply, though there was no one behind him, in fact no one but the two of them at the salad bar just then, even though the restaurant was crowded. Perhaps that explained his wanting to get to it in such a hurry.

Feeling the impatience in his voice, she passed up some delicious-looking coleslaw and some brilliantly red pickled beets, both favorites she surely would have taken, before risking another backward look at him.

Again he held the plate awkwardly between thumb and forefinger while spooning something onto it. And again a fine white powder trickled from his curled fingers under the plate into a bowl of food.

What was he doing?

She had halted without meaning to. She was staring at him. He looked up this time before bumping

3

into her, and suddenly she knew he was angry. Suddenly she knew she must leave the salad bar and return to their table. At once. Without a word of remonstrance. Without even a question.

His eyes were telling her. Or his mind again, reaching deep into hers with a command she could not challenge.

Plate in hand, she obediently turned and hurried back to her chair, leaving him to continue alone at the salad bar. He was still the only one there. Frightened and bewildered, wondering why she had ever accepted his invitation in the first place, she sat there statue-still and watched him.

Suddenly a man appeared at her side, frowning down at her and placing a hand on the table in such a way that she could not have risen had she tried to. "Sit." His voice was low but commanding; Maria would never have dared disobey such a voice. Yet he wore only an ordinary dark suit, white shirt, and a tie, not a uniform. He looked American.

She gazed up at him with apprehension, knowing now she never should have come here with Kalim. Something was terribly wrong. First Kalim, with his strange power to make her do everything he wanted. Now this. But except for keeping his hand on the table, the American seemed no longer interested in her. He had turned his head to gaze at the salad bar.

She looked that way, too, and saw something that made her gasp. Two other men had suddenly appeared there, one facing Kalim, the other a few paces behind him. They, too, were quietly dressed. Still holding his plate, which was now laden with food, Kalim had frozen in his tracks.

4

All at once he flung his plate onto the bar, where it crashed against something and made a noise that could be heard all through the restaurant. Then he whirled on one foot, away from the man facing him, obviously meaning to run. But that brought him face-to-face with the one behind him.

He froze again, gazing down at something that glinted in this man's hand. He looked up at the man's face. Then he laughed. Yes, it was a laugh, showing his wonderfully white teeth. With an exaggerated shrug he spread his hands out, palms up, in a gesture that seemed to say, "All right, so you've caught me."

Maria thought of the white powder that had dribbled from his half-hidden hand onto the various items in the salad bar. *Caught him doing what?*

The taller of the two Americans had Kalim firmly by an arm now. One hand held the arm above the elbow while the other thrust the glinting gun against Kalim's side. This was the American in charge, Maria decided. He was in his thirties, neither good-looking nor ugly, but obviously very fit and competent. He had a rather scraggly, reddish brown beard.

The second man was wiping Kalim's outstretched palm with a handkerchief, which he then folded and thrust into his jacket pocket. Producing handcuffs from another pocket, he snapped them shut on Kalim's wrists.

The sound of the cuffs clicking was clearly audible at this point, so quiet was the restaurant. All those people at all those tables . . . and yet the place was like a church, Maria thought. Everyone was watching what was happening. And now the American leader called out a name, and a man who was probably the manager of the restaurant came hurrying forward.

"Close off the salad bar." The American spoke English but Maria understood him; to work with tourists in a good hotel you had to know at least some English. And though his voice was not loud, exactly, it could be heard all through the place.

Addressing the customers next, he made it louder. "No one is to go near the salad bar. Is that clear? Does everyone understand? This man has poisoned the food here."

You could hear a gasp all through the restaurant. Then one big collective sucking in of breath as the manager repeated the statement in Spanish.

"What you are eating at present is all right," the man went on, with the Mexican translating. "Perfectly safe, so don't worry. And of course any food from the kitchen is safe. It's only just now he did it." In a low voice he said something more to the manager. Maria was just close enough to hear "Rope it off" and "Don't destroy the food here . . . Needed for evidence . . . We'll have the police here in a few minutes." Then he and his partner led Kalim away, and the man standing beside Maria's table said to Maria, "All right, you. Come with me."

Relieved to be out of that place, Maria did not even protest.

At the far end of the parking lot were two police cars. Four uniformed officers got out of them as the Americans approached with Kalim and herself. The American leader spoke to them and they hurried into the restaurant. She and her American got into one car, Kalim and his two into the other. Both machines were driven by policemen.

As usual, the city traffic was a stampede at that hour, and noisy. But Maria would have made no effort to begin a conversation, anyway, she was too frightened, and the man at her side remained grim-lipped and silent. The journey ended at a police station, where Maria was led into a back room that contained only a single massive desk and several ugly straight-backed chairs.

Moments later Kalim and his two escorts walked in. And finally a policeman, an officer of some kind, judging by his uniform, marched in and sat behind the desk like a judge in a courtroom. A judge with big shoulders and a thick neck and a bristling black mustache.

On seeing that this man was Mexican, Maria felt less terrified. The city police were not always gentle, she had heard, but at least they were her own kind of people. Why, she kept asking herself, had she ever agreed to go to dinner with a man like Kalim, a foreigner about whom she knew nothing at all? It was not like her to be so stupid.

An American emptied Kalim's pockets and placed their contents on the desk in front of the Mexican. From where she sat Maria could see a wallet, a key to a hotel room, some loose change, a pen, and a small plastic bag filled with a white powder. The American leader stepped forward and picked up the wallet. With care he examined it.

"Anything, Vin?" asked the man who had emptied Kalim's pockets.

The leader shook his head. "Anything here would be phony, anyway."

He motioned Kalim to one of the wooden chairs, and when Kalim seemed reluctant to sit, Vin pushed him. Then Vin said, scowling at him, "Well, what have you to say for yourself?"

"Say?" Seated there like a child facing a ring of teachers in a schoolroom, Kalim smiled as though it were a game he enjoyed playing. "Nothing."

"You're one of Khargi's people. You deny it?"

"Khargi? Who is Khargi?"

"Give me patience," the American said. "All right, we'll play your game if it will help any. Khargi, friend, is top man of the organization you work for, the Disciples. Khargi is the man who trained you in mind control, hypnotism, and all your other nasty talents. At least, he applied the fine edge. And Khargi is the man who assigned you to poison the food in that restaurant tonight, to kill maybe dozens of innocent people as one of the many acts of terrorism you people are carrying out all over this screwed-up world."

"I have never heard of this Khargi." Kalim shrugged, then smiled again. "Or of your Disciples."

"Then why did you poison the food at that salad bar?"

"Why did I what?"

"Listen, creep." The voice of the American named Vin was a snarl now; his hands were clenched. "We've been watching you ever since the immigration people at the airport put the finger on you. They had photos of a man suspected of doing this in Buenos Aires. Does that refresh your memory?"

"I must have a look-alike," Kalim said—as easily as if he had been asked the time of day.

The Mexican at the desk held up the plastic bag of white powder. "What is this?" he demanded.

Again Kalim shrugged. "Test it. Find out before you accuse me further."

"You could save time by telling us," Vin said. "We'll find out, anyway."

"You say 'we,' Mr. Donner. I suppose you mean Argus."

The American leader's bearded face registered surprise, then warped into a fierce scowl. "What do you know about Argus?"

"Oh, something. As you know something about the Disciples."

It was like a movie, Maria thought. Because Kalim was handsome in the way movie stars were handsome, and though a prisoner here, he was wholly undaunted, even enjoying himself. She watched Kalim and waited expectantly through half a moment of silence, and then Kalim spoke again.

"So now we are to play *your* game, eh, Mr. Donner? Well, why not? What do I know about Argus? Only what I have heard, of course. Heaven forbid I should have come by any information firsthand."

He paused. His gaze passed from Donner's face to that of the second American and then the third. The Mexican officer behind the desk apparently did not interest him. "Argus," he said, again with his delightfully eloquent shrug, "is an organization set up by your government, Mr. Donner—that is to say, the government of the imperialist United States of America—to deal with these Disciples you have been telling me about: this group of nameless people under the tutelage of the great mind-master Khargi that is terrorizing—your word, of course—that is terrorizing the world. That is, Argus is to deal with the Disciples before Khargi turns his attention to the United States, as he has vowed to do soon."

He paused again. Smiled again. Looked at all his listeners and then returned his gaze to the American leader. "You, I believe, Mr. Donner—Mr. Vincent Donner—are a former agent of the American CIA with certain talents of your own. But I think you are still very much an amateur."

The three Americans exchanged glances, obviously not happy with this new development. Maria could only stare again at the bearded man called Vincent Donner. Again she guessed he was in his thirties. Late thirties, perhaps. Manicurists knew these things. And again she decided he was not handsome but not bad-looking, either. She had seen men as old as he, and built like him, confronting the bulls at the Plaza de Toros and still winning thunders of *"Olé"* from the crowds.

The Mexican behind the desk was holding up the bag of white powder. "You will have this examined, Señor Donner?"

"In the States." Donner reached for the bag and put it into his pocket.

"You will be returning tonight?"

"Our plane is ready. Yes."

"Taking him with you, of course."

"And the woman." Donner turned to frown at Maria. "Though I doubt—"

Kalim had leaned forward on his chair. "She is

nothing," he protested, and looked at Maria with a shake of his head as though apologizing to her. "A manicurist at my hotel, that is all. You must know that a man would not dine in such a restaurant alone."

"He probably speaks the truth about her," the Mexican said. "Still—"

"Yes, still." The American, Vincent Donner, also looked at Maria now. "But we won't have time to question her here, Lieutenant. She can be sent back if she knows nothing."

Kalim said, "Please, I beg of you—"

"Sorry." Vincent Donner moved toward the chair in which Kalim was seated. "Up. It's time to go."

"May I ask what is to happen to me?"

"A ride to Washington, in a better airplane than anyone like you ought to expect. Then, since you're the first of your murderous gang we've been able to get our hands on, I'd anticipate some pretty ungentle questioning. We're going to want to know more about this Khargi character who trained you all— who keeps you at top strength with his psychic input or whatever it is—and we're going to want to know a whole lot about the Mediterranean monster, Aram Sel of Siricus, who puts up the oil money for all this."

"Surely you jest."

"Do I? Aram Sel is your real employer. You know it."

"Tell me what else I know. Can you, Mr. Donner?"

"We'll tell you in Washington. Believe it, brother. Now, damn you, get up!"

Oh God, Maria thought. Oh Jesus, Mary, and

Joseph, what have I got myself into here? Why did I ever go out with this Kalim or whatever his real name is? Now they'll take me to some American prison until I can prove I'm innocent, if I'm ever able to do so. God knows when I'll get home again. I'll lose my job. Juan will kill me for being unfaithful.

Hating Kalim with a passion, she tried to tell him so by fiercely glaring at him, even though her eyes had filled with tears.

Kalim only smiled back—the same confident smile she had seen all during the evening. Then, still seated, he lifted his head to direct his gaze at Vincent Donner.

"Mr. Donner"—his voice was almost inaudible—"I have been told *you* have powers. I wonder how true it is."

"Get up!" Donner snapped.

"Make me, Mr. Donner."

A strange thing happened then. The two men stared at each other as though the gaze of each was a magnet holding the gaze of the other, Kalim in his chair looking up, Donner, standing, looking down. And though not a word more was spoken—though it all happened in a kind of terrible silence with the Mexican watching amazed from behind his desk and the other two Americans seemingly mesmerized into immobility—Maria knew for certain that a monumental battle was going on. A struggle not of the combatants' eyes, though the eyes seemed likely to burst into flames at any moment, but of the minds behind the eyes.

The terrible silence continued and the conflict went on and on, as though it would never end—or perhaps could only end with both men dead of exhaustion. Then at long last the American took a backward step, and another, and the desk blocked his retreat. And one of the other two Americans walked like a zombie to the desk and leaned over it to pick up the key to Kalim's handcuffs. And the third American took the key from him, in a kind of slow-motion ballet, and went to Kalim and removed the cuffs from Kalim's wrists.

Then, only then, did Kalim stand up.

He looked at Vincent Donner and smiled.

"You see, Mr. Donner," he said softly, "you still have much to learn."

He walked over to Maria and touched her on the cheek. And as she sat there gazing up at him, almost in a trance herself, she tried to recall what the American, Vincent Donner, had said about the organization Kalim was accused of belonging to. Khargi's people. The Disciples. Trained in mind control, hypnotism, "and all your other nasty talents." She knew what hypnotism was. She and Juan had even been to a theater once and seen it done on the stage, the man in the black cape putting a young fellow from the audience to sleep and then having him do things that he didn't remember afterward. But mind control? What was mind control?

Was this it—the ghastly thing that had happened to Donner and the other two Americans and also to the Mexican behind the desk?

Donner still leaned back against the desk, but stared into space now. His eyes were still wide open but were twitching, as though he wanted desperately to close them but could not. His hands on the desk edge twitched, too, like a pair of crabs scrabbling to run away but unable to. And now his mouth was open and he fought so hard for breath that sweat fairly spurted from his face.

Kalim said, "Turn around, please, Donner, and pick up the lieutenant's gun." Was he saying this aloud? Maria asked herself. Or was it only something her mind was hearing? In any case, like a puppet manipulated with strings by someone invisible, Donner obeyed the order.

"When I am gone," Kalim continued in the same mysterious way—either with his voice or with his mind alone—"you will give me five minutes to be safely out of the building, and then you will use that weapon. Or your own, if you like; it doesn't matter to me in the least. And you will use it on yourself. *On yourself, Mr. Donner.* Do you understand?"

Donner's mouth quivered open as though to reply, but he was incapable of speech.

Kalim let his gaze travel almost casually now from Donner to the other two Americans to the Mexican. "None of you will interfere to stop this," Maria heard him say—either with her ears or with her mind. "Do *you* understand?"

Only the police officer responded. In a whisper he said, "*S-sí, señor.*"

Kalim then turned to Maria. "Señorita, I thank you for a pleasant evening." He smiled and shrugged at the same time. "I regret any inconvenience I have caused you."

Had he actually said this aloud? No matter, she could not respond, anyway. Her voice would not function.

"The police will let you go when they have questioned you," he said. "Don't worry. I am sure your Juan will forgive you." Then he walked over and kissed her on the cheek before turning, for the last time, to the man named Donner.

What he pressed upon the face of Vincent Donner was not a kiss. It was a cruel slap with his open right hand, followed by a stream of spittle that struck the man's right eye and dribbled down over the flush left by the slap. Then, no longer a handsome movie hero but a creature one could only hate and loathe, he turned to the door.

Still, as he opened the door and peered along the hall before stepping over the threshold, Maria knew she would not cry out to summon help. He had left a command in her head not to. And a glance at the others told her that they, too, would make no move.

This was mind control?

The door closed behind him. No one in the room had stirred. She looked at the man called Donner. Five minutes, Kalim had said. "Then you will use that weapon on yourself." If only she could rise from her chair and take the gun out of his hand!

With all her might she tried. But Kalim had ordered her—not in words, but with his mind—not to interfere.

Five minutes. Three hundred seconds. She began to count. She would have thought it a very short time, but it was not. The counting took forever. And all the time she continued her desperate struggle to go to him, to help him, but was as much a part of her chair as the wood it was made of.

Oh God, she thought, help him, and saw a movement in the hand holding the weapon. The hand shook. He, Vincent Donner, had stopped staring into space at nothing and lowered his head to look down at the gun. Maria's counting had become mechanical. Two hundred eighty. Two hundred eighty-one. Was she counting too slowly? Were the five minutes up?

"No!" she silently screamed. "No! Don't!"

The gun was higher now. His right arm was bent at the elbow and the weapon was level with his chest, creeping up toward his head. His whole body trembled. The sound of his breathing was a storm in the room. Sweat ran down his tortured face in rivers.

But now his *left* hand came up. It gripped his right wrist to stop the gun's upward motion. The battle within him had transferred itself to his hands.

No one else in the room had moved. They stared at him, transfixed, like people in a theater watching a moment of horror on a movie screen.

Suddenly a great convulsive shudder shook the body of Vincent Donner from head to foot and his right hand slowly opened and the gun clattered to the floor. Then he stumbled to the chair vacated by Kalim and slumped onto it and sat there shaking.

Time crawled. At last he lifted his head to look at the others.

"All—right," he said as if just learning to talk. "Take time—coming—out of it. He's—gone now—anyway."

Five minutes, Maria thought. Kalim had been stronger but had made a mistake in giving the American just a little too much time. But even so, Kalim had escaped.

Escaped to do what? Poison the food in some other restaurant? Murder innocent people some other way? What kind of monster was he?

Mind control. This, then, was what it meant. But perhaps it meant something even more subtle. "I am sure your Juan will forgive you," he had said.

Not once—not even once, she knew for certain—had she mentioned to him the name of the man she was betrothed to. He must have plucked it from her innermost thoughts.

1

He came into Rainy Ridge on foot, alone, wet from the morning mist and wearied to a shuffle by twenty-odd miles of walking. There are peasants in the Caribbean island of Jamaica who can walk twenty miles without wilting, but he was an outsider, an American. He had walked all night.

He wore no hat. The morning sun kindled a fire in his reddish brown hair and beard. The village watched him in wonder.

Rainy Ridge. A mountain community at a meeting of rough and rutted roads. Two or three shops, a shack marked Post Office, a tavern. He stopped at the tavern doorway to work the ache from his shoulder bones, then put his overnight case down and stepped to the bar. He nodded to the cluster of men drinking there.

"Good morning. Can you tell me the way to the coffee works?"

Silence, while they looked him over. But only a curious silence, not hostile.

"Yes, sah. It up the road here."

"Is it far?"

"'Bout a mile."

He nodded, eyeing the line of bottles behind the bar. Appleton rum. Jamaica brandy. Something called Porto Pruno, that looked as though it might have been on the shelf for years and had a label almost too dark to be read in the tavern's gloom. "I could stand a beer. Do you have a beer, miss?"

"Yes, sah. Red Stripe." She was sixteen or so and attractive; he had noticed a relaxed and easy beauty in many of Jamaica's women during his brief stay in the island. Opening a bottle, she wiped its neck with a bit of rag and passed it to him, accepting in return the Jamaican bill he fumbled from his billfold.

Pocketing the coins she gave him in return, he drank slowly from the bottle, enjoying the tickle of the beer in his throat. He was desperately tired.

At 5:30 P.M. November 8, check out of the guest house in Kingston where our man Goodwin will have been coaching you, and take a cab to the airport, his instructions from the Argus man in the States had read. *Walk about the airport, being as conspicuous as you can be. Order a meal in the restaurant and complain about the food. Inquire about flights to New York and seem to be upset because none suits you. We want you remembered at the airport, Mark Donner, so if certain people find out you went to Jamaica they will think you took a plane out of there soon afterward.*

At 8 P.M. leave the airport, board the bus that runs from Port Royal to Kingston, get off at the roundabout, and walk.

Yes, walk. Walk east along the ribbon of black ink they call the coastal highway, alone and scared and shivering in the gusty wind from the sea. Ignore the snarl of unseen dogs in peasant yards, the blare of jukebox music from roadside honky-tonks, the stare of the occasional passerby. Walk the highway through Bull Bay to Eleven Mile, which is not a village but a cluster of sleeping roadside shops, and follow the side road there that climbs into the hills. It's a long, steep eighteen miles from there to your destination, Mark Donner, but you can do it.

You'd better.

He had caught his second wind partway up the twisting ascent they called Cambridge Hill, and it was a good thing. The downgrade that followed was only a teaser; ahead were ladders of stony mountain road that slowed him to a plod, torturing his lungs and legs.

Goodwin, our man in Jamaica, will brief you carefully before you leave the guest house, his instructions had read. *In any case, it is not possible to take a wrong turn. Proceed through Llandewey, then Ramble, where you will cross a bridge only one car wide high above a swift-flowing river. Then continue on through the sprawling village of Richmond Vale. There is only the one main road until Rainy Ridge, where it meets one coming up from Morant Bay. In Rainy Ridge you will inquire for the coffee works managed by Mr. Jeff Legg.*

He had been awed by the rushing sound of the river beneath him in the darkness, but had welcomed the villages. Even though they slept, they were a relief from the awful black nothingness of the road itself—which, of course, had only nourished the feeling of helplessness that had accompanied him all the way from Connecticut. Most of all he had welcomed the first faint streak of dawn above the mountains.

His beer finished, he placed the empty bottle on the bar and turned to depart.

"You forgettin' you grip, sah."

"Oh, yes. Thanks." He picked it up and it seemed even heavier now. He was so tired. "Thank you," he said again, and turned right, up the hill.

The road was steep here, the sunlight a glitter on enameled leaves of mango trees and coffee bushes. A peaceful place, Rainy Ridge, the Argus man in Kingston—Goodwin—had said. It was that. It was water gurgling in a roadside stream, a wide-eyed lad on a gray donkey, women spreading multicolored clothes to dry on white boulders, a naked girl-child shooing a black chicken from the doorway of a zinc-roofed hut.

Whoever I'm running from, they won't find me here.

A faded sign, Coffee Works, led him up a winding drive to a shed where two men worked in a sweet reek of fresh-cut wood, building barrels. Electric lights glowed in the shed's gloom. Putting his overnight case down again to flex his cramped hand, he waited for the hammering to cease. It did when they noticed him.

"Morning. Is Mr. Legg here?"

"Him in the office, sah."

"Office?"

"That far building there."

"Thank you."

He walked again, the small case recramping his hand at once. *I was a fool to bring this. With my trunks already at Shepstowe, I won't need it.* In one of half a dozen old wooden buildings a machine of some sort whined at high speed, probably the turbine that supplied the factory with electricity. Goodwin had mentioned it when describing Shepstowe to him. Through another doorway he saw more lights glowing, and women seated before mounds of smoke-colored coffee beans at long wooden tables. Crimson berries glistened in the sunlight on coffee trees by the path.

The office was a cubicle with a small grilled window and an open door. A leather-faced man in a stained felt hat sat at a scarred wooden desk, adding columns of figures.

Mark Donner waited for the addition to be completed. Then he said, "Mr. Legg?"

The man looked up. "Sorry. I didn't see you standing there." His voice was pleasantly deep, his smile quizzical. "Morning."

"Good morning. My name is Burke. I believe you're expecting me."

"Well!" Legg got up and came to the door with hand outthrust. "So you're the one." His gaze fastened for a moment on Mark's shaggy hair and beard, and Mark inwardly winced. Why in God's name had the man from Washington insisted on a beard? But, of course, he knew why.

"You know the Shepstowe house?" Legg asked.

"No." Mark shook his head. "I'm new in Jamaica. But I know pretty well what to expect, I think. It's been described to me."

"Well, that's a start." The coffee-works manager stepped into the yard, a tall and muscled white man with a face seamed by tropic sun. "We can go up there now if you like. Where'd you leave your car?"

"I have no car."

"Oh?" The mild-seeming blue eyes could be swift with a glance of appraisal. "Well, my truck's here." He locked the office door and turned toward a pickup parked nearby. "The fellow who rented the place for you—Goodwin—says you write books."

"Yes." Inwardly Mark winced again. Of all the lies, that one came the hardest.

"First time we've had a writer here. You'll be an object of curiosity, I imagine."

"I hope not. I prefer to be ignored."

Climbing into the pickup, Legg only smiled and shook his head.

The road was scarcely a road at all now. From the coffee works' driveway it consisted mostly of boulders and ruts. There were no houses, only coffee trees in forest shade, and then on the right a stretch of scrub-grown meadow perhaps ten acres in extent. At the end of the meadow the pickup crept around a hairpin turn and came to a stop by an open iron gate red with rust.

"That's it down there," Legg said.

The old Great House had been built into an almost vertical mountainside, and Mark looked down on a crazy quilt of shingled roof slopes green with moss. Like a Tibetan monastery, he thought. Of course he had never been to Tibet, or even outside the United States until a month ago, except to go to Montreal once with the high school band. But he was fond of reading about faraway places. Below the house lay a deep valley, impressively wild, through which a thread of white water wriggled to the Caribbean.

"House was built about two hundred years ago by one of the Scots who settled this region," Legg said. "Can't say I like the way they tucked their old Great

Houses into the hillsides. I suppose they feared hurricanes." He eased the pickup down a curving driveway to the yard. "Miss Vernon's here, by the way. She came up yesterday."

"Oh."

Legg aimed a frown at him. "When your friend from Kingston rented the place for you, he asked if I could recommend a housekeeper from the district. You know she's a deaf-mute, do you?"

"Yes. He told me."

"Well, I suppose if you want peace and quiet to write a book . . . Goodwin seemed pleased when he met her." Legg shrugged and got out. "It wouldn't suit me, I'm afraid, having a deaf-mute to look after me in a place as remote as this. I'd need someone to talk to."

Mark said vaguely, "Well, I do have a book to write," and was silent. *Don't talk too much*, he had warned himself on the way out from the capital; *you could blunder and be caught.* Actually he dreaded meeting the Vernon woman. Shy with all women, a little afraid of most, he had nearly panicked when told by Graham, in Connecticut, that he must have a housekeeper. There he had kept a small bachelor apartment, doing his own cooking and housework.

He remembered Graham's annoyance—one of the few times the pink-faced Argus man had lost patience. "Damn it, man, you can't look after yourself there! It just isn't done in such a place. And with this woman you'll be safe. If you forget yourself and say something you shouldn't, it won't be gossiped all over the neighborhood."

Probably Graham had misunderstood his reluctance, thinking he didn't want the Vernon girl because of her handicap. It was not that at all. If he had to have a woman in the house, he actually preferred one he would not have to talk to.

"Consider yourself damned lucky that our man in Jamaica learned about this girl," Graham had said peevishly.

Well, yes, in a way he was lucky. He was not lucky to be the twin brother of Argus agent Vin Donner just now, or to be facing a year of solitude in an old Jamaican Great House. He certainly was not lucky to be the hare in a terrifying game of hare and hounds about which he understood almost nothing except that his life was on the line and he might end up losing it in some especially grisly way. But about the woman—yes, he was fortunate. That part of it could have been worse, he thought as he followed Jeff Legg along a fieldstone walk to the steps of a long veranda.

The double front doors of the house were closed, and the coffee-works manager leaned forward to open them. But with his hands only inches from the handsome brass knobs he suddenly froze. "Hello," he said, scowling. "What's this?"

A length of black thread ran taut between the knobs, and from it dangled something green. It was a small green lizard, Mark saw. A dead one. The thread was looped about its neck in such a way that its head was tipped forward and its beady eyes would seem to stare at anyone approaching the entrance.

"What is it?" Mark asked. "I mean what's it for?"

Legg's shrug was not a shrug of indifference. It was more the gesture of a puzzled man who did not know how else to answer. "Perhaps Eve will know."

Taking a jackknife and a handkerchief from his pocket, he folded the handkerchief about the lizard and cut the thread. Then, opening the doors, he motioned Mark to precede him.

"It's your house, Mr. Burke. You've rented it."

Not me, Mark thought with a touch of panic. *They* did. I should be back in Connecticut, teaching English at Calmar High School, God help me.

2

Entering the house, Mark found himself in a huge room with a fireplace: a drawing room, he supposed it was called here, or had been in the old days when this Caribbean island was an English colony. There were some overstuffed chairs, a vast mahogany table, a red velvet divan.

His two trunks that had been sent on ahead lay on the polished wood floor in front of the divan. Drawn by curiosity, he walked over to examine the lettering on them. PETER BURKE. SHEPSTOWE HOUSE. RAINY RIDGE, JAMAICA, W.I.

He had not seen the trunks since the day Graham called at his apartment for them. There had been no lettering on them then. He wondered idly whether Graham had done the printing himself, or did Argus have a man who specialized in such things? They seemed to have specialists for everything else.

"Lots of grand affairs been held in this room, I imagine," Legg said. The lizard was not to be discussed at the moment, apparently.

"Yes, I'm sure."

Legg gestured. "The two rooms off the side here are bedrooms, and there are bathrooms down the hall. You'll find a bigger bedroom with its own bathroom and veranda; that's the one you'll want, I should think. Kitchen's downstairs, servants' quarters are out back." He spread his hands. "No use my going into details. You'll be looking around."

"The electricity comes from the coffee works, I understand."

"Right. The water that runs our turbine comes from the stream you see down there in the valley, but our intake is high in a gorge above here. Your drinking water comes from the same place."

"I cook with kerosene?"

"No, with bottled gas. I'm to keep you supplied. I hauled two cylinders up from the bay yesterday."

"This house belongs to you?" Mark asked.

"Not to me. My place is three miles down the road that goes to Morant Bay. This belongs to the co-op that owns the coffee works."

"But you look after it."

"I look after it. Anything you need, let me know." Legg's pleasant, leathery face worked up a scowl again. "One thing you *will* need, I should think, is a car. Nearest place for food is the bay, and it's eighteen miles. Nearest phone except the one at the post office, which we ordinary souls aren't allowed to use, is ten miles." Seeming to think suddenly that he might have spoken out of turn, he voiced an uncertain laugh. "But then, maybe you have a car."

"No, I haven't." *You will not have a car*, Graham had said in a voice that forbade any argument. *It would be far too risky. Our man in Kingston will look after your needs as they arise.*

"Will you be getting one, do you think?" Legg asked.

"I'll have to give it some thought."

"Well, I'd better find Eve for you and get back to my job. She's probably out back."

Mark found himself alone. Opening his trunks with a key from his pocket, he was dismayed for a moment by the prospect of having to unpack them. He hardly remembered what they contained. Practically everything was new, and most of it, even the clothing, had been purchased by Graham or others in the Argus organization. He lifted out a portable typewriter, carried it to the mahogany table, opened it. A new typewriter, at least, was something he had long wanted. He was admiring it when Legg came back with the woman.

He was startled on two counts. First, in spite of the "Miss," he had expected someone much older. Most Jamaican country women were unmarried even when they had hordes of children, he knew from his reading. And, of course, he had expected a black woman.

She was neither old nor black. About twenty-five, she was a small, fair girl—English, he guessed, or Scottish—with actually rather pretty features, though they seemed incapable of much expression. Leaving the typewriter, he went toward her with his hand outthrust while Legg said laconically, "I found her out back, fixing up a room for herself."

28

"How do you do?" Mark wondered whether he should say more—whether she might be able to read lips—and decided against it. There wasn't much chance that a deaf-mute in a place like this would have learned lipreading.

Eve smiled and touched his hand.

"If you want to give instructions and that sort of thing, you'll have to write them down," Legg said.

"Of course."

"Best thing to do, I should think, is put it all down at once." Legg glanced at the typewriter. "Then she'll know what's expected." Almost casually he took from his pocket the handkerchief containing the lizard and unfolded it on the big mahogany table. On the back of an old envelope he wrote in pencil, "Eve, did you know this was on the front door?"

She looked wide-eyed from the written question to the lizard and then at Jeff Legg's frowning face. Slowly she shook her head. Taking the pencil from Legg's fingers, she wrote quickly in a small, neat hand, "I came in the back way with the key you gave me. I did unlock the front door—the key was in the lock, inside—but I didn't open it."

"You've no idea who might have hung this there?" Legg wrote.

She shook her head and stepped back, again staring at the dead thing on the table.

Mark said quietly, "It's an obeah sign of some sort, isn't it?" The practice of obeah, a kind of witchcraft, was outlawed in Jamaica, he knew from his reading, but it was far from being stamped out in the country districts. "Is it a warning, maybe, that I'm not espe-

29

cially welcome here? Is there a feeling against strangers?"

"Don't know why there should be." Legg frowned again as he returned the lizard to his pocket. "Unless, that is—" He glanced at Eve as though wondering whether the charm might have been directed against her, perhaps because of her handicap. Then he left the thought unfinished.

"Did many people know I was coming?"

"Well, I mentioned it at the factory, I suppose. And told a few higglers Eve would be wanting them to stop by with eggs and garden stuff." Legg made a face. "I'll ask around, see what I can find out. Meanwhile you've got things to do. I'll run along."

"You're at the coffee works every day?"

"'Most every day. If I'm not, you can always leave a message or send someone down to my place. Anyway, I'll be looking in on you."

"Thanks."

"So long, then, for now."

Mark watched him go, then took from one of his trunks a box of typewriter paper he had seen there, and sat at the table. Motioning the housekeeper to come closer, he rolled a sheet of paper into the machine. "As you probably know," he wrote, "my name is Peter Burke. Yours is Miss Vernon. Is that right?" Handing her a pen from his shirt pocket, and a sheet of the paper, he waited for her answer.

She wrote swiftly in her small, neat hand, "Please call me Eve."

"Of course," he typed. "Now, what must I tell you? The time I'd like my meals? That sort of thing?"

She nodded.

"Very well. Breakfast at eight. No, make it seven-thirty if that's not too early for you. A light lunch at noon. Dinner about six-thirty. Is that all right?"

Again she nodded.

"Right now I'm pretty tired—done a lot of walking—and would like to rest awhile. Please don't bother with lunch today. Just let me sleep."

Once more a solemn nod.

Mark hesitated, then plunged. Rapidly he typed, "I don't mind telling you I've never had a housekeeper before." About to add, "I'm just a schoolteacher," he caught himself barely in time. "If I seem to be stupid about some things, please forgive me. I hope we can be friends."

"I hope so, too," she wrote without smiling. "I have never really kept house for anyone before, except my father."

Dismissing her by taking back his pen, Mark stood up and watched her go down the hall. She was very quick, he noticed. Very light on her feet. Some of the women he knew—teachers, mostly—would have made this old wooden floor resound like a drum when they walked on it. The secret of her lightness was not that she wore sneakers, either. She wore flat-heeled white shoes that with her plain white dress made her look like a nurse.

I'll need a nurse if I don't get some sleep.

Seeking out the bedroom Legg had mentioned, he was delighted to find it nearly as spacious as the drawing room, with its own veranda overlooking the valley. The bed, neatly made and turned down for him, was a vast thing of mahogany.

He had his clothes off before he realized his pajamas were in his overnight case in the drawing room. Too tired to dress again and go for them, he got into bed naked.

Why, he wondered as he lay there feeling desperately alone and lost, had someone hung a dead lizard on the front door of this place to welcome him? What could it mean?

Was it somehow a part of the nameless threat he had been sent here to hide from? Could he have blundered somewhere along the line, to arrive not in the place of safety so meticulously prepared for him, but trapped in a cul-de-sac?

And this terrorist organization he was hiding from—these so-called Disciples with their unholy mental powers—just who *were* they, exactly?

Sleep, when it came at last, was a longed-for relief from the torment of his thoughts.

3

When he awoke and looked at his watch, it was after four o'clock. He went into the adjoining bathroom to shower and discovered there was only a tub. An interesting tub, to be sure, of enameled metal with great feet that belonged on some animal like a bear, but it could wait, he decided. Dressed, he

went down the hall to the drawing room for his overnight case, and returned to the bathroom to shave.

Eve had a meal ready for him when he finished.
He was to dine at the big mahogany table, it seemed.
She had spread a small cloth at one end of it and
prepared some canned corned beef, sweet potatoes,
some kind of pudding, and coffee. He was glad to see
she was not going to stand around and serve him.

Taking a piece of paper from the other end of the
table, he wrote on it with a pen, "Thanks. Where did
the food come from?" When he offered her the pen
for her reply, she shook her head and produced a
small slate.

On it she wrote with a bit of chalk, "I don't know."

Graham's man, Goodwin, must have brought it.
Or Legg. "Anyway, I'm hungry," Mark wrote, and
laughed.

She seemed pleased.

She went away while he ate, and returned with
more coffee just when he wanted some. On the slate
she wrote, "Can I help you unpack?"

"I wish you would. I don't know where to put anything."

Nodding, she went to his trunks. She was not curious, he noticed. While lifting his clothes out and carrying them to his room, she scarcely glanced at
them. The smaller things that he would have to attend to himself she simply stacked on the table.
When she brought his books, though, he saw her look
at the dust jackets. Then, instead of leaving them,
she carried them to a shelf above the fireplace.

There she turned for his approval and he nodded,
feeling like a fool. Four books, each with the name

PETER BURKE in bold letters on their jackets. They were actual novels written some years ago, Graham had explained. "We've just had them made up with a few alterations, to give you a ready-made reputation." Graham had an odd sense of humor.

I suppose I'd better read them now that I have the time. I ought to know what I've written.

Eve came to the table. "Where will you work?" she wrote on her slate. "In one of the small bedrooms?"

"No. Here, I should think."

"You should have a desk. For now shall I just put your writing things on a bed?"

He nodded, less interested in what she did with his possessions than in watching her wipe the slate with a bit of damp cloth from a pocket of her white dress. Her inability to speak was not such a handicap. At least, she had certainly learned to live with it gracefully. He wondered whether she had been born deaf and dumb or had acquired the handicap through some illness or accident.

Going into the large bedroom to see what she had done with his clothes, he found them neatly put away there—his suits and slacks hanging in the closet; shirts, underwear, and things of that sort in bureau drawers. She was a lot more orderly than he had ever been. Each drawer was freshly lined with paper. When she passed him on her way to the bathroom with things for the cabinet there, he was startled again by her silent way of walking.

He wanted to speak to her then. He wanted to say, "I think I'll just walk around a bit and have a look at things," for it was obvious he could not help her and would only be in the way. For the first time he felt frustrated. Paper and pen were in the drawing room. He would have to keep a pad of some sort in his pocket.

But a strange thing happened. When he looked at her, she nodded as though knowing what he wanted to tell her. A smile reinforced the nod. Then in the drawing room when he wrote the message out and waited for her, she scarcely glanced at it before nodding again.

"I know," her lips silently told him. "Go do it."

Puzzled, he went along the hall and downstairs to the kitchen. Yes, he told himself, Graham's man, Goodwin, must have brought the food. The shelves were full, and so was the refrigerator. The latter, like the stove, ran on bottled gas. It was quite a modern kitchen but gloomy, with only one window. That provided only a view of a small courtyard.

All the rooms in the lower part of the house were gloomy, he discovered. In the old days slaves assigned to household duties must have occupied most of them; Master probably never came downstairs, and Mistress only when she had to, to give orders. He crossed the courtyard and followed a path through the yard, with no idea where it might lead him.

It led to a massive hedge of bougainvillea behind which, to his surprise, stood a small shedlike building of more recent construction. The door was open and he looked in.

These were Eve's quarters, obviously. The single room contained a small iron bed, a chest of drawers, and a chair, ghastly pink, that needed repainting even if one cared for pink chairs. On the chest of drawers were things a woman would use: a hairbrush, a jar of some sort of cream, a bottle of cologne. The room was spotless.

He was still in the doorway, frowning at what he saw, when a deep, spongy voice came at him from the hedge. "Evenin', squire."

Startled, he turned to find a man standing there. "Well, hello," Mark replied guardedly.

About fifty, in black trousers and a wrinkled white shirt, the fellow came a step closer on shabby, unlaced shoes. He raised a hand to where the brim of his hat would have been had he been wearing one. "I beg you a little work, squire, to care the yard, maybe, or look about a garden for you. The times is hard on a man these days."

"I see." Mark knew he must think about this. "What's your name?"

"Zekiel McCoy, squire. I live just below here, in Mango Gut." His hand came up again to point. "You can see my roof from here."

Mark looked and nodded. "Well, I don't know about the yard. I'll have to give the matter some thought. I don't have a garden."

"I know, squire, but you should make one. Mr. Farquharson—he's the gentleman was here two, three years ago—he had a nice garden back of the garage there."

"Did he? Well, as I say, I'll consider it."

"I can come for your answer tomorrow, squire?"

"Yes, do that."

"Thank you, squire." The hand touched the nonexistent hat again. "Good evenin' to you."

After watching his caller go down the steep backyard slope and disappear into a grove of trees, Mark returned to the house. He found Eve in the kitchen, doing dishes, and beckoned her to follow him upstairs. In the drawing room he sat at his typewriter.

"A man named Zekiel or Ezekiel McCoy just asked me for some work," he typed. "Said he would look after the yard and start a garden. I suppose he meant a vegetable garden. What do you think, Eve?"

She had brought her slate from the kitchen. On it she wrote, "I don't know the people around here. I come from Trinity, ten miles down the road. Shouldn't you be careful about hiring anyone until you know who put the obeah sign on the door, and why?"

He was disappointed. It would be impossible for him to live here without some contact with the local people, and he had been counting on her to brief him, as Graham would say. "Do we need a man for the yard?" he asked on the machine.

"Unless Mr. Legg has made some arrangement."

"I'll ask him. What about a garden?"

"Yes," she wrote. "The people here grow almost nothing but scallions and carrots—they sell those—but you could grow all sorts of things at this altitude. You could grow brocolli"—she smiled as she ran a line through her mistake—"broccoli, cauliflower, good lettuce, summer squash, etc. Lots of things."

"Thank you. Now tell me about the obeah sign. What do *you* think of it?"

She shook her head. "Only the person who put it there would know what it's meant to accomplish. Every obeah person has his or her line of charms and spells. I only know it's evil, or the intention behind it is. Good people don't use obeah."

"Well, I'll find out soon enough, I suppose." All too soon, maybe, Mark thought with a twinge of apprehension.

"Wait, please," she wrote.

He looked at her, puzzled.

"Please don't think that everything you may not understand here must have its origin in obeah. There are some things about me, for instance—" She hesitated, glanced up at him, then went on as though afraid of what he might think. "The Jamaican nanny who brought me up was not in obeah, yet was still thought 'strange' by some people. I loved her. She taught me—" With another upward glance at him, she stopped writing.

"Taught you what?" he said with his lips.

"Later," she wrote. "There isn't time now. When will you want dinner tonight?"

He looked at his watch. It was already five-thirty and he had only just eaten. "Skip it, please. You must be tired after putting this big place straight. I'll raid the refrigerator when I'm hungry."

"Fridge," she wrote, smiling again. She had a wonderfully quick and pretty smile now that she had got over her shyness.

He typed, "Is that what you call them here?"

She nodded.

"Fridge it is, then. By the way, can you type?" She could, he was certain. Why was he so sure?

Again she nodded.

He rose from his chair and watched her sit down. She frowned at the keys for a moment while adjusting her fingers, then typed, "Now is the time for all good men to come to the aid of the party," and looked up for his approval. "But I'm slow," she added.

Mark was delighted. Leaning over her shoulder, he tapped out, "This is wonderful! Anytime you have something to tell me that would take too long by hand, you can type it. You're not slow at all."

"You'll be using the machine in your work," she protested.

"Just push me aside."

"Anyway," she wrote, "when we know each other better, there may be another way we can talk."

Oh-oh, he thought. Has Goodwin told her about Vin and me, and our so-called talent? Does Goodwin even know about it?

Any discussion of that would have to wait, he decided. He couldn't handle it now.

Eve was typing again. "May I go back to doing the dishes, kind sir?"

Mark had to smile at himself as he stepped back to let her rise. A while ago he had been vastly relieved to know he would not have to talk to this woman. Now he was keenly curious about her statement that when they knew each other better there might be "another way" they could talk. It was not like him to be so inconsistent. But then, she was not at all what he had expected.

When she had gone, he pulled the sheet of paper from the machine and read again what she had written. It was like remembering the sound of a voice. As he studied it, an idea came to him for the book he must pretend to be writing.

He had long wanted to try a book. It would be a failure, of course; he had never had even a short story published. Still, he had read a lot and was a better than fair English teacher. The thing to do, he had felt, was to try a novel about a high school, in which he would be on familiar ground. But there were so many such novels.

Now he had a more exciting notion.

Why not a novel based on what was happening to him now? It would be something different, at least, and would provide a legitimate reason for exploring the district. Eve Vernon could help with the details of Jamaican country life. The book might even be a good one.

He carried his typewriter through the large bedroom to the adjoining veranda and settled himself on a chair there. The sun was a crimson ball balanced on a mountaintop, doing its fiery best to blind him as he began to type.

I had no idea what the man wanted when he called at my apartment that evening. He said he was from Washington and his name was Graham. (He would have to change all the names later, Mark realized, but if he stopped to think of names now he would lose the urge to get the book started.)

When Graham had seated himself, he asked a number of questions. Was I Mark Donner? Did I teach at Calmar High School? Did I have a twin brother, Vincent, who worked for the government? He knew the answers, of course. He was simply sizing me up.

I did not care much for Mr. Graham. He was a pink-faced man about forty with unpleasantly pale eyes and a thin voice. He looked rather shabby, which I suppose was deliberate. Just when I was beginning to wish he would come to the point, whatever it was, and leave me alone, because I had a stack of test papers to grade that evening, he startled me by saying, "You don't know much about your brother, Vin, do you?"

"What do you mean?" I asked, becoming apprehensive.

"The kind of work he does for the government. He hasn't told you. In fact, though the two of you used to be close, you seldom hear from him now."

I admitted that was true.

"I am not going to enlighten you much," he said, leaning forward to tap my knee. "But I will tell you this. Vin worked with our CIA for a time and now works for a government agency we call Argus, of which I am also a member. Also, he is in great danger at present, and so are you."

I did not know what to make of this at all. "How is Vin in danger?" I demanded. "What is all this about, Mr. Graham?"

"I said I am not going to enlighten you. The point is, your brother can look after himself. He is trained to do so. But you cannot, and so we have got to protect you. Mr. Donner," Graham said, fixing me with a ferocious gaze of which his pale eyes scarcely seemed capable, "you are going to see a great deal of me in the next few days. You will probably come to hate my very guts. It can't be helped, I'm afraid. It is for your own good. Now, Mr. Donner, I want you to listen to me carefully . . ."

The setting sun had crimsoned the twisting Yallahs Valley like a forest fire. Now the fire was extinguished by a river of shadow flowing down the mountain slopes.

Fascinated, Mark moved the typewriter from his knees and stepped to the veranda railing to watch the night settle in. But it was impossible to erase Connecticut from his mind.

"You are in danger," Graham had said. "You are in grave peril of being removed from this miserable earth, most unpleasantly, by people who delight in cruelty. Unhappily they are led by the ruler of a Mediterranean country who has the oil money to finance their terrorism. I want you to think about this."

He had insisted on talking to Vin, of course, before even entertaining a thought of doing what Graham demanded. They had been reluctant to arrange that—had, in fact, flatly refused at first—but when he became adamant, they relented.

And it *was* Vin he talked to when the call came through, he was certain. There was no way they could have fooled him on that score. Even if they had rung in someone who merely sounded like Vin and knew his background, no one but Vin himself would have said, reaching back to a time when they were just kids together, "Listen, old Musketeer buddy. Hear me, Zinger. You do what they tell you."

And then with a sob in his voice brother Vincent had said, "Mark, believe me, I didn't want to do this to you. It just happened, and I wish to God it hadn't. But you have to listen to Graham. Your life depends on it."

4

Of weathered yellow brick four stories high, the building resembled a gone-to-seed warehouse. Yet it was within walking distance of the Department of Justice, if the person doing the walking were as physically fit as most of this building's occupants.

Beside its door a wooden plaque which had once been gold and black read Aragon Medical Laboratory, just in case anyone noticed people going in or coming out of a once-abandoned building. There was no Aragon Medical Laboratory in the Washington, D.C., phone book.

There was no Argus, either. At least, not this Argus.

Graham arrived for work at eight twenty-five that November morning. In a shabby topcoat, down-at-the-heels shoes, and stained hat, he looked as though he might well work for a gone-to-seed medical lab in a half-abandoned warehouse.

He had a healthy pink face, however, that Mark Donner in Jamaica had good reason to remember.

Having climbed the grimy stairs to the second floor—the only floor of this building that was presently occupied—Graham opened an unmarked door off the dusty hall and stepped into an outer office.

Four men and two women at desks there looked up respectfully and greeted him with nods. With a nod of his own he shook off his topcoat, hung it with other outer garments on a clothes tree, and proceeded to his own desk. At once he busied himself with a stack of reports someone had placed there for his perusal.

He was halfway through the stack when the door of the agency's only inner sanctum opened. Framed in the opening, a middle-aged, gray-haired man of medium height called quietly, "Winston? A moment, please?"

Graham quickly got to his feet.

Gray Hair spoke again. "And you, please, Everett."

The second man summoned would also have blended well in any crowd of ordinary people. Argus agents prided themselves on being inconspicuous. Also on being highly intelligent, finely trained, and keenly determined to carry out the very special assignment for which this elite agency had been created.

The man who wished to consult with Graham and his fellow agent was no less ordinary-seeming than they except for his eyes. His eyes matched his hair but their gray was metallic. It glinted. No one in Argus called this man anything but "Chief." Even at the not-too-distant Department of Justice, few called him anything else.

Winston Graham and Everett Kopf used the word now as the Chief motioned them to be seated and went behind his desk to sit facing them.

"We think it will be England next," the Chief said. "London."

. Graham and Kopf leaned forward together. "How?" Graham said.

"I wish we knew. But a Disciple seen there was with Kalim in Mexico City, so perhaps it will be food poisoning again."

"Who do we have in London?" Kopf asked.

"Watson. Bailey. It was Watson who spotted the man, from a description Vin supplied. But there's more than London happening now."

Graham and Kopf looked at him and waited.

"I have here"—the Chief touched a yellow pad beside his telephone—"reports, all new, of moves in Rome and Stockholm. Not just terrorist acts but the Disciples' special *kind* of cruelty." He exhaled noisily. "Why in God's name can't we persuade other so-called civilized powers to join us in hitting Siricus with an air strike? Nothing less will stop that bastard."

They let him unwind, knowing that every now and then when reports of the atrocities came in, he felt that Aram Sel's campaign of hate was directed at him personally. He knew better, of course. He knew, as did all Argus people and the Department of Justice and the White House, that the man behind the atrocities was subhuman. *And* that Aram Sel's worldwide campaign of terror was working because he had a cousin named Khargi.

Khargi. They had no other name for him. They knew what he looked like from old stories in Middle East magazines: a man of medium size who wore facial hair in an attempt to hide a scar. Yet none of them had ever come face-to-face with him.

Khargi was one of a kind. Khargi taught the oth-

45

ers. The Chief insisted he even maintained some kind of mental contact with them no matter where they were sent.

And against all this the U.S. agency called Argus—an apt word meaning "a watchful guardian"—had to struggle alone because other target countries either refused to believe there *was* a Khargi or were reluctant to offend the ruler of a country that supplied so much of their needed oil. With the Chief directing operations from this "Aragon Medical Lab" in Washington, and with Vin Donner in charge of field work because of his special training and talents, the Argus team of phantoms had to carry on without help.

"Did you hear yesterday's outburst from our lunatic?" the Chief asked.

Kopf said, "On the evening news, you mean? About India?"

"What about India?" Graham said.

The Chief actually shrugged. He did not do that often. "Some famous guru over there called Aram Sel the Devil. Not *a* devil—*the* Devil. At some very holy Hindu gathering, no less. Sel called our TV people to a press conference—you know how he uses them when he wants to—and screamed he'd have an apology or else."

"We have people in India?" Kopf asked.

"I talked with them this morning. But they're in Bombay, a long way from this holy man, and Sel may strike in a hurry to make his point."

Winston Graham of the pink face let a little span of silence go by, perhaps to make sure his Chief had finished. Then he brought his long-fingered hands together in front of him, the fingertips of one pressing those of the other, and said, "What from Jamaica, Chief?"

"Your man, you mean? He's arrived at the Great House. Goodwin phoned me last night."

"Still unsuspecting?"

"I hope to God."

Again a little silence. Then Graham, his face expressionless, said, "Do you suppose the Disciples know he's there?"

"They should know he's in Jamaica somewhere. *If* Vin's twin arrived in Mexico City while they were still hanging around seething at Kalim's failure." The Chief folded his arms. "We can always go back to Plan One, you know. When we set Mark up as a decoy, we didn't expect the confrontation between Kalim and Vin in that restaurant."

Graham looked unhappy despite his attempt to maintain a lack of expression.

"Don't feel that way," the Chief said.

"The poor guy is such a *nice* guy," Graham said. "I mean if you knew him as I do—"

"Goodwin will keep him safe. And if we want to keep Khargi out of Florida . . . Winston, do you realize what will happen when Khargi arrives at that farmhouse? How helpless we'll be to stop it?"

Another fragment of silence. Then Everett Kopf said, "Vin is there now? In Florida?"

The Chief nodded.

"Watching the farmhouse?"

"Watching the farmhouse. And the airport for arrivals. While Khargi—we hope to God—thinks Mark is Vin." The Chief stood up and frowned at his watch. "Gentlemen, if we're to get anything done to-day . . ."

Graham and Kopf left the sanctum together. They walked to Graham's desk where Graham, with a backward glance at the Chief's office to be sure the door was closed, slid open a bottom drawer and took out a bottle of Bourbon.

As he poured a meager ounce into each of two paper cups and handed one cup to his colleague, he said in a low voice, "Everett, I hope to Christ Vin never finds out what's going on here with his brother. He'll be after us the way Khargi is after him."

"Amen."

Graham of the pink face tossed off his ounce of Bourbon and quickly returned the cup to the desk drawer. "Everett," he said sadly, "I don't know how I sleep nights. When I think of what we're doing to that poor schoolteacher, I get sick to my stomach and want to throw up."

5

At Shepstowe Great House in Jamaica's Blue Mountains, Mark Donner finished breakfast and began reading over what he had written the evening before. He probably shouldn't, he warned himself. It was clumsy and stilted, and he would want to do it over. That would make it worse. He must write the whole book—he was bound to improve as he went along—and then revise it from the beginning.

Hearing a scratching noise outside, he went to the door to investigate. Zekiel McCoy stood there at the foot of the veranda steps, pressing the point of a machete into a post while rubbing its edge with a small file. Lifting the file in salute, he said, "Mornin', squire."

Mark nodded. "Good morning, Zekiel. I've been thinking over what you asked me. As you can see, the yard doesn't need any work; Mr. Legg has just had it cleaned. If you want to dig up a garden plot for me, you can."

"Yes, squire!"

"I can pay you the regular day rate on the days you work." Mark had asked Eve what he should do about that. "Understand, though, I'm not offering you steady employment—at least, not yet. I only rent this house and don't know what is expected of me in the way of keeping up the grounds and so forth."

"Yes, sah, I understand. I can start the garden now, then?"

"If you like."

McCoy said, "Thank you, squire," and raised the file in salute again before going off through the yard.

On his way to the coffee works half an hour later Mark stopped by the garage—it was actually an ancient carriage house—to watch the man at work. There was indeed an old garden of sorts at the side of the building. Weeds and scraggly guava bushes had taken it over.

As a preliminary to digging it up, McCoy was "peeling" it—there was no better word—with the sharp edge of his machete. He was remarkably adept with the tool, Mark saw. His khaki shirt hung from a bush, and sweat glistened on his muscular chest as he swung his arm.

Mark climbed the driveway and went down the road to the factory, arriving there just after eight. Legg's pickup stood before the cooper's shed. Legg himself came out of the office, carrying a wrench.

"Hello there," the manager said. "Sorry your lights were so poor last night. I'm just going to have a look at the turbine."

"Were they poor? I didn't notice." Mark smiled. "I went to bed early." He walked with Legg to the small shed that housed the turbine, and watched while the manager removed a metal plate and pulled out handfuls of wet leaves. There was a strainer at the intake, Legg explained, but the gutter that brought the water from the river was an open one part of the way, and leaves dropped into it. A hard rain or a high wind—there'd been both yesterday—always dimmed the lights.

"Well, if you're not here when it goes bad, I'll know what to do," Mark said.

"One of the men usually looks after it. He's off today."

"I see."

"But if you didn't come about the lights—"

"I came to ask if you know a man named Zekiel McCoy. At the moment he's cleaning out that old garden patch beside the garage for me, and he's offered to look after the yard. The yard *is* my responsibility, isn't it?"

Legg leaned against the turbine and laughed his easy laugh. "I guess. We're pretty informal around here, and I'm afraid I didn't discuss it with Goodwin when he rented the place for you."

"That's all right. I don't mind looking after it. But about McCoy—"

"He's not a bad sort."

"Good. After that lizard thing on the door, I thought I'd better check with you. Have you found out about the lizard, by the way?"

Legg shook his head. "I may never be able to. They simply won't talk about their obeah, even to me. McCoy can be trusted, though. We do have a few rascals in the district—obeah people and the occasional ganja grower—but he's not one of them."

"Ganja? That's marijuana, isn't it?"

Legg nodded. "The East Indians introduced it to Jamaica years ago, and it's been a curse ever since." He shrugged to change the subject. "What about Eve? Any difficulties there?"

"None at all."

"She's a fine girl. Have you discovered her special talent yet?"

"Talent?"

"I thought about it when Goodwin asked me to recommend someone to look after you. Didn't tell him, of course—he doesn't strike me as the sort who'd understand. Eve is psychic, sort of. Though deaf and dumb, she's able to read people's thoughts. Some people, anyway. Learned it from her Jamaican nanny, she says."

As Vin and I learned or acquired it from our

mother, Mark thought. But what he said was, with a scowl, "You were right not to tell Goodwin, I'm sure." Because, of course, Goodwin would inform Graham, and Graham would order him to get rid of Eve at once. The last thing the Argus people wanted was a housekeeper at Shepstowe who might learn that Peter Burke was not Peter Burke and not a writer.

"Anyway," Jeff Legg said, "I'm glad to know you and Eve are getting along. If it's all right with you, I'll take a run up with the missus this evening. Unless you'll be busy with your writing and all."

"I'll be glad to see you. Eve will, too, I'm sure."

Mark walked back up the road, admiring the coffee trees with their brilliant fruit. It was a special kind of coffee, he knew from his reading: Jamaica Blue Mountain, one of the best in the world. He would have to ask Eve about it. As he neared the Shepstowe driveway he heard voices.

The road itself stopped at the drive, or rather became the drive, but a well-worn footpath continued on down to Mango Gut, the village below the house. The voices came from a stretch of path hidden by trees, and presently a line of women appeared, chattering like birds. Pretty as birds, too, in their bright head-wraps and multicolored dresses. They were the women and girls he had seen sorting coffee beans at the factory yesterday.

"Mornin', squire," the first one said with a friendly smile.

"Good morning!"

"Mornin', sah. Mornin', Marse Burke." So they knew his name—at least his false one—already. "How-de-do, sah?"

He answered each one, delighted to know the obeah thing on the Great House door was not to make him a pariah. Suddenly he had a mental picture of himself standing on a street corner at home, being greeted this way by passing strangers, and the thought was so preposterous it made him laugh.

The last woman in line voiced a musical laugh in reply, and as she caught up with the others he heard her say, "Him a nice man, that Marse Burke."

Still, he reminded himself, *someone* had hung the dead lizard on his door, and the act had been no gesture of friendship. Be careful, Mark. You could be out of your depth here, just as you most certainly are in the game Graham is playing.

In the garden he stopped to speak to McCoy. "I find I *am* responsible for the yard, Zekiel. The job is yours if you want it."

"I would like it, squire."

"But as I pointed out before, the yard doesn't need much attention yet. If you'll get the garden ready for planting, I'll buy some seeds."

"I beg you a fork, sah, if you have one."

"I don't know whether I have or not. Did you look in the garage?"

McCoy went to the old carriage house and returned shaking his head. "No, sah. But I have one at home if I can go for it. I can do that?"

"Of course."

"Thank you, squire." He reached for his machete again. "I will go when I finish up with this."

Mark went into the house. Eve was not about, but his breakfast things had been removed from the table and his typewriter was at one end of it. He had left the machine in his bedroom last night, he recalled. She had also brought out the pages he had typed on the veranda, and placed a box of paper beside the machine.

He had to smile. He was a writer, and a writer was supposed to write. When he sat down to play at the game, he discovered she had left a message in the machine.

"I will be downstairs in the kitchen. If you should want me, just stamp on the floor. Some sounds I can feel. Or you might try sending me a message by thinking it. I have a feeling you won't believe me foolish for suggesting this."

You'd better believe I won't, he thought as he rolled a fresh sheet of paper into the typewriter and went to work.

Graham, the government man, knew a great deal more about my brother's present activities than I did, it seemed. In a way this was not surprising. Vin and I had been all but inseparable as kids and even very close through high school, but then had gone on to different colleges, he to Cal Tech and I to a liberal arts school in New England. He wanted to be a scientist, I a teacher. As it happened, he went from Cal Tech to a job in California and I obtained a teaching position in Connecticut, so the width of the country continued to separate us even after graduation.

Our mother, meanwhile, had died quite suddenly of a heart attack—she had divorced our father when we were still in high school—and so there was no home tie to bring us together again.

We corresponded for a time, but our interests lay in such different directions that the exchange of letters soon dwindled to an occasional brief note. Vin had been in Washington for months before I knew he had given up his California job. As for what he actually did in Washington, I was told only that he worked for the government. If I ever asked him what kind of work he did, I do not remember. In any case, his activities were a complete mystery to me at the time of my visit from Graham.

As I have said, Graham would shed no light whatever on the matter. "All I can tell you is that you must take a year's leave of absence and go out of the country," he said. He had already checked with the school and knew I could obtain leave. He knew, further, that there was nothing to keep me in Calmar—no romantic bond or that sort of thing.

"I'm going to send two trunks here to your apartment," he told me. "They'll arrive tomorrow. Since you don't know Jamaica, I suggest you let us provide what you'll need there—it's the least we can do for the inconvenience we're causing you. When the time comes, I'll have the trunks taken away and sent to your destination. We'll talk about that later. Your first stop, however, will be in Mexico. Do you speak any Spanish?"

I said I'd had two years of Spanish in high school and could perhaps speak a little.

"Brush up on it," he said, "though you'll be in Mexico only two or three weeks. Read up on Jamaica, too." His pale eyes blinked at me and he grinned; as I have said, this man possessed a strange sense of humor. "I have news for you," he went on. "When you leave here, you will not be a schoolteacher. You'll be a writer."

* * *

Mark looked up from his typewriter to see Eve watching him from the doorway. She smiled and came to the table, carrying a lamp with a tall chimney. Putting it down, she took up a pencil and wrote on a piece of paper, "I am taking this to your room. One to mine, too. The lights went out last night."

He pulled his story from the typewriter and on a fresh sheet typed, "Wait. I want to talk to you."

She nodded.

"Look," he typed. "I saw your room yesterday. I don't like your being way out there at the end of nowhere. I want you to have my room. I will use one of the smaller bedrooms."

She seemed startled. When he turned the typewriter toward her, she drew up a chair and wrote, "Really, I can't do that."

"Why can't you?"

"It wouldn't be right."

He was not sure what she meant. "Do you mean people would talk?"

"Yes. No, not exactly. I don't know. It just wouldn't be proper."

With his hands on his hips Mark shook his head at her as he might have at a stubborn child. "Anyway," he wrote, "think about it. Evidently we can lose our lights at any time. It worries me, your being out there alone." Guessing she would only continue to say no if he persisted, he left the typewriter but heard her tap out a message. When she had gone with the lamp, he read her final words.

"Please don't think me ungrateful. You are very kind."

In no mood to return to his book, Mark decided to see how McCoy was getting on with the garden. He found the man standing motionless at the edge of the "peeled" space, clutching a heavy fork in both hands as he scowled fixedly at what appeared to be a flag of some sort in the center of the plot.

"Something wrong, Zekiel?"

"Squire, I think we should not make a garden in this place, after all. No, sah."

"Why not?" The flag, Mark saw, was a rectangle of red cloth fastened to the top of a slender, six-foot piece of freshly cut bamboo. "What's that thing for?"

"I did find it here when I come back from my place with the fork, sah. Someone did plant it whilst I absent."

Mark felt annoyance taking hold of him. "I don't understand. Are you saying I can't have a garden here just because some intruder put up a flag?" Then he became aware that McCoy's heavy lips were quivering and there was too much white in his eyes. The annoyance subsided. "What is it, Zekiel? Is this obeah?"

"Yes, squire. It obeah."

"And?"

"I rather not make a garden here, sah. Something bound to happen if I do."

Again Mark asked himself what he knew, from his reading, about Jamaican obeah. It was African in origin and in some ways similar to the voodoo practiced in Haiti. But unlike voodoo, which was basically a religion, obeah was a wholly evil form of black magic.

The obeah practitioner worked solely for personal gain and almost always worked alone. You went to one to have some member of the opposite sex pay you the attention you so desperately longed for. Or to have a rival fired from a job you coveted. Or to bring illness or death—yes, death—to an enemy.

Were these powers real or was the whole ugly business built on peasant superstition? That was beside the point, really. Most of the island's country people *believed*, and so the expected often happened, even if only through some mysterious form of mind control. And Zekiel McCoy was obviously one of the believers.

"All right," Mark said at last with a sigh of surrender. "You'd better go home, Zekiel. Come see me tomorrow when I've had a chance to think about all this."

6

Mark worked on his book until noon, then was glad to escape from the typewriter and stretch the ache from his shoulders. When Eve served him his lunch, he did not bring up the subject of her room again. He did let her know that the Leggs might be coming that evening.

"They are good people," she replied. "Everyone likes them. It's nice you are making friends so soon."

While he was having coffee, he heard a car come down the drive.

It was a small American station wagon, and the man who got out of it was no stranger. Goodwin, the Argus man in Jamaica, had met him at the airport when he first arrived, and taken him to the Kingston guest house. It was Goodwin who had rented Shepstowe for him and briefed him on what to expect when he got here. And Goodwin had coached him in precisely *how* he must get here, including that ghastly nighttime walk into the mountains from the roundabout near the airport, even though Graham had supplied written instructions.

A tall, thin man with blond hair that shimmered in the sun, Goodwin—what *was* his first name, anyway?—left his car and came straight to the veranda steps, not lifting his gaze until he reached them. Climbing, he thrust his hand out. A faint grin touched his face. "Greetings. I don't suppose you've forgotten me."

"Hardly. Come on in."

"Got some things for you in the car, but they'll keep." The Argus man entered and dropped onto the nearest chair, clasping his hands behind his head and thrusting his long legs out. The grin returned. "How was the walk?"

"Long."

"I'll bet. I thought about you hiking that road at night as I drove out just now. One hell of a long walk, but necessary, as I warned you. Every living soul on a bus would have remembered you. Whites seldom ride the country buses here." He glanced around the room. "You comfortable?"

"It isn't too bad."

"Plenty of space to knock around in, anyway. Not much chance of claustrophobia. How about the deaf-and-dumb housekeeper? She satisfactory?"

"Very much so."

"We were lucky. I just happened to ask Legg if he knew someone who might do. Told you about herself, has she?"

Mark shook his head. "Only that she kept house for her father."

"A doctor. Died last year. Legg said he was a damned fine man, could have done far better for himself in Kingston or MoBay but felt the people here needed him. English. How he happened to land out here in the country I wasn't told."

"Was Eve born that way, the way she is?" Mark asked.

"I didn't ask. All Legg said, she was living there alone and needed work and might be a good bet for someone who wanted peace and quiet, so I propositioned her. At first she said it would be too much. I had to tell her you were a real nice guy, understanding as hell and easy to get along with."

"Thanks," Mark said wryly.

"Well, you are."

"Someone out here apparently has different ideas about me. There was an obeah sign on the door when I arrived, and another in the garden this morning."

Goodwin came out of his slouch. "Obeah? What kind of signs?"

Mark told him. "So apparently I have enemies. Could there be people here who don't want a stranger moving into Shepstowe?"

The man from Kingston slowly rubbed his jaw. "Have you done anything? Offended someone?"

"I've hardly opened my mouth yet."

"I don't like this, Donner. Don't like it at all."

"Nor do I. Believe me."

"And you haven't a clue?"

Mark shook his head.

"Can't Legg find out what's behind it?"

"He says he isn't hopeful."

"Well"—Graham's man looked unhappy—"you'll know before long, I imagine. But the obeah person is not your problem, of course. He—or it could be a she—is being *paid* to do a job on you. Your real enemy will be the one doing the paying." He gave his head a final angry shake and pushed himself to his feet. "I'll bring in your things. Come lend a hand if you like."

Mark went to the car with him and carried a box of supplies to the house. Goodwin carried another. "Begun your book yet?" the Argus man asked as he lifted things from the boxes and stacked them on the table.

It was on Mark's tongue to say yes, but he decided against it. The thought had come to him, when Goodwin was commenting on the long walk from Kingston, that he should not be writing what he was writing. A book, yes, but not that book.

He had been provided with a deaf-and-dumb housekeeper so he would not betray himself with a spoken word, yet he was putting down on paper the very words he was not supposed to speak. There was probably no danger—Eve was not one who would read a manuscript unless invited to—but he was glad she had moved his typewriter and papers when setting the table for lunch. Goodwin, he felt, would not hesitate at all to look at anything lying there.

"No," he answered the man's question. "Not yet."

"Well, I don't suppose writers write all the time. Don't wait too long to get started, though."

"I won't."

Goodwin lifted a bottle of Appleton rum and one of Scotch from one of the boxes. "Graham says you don't drink much, but you may need this. People could drop in."

"Yes. Thanks."

"Matter of fact, you might offer me . . . No, I guess not; I can't stay that long. Look, there's food here. Meat, eggs, butter—I don't think I've skipped much. Have a look, and if there's anything else you want, I'll bring it next time. I expect to be out once a week."

Mark examined the things on the table, which now looked a good deal like a supermarket. "I'd like a whistle."

"A what?"

"Miss Vernon is alone at night in that place out back. It scares me a little. I'd feel safer if she had a whistle."

The golden-haired man produced a pad and pencil. "This obeah thing has got you worried, hey? All right, one loud whistle. Anything else?"

"Some seeds. I'm starting a garden." If not where the flag is, then somewhere else, Mark thought angrily. I'm going to have a garden!

"Good idea. It'll take your mind off the witch-doctoring. What kind of seeds?"

"Well—broccoli, cauliflower, lettuce, summer squash, radishes—"

"Some of everything," Goodwin said, scribbling. "Anything else?"

"I don't think so."

"Then I'm gone." Returning the pad and pencil to his pocket, he thrust his hand out.

"Suppose I want to get in touch with you between visits," Mark said.

"Send a telegram from the local post office to the U.S. Embassy. They'll know where to find me. Just 'need you'—no signature. But don't unless you have to."

"One other thing. Do I pay Miss Vernon? If so, how much and when?"

"You pay her. Weekly. First payday Saturday, one hundred U.S. dollars because the exchange rate keeps fluctuating." Goodwin grinned. "You ever heard the one about the old Chinaman in the States who kept getting money from home, and the bank kept giving him smaller and smaller amounts for it, telling him the rate kept fluctuating? And one day when they told him that, he just shrugged and said—"

"Ah so. Fluct again."

"You're a stinker, spoiling a man's joke like that. Anyway, you pay her a hundred a week out of this." Goodwin lifted a white envelope from among the things on the table and let it fall again. "Okay, Mr. Peter Burke. See you." With a nod he walked out.

Mark looked around the room. For some reason that he could not quite put a finger on, he felt a need to get out of it for a while to relieve the tension that had been building up inside him all through Goodwin's visit. He ought to go for a walk. But first he must help Eve put away the food the Argus man had brought.

He repacked a box and carried it down to the kitchen, telling Eve on her slate where it had come from. She went upstairs for the rest. When they were finished, he wrote, "I understand there are coffee fields on the estate here, maintained by the co-op. I'll just go look at some of them, I think, for the exercise. That is, if I can find them."

"A good idea," she replied. "You've been working hard. Just follow the track through the meadow at the top of the drive."

Climbing the driveway, he located the path and contentedly strolled along it through a tangle of thorny brush and tall, tough guinea grass—a likely place to hide if ever he had to, he thought wryly. Then the track led him up a forested slope into a mountainside of coffee.

An aluminum disc nailed to a tall shade tree bore the number "1" and the coffee bushes in field 1 were dark green, obviously healthy, heavy with bearing. Jeff Legg must be good at his job if it included supervision of the fields here. Presently a "2" sign appeared, and then a "3."

He was enjoying himself, with no intention of returning soon to the house, when his little escape from fear and brooding was abruptly terminated. Hearing his name called, he turned to find Zekiel McCoy toiling up the track after him.

McCoy handed him a note in Eve's handwriting. "Mr. Burke," it read, "something seems to have gone wrong with the water system. Suddenly we have no water at the house."

Mark frowned at the message, then peered at its bearer. "Have you read this, Zekiel?"

McCoy shook his head. "I never did learn to read, squire."

"Miss Vernon says there is no water at the house." Mark's frown deepened. "By the way, what were you doing there? I thought you went home."

"I did come back to look some other place to make a garden for you, sah."

"Oh. Well, what about this? Is there some trouble at the intake, do you suppose?"

McCoy thought about it and shook his head again. "It not likely to be there, squire. I know for a fact Mr. Legg's people was up there yesterday, cleaning it. More likely is the gutter line. I can walk it and look."

An opportunity, Mark decided, for him to become acquainted with the gutter line, too. There might come a time when he would need to know about it. "All right. I'll walk it with you."

It was not easy. A wooden trough lined with zinc, the gutter proved to be more than half a mile long, twisting through the estate like a giant snake. In places it was half hidden in the jungle twilight of dense bush. In others it glittered like a thread of mercury across bare, steep slopes of greenish black rock. In still others, on spider-leg trestles of poles, it spanned deep gullies through which McCoy and he had to claw their way one wary step at a time.

I should have gone to Legg, Mark thought when they stopped to rest. But I ought not to run to the coffee works every time there's a problem. Not if I want to keep Legg's respect and friendship.

They found the trouble at last. A boulder two feet

in diameter had dislodged itself from the slope above and crashed down on the gutter, breaking it. The water from the river, meant to glide on to the Great House and the coffee works, swirled out through the break instead. While Mark stood there wondering how to repair the damage, he heard voices.

They belonged to workers from the factory, walking the line as he and McCoy had done. They were surprised, obviously, to find him there before them. When they examined the break, though, and looked up at where the boulder had come from, they seemed even more perplexed.

"We never have no trouble here before," one said. "This not a place where rain make the earth slide."

"Is no path up there a man could be walking on, loosening rock-stones," another said.

They directed their frowns at Mark, as if to imply that only he could provide an explanation.

"You think this was not an accident?" he said.

No one answered him. Then when the stillness began to seem ominous, one man said matter-of-factly, "Well, we will fix it, Mr. Burke. No need for you to worry youself."

Mark watched them at work for a time, then he and McCoy departed. *Had* it been an accident? Or did someone want him to become so disenchanted with living at the Great House that he would give up and go away?

With McCoy at his side he trudged down the curving Shepstowe drive and saw the red obeah flag still fluttering from its bamboo pole near the garage. "Did you find another place for the garden?" he asked.

"Yes, squire. An even better one, I think."

"Where?"

McCoy pointed to a row of coffee trees closer to the house. "I can take up that old coffee there, squire—it don't bear nothing much no more—and with some manure forked in, that will be real good garden soil. I ready to start right now, squire."

"What if you find a red flag flying *there* when you come tomorrow?"

"I will take my chances. I need the work."

Why the change? Mark wondered. Was it because I was able to walk the gutter with him without breaking my neck?

Whatever the explanation, he was pleased. Striding through the weeds to the pole with the red flag on it, he tore the flag off and threw it to the ground.

As he walked on toward the house, he looked back and saw Zekiel McCoy standing motionless, staring after him.

7

Their tutor, the great Khargi, had said fiercely to the two of them, "We have a score to settle with the Voice of India—the guru Babananda—who has publicly called my esteemed cousin, your leader, the Devil. Not *a* devil, but *the* Devil. Do you understand the magnitude of the insult?"

Staring back at him, they nodded and waited.

"India, then," Khargi continued, "is where your supreme test will take place. There we shall find out how much you have absorbed of what I have tried to teach you. Because your target is a Siddha Mahatma, the highest saint, and is revered by many as a god. Listen now with care to what you will do."

This conversation took place at Khargi's headquarters in Siricus, and the pair to whom Khargi addressed himself were two of his most apt pupils. Already they had proved their skills in Italy and Sweden.

Now they were on the last leg of their journey.

Two days ago they had arrived at Calcutta's Dum-Dum airport and boarded a northbound train at Howrah Station. All the way north toward the Himalayas, whenever the crowded condition of the train permitted, they had reviewed Khargi's instructions for carrying out their assignment.

Arriving at their destination, each had known exactly what was expected of him.

It was not a large town, nor was it as high in the mountains as those farther north. But the day was bleak, the skies gray, the road unpaved. They would find Babananda's temple-school, his ashram, on the right about two miles from the station, they had been told. "Despite Maharajji's great reputation, it is a modest kind of place with a long front veranda. All strangers are welcome. You will not be turned away."

Through a mist that had floated down from the

mountains they saw it now ahead of them. Small, yes, compared with some other schools and monasteries they had seen from the train. But only five weeks ago, at an event celebrating the twentieth anniversary of its founding by the same Babananda, other well-known religious leaders, and some non-religious ones as well, had assembled here from all over India.

It was at that gathering, while commenting on world problems, that Babananda had made the remark he was now to be punished for. Because the remark had traveled far beyond India's boundaries. The world's communications media had spread it far and wide.

In any case, Khargi's two pupils had been in India long enough now to know that some of the greatest saints maintained humble ashrams. "Don't be misled by what we see here," the smaller one warned as they approached the gate in the wall. "What we have to *do* here won't be easy."

The gate stood open. They walked along a gray flagstone path to a flight of steps leading up to the long veranda. Strange, but the ashram seemed to be deserted. No living thing moved on its lawns and walkways. Finding an open door off the veranda, Khargi's men walked unchallenged into a large room that contained a number of the wooden platform beds called tuckets and a few other pieces of furniture.

On a wooden chair against the wall on their left sat a man of sixty or so, white-haired, unshaven, barefoot, clad only in soiled blue cotton pants. He was asleep.

Perhaps jarred from his dreams by the trembling of the floor, the fellow awoke with a start as they crossed the room toward him. He scrambled to his feet, greeting them in Hindi.

They had been coached in certain Hindi phrases, but did not know enough of that tongue for a conversation. Babananda, of course, spoke English. This man did, too, they discovered on asking him who he was.

He was the *chaukidar*, he said. The gatekeeper.

"We seek Babananda."

"Maharajji is not here. The ashram is closed."

"Closed? Why?"

"Two of the students were found to have an illness as yet unidentified. Until the authorities can be sure it is not contagious, no one may live here except me. The students and teachers have dispersed to their homes. Maharajji is staying at the home of a teacher in the town, so as to be available."

"You are alone here, then?"

"I am alone here, yes."

"Tell us, please, how to find this house where your guru is staying."

"Of course." The fellow stepped to a blackboard and took up a piece of chalk. "Where have you come from?"

"The railroad station."

"Well, then"—he drew a small rectangle with the chalk—"here is the station. And here is the road by which you came here. Now you must continue along the same road"—he indicated it with a wavering line—"for another mile or so until you reach the town. In town you will go past the bazaar"—another squeal of the chalk, this time to create a circle—"and after a short row of houses, the pharmacy." He indicated the pharmacy.

"And?"

"The house where Maharajji is staying is the third one after the pharmacy, an old gray wooden house with a narrow veranda fronting the road. More than likely you will find Maharajji there on the veranda, where people passing by can speak with him."

The *chaukidar* paused, suddenly wide-eyed with alarm. "What are you doing, please? Why do you look at me that way?"

"Sit," the tall Disciple ordered.

"I must not. It was wrong of me to be asleep when you arrived. I must sweep the walks and mow the lawn and—"

"Sit."

"But I have told you I—"

"*Sit!*"

The Indian lowered himself onto the edge of the chair on which he had been sleeping. Slowly, as though it might burn him, he slid back until his head touched the wall. The two from Siricus never stopped gazing at him, and he seemed physically unable to stop staring back.

Even when the tall one signaled the other with a nod, and both walked out of the room, the gatekeeper continued to sit there, staring vacantly into space. Only the faint sigh of his steady breathing indicated he was still alive.

When Khargi's two Disciples arrived at the house where Babananda was staying, the guru, as his *chaukidar* had predicted, was seated on the veranda. Possessing the frail body and round, soft face of a child, in meditation he seemed scarcely more alive than the gatekeeper they had left under their control at the ashram.

Aroused by the sound of his callers' footfalls on the veranda steps, Babananda opened his eyes. At once something in his mind warned him he was in danger.

Very great danger, in fact. But what to do? Physically he was no match for either of these intruders, not even the smaller one. And the owner of the house was absent.

As his visitors came along the veranda, Babananda abandoned his lotus position and uncrossed his legs, but did not rise. Despite the weather, he wore only a dhoti and a blanket. Adjusting himself on the wooden bed, he pressed his palms against it and sat up straighter to greet the callers.

They were not Indians. Having carried his teachings to all corners of his country, he was sure of that. The small one's thin, sharp face suggested a blend of many genes. The other might be from that Mediterranean country now called Siricus, whose ungodly leader, Aram Sel, was presently exporting terror to half the world along with the oil that kept him so dangerously able to do so.

Is that why my toenails tingle and a warning bell rings in my head?

The two halted before him on the veranda, and a lone passerby on the far side of the road paused to look. It was a sight to arouse curiosity, without a doubt: two strangers so different in stature confronting a seated Indian holy man who could be forty years old or—what? Some said Babananda was at least two hundred.

The mist in the road had thickened a little. There was a streak of darkness in the sky where one would have expected something more blue. The tall and the short bent forward from the waist in a gesture of respect. Why did Babananda feel it was only a mock gesture?

"Greetings, Maharajji. We come for *darshan*."

For spiritual guidance? Really? Then why the tingling in his toes, and now in each separate fingertip of both hands?

As if to prove their statement, they placed a *prasad* on the veranda before him, in front of his tucket. An offering of fruit in a basket. Then they respectfully reached forward to touch his bare feet. To touch the bare feet of a Siddha Mahatma was to touch those of God.

Still unsure, because the hour was somehow wrong and they, too, were somehow wrong, the guru leaned forward, took up a handful of pomegranate seeds, and slowly chewed one.

Yes, he was in grave danger. Every sense told him so. He was in danger of being killed.

Well . . . he was not young anymore, was he? And he had been ill for a long time with complaints even the best medics in Calcutta seemed unable to conquer. Why should he be reluctant to leave this old, ailing body and go on to the next? Except, of course, he preferred to do it his own way in his own good time. With this in mind he fixed his gaze on the two men before him and said in English, "Who are you? And where from?"

"From far, Maharajji. Who we are is of no consequence."

73

"Perhaps. But you have not come here for *darshan*. You seek no spiritual guidance."

The lone passerby across the road had moved on, his curiosity apparently satisfied. One of the two callers stepped to the open door of the house, peered in, and made a sign to his companion. Reassured that Babananda was alone, both seemed to become even more confident. The tall one even dropped his pretense of respect and allowed a sneer to twist his face. What had before been a rather handsome countenance subtly became ugly and menacing.

"No, we have not come for *darshan*, Maharajji."

Maharajji, he thought. When my people say the word it means "Great King." But not the way this man says it.

"I fail to understand why you are here, then." Still seated on his wooden bed, still gazing up at them, Babananda wondered if—when—one of them would produce a knife or a gun and release him from his body. Because if they did that, would he not join the highest saints now? Would he not become one with Christ, Ramakrishna, Sivananda, and those others with whom he longed to spend eternity and had devoted his whole long life to earning the privilege?

"About five weeks ago you were greatly honored here," the tall one said.

"Not I. My school."

"You gave a speech."

"A little talk. It was expected."

"In it you chose to mention the name of a man far greater in the world's eyes than you. A man called Aram Sel. You called him the Devil."

"Yes." Why was it he felt he had to be truthful?

What power did this man—these men—have to make him give only honest answers when he knew them to be wholly evil?

"We are followers of Aram Sel. Do you understand now why we are here?"

In the silence that ensued, Babananda looked at them and they at him. He had not encountered such eyes before, ever. Or such minds. He knew what the eyes and the minds were doing to him, and he fought against letting it happen, but the longer it went on the more he realized he would have to call upon all his powers to defeat them.

He would defeat them—perhaps—if he could convince them they had won the struggle. Yes, yes! They must be made to believe they had conquered him. Whatever they wanted him to do, he must pretend to do or promise to do. Otherwise they would destroy him.

"What is it you want of me?" he asked humbly. It was easy to be humble. All his life, to *his* gurus, to the politicians who sought to use him, to the non-believers who called him a charlatan, he had been humble.

"What we want of you is your total obedience, guru." The voice of the tall follower of Aram Sel cut into his brain like a dagger.

"Yes." He must pretend to be wholly in their power even now. As he almost was, but not quite. If they felt it necessary to plunge the dagger deeper, he would be lost. "You have greater powers than I." He made his voice a whimper to convince them. "What must I do?"

"Where do you keep pen and paper?"

"I think in the desk in the study. This is not my home."

"Show us."

He knew where pen and paper were kept; he had used them more than once since coming to this house. Still pretending to be completely in their control, he led them inside to the desk and said, "Here, I believe."

"Sit."

He sat.

"Take a sheet of paper. Write on it what I am telling you to write. I am telling you in English and you will write it in English because all important people in this country speak English. But you will also write it afterward in Hindi, for those less educated. Are you ready?"

He was seated and ready, and suddenly the words assaulted his mind. Each word, each syllable, was a separate agony almost too monstrous to be endured.

Knowing they would read it over when he finished, he put down each and every English word exactly as their minds dictated the message. Then, as instructed, he wrote it again in Hindi.

Finished, he handed them the paper. They read it together and seemed satisfied. "Very well," the tall man said. "Go!"

Babananda struggled to his feet. He had written what they ordered him to write. He knew what he was supposed to do next. He knew he still had the will to resist.

There was but one question. Suppose he could not convince the superintendent of police—who might or might not be in the town at this time—suppose he could not convince that sometimes pompous individual of the seriousness of all this? Still, he must go. And pray that his mind would still retain its grain of defiance, and things would turn out all right.

Leaving the house, knowing the two from Aram Sel were surely watching him, he turned to his right along the road to the ashram. But there were side roads. After passing the first he turned down the second, hurried to the next corner, then turned again and was on a road parallel with the one he had first taken. But now he hurried in the opposite direction.

Not toward the ashram. Back toward the center of the town.

The mountain mist had burned away. The distant sky was a blue glow framing snow-clad mountains.

Barefoot, still wearing dhoti and blanket, the guru who some said was more than two hundred years old walked on with a firm step. Totally obsessed with the seriousness of his mission, frightened that he might fail despite his resolve, he turned another corner and was within a block of his destination.

What was he to say to the superintendent, who had *not* attended the twentieth-anniversary gathering at the ashram and did not believe India's holy men were holy? First, of course, he must describe his two callers and repeat what they had told him. Explain who they were—for this superintendent of police might not know that much about events outside India.

Then he would have to say, "Sir, let me pretend to be obeying these terrible people. Let me grovel to them. And while I do this, you and your men will arrest them and put an end to their reign of terror."

Even an unsympathetic SOP should agree to that.

But wait. The torment inside his skull was becoming intolerable. The dagger was being turned, twisted, driven deeper, and turned again. As if they who had thrust it there were reading his thoughts at this very moment and were taking steps to change his thinking.

Now he was not able to think at all. Some other mind was telling him what he must do. "Stop, guru. Stand against the wall there to your left." The wall was that of a very old storehouse, long abandoned, just waiting for some bulldozer to raze it so a more modern building could be erected in its place . . . after all, his beloved India was a mindless giant now, discarding the past as though it were an abomination.

Obediently he turned to the wall and let his shoulders slump against it. Babananda, the Siddha Mahatma, the highest saint, was now too full of suffering to take even one more step in defiance.

How could the Disciples of the infamous Aram Sel be so powerful? Where were the guardians who were supposed to protect the world from such monsters?

He leaned against the wall and looked at nothing. His eyes filled with tears. Only one block more and he would have reached the new brick building in which the superintendent of police for this district maintained an office. Only one block more, to save his ashram and himself from oblivion.

"Why did you think you could do this, Maharajji? Are you suddenly stupid?"

The dagger drove the words deep into his brain, and each was a new, more terrible agony.

"The superintendent cannot help you, guru." This time the voice was a thunderclap that threatened to blow his skull apart. "No one can help you now. You know what you were told to do. Go and do it."

He had no choice. There were people close enough to hear a cry for help, but his tongue would not work. Only a few steps from the one man in the entire district who might have saved him, he was forced to stagger away from the wall and return to the town's main road. The pain was more than even he could bear any longer. Only absolute obedience would cause it to diminish.

On reaching the main road he did not turn back toward the house from which his nightmare journey had begun. He went in the opposite direction, toward the ashram.

The walk was unreal.

He passed people who spoke to him—students, old friends, a woman from the pharmacy—but was unable to return their greetings. They seemed bewildered by his behavior. One young student followed him a little way, caught up with him, and tugged at his hand. "Maharajji, are you ill?"

He could only shake his head. The men of Aram Sel would allow him that much, it seemed, but had stolen his voice.

When he stumbled through the ashram's open gate at last, he knew exactly what he had to do. He, Babananda, who could go for weeks without food if need be, who could appear in some distant city at will while still seated in meditation on the ashram veranda, now had to obey every smallest command of two terrible men who controlled his mind.

From the gate he crossed the lawn to a small building at the back of the compound, in which the lawn-care tools were kept. There he took up a nearly full, five-gallon can of gasoline for the mowers, its weight causing him to struggle for breath as he went toward the ashram.

All parts of this ashram were connected: the Hanuman temple, the dormitories, the kitchen, the meeting rooms. At each door he entered and methodically splashed gasoline about. Then a stream of gasoline wet the veranda floor behind him as he stumbled along to the big main room.

At the far end of that room the old gatekeeper still sat on his chair, gazing wide-eyed at nothing. Babananda glanced at him but went past without a word, to spill gasoline in all parts of the chamber. That done, he emptied the remaining fuel onto one of the wooden platform beds, discarded the can, and seated himself on the bed with his legs folded.

The box of matches he drew from his dhoti was one he had picked up in the ashram kitchen. He opened it as though in a trance and took out a single match. Then without even a prayer for the safe passage of his soul—for the Disciples in their cruelty denied him even that—he rubbed the match against the box and let it fall blazing from his fingers.

On the veranda of the house in town the Disciples had been silently gazing in the direction of Babananda's ashram for some time. Now they saw what they were waiting for: a mass of dark smoke suddenly boiling up into the sky.

"Need we investigate, do you think?" the small one asked.

"No. He obeyed us. All that remains is to post this letter." Even while speaking, the tall Disciple stepped forward to thumbtack Babananda's letter to the door beside him.

As he did this, others in the town saw the distant smoke and sent up an outcry. The road filled with shouting figures, all of them running in the direction of the ashram. But the volume of smoke in the sky had already told them they would not arrive in time.

The two on the veranda watched for a few minutes in silence. Then as the babel died away in the distance and the road became empty again, the tall one said, "Come," and they departed. Side by side they strolled down the road and disappeared.

Behind them on the house door the letter they had forced Babananda to write awaited its first reader. Throughout the world there would soon be thousands.

In English the guru had written:

"To all those who heard me speak of the ruler of Siricus as 'the Devil,' and to all those who may have heard or read that I said it, be advised that I have decided to punish myself for sinning against such a great and good man. I go now to the ashram to do this thing."

But in Hindi the guru had dared to make a few alterations. Suspecting his murderers could not read that Indian language, he had written:

"To all those who heard me refer to the ruler of Siricus as 'the Devil'—know that what is about to happen to me is his work, intended as punishment. Ignore what I have written above under duress, with two of that Devil's disciples standing over me."

8

When the Leggs came to call, Mark learned more about Eve Vernon. But only because they came so late in the evening that she had already retired to her room at the end of the yard, and he felt free to ask questions.

"No, indeed, she wasn't born handicapped," Mildred Legg said in reply to one question. "She was a perfectly normal child until just a few days after her third birthday. An absolutely adorable child. Then she had scarlet fever and nearly died, poor thing, and it left her the way she is today."

She said this so softly that Mark might have thought her overwhelmed with sadness, except that she had already discussed a number of other matters in the same whisper. It was her natural speaking voice. She was a featherweight woman scarcely half the size of her husband, with white hair and a wonderfully pretty face.

"We loved Eve's father," Mildred went on. "Everyone did. I don't suppose there ever was another doctor who gave so much of himself for the people of these hills."

"How did he happen to settle here?"

"He came out from England the year Jeff and I were married. First he tried Kingston and didn't like it. He was a country bumpkin at heart, he always said. Then he met Lydia Baylor. She was English, too. She taught school at Royalton—that's a big estate near Holland Bay—and disliked the city as much as he did. So when they were married, they bought the old Forsythe place in Trinity."

Mildred seemed to enjoy talking about Eve's parents. "They were heartbroken, of course, when Eve was stricken. They did absolutely everything: took her to specialists in England and the States, and to that Episcopalian sister in Haiti who does so much for handicapped children—but it was just hopeless. I'm sure Lydia died of a broken heart. But Dr. Vernon never stopped trying. Even last year, just before *he* died—he died suddenly at the wheel of his car, you know, of a heart attack—even last year he went to Canada to consult with still another specialist. Poor man, he spent just all he had, trying to help Eve."

"She still has a home, though?" Mark asked.

"Yes, the house. But it's old now and run-down. She needs this job, believe me."

Mark wondered what Eve would do when he left Shepstowe. A year was not such a long time, after all, and more than a little of it was already gone. He did not like to think about it.

"Are you writing about Jamaica?" Mildred asked. It was high time, she went on without waiting for an answer, that someone wrote a good book about the Jamaican country people. Not a travel book—there were several good travel books, actually—but a

novel in which a writer of sensitivity and understanding could depict the country folk as they were.

She read a lot, it seemed, and did not care much
for most novels with a Jamaican background. "When
they're written by Jamaicans," she said, "they're full
of the most awful rubbish about how much better
our people are than any others in the world—better
at absolutely everything, mind you—and when written by outsiders they make us all seem stupid. My
goodness," she said, "we're just the same mixture of
sense and nonsense as any other people, I'm sure,
and if you write about us, Mr. Burke, I hope you'll
say so. You *will* be writing about us, I suppose."

"I'm afraid so," Mark said.

"Not another travel book?"

"No. A novel."

"In which, I'll risk a guess," Legg said with a
smile, "some character has to walk a country road at
night." He shook his head in wonder. "I had no idea
an author worked so hard to be authentic. Did you
know," he said to his wife, "that this man *walked* out
here from town? And at night?"

Mildred looked astounded, and Mark said with a
frown, "How do you know I did?"

Legg chuckled. "A shopkeeper in Llandewey saw
you. Asked me today if I knew who the man with the
beard was. Woman in Richmond Vale says you
started dogs barking and woke up the village."

So Goodwin was wrong, Mark thought. I might as
well have taken the bus.

He was wryly pleased to discover that Argus could
be wrong about something so important. There was
a certain satisfaction in it, even though his safety ap-

parently depended on their being more often right. "In the book I'm doing," he said, to satisfy any curiosity the Leggs might have, "a man *will* have to walk here from the city at night. I thought I'd better find out what it feels like."

"It's obvious you don't believe in duppies." Mildred chuckled. "That's one thing I do have against our country people. They're afraid of the silliest things."

"I wouldn't know a duppy if I fell over one." Mark gestured helplessly. "What are they, exactly? Books on Jamaica mention them often enough, but no one ever seems to come up with a definition."

"Well," Mildred said, "a duppy is a ghost or spirit. Someone dead come back to life, to do some kind of evil. No one ever does seem to define the word, really—you're right about that—but the place you're most likely to encounter one is near a graveyard, at night." She smiled. "Anyway, Peter Burke, when the people find you walked that road at night, they'll think you a brave man."

"Don't be so sure," her husband warned. "They just might decide he had no reason to be afraid."

"Meaning what, for heaven's sake?"

"You know them, Milly. If they think you *ought* to be afraid of a thing and you're not, there's something strange about you."

"Well," Mark said, "they probably think a writer is an odd duck, anyway. By the way, I—"

He had been going to mention the obeah signs again, and it seemed Jeff Legg had the same thought. Or was it that he, Mark Donner, had projected the thought so strongly, as he sometimes did without meaning to, that Jeff had picked it up? Whatever the answer, Jeff spoke just as he did, saying, "About our lizard—" and then both were silent, each waiting for the other to continue.

"About the lizard?" Mark echoed. "Yes?"

"I've done some more probing among the factory workers, but can't find out anything. They *are* afraid of certain lizards, these people—foolishly so, because there are no really harmful ones in the island—and obviously the thing was meant to give you something to think about. But I still haven't a clue as to who might have done the job."

Mark told about the red flag in the garden.

"Someone has hired an obeah person to work on you, it would seem," Jeff said. "But why? No one out here even knows you yet."

"Did your coffee-works people tell you about the gutter this morning?"

"They think it was done deliberately. I don't understand that, either. We do have troubles of that sort once in a while, usually after firing someone, but I haven't had to fire anyone lately."

"In other words, this was aimed at me. To shut off the Shepstowe water and give me trouble."

"It would seem so. If it *was* deliberate."

When his callers had gone, Mark thought about them while getting ready for bed. Jeff was obviously a solid, down-to-earth man with no pretense, and Mildred was warm and friendly. He would have to ask them to dinner one evening. Before then, though, there must be some changes made around the place—changes he was determined to make, anyway. It might be necessary for Eve Vernon to work as a housekeeper, but it was neither necessary nor right for her to be the sort of servant she had elected to be.

First, though, he must persuade her to change her quarters.

He brought up the subject again the next day, but again met resistance. Two kinds of resistance. Openly she insisted she was not afraid to be alone in her room out back, and there might be talk if she moved into the house. But behind her written words he caught something else—after all, she had admitted to a knowledge of ESP and was fairly good at it. He should realize how it would look, she was thinking, if he had callers who stayed late and heard her moving about in the bedroom they would naturally assume was his.

He was not amused. "I don't give a damn what people might think," his mind retorted while his fingers tapped out a more polite reply.

Before even glancing at what he had written, she looked at him curiously, as though she had received the telepathic message. Then she read the typewritten words asking her to reconsider, and shook her head at him.

This happened at lunch. In the afternoon he went out to the garden and found McCoy industriously forking the strip of earth where the gone-wild coffee trees had been. A second man slashed at weeds. Perhaps because of his failure with Eve, Mark was annoyed.

"I didn't tell you to bring a helper. I can't afford two people."

McCoy seemed upset by the criticism. "Him is not

workin' for pay, sah," he explained, lapsing more deeply into the patois than he usually did. "Him is only my woman's brother that live with we." He tapped the side of his head to indicate a shortage of intelligence. "Him not bright up here, squire."

Mark looked again at the helper, who seemed oblivious of his presence. There was indeed something wrong. The youth was about eighteen and could work well enough—in fact, was built like a professional football player—but attacked the weeds as though they infuriated him, and muttered to himself as he worked.

Suddenly he laughed and stood up, holding out by its tail a large green lizard whose head he had chopped off.

McCoy backed away, wild-eyed. "Put it down, that!"

The youth giggled, gleefully waving his trophy back and forth.

"Put it down, me say!" McCoy hoarsely shouted. "It the kind make you turn green all over like itself!"

With a shrug the boy tossed the headless thing away and returned to work. McCoy stopped breathing so heavily. Mark, not eager for a peasant lecture on lizards, said quietly, "What's his name?"

"We call him 'Iron,' squire."

"Iron?"

"Him strong. Him truly powerful." McCoy glared at the fellow for a moment, then smiled and added in his normal spongy voice, "You leave him to me, sah. He can ease the work for me and it cost you nuttin'."

"Well, we'll see."

"Thank you, sah."

9

Mark returned to the house and tried working. It was no use. For a while he sat at the table, wondering whether real writers faced times when every thought led to a dead end. Then he decided to have a look at the village called Mango Gut, where McCoy and Iron lived. It took only a moment to tell Eve where he was going.

At the top of the Shepstowe driveway he took the footpath along which the women had appeared. It was a pretty path. For a time it wriggled through tall, lacy-leaved trees—he had no idea what kind they were—and then it dipped sharply downhill between walls of red earth.

This was the mountainside below the Shepstowe veranda, he realized, but from there the path was hidden by forest. He came presently to a leaning bamboo fence—the rocky slope behind it was a carrot garden—and then to a wattle-and-daub house.

A woman washing clothes at a tub in the yard was pure peasant, but said, "Good morning, sir," not "Mornin'" or "sah." They had different ways of talking, he now knew. Even the same person might word things differently at different times, as McCoy did.

Perhaps it depended on how they felt at the moment. Returning the woman's greeting, he was amused by an octet of round eyes, all nearly the same height, peering at him from the doorway.

He passed more houses. All were of the same rough construction, with roofs of corroding zinc. They varied in size and, from what he could see without rudely staring, in the way they were furnished. Apparently the status symbol was a bed. If you had money enough, you bought a big one layered with varnish and decorated with flowers that looked like no flowers on earth.

There were gardens, too. Gardens everywhere. Little ones at the sides of the houses, big ones that sprawled up and down hillsides lumpy with boulders. Men and women at work in them paused to greet him with smiles, some using his assumed name. Friendly people, good people. I wish I could actually make a living as a writer, he thought. I might stay here.

The path widened now to become a sort of village green or common. The grass was short—they used machetes on it, he supposed—and there was a straight strip of firmed earth that must be for cricket, the most popular outdoor game in the island. He went into a shop and bought from the man behind the counter a bottle of something called kola champagne, too sweet for his taste but cooling after his long walk in the sun.

"We is glad to know someone is living in the Great House again," the shopkeeper told him. "It don't look good to have that big place standing empty." Old and bent, with hair white as sugar, he must have known many an owner or tenant at Shepstowe.

"I'm glad to be here. I like it here."

"It seem so, you walking about already to get acquainted."

Mark smiled. "I must confess, though, that I didn't know there was a village this big down here."

"We is not truly a village. Only what you see."

"Whatever you are, it's very pleasant."

The old man said his name was Henderson. He said he understood Mr. Burke was a writer, and when Mark nodded, he said it must take a great deal of learning to be a writer. That was what the district needed: men with learning. "We have problems here. We need good men to show us how to solve them. Take we carrots and scallions, for instance. They sell in Kingston for a good price, especially in the supermarkets, but do we get that kind of price for growing them? We do not."

A woman and two men came into the shop then, and Henderson gravely introduced them as Mr. Shepherd, Mr. Crosdale, and Miss Weeks. Mr. Burke was a fine man, he solemnly informed them, a man truly interested in their problems. Look at how he had walked all the way down here from the Great House to make himself known. Only a truly good man would do that so soon after moving into the district.

The three listened and nodded, and the two men said, "Yes, yes, true," and "What you say is so." Miss Weeks, though, studied Mark in silence for a moment. About thirty and very much a female, she finally said, "Tell we something, Marse Burke. Is it a fact you did walk here from Kingston in the nighttime?"

Mark laughed. "Not all the way. But I did walk, yes."

"Alone? By youself?"

"Yes, by myself."

She backed away, still studying him. She had exceptionally bright eyes, he noticed; they seemed to flicker like bits of glass with flames behind them. "I is not meaning to be rude," she said, her voice falling to a whisper. "I is just asking because I hear people talk."

"Why? Shouldn't I have walked?"

"Oh yes, sah! There's nuttin' wrong with walkin'!"

But, of course, there was.

This is something you didn't know, Goodwin, Mark thought as he strolled back up to Shepstowe: that a stranger walking these country roads at night is more suspect than one on a bus. Or was it Graham who had decided he should walk?

He would have to make a list of Argus's little blunders and present it to them someday. In a year the list should be impressive. Still, it was probably too much to expect a man in Washington, or even Kingston, to know everything about a place such as this.

On reaching the house he found Eve in the kitchen, preparing dinner. With gestures he tried to tell her it smelled good, and she smiled. Needing no more encouragement than that, he perched on a stool and watched her.

"In case you don't know it," he said to her back, "I've done quite a bit of cooking myself. You've never asked me, but I happen to be a thirty-three-year-old bachelor. An unmarried man that old has generally done more than boil an egg or two."

She heard nothing, of course. Yet she turned to look at him as though she had.

Taking a chicken from the oven, she began to put a salad together. There was no need whatever for him to offer assistance, but on an impulse he slid from the stool and stepped to her side. She did not protest when he took over the salad making.

It was pleasant to be working beside her. Much more so than sitting upstairs on the veranda, waiting for her to let him know the meal was ready. The lack of conversation did not trouble him. He kept glancing at her face as she moved about, and when she caught him doing so, she smiled. There was a kind of communication that was in some ways better than words.

Mark wondered about his feeling of ease with her. Was it because she could *not* talk? That could well be the answer. With a woman who did talk he might have felt a need to keep his distance. He was not proud of being shy, but the shyness was there and he had learned to live with it. Other men had to live with ulcers, he thought whimsically. Or false teeth. Or hearing aids.

While he was carving the chicken, Eve took two plates from a shelf. One she placed on a tray with the serving dishes that contained his dinner. The other, he supposed, was for her own dinner when she returned to the kitchen.

He placed her plate on top of his own and picked the tray up.

She shook her head violently in protest.

He spoke aloud to her. "I am not going to eat my dinner alone. Don't argue." When she reached for the tray, he turned from her hands and marched to the door.

She followed him upstairs. He ignored her. Agitated now, she fluttered about him, trying to stop him as he rearranged the table to make a place for her. It was then that he snatched pencil and paper and furiously scribbled, "Listen to me, please. I do not like dining alone!" and underlined the words twice.

She stood very still, looking at him.

He wrote then, more slowly, "Please, Eve. We are two people in a big, empty house. You are a doctor's daughter and I am"—he almost wrote "a school-teacher" but remembered in time—"just a man who writes books. Can't we be friends?"

She looked at what he had written, but did not lift her gaze to meet his when she had finished. Stepping around her, he drew out a chair for her at the table. After a moment, still with her gaze lowered, she sat down.

She seemed about to cry, and when at last she lifted her head, there was indeed a kind of liquid brightness in her eyes. She had brown eyes that matched her hair, Mark noticed for the first time.

He smiled at her and shaped the words "Thank you" with his lips. After a time she shyly smiled back.

10

Again this time the assignment called for only two of Khargi's people.

"For now it is best we keep a low profile," their tutor explained. "Also, if we operate only in pairs at this stage, while preparing to move against the imperialist Americans, the damage to our organization will not be so great should anything go wrong."

The target on this occasion was a small, mountainous country to the east of the Disciples' Mediterranean base, to be taught a lesson because its ruler had dared to call Siricus a land of murderers and declare Aram Sel's envoy persona non grata.

On the day the dismissed envoy arrived back in Siricus, Khargi dispatched Disciple No. 7 and Disciple No. 13 to "let the world know we do not accept such insults."

Armed with false passports, they entered the target country as citizens of Turkey. In customs their small suitcases appeared to contain only the personal things any two men might need for a brief stay.

After all, what immigration or customs officers would challenge men who, simply by staring at them, told them what to *think*?

Two days later the two Disciples lay on a ledge of rock high in the mountains, peering down a forested slope at a body of water that caught the high-noon sunlight and threw winks of silver back into their eyes.

"Not very big," Seven said with a shrug.

"But deep. Khargi pointed that out. It is very deep."

The lake's name appeared on no list of the world's most important. Still, it was surrounded by a high chain link fence, topped with spirals of barbed wire, that would have been more appropriate around a prison. In keeping with the prison likeness, two tall guard towers, manned day and night, allowed specially trained watchmen to look and listen for possible intruders.

Khargi had told them what they would find. Khargi had carefully instructed them what to do about it. Because this mountain lake supplied all the water consumed in the country's capital, population just under 300,000, that sprawled so prettily over the foothills below.

The ruler who had dared to call Siricus a land of murderers lived in a palace there. He drank this water.

He and all the others.

"If you are ready," Seven said, "let's begin."

Opening the two suitcases which had seemed so innocent in customs, they took from one what appeared to be an electric razor in its case. From a compartment behind the lining of the other they removed an assortment of balsa-wood shapes and a telescoped antenna.

Now for a few minutes they worked swiftly, in silence, to combine these items. And when all the parts were in place they had a model airplane.

Gazing at it with satisfaction, Seven reminded his companion how, back in Siricus, its creator had laughed loud and long when they jokingly suggested he smuggle himself into the U.S. and earn huge sums of money doing such things for that country's Central Intelligence Agency.

Thirteen smiled in reply as he removed from his left ear a small, flesh-colored, plastic hearing aid to which the customs men at the airport had paid no attention. Of course, if it *had* aroused suspicion, the cold stare of its owner would at once have removed any such thoughts from the man's mind.

With the thin blade of a small pocket knife Thirteen opened the plastic button, and with a pair of tweezers he very carefully lifted out of it a small gray-blue tablet. This he transferred to a receptacle under the body of the plane, swinging into place, to hold it there, a little disc of some sugarlike substance that would dissolve on contact with water.

"It seems small for the job," Seven observed with a frown.

"Khargi said it's big enough to handle a reservoir twice the size of this."

"Where did he get it?"

"You're asking me? Where does he acquire half the weapons in our arsenal? He brought a Russian scientist into our organization last month, if that means anything." Thirteen shrugged. "I can tell you this: Without Khargi, Aram Sel would have no organization. Khargi built it, he trained everyone in it, he *is* it. Right this moment his directed thoughts are telling us what to do here, whether you're aware of it or not."

"What to do, eh? Which is to stop talking and direct *this* little thought"—Seven tapped the model airplane—"on its mission."

The tiny plane was painted silver with spots of green, to blend first with the sky and then with the mountain-slope forest as it descended over the lake. And finally to blend with the winks of silver created by the high-noon sunlight on the reservoir's surface.

"Bon voyage, then," said Thirteen, who already had the remote-control device in his right hand.

The winged death took off from Seven's fingers and spiraled down upon the lake. Even alert eyes in the guard towers would probably not have seen it, and at this hour when high-noon heat made human eyelids heavy, Khargi's prediction had to be correct.

"They will never notice it," the great tutor had said with his usual assurance. "They will never see the splash, either, when you fly it into the water. That will be simply a fish rising to an insect.

"So then you will get out of there," Khargi had instructed. "You must be out of the country within two hours at the most—before they begin to realize it is the water that is killing them off."

Thirteen looked at his companion. Below them the model plane had plunged in among the silver winks of the lake's surface. "Done without a hitch," he said. "Khargi will commend us."

"As he should," said Seven. "And Aram Sel, too. These people will be burying their dead for weeks."

11

Mark sat at his typewriter, reading over what he had written. He had not accomplished much, he realized with a twinge of frustration. He was hopelessly slow. Sooner or later, too, he would reach the end of what actually had happened to him and would have to start inventing. Then his troubles would begin in earnest.

The two trunks had been in my apartment for several days, empty because Graham had said he would take care of what I needed. I knew they would somehow change my entire life, wrenching me out of my placid schoolteacher existence and thrusting me into adventures for which I was in no way prepared.

Then Graham came again.

He came on a Friday evening, late, with a number of department-store boxes containing clothes for me. As he emptied them into the trunks, he told me there would be others arriving the next day. Then he handed me a large brown envelope from his inside jacket pocket.

"Look at these papers carefully," he said. "If you have any questions, I'll try to answer them."

I sat down and opened the envelope. It contained a passport issued not to me, but to a Peter Burke. The photograph puzzled me, too. "This isn't a picture of me," I protested.

"Look again. It's you with a beard. You'll grow one in Mexico."

"How did you do it?"

"You ask too many questions."

I examined the passport again. "All right, but I'll ask another one. You say I'm to go to Mexico, but this is a Jamaican visa."

"You won't need one for Mexico; you won't be there that long. Until Jamaica you won't need this passport at all."

I could only shake my head.

"Have you brushed up on your Spanish?" he asked.

"As much as I could in such a short time."

"Good. Now listen carefully. You leave here next Wednesday for Mexico. Your tickets are there in the envelope with the dates on them; no need to take notes." (He saw I was frantically scribbling.) "You'll arrive in Mexico City that evening and you have a reservation at a little hotel off Cinco de Mayo. It's all in there; study it later. You're to stay in the city ten days."

"Doing what?"

He still had his twisted sense of humor. "Mostly starting the beard you see in that passport photo. What else you do is your own affair, so long as you keep out of trouble. You'll have some money. In fact, you'll have much more money for the next twelve months than you would earn as a teacher."

"I'd rather be a teacher."

"But not a dead one, I imagine. And the chances of your being dead if you don't follow directions are about ninety-nine to one. As I've told you, or maybe tried not to tell you, you have innocently become a key figure in—" Just when on the verge of perhaps revealing himself to be human, after all, he pulled up short. "Sorry. Let's get back on track."

"I was hoping you'd become untracked."

"Uh-uh. We were in Mexico City."

I waited, keenly disappointed.

"All right," he went on. "You'll be there ten days, as I've said. Then you check out of your hotel and take the train to Mérida."

For the first time I was pleased. I had read at least three books about the Yucatán and the Mayan ruins there, and the prospect of visiting that part of Mexico thrilled me. I could have been one of those game-show contestants who win a vacation abroad and delight the television audience—or, at least, the producers—by jumping up and down in glee.

"How long am I to be in Mérida?" I asked eagerly.

"A week. All the dates are in there." He indicated the envelope again.

"Staying where?"

"Well, not at a fancy tourist hotel. But I imagine a nice little back-street *pensión* will suit you better, anyway."

"And I can do as I please?"

His grin returned. "You know about the Chichén Itzá ruins, do you? All right. I've been there, and they *are* something. Be our guest."

"But why send me there at all?"

"Our man in Jamaica has to set things up for you. When you fly from Mérida to Kingston—Mexicana has a direct flight—he'll meet you at the Kingston airport and drive you to a guest house. There he'll provide further instructions which—let me make this clear—you are to carry out to the letter."

There was a long silence. Then Graham said, "Any questions?"

"You told me last time that I'm supposed to be a writer."

"Correct. Not in Mexico, though. You won't be there long enough for anyone to wonder what you do for a living. If you *are* asked, you're a writer on vacation. In Jamaica you'll *be* a writer."

101

Proud of myself for having found a flaw in his plan, I said, "If I claim to be a writer in either place, someone is sure to ask me what I've written."

He narrowed his pale eyes at me. "My, my, aren't we smart? But you're right. You won't know what you've written until you get to your final destination. If anyone in Mexico or Kingston should question you, tell them you *sell* books. Schoolbooks. You'll be on safe ground there."

"Why should anyone at my final destination, as you call it, believe I'm a writer?"

"Because you'll write. There'll be a typewriter in one of these trunks. And there'll be books. Your books."

"I haven't written any books."

"*You* think," Graham said with a chuckle. (That warped sense of humor again.) "We'll attend to that. I should say we *have* attended to that." I must have looked puzzled, for he added with a shrug, "Take your time, friend. If you try to swallow all this at once, you'll choke."

"I wish you would be honest with me and tell me why I have to do these things," I said.

"I *am* being honest. You have to do them to go on living."

"That isn't an answer."

"Sorry." He shook his pink head, and for the first time seemed genuinely sympathetic. "Actually, Donner, you're better off not knowing too much. If you did, you might start thinking for yourself instead of letting us think for you. We've had experience in this sort of thing. Or if not in this sort of thing, we're at least professionals. You're an innocent."

"And it will be for a year?"

"More or less. Probably much less if things go well. As I say, I regret it but it just can't be helped. If you and your brother were not identical twins—but, my God, you look so much alike it gives me the creeps to be sitting here talking to you."

"Where is my brother?" I asked. Vincent had said he could not tell me that when I talked to him earlier, in the telephone conversation they had arranged for us.

When Graham offered no answer, I glared at him and repeated the question. "Where *is* Vin?"

"As I told you before, he can take care of himself." The man from Washington rose to depart. "That's all I can say, so help me, until—" He shook his head.

"Until what?"

"Well—" And now suddenly I sensed a fear in him that refused to be bottled up any longer. It showed in his eyes. It had crept into his voice. "Until we either win out over those creeps or they turn us into zombies, damn them!" After a shudder that seemed to rack his whole frail body, he pulled himself together. "You've talked to your brother," he said defensively. "You know what he said."

"I know what he said. That doesn't mean I understand it."

"For now it's better you don't," he growled. "Let's keep it that way, shall we? When the time comes for you to know more, I'll see that you do."

Then, before turning to go, he surprised me by offering his hand. "Oh hell, it won't be so bad," he said, resorting to that warped sense of humor again—as though he could not continue playing the

103

game without it. "Think of all the tourists who pay through the nose to spend just a few days in Mexico or Jamaica. All those lovelies in bikinis on the beaches."

12

The "simple" country life was not so simple, Mark discovered. He wanted to explore Shepstowe's five hundred acres—after all, he rented the estate and would be here for months—but there was no time for it. The old Great House seemed maliciously determined to keep him busy.

One day the kitchen stove refused to function. A stranger to that type of stove, he wasted most of the morning on it before discovering the trouble was outside at the cylinder of gas, where a connection had worked loose or been loosened.

Again, the lights failed one night even though the generator at the factory was working properly. It took him half the next day to discover that the line from the factory, strung from pole to pole through the big flat called the meadow, had broken or been cut. Of course, the break was in a clump of trees where it had escaped the notice of the coffee workers going to and from their jobs in the fields.

Small troubles, yes. But after the obeah signs and the broken gutter, they made him jumpy. *Was* there a conspiracy afoot to make him give up and go home? If so, would the little annoyances grow into more sinister uglies when he refused to be shaken?

He did walk enough of the estate to learn one significant thing about it. It was a crazy quilt of all-but-vertical mountainsides and deep ravines, and there was a wild white stream through parts of it that produced a ceaseless thunder. Maybe it was foolish of him even to think of exploring such a terrain by himself. But he hoped to try.

Then one morning Eve came into the drawing room while he was working on his book, and when he looked up at her, she held up her slate. On it she had written, "Of all things, we are out of matches. I'm sorry. Shall I try to borrow some at the coffee works?"

He welcomed the excuse to stop working. "Let me," he wrote. "I want to see Jeff, anyway."

Before leaving the house he put his manuscript away. It was about time for friend Goodwin to come again, and there might be trouble if Our Man in Jamaica walked in and found it. Near the factory, women were harvesting the red cherries from coffee trees on the co-op property, and he walked slowly so as to watch them. The trees with their glossy dark green leaves and cranberrylike fruit were truly handsome now, and the women nodded and smiled, greeting him as they had before.

Jeff Legg was at the factory, standing by a machine that squeezed the coffee beans from the cherries—a pulper, he called it when Mark asked.

"Needs watching or it can crush the beans," he said. "At least, ours does—especially if the coffee is not quite ripe. Our women are pretty careful to pick only the ripe ones, though. We're proud of our quality here."

"What happens after the pulping?"

"The beans float down to fermenting tanks. Then they're washed and moved out to those concrete platforms—barbecues—you see through the windows there. When the sun has partially dried them, they go into a machine dryer to finish the job, then to another machine that rubs the parchment skin off, and finally through a sizer. At the end they're picked over by hand here—you've seen the women doing that—to remove any broken or bad ones."

"It seems a cup of coffee is a major operation."

"Think of that next time you groan about the price," Legg said dryly.

"Tell me something. Do you know the history of Shepstowe House?"

"Some of it."

"Is there anywhere I can get it all?"

Legg's leathery face took on some deep creases. "I'm not sure. The Institute, maybe. That's on East Street in Kingston. They have a whole section of books about the old days."

Mark knew he could not go to Kingston. "There's no library around here? I want to use the house in the novel I'm writing. The more I can find out about it, the better."

"I'll have a look at home," Legg said. "Milly has some old books about this parish that might help you." He chuckled. "So the old Shepstowe place is going to be in a novel, is it? That's one book I'll have to read."

You probably never will, Mark thought.

"And it's odd you should ask about the house," Legg added. "I've got a letter for you. Come on to the office."

In his cubbyhole of an office the manager took an envelope from his desk. "As you can see, it's addressed simply to Shepstowe House, Rainy Ridge, Jamaica. That's why I opened it. But it's your kind of thing, not mine."

Mark frowned at the printed return address. Stellar Publishing Company, 1017 N.W. 30th St., Miami, Florida? It must be a small company or a new one. He had never heard of it.

The typewritten sheet inside bore the same printed information as the envelope, and read:

Sir:

Our company recently acquired reprint rights to a much admired book about Jamaica which you may well be familiar with: *An Island to Remember* by Carroll Hughes. Mr. Hughes had agreed to make certain alterations to his book, mostly to update it. Unfortunately he passed away of a heart attack before he was able to do the work.

His widow, Catherine Hughes, has graciously consented to my doing the necessary updating, and so I am writing to you in the hope that you may be willing to help me.

It is my desire to expand the chapter titled "Jamaican Great Houses" to include a description and brief history of Shepstowe. Could you possibly supply this information? There would be no need for you to polish your prose for publication; I will do that. I need only a letter from you conveying the information in your own words.

We are not a large company, but can offer you a token payment of $50 for your assistance and would, of course, send you a copy of the book upon publication. In addition, you would be given full credit for supplying the information on which the paragraphs about Shepstowe will be based.

I look forward to hearing from you. Please use the enclosed envelope in replying. I work at my son's home these days while struggling with an arthritic hip, and am temporarily picking up my mail at a post office close by.

Sincerely yours,
Alan H. Koch, Editor

Puzzled, Mark looked at the enclosed return envelope. It was addressed to the writer at General Delivery, Coconut Grove Sta., Miami, FL 33133. "It's an odd one, all right," he said to Jeff Legg.

"Will you do it?"

"Well, as I told you, I want to bone up on Shepstowe's past for my own book. So why not? That is, if you don't mind."

"Me mind? Lord, I'm no one to answer it!"

Mark glanced at the reply envelope again. It had no stamp on it, but then, where would a man in Florida buy Jamaican stamps? He pocketed the whole thing and remembered what he had come to the factory for. "By the way, I need some matches if you can spare some. We're out, Eve tells me."

Legg found a small box of them in his desk. "I can get you more by asking the workers."

"Uh-uh. I'll walk down to Rainy Ridge and buy some. Want to see it, anyway. I didn't pay much attention that first morning." And will have to describe it in my book, Mark thought.

"Have fun," Legg said with his usual dry smile. "Today is market day."

The road seemed shorter this time. He hadn't walked all night, of course, and was not exhausted. In fact, he felt better here in the Blue Mountains of Jamaica, physically stronger and more alive, than he had felt in a long time. It must be the mountain air.

As he neared the village he met women with baskets of produce on their heads. They had done their marketing and were returning to their homes, he supposed. Many spoke to him. In the village itself both sides of the road were lined with displays of foodstuffs, and the lane between was a slow-moving river of humanity. A car could not easily have got through.

He was greeted now from all sides. Higglers beckoned him to come look at their wares and made mock-solemn faces at him when he insisted he needed nothing. Men nodded and saluted him and called him "squire" or "Busha." A boy bawled at a laden donkey to get out of Marse Burke's way.

He went into the largest of the shops and was not surprised to discover it was run by a Chinese. Practically every country village in Jamaica had its "Chinaman's shop." The proprietor of this one stood behind a dingy, cluttered counter with his thin hands flat on the countertop. His toothy smile was marred by a broken incisor.

The island Chinese had first arrived when the slaves were freed, Mark remembered reading. The big sugar estates were struggling for survival at the time, desperate for workers, and the Chinese had been brought in as indentured labor to work in the fields. Now they all but controlled the retail grocery trade. In a village such as this they mixed only a little with the people.

"I'd like some matches."

"Yes, yes, Mr. Burke. Matches." So his name was known here, too. "A carton, yes?"

"Please."

Matches on the counter—slap!—and the proprietor was a statue again behind it, teeth on display and hands flat. It was slightly incredible. Mark had not even seen where the matches came from.

This was worth a further demonstration, he thought. "I could use some pencils, too. Do you have any?" No matter what he asked for, it would be here somewhere, without a doubt. The grubby shelves seemed to hold everything from machete files to jars of instant coffee. *Instant*, when one of the world's best coffees was produced just up the road? From the rafters hung an English bicycle, upside down.

"Pencils, yes." Slap! A package of yellow pencils appeared on the counter, and the fellow was all teeth again.

"I think that's all, thanks."

The proprietor took Mark's Jamaican ten-dollar note and gave him change. "You come from America, huh?"

"Well, yes."

"Very nice people, Americans. I have son in America, go to school in New York."

"Really?" Mark was surprised enough to be curious. "Where does he go?"

"You not know, I think. Place call Omega Art School. Son have great talent."

"I'm sure he must have."

"You be here long?"

"Maybe. I'm not sure."

"You write books, hey?"

"Yes."

"Next time in Kingston, I buy some. Go to book-shop." He beamed now. "Have to be very smart man to write books, yes? I come to Shepstowe sometime, call on you."

Mark felt a breath of panic chill his face. "When I've had a chance to get settled, please. I've only just got here, you know."

"Yes, yes, when you settled."

It might have gone on longer—Mark could see no way to end it without offending—but just then some customers walked in.

Picking up his purchases, he left in a hurry.

13

Past the coffee works, climbing a boulder-strewn grade, Mark heard a patter of small feet and turned to find a barefoot, breathless little girl running after him. Laughing gaily at her accomplishment in overtaking him, she promptly clutched his hand.

"Well, hello," he said, delighted. "Who are you?"

She laughed again, a sound like tiny bells. "I can walk with you?"

"Certainly you can walk with me. But what's your name?"

"Merlinda McCoy." It was a solemn declaration.

Mark repeated it, and they continued up the road together.

She discovered the watch on his wrist and made him stop again so she could examine it. After bending her head to put an ear against it, she looked up at him and laughed her little laugh again. When she tried to tug the watch off his wrist, though, he stopped her.

"No. You'll break it."

She pouted. The pout vanished. She laughed again and pulled him on up the road.

"Merlinda McCoy?" he said suddenly, frowning down at her. "Where do you live?" They were almost at the Shepstowe driveway.

"Down there." She stuck one small finger out of a clenched hand to point. "With my gramdaddy."

"Your gramdaddy works for me?"

"Uh-huh."

"I see. Well, then, I'm glad to know you. I'd be glad to know you, anyway."

She laughed again and pulled him down by his arm so she could plant a quick, wet kiss on his cheek. All the way down the driveway she clung to his hand, bouncing along beside him on her small bare feet. Then in front of the carriage house she abruptly said "G'bye!" and ran off to McCoy in the garden where the coffee trees had been.

* * *

Goodwin, the golden-haired man from Kingston, came that afternoon with supplies. Producing the packets of seeds Mark had asked for, he flipped them onto the table as though dealing cards.

"Lettuce," he said. "Radishes. Broccoli. Cauliflower. String beans. Salsify, whatever the hell that is. Chinese cabbage—grow some for the Chinaman if you don't like it; he'll be your pal for life. Summer squash. Cucumbers. Tomatoes—damned expensive in town, I can tell you." He threw the rest down in a heap. "You know something? If you grow all this, I'm coming out here to live with you. There are some flower seeds in there, too. I figured Eve might like some. Everybody in these hills grows flowers."

"She'll be grateful, I'm sure."

Eve had come into the room while Goodwin was talking. At least, she had come as far as the doorway and stopped there. The blond man noticed her now and waved a hand in salute. At the same time he said, "This time I *will* have a drink, if you don't mind."

Passing Eve on his way to fill the request, Mark was puzzled by her expression. Her gaze was fixed on Goodwin, he saw—actually on Goodwin's face, as though she were trying to read the man's lips. When he returned with the drink, she was still standing there. It annoyed him to think she might be waiting for Goodwin to give her an order, as though she were a servant.

Downing his drink, the golden-haired man produced from his pocket the whistle Mark had requested. "Any more obeah signs?"

113

"Well, not really." There was no point in telling him about the other things, Mark decided. He had no proof, after all, that any of them were deliberate. Or even if deliberate, were aimed at him.

"You explored the whole place yet?"

"Far from it. The days aren't long enough."

"Take your time. You'll see it all soon enough. Myself, I predict you'll be heartily sick of Shepstowe before you even know where the boundaries are." Goodwin grinned. "Well, I'm gone again. See you next week." Again he saluted Eve, and again, gazing at him in her strangely intense way, she answered with a nod.

When the man from Kingston had departed, Mark handed Eve the whistle and explained on the typewriter why he wanted her to have it. He was puzzled by her reaction to Goodwin. Did she dislike the man for some reason? Had something happened between them when Goodwin approached her to be housekeeper here? She seemed almost afraid.

It was not his business, he decided. He certainly had no intention of trying to force the fellow on her as a friend just because Goodwin would be coming once a week with supplies. "Try it," he wrote, meaning the whistle.

Reluctantly she did so, and he was satisfied. It produced a blast that would certainly wake him, no matter how soundly he might be sleeping. He was a light sleeper most of the time, anyway.

"Would you like part of the new garden for flowers?" he asked.

"Oh yes!"

"Fine. If you're not busy, why don't we do some planting?"

They went to the garden together and found Mc-Coy and the not-bright Iron at work there, with Mc-Coy's granddaughter perched on a stump, watching. The garden was larger than Mark thought it should be. He ought to have been more specific, he supposed. It was nearly finished, however. McCoy could move on to other chores tomorrow.

It was a good piece of work, forked up in rectangles separated by wide paths that would be easy to move about on. The pattern resembled some sort of game board and gave Mark an idea.

He had succeeded in convincing Eve that she ought not to stay alone in her room every evening. When finished in the kitchen now, she usually sat with him in the drawing room, reading or sewing while he worked on his book. But why not acquire some games? There must be many they could play together. And he had cards—Graham had tucked a pack into one of the trunks—although he was not too bright at card games.

He must remember to ask Goodwin.

He handed Eve the flower seeds and indicated she was to plant them where she wished. She selected a part of the garden she would be able to see from the house. When he went to work, himself, McCoy's granddaughter hopped from her stump and came dancing down a path to his side. Then McCoy came to help. The not-bright Iron leaned on a fork, idly watching.

Some time passed before Mark happened to glance in Iron's direction again. What he saw disturbed him. The youth was watching not him but Eve, he realized, and was doing so with eloquent intentness. With her back to him as she bent over to plant, Eve was unaware of his interest. The bending drew her dress tight—she wore the white one Mark had first seen her in—and her legs were exposed for several inches above the backs of her knees. She had lovely legs.

"Tell your man to get to work," Mark said sharply to McCoy, and McCoy did so. But it was too late. The boy was aroused, no doubt of it. Even while working he continued to stare.

Mark found it impossible to pay attention to what he was doing, or to answer the little girl's chatter. If Eve would straighten up . . . but she didn't. Just when he had made up his mind to go over to her and take her back to the house, the child tried to tug his watch off again, laughing her little bell laugh.

It was nearly four o'clock, Mark noticed while pulling his hand away. McCoy stopped work at four. He straightened and turned to the man. "All right, Zekiel. You and Iron may go now."

"We can finish here, squire."

"No. It will keep."

It was a relief to see them go, though he had to smile when the little girl remembered her manners and came scampering back to bid him good night. She trotted over to Eve, too, then went racing along the path after the others, shrieking at them to wait for her. Mark walked over to Eve.

She did not want to stop, he realized. She was enjoying herself. Well, he himself had no desire to quit now that Iron was gone. He watched her for a time, winning a smile from her when she glanced up from her work. Then he went back to his vegetables.

It was dark when they finished. Dark early this

evening, because the sky was murky with clouds moving in from the northeast over the mountains. Most of Shepstowe's weather came from that direction, Mark had discovered. Perhaps there would be rain tonight, to give the garden a good start. The November rains he had read about were to be late this year, it seemed.

He helped Eve with the evening meal, knowing she must be tired, and they ate together in the drawing room as they always did now. Afterward, ignoring her headshakes of protest, he went down to the kitchen with her to help with the dishes.

There *had* been some games in one of the trunks, he remembered then, while standing beside her at the sink. Graham had packed some, evidently anticipating he might need something of that sort to counter the loneliness. There had been a Scrabble game, and he thought he recalled having seen a backgammon board. When he had dried the last dish and hung up the towel, he reached for Eve's slate.

"Are you tired?" he wrote.

She shook her head, smiling at him.

"I have an idea, then. Come on."

He led her upstairs, found the Scrabble game, and sat her at the big mahogany table. He could easily teach her the game if he had to. But he did not have to. She knew it well—even better than he did. When he challenged some of her words that were strange to him, the dictionary more often than not proved her right. He was delighted.

"You've played this a lot," he wrote on her slate.

"With the Leggs and other friends. I've always

done crossword puzzles to amuse myself, too. There's one in the *Gleaner* every day."

"You're wonderful."

Her laugh was like Merlinda's, a sound of bells.

He really should not blame the boy in the garden for staring at her, he realized. Of course, the fellow had no right to stare *that* way, but a man would have to be blind not to see how lovely Eve was. All right, he himself had been blind at first. Blind through apprehension, probably. Even then, though, he had noticed some of the things that contributed to her loveliness. Her way of walking, for instance.

There was more, he knew now. So much more. She was able to talk with her eyes. Her face, which he had stupidly thought expressionless that first morning, was actually a storehouse of expressions more eloquent than words. Above all, she was warm and gentle.

He was falling in love with her, wasn't he? He who had always been shy with women, half afraid of them, was being drawn toward this girl as by some sweet, warm magnetic force that had trapped him and would not let go. And he was not resisting. He did not want to resist.

They played until nearly midnight, and when they arose from the table it was all he could do to keep his hands at his sides. So strong within him was the desire to take her in his arms, to make her aware of his feelings for her, that he actually began to tremble. Then he remembered the letter.

"Wait," he wrote on her slate. "I've something to show you."

The envelope had been in his hip pocket all this

time and was badly wrinkled now. Warm, too, from the warmth of his body. He fished out the enclosed sheet of paper and handed it to her. She would have to help him if he undertook to write even a brief history of Shepstowe, of course, unless Mildred Legg had some books he could refer to. It would be great fun, though, working with Eve on such a project.

Suddenly, glancing at the letter in her hands, he saw it had undergone a remarkable change. Between the typed lines that he had read at the coffee works, another kind of message had become visible. This one was in a heavily slanted script that he recognized.

Puzzled, he reached for the paper just as Eve turned to him with an expression of bewilderment. How had his brother done this? By using some chemical—some sophisticated version of the "secret ink" they had concocted with their chemistry sets when kids? Something that, after exposure to light or atmospheric conditions when the envelope was opened, slowly became visible?

"Your brother can look after himself," Graham had said that day in the apartment. "He is trained to do so."

Out of its envelope, the handwritten message grew darker even as Mark stared at it, as though reacting to the very intensity of his gaze.

"They have tried to keep me from finding out where you are," it read, "and I have to be certain I have really located you. Answer Koch in the enclosed envelope. Work in your old nickname from our Three Musketeers kid days. Also the name of the third Musketeer. Then I'll know it's you and not someone else, and I will get back to you at once.

"Don't delay! You have to know what you are up against, so you will make the right moves to protect yourself. I thought my people had told you, damn them. They assured me they had. Instead, by keeping you in ignorance they may have put you in even greater danger."

Eve was holding her slate out to him when he finished. "Is something wrong?" she had written.

He took the chalk from her fingers to answer her. "I don't know. I must think about this."

She looked at him, and a thing happened that did not greatly surprise him. Jeff Legg had talked about her ability to communicate, and she was doing so now, just as he and Vin were able to. While she looked into his eyes and he into hers, her mind was sending a message and he was receiving it as clearly as though she were speaking aloud.

"Tell me if I can help."

He tried to answer her in kind, but her frown told him the flow of thought did not work as well in reverse. All right. He and Vin had not played this game since they were kids, but it would come back to him; he knew it would. With Eve helping him, it was bound to.

Folding Vin's letter, he returned it to his pocket. "Thanks for your offer to help," he wrote on her slate. "But it's a long story and we're both tired. I'll tell you tomorrow."

Tomorrow he would tell her everything. He had kept it to himself too long. But even more important, he would work with her on their ability to communicate.

As he touched her hand by way of saying good night, she smiled. And again his mind picked up a thought of hers, this one letting him know that *she* had understood *him*.

"Yes, oh yes," she was telling him. "We must do that! All we need is to practice!"

14

Mark found it almost impossible to get to sleep that night. The letter had created questions that kept his thoughts churning.

Why the *double* letter, with the important part hidden behind a camouflage? Was Vin being watched? Had he been fearful the envelope would fall into wrong hands after he mailed it?

Into wrong hands where? Miami? Or—and this was surely more likely—here in Jamaica? Meaning when it arrived here at the village post office in Rainy Ridge.

If Vin feared that, he must have reason to believe the false-identity game was a failure. The detour through Mexico City and Mérida. The stupid nighttime walk from Kingston. The pretense of being not Mark Donner, fugitive from God knew what, but Peter Burke, writer.

"Don't delay! By keeping you in ignorance, my people may have put you in even greater danger."

My people? Did he mean Graham? And "our man in Jamaica," Goodwin?

He did doze off at last, only to awake to a sound of rain on the shingled roof and a feeling that some other sound, more ominous, had disturbed him. The light in the hall was a mere glow. He looked at his watch. He had slept a few hours in spite of the letter. The time was 4 A.M.

The sound came again: dry branches snapping in heavy brush on the slope beneath his veranda. Some animal floundering about in the rain and darkness, perhaps. Someone's cow or mule or donkey? It made him uneasy, though—perhaps because the message from Vin had stretched his nerves taut.

He reached to the small table beside his bed for the flashlight he kept there. With the lights failing so often, it had seemed a good idea to ask Goodwin to bring flashlights and a supply of batteries for both Eve and himself.

Without using the light he went barefoot across the room and through the open doorway to the veranda. The rain was not a downpour, just a light, steady pattering. He stepped to the veranda railing and looked down.

Nothing.

He would have to get used to this, he told himself. On his walk from Kingston that night he had encountered all sorts of stray animals, and on the road to Rainy Ridge yesterday there had been others. The farmers seemed not to care where their creatures wandered. As he stood there listening to the rain, shivering slightly in a cool breeze that came up the valley, he heard the sound again.

This time it was close at hand, at the end of the yard, and different. Not a crackling of brush, but a single sharp report, as though someone had picked up a stick of some size and snapped it.

He walked to the end of the veranda and saw something in motion at the side of Eve's little cottage.

The beam from his flashlight shot downward at a slant, boring through darkness and drops of rain as he leaned over the railing to aim it. His aim was good. The shaft of brightness touched a crouching shape at Eve's window, trying to pry the sash open with a broken stick. The man's upthrust shoulder hid his face, but Mark knew at once who it was.

"You, there! Iron! What are you up to?"

The light had startled the fellow, and the challenge finished the job. He lurched about and looked up, the beam full on his face. Mouth open, he pawed at the glare for a few seconds as though fighting off an attacking bird, then flung himself away from it and fled.

Mark heard him go thrashing down the slope, loosening stones with his flying feet. Heard the stones rattling after him. Heard an empty can of some sort—the garbage hole was down there somewhere—clatter against one of the old slave-built estate walls.

He waited for no more. Certain that Eve must have been wakened by the flashlight's beam on her window and had seen the fellow trying to break into her room, he went pounding back through the bedroom and down the hall. Though barefoot, he took the stairs two at a time and raced along the walk to the cottage.

There was no sound inside.

He spoke her name softly so she would not be frightened, then remembered she could not hear even if he shouted. He tried the knob; the door was locked. Feeling like a prowler, he went to the window and looked in.

She kept a light burning at night, he saw, just as he did in the big house. A small night-light screwed into a socket above her dressing table. With the power so poor tonight it was hardly a light at all, just a wire glowing yellow inside a bubble of glass. By the glow, though, he could see her in bed, sleeping, with her face turned away from the window where that other face had been.

He was suddenly weak with relief.

For a time he lingered there, not at the window, but near it, wondering what to do. Wake her and insist she come into the house? To wake her he would probably have to shine the flashlight on her face, and she would be frightened. Anyway, she was in no danger now. The fellow might be less than bright, but would not be stupid enough to come again.

Returning to his room, Mark got dressed and carried a chair onto the veranda. It was cold there. He went back to the bedroom for a blanket, then sat on the chair with the blanket wrapped around him, the flashlight on the railing in front of him.

He was still there at daybreak when the cottage door opened and Eve came along the walk to the kitchen.

In the drawing room, at his typewriter, he wrote, "Eve, listen to me. Last night the boy who has been working with McCoy, the one called Iron, came up through the yard to your cottage. I heard him. When I got out on my veranda with a flashlight, he was at your window trying to open it with a stick. I yelled and he ran.

"Eve, if you had seen him looking down at you in the garden, when you were planting your flower seeds, you would know what he wanted. He won't work here again, of course; I'll see to that. But there may be others like him, and you are not safe out there. No matter what people say—and I've already told you I don't care about that—I want you in the house at night."

He carried the message to the kitchen and handed it to her, too upset to return her smile of greeting. Her hands began to shake as she read it. There was fright in her eyes when she finished and looked at him.

He motioned her to follow him, and she did. He walked upstairs to his bedroom and started to strip the big mahogany four-poster of its sheets and blankets.

She reached for her slate. "I'll move," she wrote. "But why can't I have one of the small rooms?"

"This one has its own bathroom. Better for you."

"But it isn't right."

"Don't argue."

She looked at him in resignation. "Very well, if that's what you want. I'll get breakfast first. Then I'll move."

After breakfast, Mark carefully followed instructions in replying to his brother.

Dear Mr. Koch,

Thank you for your letter addressed to Shepstowe House. As the present "occupant" I shall be happy to provide you with a brief description and history of the house, as requested, and will begin work on it at once. There is in existence, by the way, a book called *Jamaican Great Houses* by one Dempsey Zinger that was published, I believe, in England. Unfortunately I do not have a copy and probably could not find one here, but perhaps one of your excellent American libraries could track it down for you.

Sincerely,
Peter Burke

"Zinger" was the boyhood nickname his brother had asked for by way of identification. Eddie Dempsey, a neighbor, had been the third member of their backyard trio when their favorite tale spinner had been Alexandre Dumas and their book of books, *The Three Musketeers*.

There was no way he was going to entrust this letter to a messenger. Carrying it to Rainy Ridge himself, he stood at the window of the little wooden post office and kept the postmistress in conversation long enough to see her cancel the stamp and thrust the envelope into a sack of outgoing mail. Before long the mail van would come by to carry the sack to Morant Bay, for the trip to Kingston.

It was the best he could do.

15

Though hardly the size of a chain supermarket, "Mr. Thornton's" was no small establishment. In this garden suburb of London there were few better stocked.

The blond young man with the spectacles had passed the tins of assorted fish and tubes of anchovy paste twice without being able to do what he had come here for, and was now approaching them for the third time.

Thus far he had managed to avoid suspicion by pretending to have difficulty reading labels. Pushing his wheeled basket along, waiting for the aisle to empty itself of other shoppers, he had killed time by taking things from the shelves and peering at them. One sympathetic soul had shaken her head in understanding and remarked, "They make the print so small now, don't they?"

Until today Paul Vassell had never worn glasses. These had been handed to him, with instructions, by the two men responsible for his being here at Mr. Thornton's on his mission of dread. Their lenses were of clear glass.

Vassell himself was a twenty-seven-year-old bookkeeper from the East End whose only claim to fame was having been fairly good at soccer before a broken ankle two years before took even that away from him.

Now for the third time he approached the tubes of anchovy paste, and this time the aisle was empty, thank God. With a final quick look behind him to make sure, he dropped four tubes of the paste into his basket and swiftly replaced them with identical ones from his jacket pockets.

The four from his pockets had come from another market about an hour before.

Breathing less heavily now, shaking hardly at all, he wheeled his cart to the checkout. There he paid for the anchovy paste, plus the items he had picked up to avoid suspicion while awaiting his chance (two tins of tomato soup, a box of biscuits, a bottle of vinegar), and then he walked out of Mr. Thornton's with his purchases.

His eight-year-old blue Anglia was parked halfway down the block. Making his way to it, he tried to look as innocent as possible without wasting any time.

Having unlocked the boot, he tossed his purchases in. All but the tubes of anchovy paste. Those he carried with him into the car and placed on the seat beside him. From the glove compartment he took a hypodermic syringe and a small glass jar half full of a colorless liquid.

With a glance up and down the pavement to make sure no pedestrians were likely to pass by and be curious about what he was doing, he swiftly filled the syringe from the jar, removed the caps from the tubes, and needled the liquid into the paste. What the liquid was he had no idea. They had not told him.

What they had told him, after bringing the first four tubes of paste to his house and showing him how to use the needle, was that he must visit three markets today. "At the first you will leave these four tubes and buy four others. Those you will treat in your car and leave at market number two, taking four more which you will treat and leave at number three." He had been given the names of the markets.

Yesterday it had been chemists' shops and tubes of toothpaste. What tomorrow?

The caps back on the tubes and the tubes safely in

his jacket pockets, he took from the glove compartment the paper on which he had written—with the two strangers looking over his shoulders—the names of the markets he must visit. Two down and one to go, he thought. Number three was a mile away.

He looked at his watch. In a few minutes the time would be 2 P.M.

I wonder why I am doing this.

It was after three when he arrived home. The two strangers had said they would be waiting, and they were. They sat in the small backyard garden on two wooden chairs he had knocked together himself just after Doreen and he took the place last year. Doreen was on her knees weeding a flower bed, and little Brian was helping her. She knew why the two men were there, of course. Or if not exactly why, she at least knew they possessed some awful power to make people obey them, including herself. She'd been present in the house when they told him what he had to do and had been just as helpless, just as unable to protest, as he.

For just a little while in the beginning, before they took over his mind completely, he had been able to wonder who they were and why they had chosen him. Both questions were still unanswered. Both of them spoke English with an accent that sounded sort of Middle Eastern. Both of them *looked* sort of Middle Eastern, he supposed, though if told they were Pakistanis or Indians or something like that, he would not be surprised. He was no expert about such things.

Anyway, one was bearded and one wasn't, and

aside from that they could have been brothers, each not quite as tall as he was or quite as heavy, and probably a few years younger as well. What got you about both of them was their eyes: dark, dark eyes that could stare at you without blinking for the longest time, and seemed to have some sort of fire burning deep inside or behind them.

When those eyes looked at you, you were quite helpless.

He had first encountered those eyes at the river, which was just at the end of the street here. Evenings, when the weather was nice, he liked to go down to the small dock where he kept the boat he'd bought soon after Doreen and he took the house. He'd lived within sight of the Thames most of his life, and it never failed to work a kind of magic on him. You could have your airplanes and motorcars. What he'd longed for, even as a boy in Tilbury, was a job on one of the big ships heading down that great river to the sea and then to some romantic port half a world away. And he'd been thinking of just that the evening before last while standing there by his boat, when the two strangers came along the shingle and stopped to chat.

Was this his boat? Did he live up the street here? What sort of work did he do? Was he married? Any children? They were a nosy pair, for sure, and even while answering their questions he wondered why he was doing so. It seemed he had no choice, with the two of them standing there staring at him. He couldn't turn his back on them, either. Just had to stand there. And when he had finished telling them who he was and what he did and where he lived, and about Doreen and Brian . . . then they said they would go home with him, and they did. And talked until midnight, telling him what he had to do for them. And then stayed the night, sleeping—if they actually did any sleeping—on chairs in the front room because Doreen and he hadn't anywhere to put guests.

Next day, instead of going to his job, he had visited the chemists' shops with the toothpaste. And found them waiting at the house when he got home, to question him and give instructions for today. And today the markets, with the anchovy paste.

And here they were again, this time in the garden, waiting as before.

As he approached, they rose from the chairs to confront him and he found himself gazing into the eyes again.

"Did everything go as planned?" the bearded one asked.

"Yes."

"You came straight home?"

"Straight home."

"Talked to no one?"

Paul Vassell shook his head.

The two exchanged glances, and Beard said, "We have a reward for you. While you were following instructions today, Ahmed went and rented a boat. We have planned a pleasant evening cruise on your lovely river to show our gratitude. Come."

"Just me? Alone?"

"Of course not. All of you."

Doreen had risen from her knees at the flower bed to listen to the conversation. She stepped to her husband's side now and took his hand. Vassell thought there was an unusually passive note in her voice, a kind of melancholy, as she said, "A cruise on the river will be nice, Paul."

But their six-year-old Brian, always independent for his age, had his hands on his hips and was saying, "Well, I don't want to. I'll stay right here, thanks."

Beard and No-Beard turned to look at him. With a shake of his head that tossed his hair about, he defiantly showed them his back. Seconds passed. No one spoke.

Very slowly, as though fighting the pull of an invisible rope, the boy swung back to return the gaze of the strangers. No-Beard extended a hand. "Come here."

Brian's reluctant feet tore tracks in the grass as he struggled to refuse. But he took the necessary steps and reached for the outthrust hand.

"That's better. Now then, the boat," No-Beard said.

With the two strangers in the lead, No-Beard still clutching Brian's hand, the five of them walked out of the Vassells' yard and down the street to the river. There at the dock were Paul's old rowboat and a larger craft with an outboard motor. A haze lay over the river, making the distance to the far shore seem even greater than it was.

To Paul the river seemed unreal. Nor did it seem right for him and his wife and their child to be getting into this strange boat with these two Middle Eastern strangers. Yet his mind told him it had to be done, and without any discussion.

While the strangers stood there silently looking on, he helped Doreen into the craft and watched her go forward to the bow. Then he watched Brian follow and sit beside her, both of them facing forward. And then he, Paul Vassell, went and sat on the thwart behind them, staring at their backs.

His own back was toward the strangers now, but there was no lessening of the power they had over him. With no will of his own he could do only what they told him to. Somehow he knew his wife and son were wholly under the strangers' control as well.

As the craft cleared the dock he was aware of the drone of its motor and the gurgle of water along its hull. Once more he felt that his beloved river had become a stranger, somehow sinister in its veil of haze. Silently forbidden to turn around, he did not know that his own small boat was in tow as the larger craft headed for deep water and then turned downstream.

Time crawled. Or perhaps it only seemed to. The haze hid both banks now, and when the sound of the motor suddenly ceased, and the forward motion of the boat slowed to a mere tidal drift, there was almost no sound anywhere. I must be dreaming, Paul thought. Were they telling him to think this, or was the thought his own?

I must be dreaming . . .

"Yes, you have been dreaming." No one had spoken aloud, but still he heard the words clearly. "You have been dreaming, Paul, but you are awake now and it is time to go home. Get up now and go home."

He looked down at his knees and, yes, he was sitting on a bench in front of a greengrocer's just up the street from his house. And he did want to go home, to be with his wife and son and perhaps to have a Guinness to clear his mind of the haze that filled it.

"Go," the voice said again. "Go now, Paul. Go home."

He stood up. As his right foot reached for the gunwale, his weight caused the craft to tip and he put his hands up to keep his balance. So instead of stepping over the gunwale into the river he went into the hazy brown water headfirst. But where a man who knew he was drowning might have struggled, Paul Vassell did not. He simply inhaled water as though it were air, and sank slowly from sight.

Then while the two strangers silently watched, Doreen rose from the forward thwart and walked to *her* death, except that under her lesser weight the boat did not tilt and she simply stepped out into the river and disappeared feetfirst. All that marked her passing were the bubbles rising through her hair as it floated for a few seconds like a patch of seaweed.

And finally the boy. Without a struggle. Without an outcry. Almost without a splash.

No-Beard, in the stern, hauled on the tow rope then and drew the Vassells' own boat alongside, where he untied the rope. Standing elbow-to-elbow, he and Beard turned the craft over and gave it a shove. Upside down, it slowly drifted off into the haze.

"It will seem to be an accident when they are found." Beard spoke not in English now, but in the tongue of Aram Sel's Siricus. "A simple boating accident—boat overturned, three people drowned. It's almost a pity. He was so adept at what we had him do, I was tempted to suggest we use him longer."

"And incur Khargi's wrath?" The other shook his head. "The great one's final words to us—in fact, I am receiving the same message this very moment— were that we must not use any man long enough for suspicion to fall on him." He shrugged as he stepped to the stern to start the outboard. "Who is next?"

"A man named Will Partson, in the production of cough syrup at Myert Pharmaceutical."

"Living where?"

"In Belgravia. In a home left him by his parents— better, probably, than he could afford on his own."

"We go there tomorrow?"

"We go tomorrow. Early. Before he leaves for work."

The home of the Partsons, in that part of London called Belgravia, was indeed probably more than Will Partson could have afforded on his salary as chief chemist at Myert. On one of Belgravia's lovely, oh-so-quiet residential streets, it could hardly have welcomed two foreign visitors at seven o'clock the following morning. But the Partsons were up, Will having his breakfast, and, having no servant to do it for her, Emily Partson answered the doorbell.

"Yes?"

Beard and No-Beard were not at all the kind of callers she or any of her immediate neighbors were in the habit of receiving. Startled, she took a backward step. The street outside was empty. Her two little girls were dressing themselves upstairs.

The eyes gazed at her. Those almost black eyes with the flames blazing deep behind their pupils, seeming to set the whole iris on fire.

"We wish to speak with Mr. Partson, madam." The accent told her she was right to be afraid.

"He—he—" Then her mind stopped struggling and accepted the fact that they meant no harm to her beloved husband. Of course not. How silly of her. They were friends. She could trust them.

"Come in. Please do. He is just having his breakfast."

They followed her through the house into the kitchen, where her husband sat looking bewildered with a spoonful of cereal half lifted to his lips. Her two little girls came trooping in from the hall.

Will Partson put his spoon back into the bowl of cereal and stood up, wiping his mouth on the back of his hand. The little girls—twins, five years old and looking like elfin pixies in their pale blue sleeveless dresses—stood there gazing up at the strangers as though hypnotized.

"Mr. Partson," Beard said, "we have come a long way for this. May we speak to you privately, please?" His eyes engaged Will's. The fire blazed. Will Partson rubbed a hand hard against *his* eyes as though to clear a suddenly blurred vision.

"Who are you?"

"Friends. From afar."

It was not necessary to explain. It never was, even with subjects as sharply intelligent as young Will Partson. Whenever it became difficult, they could always fall back upon Khargi, anyway, having reached that level of their training at which they could communicate with him no matter where they were.

Right now, for instance, Khargi was in Mexico or Jamaica, seeking a confrontation with that vexing

Argus adversary, Vincent Donner. No matter. They could reach him if they had to. Or perhaps he was present, anyway.

"Of course," Will Partson said, still staring back at the eyes. "Yes, of course. We can talk in my study."

They bowed to his wife. They smiled at the two staring little girls who now resembled daffodils lifting their yellow heads to sunlight. They followed Will out of the kitchen, down the hall, into a small, book-lined room where the shades were still drawn at the windows.

Most of the books on Will Partson's shelves had to do with chemistry and medicine. After all, he was chief chemist with a company that produced a number of popular concoctions sold over the counter in chemists' shops.

"Sit down, Mr. Partson," Beard said.

Will sat. He was the right age to have twin daughters aged five. He had the looks which, combined with those of his wife, would explain quite easily the twins' loveliness. Though he had inherited this home on one of Belgravia's best residential streets, he no doubt would in a few years be able, if need be, to buy such a home with his own earned money.

"Mr. Partson, you supervise the manufacture of the products of Myert Pharmaceutical, do you not?"

"Yes." Staring.

He had to stare. They would not stop staring at *him*. And the fires behind their eyes were searing his brain.

"We have a certain favor to ask of you, then."

"A certain favor. Yes. Of course."

They told him what he must do at the place where

137

he worked. Then Beard produced a sizable vial of the same colorless liquid Paul Vassell had injected into tubes of toothpaste and anchovy paste. "You will begin this morning. Do you understand?"

Will Partson looked at the vial. He seemed to shudder, but it endured only a few seconds and then he was in control of himself again. As though drawn by a magnet, his gaze left the vial and climbed again to focus on Beard's eyes. Then it shifted to focus on No-Beard's eyes.

He nodded. "I understand."

"You may go, then. No need to say good-bye to your wife and children. Just go to work. When you return this evening, we shall be here waiting."

"Yes." Will dropped the vial of liquid into his pocket and departed. He had been ready to drive to work, anyway, as soon as he finished his keep-trim breakfast of cereal and skim milk and kissed his lovely wife and children farewell.

The door of the study closed behind him. Beard looked at No-Beard.

"This, of course, will take only a day," Beard said in the tongue of their Mediterranean country. "The products they make are sold in most of the chemists' shops in London."

"A stupid name. I prefer our 'drugstores.'"

Beard ignored the interruption. "About how to dispose of this man and his family, I think we should consult with Khargi."

"Yes."

The two were silent. Each placed his hands limply on his knees and closed his eyes and lowered his head. They remained thus for several minutes, as though in deep meditation. Then Beard shook himself like a dog emerging from a lake, and stood up.

"Khargi feels that Partson will be suspected as soon as the poisoning is discovered, so we are to dispose of him tonight before he can be questioned. Did you receive that?"

"I did. Tonight, before we leave, he must first poison his wife and children, then himself. No one must be left to identify us."

"Did you also receive Khargi's message about Jamaica?"

"He is there now, with Ling Gan and the Haitian, closing in on the Argus man, Donner, who he believes has set up a secret command post there, being afraid that our people will find and destroy the one in the U.S."

"And *our* next move?"

"We are instructed to go now to the farmhouse in Florida, to prepare for the attack on the Americans."

16

The tension of waiting to hear from his brother again was more than Mark could bear with equanimity. He must get away from the Great House, he decided, even if only for a day. But if he was truly in danger, where could he go without increasing the peril?

Above the intake in the river were pools where one could enjoy a swim, Jeff Legg had told him. He was delighted when Eve agreed to a Sunday of exploration.

They left the house soon after seven, Mark carrying a basket in which Eve had packed a lunch. It was no light load. She was still determined to "care him," apparently—that would be the local way of putting it—even though she was more like a sister than a housekeeper now. And if Jeff's laconic description of the route to the pools was not an exaggeration, the basket would seem even heavier by the time they got there.

Well, he would welcome a little physical fatigue instead of the continued mental strain. A seemingly endless string of obeah threats had kept him off balance since the arrival of Vin's letter. New ones had appeared on garden walks, the front door again, even at windows.

Sooner or later the threats would erupt into some sort of actual violence, he supposed. When it happened, it might be almost a relief. But he still did not know the why of them, unless they were part of the peril Vin had written about.

Life during the past week had not been altogether negative, however. Mildred and Jeff Legg had come to dinner once, and it had delighted him to see how effortlessly Eve was able to participate in an evening of games and talk.

He was not quite sure how she did it. At the games she was not handicapped at all; Scrabble was only one of many at which she excelled. And with only a little help from him on her slate, she seemed actually to take part in conversations as well. He knew a good many so-called normal people who enjoyed themselves less and were less gracious.

They had gone down to the Leggs' once, too. Walked down, and Jeff had driven them home. It was becoming a bit awkward to explain his not having a car. Even Eve must think it strange, for he had not, after all, obeyed his impulse to tell her the truth about himself. It had occurred to him that she might decide she did not want to remain at the Great House with a man who had come there under false pretenses and an assumed name. He simply could not risk it. Were she to leave him now, he would be devastated.

"If I buy a car," he said to Jeff almost apologetically, "it will only sit in the garage, you know. I've a deadline to meet on the book"—that's another stupid lie you've forced on me, Graham; I hope you're proud of yourself!—"and it isn't going well at all. There's just too much about this country that I don't know."

It was true, though, that the book was going badly. Time and again he'd been tempted to drop it. But if he dropped it, what would he do to escape boredom? Work in the garden? Walk about the estate? That wouldn't be enough.

He had written at great length about his stay in Mexico City, including the hours he had spent in the great central square, the Zócalo, viewing the intricate stone carvings on the recently discovered Aztec temple there. And about the long train trip to the

Yucatán Peninsula and his visits to its Mayan ruins. But he was aware now that the novel would never be considered for publication unless he went back and injected some suspense into it. A mystery novel could not be a travel book.

What he might do, he supposed, was work up something sinister about the little South American priest on the train. After all, the fellow *had* seemed to be part of the immediate background rather often, occupying a nearby table in the dining car at mealtimes, hovering suspiciously close when the train stopped at little stations where the passengers eagerly piled out to buy fruit and spicy fried chicken and native handicrafts from crowds of Indian women. Then hadn't he turned up later even at Chichén Itzá?

I could bring him into the story again here in Jamaica, Mark mused. I could have him questioning the Chinese shopkeeper when I go down to Rainy Ridge one day. The hunters closing in on their quarry, so to speak.

He made himself stop thinking about the book. The whole project was a sham, anyway; no one would ever publish it. Eve and he had been following the easy, well-worn track to the river—worn because it was used by men from the coffee works going up to clean the intake—and now he heard the stream itself. Only a murmur at first, the sound suddenly became a roar as they turned a corner and found themselves at the edge of a cliff, looking down on swift water.

Mark had been here before, but had not gone beyond this point. They would have to descend the cliff and ford the stream, Jeff had warned. "Safe enough in daylight, but be sure you get back before dark." Mark went first with the lunch basket, using his free hand to steady himself and anxiously watching Eve as she followed. He needn't have worried about her, he quickly realized. She was far more agile than he, and quite unafraid of falling.

They crossed the stream by stepping from boulder to boulder—it *would* be tricky in darkness—and had to climb a cliff on the opposite side. The river was like that, Jeff had warned. "You won't be able to go up the stream itself. It's all cascades and deep gorges for miles. In fact, the track isn't even close to it at times, and you may think you're lost. Don't fret, though. There's only the one track, so stay on it and you'll reach the pools eventually."

"People do go to the pools, then?" Mark knew his disappointment was showing. He had hoped Eve and he would have the place to themselves.

"No, they don't bother. But some sawyers were in there a while ago, cutting juniper. They cleared the track to head the boards out."

"That sounds better."

"There's one thing, though. If you go past the pools, you *may* get lost. That's wild-hog country up there. Hog tracks everywhere. Don't mistake those for paths, or we'll be sending a search party."

Jeff was right about the river. They kept losing sight of it, and at times even the sound died away, leaving only bird cries in a deep green stillness. At the top of one especially difficult climb they came upon a flat black stone as big as the table in the Great House drawing room, and sat to rest.

Opening the lunch basket, Eve took out her slate. "Enjoying yourself?" she wrote.

Mark touched her hand and smiled. She smiled happily in return and then, with her arms upstretched, lay back on the stone as a child might have done. She *was* a child in some ways, he thought. It simply did not occur to her that in lying back that way, with her lips parted and her blouse pulled tight across her breasts, she might be inviting him to lean over her.

True, she understood quite well what Zekiel McCoy's helper had wanted, but that was a thing apart. A boy like Iron would not care that she was different from other women. That Mark no longer considered her different had not occurred to her.

A sudden snorting sound in the undergrowth made him stop looking at her and swiftly turn. It came again, a kind of throat-clearing grunt. He saw an animal of some sort, brownish black and about the size of Jeff Legg's bull terriers, moving away through the brush.

His abrupt movement had caused Eve to sit up, and apparently she, too, saw the animal before it disappeared. When he looked puzzled, she reached for her slate.

"Wild hog," she wrote swiftly.

He frowned as he answered, "Here? Are you sure?"

She nodded. When she slid from the black rock and picked up a stone, Mark picked one up, too. The wild hogs were dangerous, Jeff had warned. Powerful creatures with an ugly disposition, they were likely to charge without provocation. To be sure, their sight was poor and they kept to their runways

144

mostly, but if encountered in such a runway they could give trouble. They frequently killed the hunters' dogs, who were powerful brutes themselves.

But there would be no danger this side of the pools, Jeff had assured him. Occasionally one came down from the high forest when food was scarce—the wild pigeons did that, too—but the fall rains had been too mild as yet to affect the food supply.

Mark thought of his conversation with McCoy, the day after the Iron incident. Brazenly the boy had come to work that morning as though nothing had happened. Mark had ordered him off the property. McCoy, of course, had to be told why.

Mark had never seen a man so angry. The boy himself had been merely sullen, throwing him a look of hatred and mumbling as he slouched away. But McCoy had flown into such a rage that his speech became almost unintelligible.

"Him is purely no good!" the. gardener shouted. "Me know it from the beginning, but me woman keep insisting me care him! Now me putting him out once and for all time. God be witness to what me saying!"

"What will he do?" Mark asked. After all, the boy might not be capable of looking after himself.

"Oh, him will manage, never fear. Likely him will hunt the wild pig to sell."

"Can he live on that?"

"Him?" McCoy snorted. "That worthless boy been hunting the wild pig for years, and by himself, too, without no dogs. Him know the high mountains like him hand. Certainly him can live on it! A pig fetch good money."

It was something to think about, Mark reflected as he stood at Eve's side, stone in hand. A hunted hog might run from high ground, too. If Iron *had* turned to hunting hogs, might they not encounter him before the day was over? But, as for the animal he had seen, no further noise came from the undergrowth, and presently Eve indicated they had nothing more to fear.

They went on. The track descended to the river now, and there was a pool. It was not a natural one, however, but one created by boulders thrown or rolled in to make a fording. The sawyers, probably. He followed Eve across, marveling again at her agility and grace. Then the path led them upstream through a deep gorge pink with wild begonias, to the pools Jeff had described.

Mark was delighted. The setting here was a world unto itself, a forest glade in which the river seemed weary of its wild plunging and welcomed a chance to rest. Three broad basins of stone held water deep enough for swimming, and the stream's flow from top to bottom was a gentle glide.

The track ended here. At least, it crossed the river here and sharply climbed on its way to the high, wild-hog country Jeff Legg had warned against. The river itself flowed out of deep shadows above the pools—a clearing of some sort on the left, a cliff on the right with grotesque trees leaning out from what appeared to be, but of course could not be, solid rock. How could a setting be so peaceful, yet at the same time so spectacular?

Never mind. They were here. The fears inspired by the letter from Vin had no place here and could be

146

forgotten, at least for a time. With gestures Mark urged Eve to choose a place to picnic, and she climbed to a ledge of stone beside the topmost pool. "Shall we have lunch before we swim?" he asked on her slate.

"I'm famished," she answered. "And why don't we practice talking to each other while we eat?"

"You'll have to tell me how. I mean, my brother, Vin, and I were able to do it as kids, so I must have a talent for it, but—" He looked at her and she nodded.

"Think of me and ask a question," she wrote.

"With my eyes closed?"

"It doesn't matter. Ask me something."

Continuing to look at her, he let his mind ask if she was tired from the long walk.

She smiled. "No," came the reply—just as clearly as though she had said the word aloud. "But, as I told you, I'm hungry."

It filled him with awe, what happened then. He sent thoughts to her and at least half the time she received them, sometimes answering on her slate, sometimes by silently shaping a brief reply with her lips, and sometimes—this was the wonderful part of it—by sending her answers directly into his mind. And while they did this she set out the lunch, using the ledge for a table.

"Next time we'll have radishes from the garden." She hadn't used the slate to say it. Hadn't moved her lips. All she had done was turn her head toward him.

"And lettuce," he replied.

"Yes, and lettuce."

But then the power left him—perhaps it demanded too much of some mysterious inner energy at this stage—and both of them concentrated on satisfying their hunger. But never mind. She *had* said, "Next time we'll have radishes from the garden." And he had received the thought and *replied* to it.

The garden gave them a lot of pleasure, he thought as he ate. Perhaps that was why the image had come across so clearly. Every day they managed to spend some time together there. When he was faithfully carrying out his instructions to "act like a writer," Eve went there without him.

Someday when she was in the garden and he at the typewriter in the Great House drawing room, he must try sending her a mental message. To find out if they could communicate without being close to each other. He had sometimes been able to communicate with Vin at a distance when they tried hard. And both he and Vin had done so with their mother—from whom, no doubt, they had inherited whatever gene it was that made such mental exchanges possible.

The garden, he thought again. McCoy's granddaughter, Merlinda, went there with Eve sometimes. Hardly a day passed now without a visit from the child. Trotting up in the morning from Mango Gut, she would march into the drawing room to greet him and watch him at work for a while, then chase after Eve to help—if that was the word—with whatever Eve happened to be doing.

She spent hours in the kitchen, and got herself so grubby in the garden that Eve sometimes had to give her a bath. Whether she helped or hindered in the garden Mark did not know and was quite sure that to Eve it did not matter, but he felt fairly certain that between them Eve and Merlinda would soon have the house gay with flowers.

He watched Eve with more than a little curiosity as they finished lunch. She had put on a swimsuit under her blouse and skirt, he knew. They had agreed that the less they had to carry, the easier the day would be. Would she go off somewhere now to disrobe in private?

She seemed to be in some doubt, herself, about what she ought to do, for after putting the picnic things back into the basket she stood up, looked around as though in search of a suitable place to retire to, and then turned her back on him while unbuttoning her blouse, as if that were at least something.

Thinking she would have on an old-fashioned bathing suit, he was delighted when she stepped out of her skirt wearing no such thing. It was a white bikini in which she looked stunning. When she paused on the edge of the rock to study the water before committing herself, he could not take his gaze off her.

They did not swim long. The mountain-stream water was too cold and, besides, their swim attire would have to dry before they could dress for the long walk home. They lay side by side on the rock, and Mark dozed. On opening his eyes he discovered Eve was gone.

In sudden panic he scrambled to his feet and called out to her, forgetting she could not hear. "Eve! Where are you?" The steep cliff above the pools tossed his yell back at him in fragments. Then, quite clearly, he heard Eve answer.

"It's all right, Mark," her voice said in his mind. "I'm just up here. See?"

Turning to look upstream, he saw her waving.

So they *could* communicate without being close, he thought with a touch of wonder as he waved back. There was no need for experimenting while she was in the garden and he at his typewriter. Awed by the discovery, he saw she had put her clothes on and gone upstream to the shadowy clearing on the opposite bank. For the first time he noticed what appeared to be a small shelter of some sort not far from the water's edge.

Thinking of the boy called Iron, he stepped into his own clothes quickly. If Iron had indeed turned to hog hunting after being driven from home by McCoy, the place could be his camp.

At times finding it necessary to leap from boulder to boulder, he hurried along the stream's edge. He would not like to encounter McCoy's helper here, he thought. But then, he would not like to face him anywhere if the boy were bent on revenge for having been fired.

Eve was inside when he reached the shelter. The place was a cabin of sorts, and she was examining a mattock and heavy fork that leaned in a corner. As he stepped toward her, she broke a lump of dried red clay from the mattock and peered at that; then she heard him or felt the vibration of his footsteps and whirled, seemingly frightened, to face him.

But there was nothing for them to fear, he saw with relief. At least not now. The place was simply a rude shack made of untrimmed boards, with a roof of saplings and grass. At each end of the single room a frame of poles supported a bed of old burlap bags. A board table against one wall was littered with bush-rat droppings. Obviously no one lived here.

On a pad of paper from his pocket (he never went anywhere now without such a pad!) he wrote, "Jeff said there were sawyers here some time ago. This must have been their camp." Eve read it and at last nodded, though not without a glance at his face that puzzled him.

He wrote then, "We ought to be starting back, don't you think?"

Again she looked at him strangely, as though about to ask a question. But after a brief glance at the tools in the corner, she turned to the door.

Something had gone awry with the day, though, he felt on the walk back to the Great House. There at the cabin Eve had been deeply disturbed about something—more than by the many obeah signs or even the letter from his brother. Not once on the return journey did he win a real smile from her, and on reaching the house at sundown she took the picnic basket from him and went straight to the kitchen.

When he followed and would have used the slate to talk to her, she shook her head. "Please, not now," she wrote. "I must start dinner."

He would wait until evening, he decided. Whatever it was, he would find out about it then.

Half an hour later he heard a car descending the drive and went out to investigate, thinking it must be Jeff Legg.

The car was not one he had seen before, though, and the man who got out of it was black. Blacker than any Jamaican he had yet encountered. Slender, supple, about thirty and wearing sport clothes, the fellow said with an apologetic smile, "I'm afraid I'm lost. If this is the end of the road, as it seems to be, I know I am."

"You are unless you're looking for the Shepstowe Great House."

"But the sign in Rainy Ridge said Kingston was this way. I'm sure it did."

"It did. To be exact, it said, 'Kingston 23 miles via Gordon Town.'" Mark could not help smiling at the fellow's bewilderment. "Under that, though, it said, 'Not a driving road.'"

"Oh-oh. I'm to go back over those bumps?"

"I'm afraid so."

"Well, I suppose if I must . . . Might I trouble you for some water first? I wonder. The car sounds like a whistling teapot." Shaking his head, he leaned into the machine and pulled a lever to lift the hood.

"Of course. No trouble." Wondering at the man's accent, Mark dragged a hose from the near end of the garden and turned on the tap. What accent was it, actually? Not Jamaican. Not really English, despite its overlay of English idioms. It seemed to have a French intonation.

The car, too, puzzled him. It was not really hot, he noticed at once—a good thing it wasn't, for the fellow spun the radiator cap off much too carelessly and might have got a nasty scalding. It took a surprising lot of water, though. Perhaps the radiator was larger than it looked.

While he was standing there holding the hose, his visitor gazed at him in silence. Gazed at him as though—well, as though trying to see past his recently grown beard, perhaps. It was slightly disconcerting. When the job was done, though, he smilingly said, "Thanks very much!" and drove away with a cheerful wave.

A black man who spoke English with a French-sounding accent? Mark thought about it on his way back to the house. Suddenly an answer came to him.

"Probably Haitian," he said aloud. "Of course." Haiti as a country had always fascinated him, although he had never been there, only read about it. He had long wanted to know more about its voodoo and sorcery and zombiism.

I should have asked him in, he thought. It might have been interesting.

17

He was not to talk to Eve that evening, after all. Just as they finished dinner and were preparing to begin a conversation on the typewriter—with, of course, more experiments in telepathy—Jeff Legg arrived.

"I've another letter for you from that publisher in Miami, Peter. They asked at the post office if I'd be coming up here, and I said I'd deliver it. Meant to drop in on you, anyway, with these books Milly found for you." He dropped some old-looking volumes on the table. "She's having a hen session with some of her old Hampton schoolmates."

Jeff had not opened the Miami letter this time. It was addressed to Peter Burke at Shepstowe House. But Mark, suspecting it contained the information he had been so anxiously awaiting, did not open it, either. By casually tossing it onto the table, he tried to indicate it was not that important.

Jeff was full of talk, mostly about a large order received from Japan for the co-op's coffee and the problems he anticipated in being able to ship it soon enough to suit the buyers. Eve excused herself and went to her room. It was after ten when Jeff at last departed.

Almost frantically Mark snatched up the letter and tore it open.

No invisible ink this time. The letter was openly typed and quite long. As he read it, he felt a film of cold moisture forming on his face.

They call themselves the Disciples. By that they mean disciples of the ruler of Siricus, Aram Sel, so a better name for them would be the Devil's Disciples. Their leader—their trainer, if you will—is the world's leading master of mind control, a cousin of Aram Sel's named Khargi.

Aram Sel, as I'm sure you know, is a screaming madman who hates and would destroy the civilized world. With this organization and his fabulous oil wealth, he just may succeed.

So far the Disciples have operated in Mexico,

South America, India, England, and a number of smaller countries that have called Aram Sel insane or offended him in other ways. But their avowed number one target is the U.S. Here they have set up headquarters in an old farmhouse south of Lake Okeechobee in Palm Beach County—which, let me tell you, took us months to find. It is being watched by people of the Argus organization I toil for. (No, I no longer work for the CIA. I was put in charge of field work in this new outfit which was set up specifically to deal with the Disciples. Why me? Probably because of certain talents I possess that you also possess, if you remember how we used to read each other's thoughts as kids.)

As I say, the hideout is being watched, and we could take the place anytime. But the man we want and must have in order to break up this nightmare is their instructor and leader, Khargi, and he hasn't arrived yet. Some of us think Khargi is in telepathic communication with the others wherever they are, and acts as a sort of spirit guide in whatever they do. Each and every one of them, you understand, is high up in some sophisticated phase of mind control. And they come from all over—from the Near East, China, Russia, everywhere. There's even a former Catholic priest from Brazil and a voodoo *houngan* from Haiti.

But about you, old buddy—believe me, when I learned that Graham had packed you off to Jamaica without telling you what you were running from, I was furious and still am. The very idea of expecting you to be alert for danger when you weren't even told what to look out for—well, I'll never forgive the bastard. I thought all along he had *told* you before you left the States.

Now listen carefully, please. I will keep you up to date as best I can on what is happening here. Meanwhile, as a writer in the mountains of Jamaica you probably have as good a cover as we can provide. *If* you don't get caught napping.

Don't move around too much. Don't talk. Be suspicious of all strangers. Plan *now* what you will do if suddenly you feel you have been discovered. Because—let me be emphatic about this—you won't have time to do any planning after the fact. These people go after your *mind*, and they are good at what they do.

Zinger, old buddy, I'll get back to you as soon as I can. Take care of yourself.

There was no signature.

And, Mark thought after reading the letter over more slowly, there were still some unanswered questions. One of them went to the heart of the whole frightening affair.

Brother Vin was in charge of "field work"—whatever that meant—of a group of specialists set up to protect the U.S. against Aram Sel's Disciples. He had been chosen for the job because of his CIA training and special talents in ESP and telepathy. So, then, the Disciples felt they had to remove him before launching an attack on their number one target, the United States.

All right. But why should they be confusing an innocent schoolteacher named Mark Donner with Vin Donner, even though the two were twins?

And—even more disturbing—why should the top brass of Vin's organization have *anticipated* their doing that?

* * *

It was too late to show the letter to Eve. He did listen at her door, hoping to hear her moving about, but the silence told him she was asleep. In the morning, though, he was up before her, waiting at the big mahogany table for her to appear.

It was time, he had decided, to tell her everything, and the best way to tell her was to let her read the book he was writing. It would take hours of typing to convey the same information in a letter.

When she came from her bedroom, he beckoned to her and pushed the manuscript toward her. With it was a letter he had written in his bedroom during the night, and the one from Vin.

"Eve, please read this book I have been working on. It is not a novel, as I have led you to believe, but a true story—my own story—and it will tell you who I am and why I am here. I should have told you long ago. Time and again I wanted to. But always I was afraid it might mean the end of our friendship and cause you to leave me. When you have read the book, please read this letter that came yesterday from my brother. Then we can talk."

Leaving her, he went to a chair on the far side of the room and sat down.

A little frown twisted her mouth as she began to read. It deepened as she turned the pages. Every few moments she stopped reading and turned her head to direct the frown at him. But he did not interrupt her.

The book finished at last, she took up Vin's letter and read that. Then she moved the book manuscript aside and reached for the typewriter.

When he saw her do that, Mark left his chair and went to stand beside her again.

"This is all true, you say?" she wrote. "All this about you and the man named Graham?"

He nodded.

"And the letter from your brother—it means that you are in some terrible danger, doesn't it?"

Leaning over her, he tapped out, "It would seem so. All I know is what he says."

"He must be a very important man, if they felt they had to tear your life apart just because you're his twin."

"He must be. Yes."

"Will you learn more about all this, do you think?"

"Well, Vin says he'll write again."

"Meanwhile, you just have to stay here in Jamaica, pretending to be a writer named Peter Burke, and hope these awful people are caught before they track you down? Is that it?"

He had drawn up a chair close to hers so they could communicate more easily. "They may have tracked me down already," he typed. "While you were preparing dinner yesterday I had a visitor."

In detail he told her about the man in the car with the not-hot but half-empty radiator. "I believe he was Haitian. Who knows—he may have been the Haitian Vin mentions, coming here to get a close look at me. He did stare at me, as if trying to decide what I would look like without this beard.

"And there was a South American priest on the train to Mérida," Mark went on. "I didn't put him in the book, but he seemed to be always in a position to watch me. I saw him again later at the Mayan ruins in Chichén Itzá. Eve, I hate to say this—God knows how much I hate to say it—but you mustn't stay here at Shepstowe any longer. You could be in danger here because of me."

She had watched the words appear on the paper. Now she read them over and shook her head.

"The man with the car could have been anyone. We have lots of Haitians in Jamaica; it's only a short flight from Port-au-Prince to Kingston. And the priest in Mexico—aren't you letting your imagination work overtime? I mean, you had every reason to be apprehensive, the way Graham and his people had turned your life upside down, but a priest on a train—that could be quite innocent, really."

"I saw him again at the ruins, I tell you."

"That doesn't prove anything, either. The train was going to Mérida. If he was on it, why wouldn't he go to the ruins? All sorts of people do. No." She shook her head again. "I'm not leaving. Not unless you make me."

Mark rose and paced to the fireplace, trying to think the thing out. Perhaps he *was* letting Vin's letter shake him up too much. It was a frightening letter, no question of that, but Vin had not advised flight; only to be wary of strangers. And the only stranger so far had been the Haitian—who might honestly have misread the sign in Rainy Ridge and just happened to have a car with a noisy radiator.

Perhaps he had been alone with his fears too long and was overreacting. Just being able to discuss the situation with Eve had brought some relief. She was a woman, and with a woman's intuition might see perils or pitfalls he had overlooked.

159

And she cared. That was the big thing.

When they had continued the dialogue a little longer and Eve knew everything, she sat at the typewriter and wrote him a summing-up—partly to put her own thoughts in order, he guessed.

"As your brother says, we must be sure we are taking every possible precaution. It is so easy to be careless, Mark, and we must not be, even for a moment. Remember, we don't know what we are defending ourselves against, really, and that makes it so much harder.

"You should burn your book, don't you think? If someone came while we were out and found it—yes, burn it right away. And all these pages we have been talking on—burn them, too. And after this, whenever we discuss the matter, we ought to destroy what we have written as soon as we finish.

"So far," she continued, "there has been no indication that they, whoever they are, have traced you to Jamaica. If only we knew what sort of danger we are dealing with, and what to look out for. 'Mind control' sounds nightmarish, like hypnotism, only much more terrible. But we have one advantage. The people of this district are Jamaican country folk, and those hunting you will not be. As Vin says, we must watch out for strangers. And we should heed his advice and plan ahead, too. We must know what to do, even a number of alternative steps we might take if danger does come. It may come swiftly."

We, he thought, feeling a strange and wonderful warmth in him. All down the page she had written *we*, not *you*. "Do you think there may be a connection between the Disciples and the obeah I seem to have stirred up around here?"

She thought about that and shook her head, though apparently without much conviction. "I shouldn't think so. But obeah is a kind of mind control, too, you know. I've known our superstitious country people to die just because they were told there was a curse on them. At least, I've heard of it."

"I've read about that."

"And"—she hesitated with her pretty hands poised over the keys, then apparently decided to go on in spite of some inner reluctance—"do you remember our trip to the pools?"

"Something was wrong there, wasn't it?"

"Yes, in that old cabin. I felt something threatening us. Even now I keep thinking about it, wondering what made me so afraid."

"I sensed it in you," he replied. She was, of course, a woman whose mind picked up vibrations that less sensitive people might not be aware of. And because of that, having her here at Shepstowe might be a fortunate thing for him. Like having a smoke alarm in an old house where a fire could break out at any moment.

On the other hand, if the people Vin called the Devil's Disciples were adept at mind control, it might make her especially vulnerable and put them both in added danger.

With that thought contributing to his apprehension, he carried his aborted book and their typewritten dialogue to the fireplace. Tossing the book into the flames caused him no anguish; it was only an amateur thing, anyway, better looked upon as practice. He wished he could save some of his dialogue with Eve, though. *That* was practically a love story. But when he hesitated over it, Eve determinedly took it from him and tossed it, too, into the fire.

They stood shoulder-to-shoulder, watching the mass of papers flare up in a swirl of white smoke that poured back into the room for a moment before finding its way up the old chimney. To Mark it seemed to end a part of his life. There in the smoke went Graham's fantastic visits to his Connecticut apartment, his wanderings in Mexico, his arrival at Shepstowe.

He had no regrets. What was burning was the "I" in his life, a lonely "I" even before Graham's intrusion. By helping him destroy it, Eve was committing herself to be a partner in what was to follow . . . wasn't she?

It did not occur to him until later, when she was downstairs preparing breakfast, that Eve had rather obviously contradicted herself. Early in their conversation she had scoffed at his suggesting the Haitian caller might be Vin's Haitian; then later she had stressed the need for them to be on guard.

Was she reluctant to leave Shepstowe for the same reason he so desperately wanted her to stay? Because she, too, was in love?

Could he even hope it might be that?

18

So, then, the tale of the Connecticut schoolteacher's flight to Jamaica was finished. But he was still supposed to be a writer, wasn't he? The Leggs could not be told the truth—at least not yet. And even little Merlinda McCoy might think it strange if he was not working at the typewriter sometimes when she called.

Why not a novel about the Great House, laid against a background, say, of the early settlers and their struggle with the wilderness, the beginnings of the island's famous Blue Mountain coffee, the slave uprisings? Some heavy research would be necessary, of course. He would probably have to go to the Institute in Kingston and the archives in Spanish Town. Graham and Goodwin would have fits. But why should he tell them?

He thought of the old books Mildred Legg had found for him. Busy with the tale of his flight to Jamaica, he had scarcely glanced at them. Collecting them from the shelf above the fireplace mantel, he carried them to the table and began to browse through them.

Before long he was eagerly typing notes for the new project.

He was not startled when McCoy's granddaughter appeared suddenly in the doorway. She had been with Eve in the kitchen most of the morning. With a nod to her he went on typing.

She marched to the table, wriggled onto a chair, and sat to watch him. It was one of her favorite diversions. After a while she said, "I like to know something, Marse Burke. Why Miss Eve don't hear me when I talk to her?"

His fingers stopped moving and he looked at her. He had been expecting something like this for a long time.

"You know what a fever is, don't you?"

She nodded.

"Well, when Miss Eve was a little girl about your age, she caught a fever. It was a kind of fever that made her sick for a long time. When she got over it, she couldn't hear anymore."

"Couldn't hear?"

"Not a word. Now remember, she was only a little girl then, just learning to talk. All at once she couldn't hear other people talk. So she never learned how." He waited for a nod of understanding but failed to get one. This was not going to be easy, after all.

"Take yourself, for instance," he went on. "You live with your grandfather and hear *him* talk, and that's how you learn to say things, mostly. But if—"

"My gramdaddy don't talk much. Is Miss Roselda I talk to."

"All right, you talk to Miss Roselda." That would be McCoy's woman, the sister of the not-bright Iron. "But suppose you couldn't hear *her* when she talked to you. Suppose, for instance, you didn't know what a yampie is and you asked her, and you couldn't hear what she said. You wouldn't ever know what a yampie is, would you?"

"I could ask somebody else."

"But if you couldn't hear *any*body. Miss Eve couldn't hear anybody at all, remember."

The child made a small circle of her mouth and said, "Oh."

"Then what happened, Miss Eve forgot how to speak the few words she already did know, because she never heard them again. She forgot how to talk at all. Then she was not only deaf, but dumb."

"She can hear *you*," Merlinda protested.

"Not really."

"Yes, she can. The two of you talk to each other."

Mark had to smile. It pleased him that the child was aware of the communication between Eve and himself. He could think of no way to explain it to her, however, so he said simply, "Well, *I* can talk to her because I know special ways."

"I see."

"Now run along. I have work to do."

Obediently the child slid from her chair. But before running from the room she stood for a few seconds by the table, curiously staring at him.

After lunch Mark plunged again into the books Mildred Legg had lent him. There were three. One was the privately printed journal of a former governor, remarkable for its descriptions of island life in colonial times. The second was an old government publication full of statistics. (There had been 138 slaves at Shepstowe at one time, he discovered.) The third was a history of the Parish of St. Thomas—this parish—containing a treasure of information about the old Great Houses.

By five o'clock he had found something that brought his enthusiasm to the boiling point. It was about Shepstowe.

In 1834 the Great House changed hands for the fourth time, the buyer on this occasion being one Jabez Willoughby. Born in Staffordshire, England, Willoughby had come to Jamaica only eight years before, bringing with him his wife, Sarah, to establish a printery in Kingston. The oppressive heat of the city affected his health, however—he was not a young man—and he sold the printery to settle in the mountains at Shepstowe and become a coffee planter.

Willoughby owned Shepstowe for thirteen years. Though he was apparently successful as a planter—or rather as a grower, for the coffee trees were already on the property when he bought it—his wife, Sarah, died in 1846 and he then lost interest. In letters written to relatives in England at this time he complained of being "wretchedly lonely" and "feeling sometimes as if I might go mad here with no one to talk to." A year after Sarah's death he made arrangements to return to England and placed the property in the hands of an attorney, with instructions that it be sold.

The vessel on which Willoughby was to return to England was scheduled to depart from Kingston on the 15th August 1847. He had arranged to travel to the city by carriage on the 10th. On the evening of the 9th, according to a statement made by one Imogene Shepherd, his housekeeper, he left the Great House just before dark and walked down to his wife's grave, on the hillside below the house. He remained there for some time, making his farewells. Then he walked slowly back up to the house and sat for more than two hours on the veranda adjoining the large bedroom. He refused supper, saying he did not feel well. He was still sitting there when Shepherd retired to her quarters, but soon afterward she saw the windows of his room darken and knew that he had gone to bed.

In the morning Willoughby did not appear at his usual hour, and Shepherd knocked on his door. Getting no answer, and alarmed that he might be late in starting for Kingston, she went into his room to arouse him. The poor man, sad to say, was past being aroused. He had passed away in his sleep, and was buried two days later by his wife's side. It would seem that Sarah was determined he should not leave her alone there.

Mark looked at his watch. There would be time, he decided, to visit the graves before dark, if he could find them. He was excited. He had not known there was a "burying ground" on the property. If it still existed, a study of the stones might provide valuable information about Shepstowe's past.

"On the hillside below the house." That must be the slope down which Iron had fled after trying to break into Eve's old room. He hurried into the yard. The area confronting him was a five-acre wilderness plunging toward the zinc roofs of Mango Gut, where McCoy lived.

A graveyard in this place? But, of course, in the old days when there were slaves at Shepstowe, the slope must have been kept clean. The brush now was all but impenetrable. As he scrambled down through head-high tangles of the wickedly thorny shrub they called "wait-a-bit," he began to wish he had been less impulsive.

He searched through the wait-a-bit jungle until exhausted, then gave up, turned back, and came upon the graves quite suddenly, actually clutching at a headstone to steady himself without knowing what it was.

There were seven graves. Six of the stones had fallen over and were nearly hidden by brush and grass. Patiently he cleared around them, gashing his hands so badly that when he copied the inscriptions into a notebook, blood dripped onto the pages.

Seven graves. They were those of Jabez and Sarah Willoughby and other owners of Shepstowe mentioned in Mildred Legg's book. Should he clean the place up and put a fence of some sort around it? He must ask Eve what she thought about that. Returning the notebook to his pocket, he started back up the slope.

But night had fallen now. Lights were on in the Great House high above him, and the hillside up which he must struggle was a dark no-man's-land of brambles and boulders. If he went to his left instead, he would come out on the track by which Mango Gut people walked up to the coffee works.

He turned to his left, and for a time the move seemed a good one. Then the torment began. In the dark a second jungle of man-high wait-a-bit closed around him, each branch armed with hundreds of thorns as cruelly barbed as fishhooks. Too late he realized his blunder and tried to retreat. The wall of thorns had closed behind him.

He fought his way forward, the barbs tearing at his flesh and clothing. The slope there was steep and rocky. Stones rolled under his feet and he stumbled, but the wait-a-bit would not let him fall. It held him grotesquely off the ground like an insect struggling in a web, and the effort to right himself again was an agony worse than the falling.

A final disaster awaited him at the end of the yard. Clear of the thorns at last, stumbling to his feet after a twenty-yard crawl on hands and knees with his shirt in shreds and his face afire from scratches, he stepped on still another loose stone. This time his forward lunge, with arms flailing, carried him head-long into a barbed-wire fence by the trackside. His cry of pain climbed to heaven as wire ripped his out-flung hands.

Moments passed before he was strong enough to sink to the ground in the dark and crawl under the wire. The path from the Gut was just beyond. As he straightened, a flashlight beam leaped from it to fasten on him, and he stood there in its glare, a living scarecrow, swaying.

It was the woman he had seen in Henderson's shop by the cricket field—the sharp-eyed Miss Weeks who had questioned him about walking alone at night from Kingston. He recognized her even though the light all but blinded him. Statue-still, she stared as though at a ghost. On her head she carried a bundle of firewood.

She was frightened, Mark realized. He had better say something to reassure her. "Hello—good evening," he offered weakly, lifting a hand in greeting.

She did not reply. For a few seconds more she stared, not at his face now, but at his upraised hand—a hand gouged by wait-a-bit thorns and the wickedly sharp barbs of the fence; a hand gloved in glistening blood. Then her light abruptly went out and she screamed.

The sound was like nothing human. It was the shrilling of some weird electronic device meant to reach and shatter the stars. Like a rocket it soared into the darkness where it exploded into uncount-able fragments. Then the fragments burst into fragments and the night was full of them. Trees and slopes and cliff walls hurled them back to make a whirlpool of echoes, and the sound was everywhere.

Long after the woman had dropped her head-load of firewood and raced past him down the road in the dark, the screaming held Mark paralyzed.

The stillness returned in time. He stumbled into the track, past the abandoned bundle of sticks, and trudged on up to the Great House. As he neared the house a light came weaving down toward him.

It was Eve. Had she simply missed him and worried, or had he somehow managed to send her a mental plea for help? As she shone her light on his face, her lips came apart in a soundless cry and she seemed frozen with fright. But she recovered quickly and, stepping forward, touched his hands, wincing as though she could feel the pain in them. Taking him gently by an arm, she helped him up the steps.

He was grateful when she sat him down and made a fuss over him, bathing his face and arms with warm water and doctoring his cuts with something soothing from a tube. She worked over him a long time. When she had finished, he was strong enough to take a shower and change his clothes. The clothes he had worn in the graveyard were in shreds, smeared with blood. The peasant woman must have thought him some kind of monstrous apparition.

Later, when some of the soreness had left his hands, he sat at the typewriter and told Eve what had happened. The expression of concern on her face worried him as she took over the machine to reply.

"You should not have done it. Not at night. You simply don't understand these people and their superstitions. They know those old graves are there on the slope; be sure of it. Now by morning the entire district will have heard that she saw you coming from them with blood on you." She went back to underline the words "with blood on you" and then wrote, "Only an obeah person would disturb a graveyard. Especially at night."

"But they can't believe I'm into obeah," he protested. "Ever since I came here, someone in obeah has been trying to drive me away!"

Eve shook her head. "You're trying to apply logic, and logic doesn't enter into this. These people live in fear of obeah. Now they, too, may try to drive you away. I'm not trying to frighten you, Mark. I just want you to know what can happen."

He would have discussed it at greater length with her but his fingers had begun to bleed again and he was exhausted. With a shake of his head he abandoned the dialogue.

19

The best part of a Shepstowe day was the evening, Mark decided. McCoy was not in the yard then, likely to come to the house with some question. Merlinda was gone with her chatter. The day's work was over for Eve and she could relax with her sewing or a book, or play a few games of Scrabble with him. The old house seemed less enormous in the evenings.

He was working this evening, but not hard. Working because he wanted to, lazily. He sat on the old red divan with the typewriter on his knees. Eve, with her shoes off and legs tucked under her, was curled up with a book in one of the overstuffed chairs.

Mark had hit on a way to use the Willoughby story in his new project and was playing around with it. How had the man felt, living alone in this huge place after the death of his wife?

How would I feel without Eve?

The days would be lived through somehow, of course. One had to survive. But they would be long and full of brooding. And what about the evenings? If alone, he would have to have music of some sort: a record player, say, or a tape player. The radio would not be enough.

Had Willoughby owned a phonograph? Had they been invented then? He would have to look it up. There might have been a piano here. The ladies of the old estate houses went to great expense to import pianos.

He stared at the blank wall behind Eve's chair until he could actually see an old upright standing there, with a white-haired man seated at it, playing to hold back the silence.

Strange. The room was silent now except for an occasional rustle as Eve turned a page of her book. But it did not *feel* silent. Her being in it made the difference. To Willoughby, after his wife's death, it must have seemed a tomb.

Eve, he saw, was reading one of the books Mildred had brought: the colonial governor's journal. He had spent part of the afternoon with the same volume and found it fascinating. The writer had been one of Jamaica's best governors. An early chapter contained an intriguing account of his courtship of his lady, with a description of a gift he had given her on the day of their wedding.

The governor, it seemed, had been a romantic. At his insistence a Kingston goldsmith had made for him a brooch—just a simple circle of gold with nothing more than a ring of words engraved on it. "My love, like this circle, shall have no ending."

The lady liked it, apparently. "I think she was pleased," the governor wrote in his journal, "for she did come into my arms and kiss me as though I had given her something of wondrous value. And so I had, she insisted when I questioned her, for the love of a good man was no small thing, she said."

Picturing the scene, Mark smiled. Then he began to type.

There was no faltering now; he knew precisely how Willoughby had felt. His fingers had to fly to keep up with the flow of ideas.

They flew too fast. His left hand, badly gashed in the cemetery, began to drip blood again.

He paused to take a handkerchief from his pocket and wipe his fingers. When he began to type again, Eve came and stopped him by lifting his hands from the keys.

She looked at his hands and shook her head. She went away for a moment, through the big bedroom into her bathroom. Returning, she placed a basin of water at his feet and knelt before him.

He was much more interested in her than in what she was doing. She had come to him so swiftly, she must have been watching him. Why? For the same reason he glanced at her so often, even when working? To keep alive the comfort of knowing she was there, as one kept a fire glowing by constantly replenishing it?

He enjoyed having her "care" him. The little frown of concentration on her mouth was so typical of her. She was so anxious to help, so sure he wanted her help. When she had finished, it seemed entirely natural for him to lean forward across the typewriter on his lap and lift her face to his, and then to kiss her.

She pulled away so swiftly that the typewriter would have fallen between them had he not caught it. Still on her knees, she rocked back and stared at him like a terrified child, violently shaking her head. Had she been able to speak, she would have screamed "No!" at him in a voice as frantic as her eyes, he was certain. In fact, she did scream it mentally, and the world blazed in his mind as he received it. Then she rose from her knees and backed away, thrusting her hands out as though afraid he might leap at her.

Mark was the frightened one then. Numbly he watched her run to her room. He had been so sure of her feelings for him, and now there was nothing. Now whatever there might have been was lost because of his stupidity. He sat without moving, the typewriter on his knees, the basin of water on the floor between his feet. He was dead inside.

In despair he waited for her to reappear. When it seemed certain she would not, he turned again to the typewriter. There was no make-believe now in what he wrote.

"Eve, my darling, forgive me. It was not a mere impulse, but I should have spoken first. So many times I have wanted to speak, but was afraid it might be too soon. Now, God help me, it may be too late.

"You must know that I love you. You could not have lived here all this time without being aware of it. True, you knew little else about me for a long time, but you know everything now.

"Marry me, Eve. Loving you the way I do, I can never live without you."

He went to her door. Like all the doors in the house, this one had shrunk and there was a space under it. On his knees he slid his letter through the gap. When he heard her come and pick it up, he returned to the drawing room to wait.

Nearly an hour passed before she appeared. Her eyes were red from crying and filled with anguish. Standing up as she came to him, he held out his hands. But she halted, shaking her head. With gestures she told him she wanted to use the typewriter, which he had returned to the table.

He held a chair for her, then stood beside her as she typed. So apprehensive was he, he could scarcely breathe as the words appeared.

"Mark, what can I say? You know I can't marry you."

"Why can't you? Why? Why?"

"It might work here, perhaps. Just the two of us. Life is simple in these mountains. But you will be going home. Everything in America is more complicated, and you are a teacher. A teacher with a deaf-mute wife? No, no, no!"

"You're building obstacles where there are none. I

love you." He underlined the word "love" with such force, the typewriter walked over the table.

"It wouldn't work. We hardly know each other. And this other thing, this trouble you are in because of your brother—we would have to wait for that to end in any case, Peter. There, you see? I'm still calling you Peter." She looked up at him and smiled, but it was only a fleeting thing; actually she was crying again.

Mark knew he must put an end to the discussion. It would be cruel to force her to continue tonight. "You are too tired for this now," he wrote. "Go to bed, my darling. But sleep on this: I love you with all my heart and soul, and someday I'm going to persuade you to marry me, no matter how long it takes."

When she stood up he did not touch her, though he longed to take her into his arms at that moment. It was she who touched him, pausing briefly to lift his injured left hand and frown at it before she left him.

After her departure he remained at the table an hour or more, reading and rereading the lines they both had written.

20

Mark had walked to the coffee works to borrow a pipe wrench. It would be nice to run a water pipe from the Great House to the garden, Eve had suggested; having to maneuver long sections of hose was a bother. There were some lengths of pipe in the garage that he could use.

When he inquired for Jeff Legg in the factory yard, he was directed to the sorting room.

Only a handful of women were at work there this afternoon. They looked up as he entered. Knowing most of them now, he smiled and said "Good evening" as he walked between the twin rows of tables.

It surprised him when they did not respond. He had expected the usual "Evenin', squire" or "How-de-do, sah" but met only stares and silence. Even more strange, they stared not at his face, but at his hands. Or, rather, at his left hand. Before working on his book this morning he had put some strips of bandage on it to keep it from bleeding again.

But surely the factory women knew what bandage strips were. Even the local shops sold them. The stares puzzled and disturbed him.

Jeff Legg was on a ladder at the end of the room, repairing a skylight. "Hello there," he said, glancing down. "Be with you in a minute."

Mark turned to look at the women again. They still stared. It was as though he were a stranger, or they were afraid he had come to lodge some complaint against them. One by one they pretended to concentrate on their work, but with their heads lowered over the trays of coffee beans they whispered to one another.

Jeff came down the ladder, and Mark inquired about the wrench.

"That's easy. Come along."

As they walked down the aisle, Jeff scooped a

handful of gray-blue beans from a tray to examine them. Mark was more interested in the sorter, who eyed his bandaged hand as though it were a snake that might suddenly lunge at her. Her name was Sadie and he had exchanged greetings with her often, even talked to her at times when she came to the house with scallions to sell. But she was so afraid of him now that he half expected her to leap from her stool and run away.

It was a relief when Jeff returned the beans to the tray and strolled on out into the sunlight.

While wiping the wrench with a bit of waste before handing it over, Jeff said, "Mildred and I are going to town tomorrow. Soon be Christmas, you know, and she wants to do some shopping. Come along, why don't you? You and Eve."

Christmas was only two weeks away, Mark realized. "Well—"

"Do you both good. All this obeah business and your troubles at the house—you need a change."

"I'd like to, Jeff, but—"

"We'll pick you up about eight." Jeff finished wiping the wrench and handed it over. "When you use this thing, don't get brutal or you'll strip the pipe threads. Pipe today is miserable stuff. What we get here, anyway."

"About tomorrow," Mark said, "I'm not sure I—"

"You're thinking of Eve? The big city won't frighten her. She's been there before."

Graham would have a fit, Mark thought as he walked up the road with the wrench on his shoulder. *"You will not have a car; you will not leave Shepstowe."* But then, how would he know?

And it was only fair to Eve. She, too, would want to do some Christmas shopping, probably. She must have friends, though none had yet come to visit her.

Goodwin was responsible for that, no doubt. When hiring her, he would have warned her not to encourage friends to come. "Mr. Burke has a book to write and must be disturbed as little as possible."

Why had the women in the sorting room stared so intently at his bandaged hand?

When he told Eve about the women's strange behavior, she was instantly alarmed.

"They looked at your *hand?* Are you sure?"

"Positive."

"Then the woman you met when you came from the graves has been talking. Her screams must have been heard in Mango Gut, anyway. This is what I was so afraid of, Mark. *You* are an obeah man now."

What a fool he had been to look for those graves at night. But how could he have known? Unable to think of anything more to say on the subject, he dismissed it and wrote almost defiantly, "Jeff and Mildred want us to go to Kingston with them to do some Christmas shopping."

Eve's eyes brightened with excitement, and she clapped her hands like a child. Then suddenly she became fearful. "Should we?" she wrote.

"Why not? Whatever I'm hiding from is more likely to be here than in Kingston, don't you think?"

"Will you tell Goodwin? He'll be bound to report it to Graham if you do."

"Why should I tell him? Why not just drive to town with Jeff and Mildred, have a grand time, and keep it to ourselves?"

179

Again she hesitated, wanting to consent, obviously, but afraid for him. "Well," she finally wrote, "you do need to get away from here, even if only for a day's outing. It would be so good after all the strain you've been under."

"Then you agree? We'll go?"

"Mark, it's for you to say. Not me."

"We go, then," he wrote with a triumphant grin. "Hooray!"

Kingston with its horde of holiday shoppers was a beehive.

"Eve is coming with me," Mildred Legg said. "You two men can just be off about your business, and we'll meet you later." She reached for Eve's hand. "How about twelve o'clock at the post office? We can walk up to that Chinese place on Princess Street for lunch."

They were standing outside a parking garage on Duke Street where Jeff, after vainly touring the lower part of the city for twenty minutes, had at last found a place to leave the car. Jeff looked at his watch. "Well, all right."

"We're gone, then," his wife said, and briskly marched Eve away.

Jeff grinned at Mark. "Determined woman, my wife. Well, we've an hour and a half to kill. What's on your mind? The Institute?"

"Not today. I want a present for Eve."

"Fair enough. What sort of present?"

"If you won't be inquisitive and ask me why, I'll describe it exactly. I want a gold pin—a brooch, I guess you'd call it—in the shape of a small circle."

"Uh-huh." Jeff took his pipe from his mouth and nodded. "Swiss Store, I should think. Good place to start, anyway, and it's just along Harbour Street a way."

The Swiss Store, Mark thought, and was suddenly weeks back in time, desperately alone, trying to carry out the instructions of the man from Washington.

"At 5:30 P.M. check out of the guest house in Kingston and take a cab to the airport. Walk about the airport, being as conspicuous as you can be. Order a meal in the restaurant and complain about the food. Inquire about flights to New York and seem to be upset because none suits you. We want you remembered at the airport, so if certain people find out you went to Jamaica they will think you took a plane out of there soon afterward."

If Graham had been trying to get him to Shepstowe without leaving a trail for the Disciples to follow, did this really make sense? Wouldn't it have been relatively easy for trained men to find out he had *not* booked a flight out of Kingston? And, having learned that, wouldn't they logically have said to themselves, "He went to such trouble to fake it, he must have been planning to *stay* here in Jamaica?"

Come to think of it, since the letter from Vin, *none* of Graham's instructions seemed to make much sense. The whole orchestration was full of discords.

Thinking about it frightened him.

Anyway, there'd been a branch of the Swiss Store at the airport, with a striking display of handmade jewelry, so the main store here in town might be just the place.

On Harbour Street traffic crawled and the growl of trucks made conversation all but impossible. The sun beat down through a reek of gasoline and diesel fumes. Pedestrians dragged their feet.

All kinds of pedestrians, all hues. Coloreds from off-white to black. Chinese in shades of yellow—the little Chinese office girls, pert and pretty, were so much alike they might all have been sisters. East Indians were part of the scene, too, fine-featured and haughty-seeming. "Out of many, one people" was the country's excellent motto. There were indeed many.

The Swiss Store had a fine display of things in gold, and a young woman behind the counter promptly produced what Mark wanted. She knew its significance, too, apparently. "Will the lady understand?" she asked, smiling. "You could have something engraved on it, you know."

"Thank you. That won't be necessary, I'm sure."

He hoped he was right. At least, Eve had read the book; he was sure of that much. He paid for the gift and put the box into his pocket.

"What was that all about?" Jeff Legg asked as they left the shop.

"I told you not to be inquisitive."

"So you did. Well, what next?"

"Something for McCoy's little granddaughter. And a few Christmas cards." He wouldn't, of course, be mailing cards to anyone in the States; that would be carrying his insubordination too far. But he did want a card for Eve, and one for the Leggs.

"Woolworth's, on King Street," Jeff said. "Not far from here, but what about a Red Stripe first? I know you don't drink much, but this heat brings on a thirst." He must have known there was a bar just ahead, for in the next breath he added, "Here we are," and thrust open a swinging door.

It was a small, hushed place. Dark mahogany tables. A framed and faded photograph of Elizabeth II on the wall. An aproned man polishing glasses behind a tiny bar, and a waitress reading a magazine. "Always quiet like this," Jeff remarked as they seated themselves at a table. "Wonder sometimes how they stay in business, but the place has been here for years." The waitress put her magazine down and came over, and he ordered two beers. "It *is* beer you want, isn't it?"

"Fine."

They were silent for a moment, Jeff puffing his pipe, Mark thinking of the gift in his pocket. The girl came with two glasses and two bottles of Jamaican beer, named for the red stripes on the trousers of the island constabulary force. She filled the glasses and went away, leaving the bottles on the table. When Jeff had satisfied his thirst, Mark took the jeweler's box from his pocket and said, "If you're still wondering, I'll tell you about this."

"I think I know what it is." A smile spread on Jeff's leathery face. "I've read the governor's journal, too."

"I'm in love with her. Were you aware of that?"

"Guessed it. I'm not surprised."

"That's why I'm telling you—because I didn't think you would be surprised. I might also tell you, since you've known me only a short time, that I'm not married, never have been married, and have never felt this way about a woman before."

"Does Eve know how you feel?"

"She knows, but thinks it can't work."

"Can it? When you go back?"

"It can. It will. But I have to convince her." Returning the box to his pocket, Mark sipped his drink and directed a wry smile at his companion. "You know why I'm telling you this, of course. You and Mildred are fond of her, and she trusts you. If you think I'm worth the effort, you could help me."

"I'm not so sure. She's a girl who thinks for herself."

"That I know."

"I can tell you something else, too. My wife would want to be absolutely certain you've thought this through. That girl has had a hard enough time without making a mistake in a matter of this weight."

"I don't blame Mildred, or you, either. You don't know me."

Jeff put some money on the table to pay for the drinks. "I like what I do know," he said, rising. "Will that do for a start?"

It was an odd thing, Mark thought as they faced the crowded sidewalk again. He had known this man only a few weeks, yet felt for him a depth of friendship he had never known for any man before. There must be a reason for it. Shepstowe was part of the answer, probably. Life there was so basic that one had time to get hold of an emotion and think about it.

The coin had two faces, of course. He remembered an observation in one of Mildred's books about the "emotional instability" of the peasants. They, too, had more time to dwell on their feelings than did people who led busier lives. As a result, a dispute over something as simple as a stray goat in a neighbor's garden could lead to months of feuding.

He hoped the people of Mango Gut would not think too hard about his bandaged hand. Or, worse, about the blood the woman from Henderson's shop had seen on him when he stumbled out of the cemetery.

21

At Woolworth's Mark bought a doll for Merlinda and the cards he wanted. Then he and Jeff walked down King Street to the post office, where they found Mildred and Eve waiting. Both women carried shopping bags.

"Been spending all your money, eh?" Jeff said, and Mark jokingly reached for Eve's bag to peer into it. She pushed him away, smiling, and Mildred said, "It isn't Christmas yet. Don't be nosy."

The congestion worsened as they turned up Princess Street. Humanity flowed like a sluggish river down street and sidewalks. Cars inched through with a querulous bleating of horns. Every second

shop appeared to be a wholesale grocery establishment with a Chinese name. Mark held fast to Eve's
arm as the crowd pressed against them.

They were out of it soon, climbing a murky flight
of stairs to the restaurant Jeff and Mildred had selected. After the street and the stairway, Mark was
pleased to find the place itself spacious and attractive. The waiter led them to a table for four near the
center of the room.

"I hope you like Chinese food," Mildred said. "I'm
afraid we didn't ask you."

"I do."

"I know Eve does. She's even good at preparing
it." She looked at Eve and smiled, though the younger woman could not have heard what she said.
"Well, then, suppose we order the family meal. Choy
Fan, they call it. They bring all sorts of goodies and
you just help yourself."

"Meaning," Jeff said with a chuckle, "you'll help
yourself to my share of the sweet-sour pork and the
duck, and leave me wallowing in rice."

"I won't, I promise." She laughed gaily. "I'll be a
proper lady."

Mark enjoyed the meal. It included a number of
Chinese dishes he had not tasted before, and he
could well understand why the restaurant was
crowded.

The patrons formed a cross section of Kingston itself, he noticed. The Chinese office-girl sisterhood
was well represented: so many of the same doll-like
faces that the room seemed full of mirrored reflec-
tions. At other tables were quartets of neatly dressed
young businessmen, both yellow- and dark-skinned,

who kept the room filled with a beehive hum of conversation. At still others were older Chinese, silently intent upon their food, looking for all the world like illustrations in an old-style travel book. And there were a few whites: whether Jamaican whites or tourists, one had no way of knowing.

Suddenly he saw a face from Mexico.

He was not sure at first. The man on the train to Mérida had worn a black cassock, if that was the proper name for a priestly robe in Latin America. This man's attire consisted of dark trousers and a white sport shirt.

It can't be the same fellow, Mark thought with a mental shrug. They just happen to look alike. Much to blur his memory had happened since the train trip. Yet the man he was gazing at had the same features, not Jamaican or Chinese, but Latin American without question, and the mere thought that it *could* be the same man had caused him to begin trembling.

What had Vin written about the Disciples? "They come from all over. There's even a former Catholic priest from Brazil and a voodoo *houngan* from Haiti."

A moment later he was certain.

Two other men had come into the restaurant together and gone straight to the same table. Without even speaking to the one seated there they pulled back chairs and sat. One of them was young, slender, and very black.

Without question it was the fellow who had wanted water for a car that was not hot enough for him to know it needed water. The black man who spoke English with a French intonation.

". . . *even a voodoo* houngan *from Haiti.*"

Mark suffered an increase of dread so sharp it all but iced his blood.

Now the three conversed, and the identity of the man in the white sport shirt was no longer to be questioned. The tilt of his head while he listened, as though he had a stiff neck—the habit he had of lifting a finger to rub a corner of one eye—Mark could almost feel the sway of the train and see the Mexican landscape blur past outside a grimy window.

And the third man? This one he had not seen before, he was sure. Dressed in a dark gray business suit, he was shorter and older than the others. Black hair and a black beard set him apart. So did flashing black eyes that seemed constantly in motion as the three men talked. And marking him even more was a zigzag scar that disfigured his pink lower lip.

Mark had forgotten he was at lunch with the Leggs and the woman he loved. Mildred brought him back by saying suddenly, "What is it, Peter? Is something wrong?"

He managed somehow to make himself smile, and to sound merely embarrassed. "No, nothing wrong. I thought I recognized someone over there. I'm probably mistaken."

"You easily could be, here," Jeff said. "Someone from our district, you mean?"

"No. A man I met in Mexico." With no small effort Mark concentrated again on the lunch.

He had had to turn partway around on his chair to look at the table where the three men sat, and now for some twenty minutes he forced himself not to do so again. With the lunch nearly over, he began to lose his fear. Then suddenly he felt something at the back of his head.

It was an itching of sorts. A feeling that something with many legs had crept into his hair and was wriggling over his scalp like a centipede through grass. His head began to ache. His ears filled with a humming that slowly became almost too shrill to be endured.

Something was telling him, commanding him, to turn around again.

Did they want to see his face? Had they become curious? Four whites, seated together in this restaurant where even the Jamaican patrons were outnumbered by Chinese, could hardly have escaped attention.

He struggled against the command as he would have fought to extricate himself from the terrors of a nightmare. He must *not* turn around! He must *not* let them look at him! In some deeper recess of his mind he could almost hear the Haitian giving the others a report of his ruse with the car that day. "Yes, I talked to him. I think he is our man. But we need to be sure."

"Shall we have some dessert?" Mildred Legg was gaily asking. "They have some wonderful things here."

Get out, Mark told himself. Get out now, before it's too late. But he knew it was already too late. The command to turn around was eating at his mind like some monstrous maggot, devouring his will to resist.

Suddenly another voice entered his mind. Eve's

voice. "Don't do it, darling! Don't listen to them!" Had she screamed it aloud it could have been no more distinct.

He looked across the table at her. How could she know what was happening to him?

She knew because she was facing the table where the three men sat, he realized. She was staring right at them. And because her mind was more receptive than his to this kind of mental telepathy, she was intercepting the command they were sending him.

"Don't do it!" she told him again. "Don't turn! I'll say I'm ill so we can leave."

My God, he thought, she could be *talking* to me. Her voice is louder than theirs!

Eve had reached for the notepad she always kept handy. On it she scribbled hastily, "I don't feel well. Can we go, please, Peter? Now?" Her underlining of the word "Now" was so frantic it caught Mildred Legg's eye and caused Mildred to look at her in alarm.

Eve thrust the note at Mark. As he handed it to Jeff, he felt the torment building up inside his skull again and had to fight for control of himself. "Jeff—" He struggled to his feet. "Can you take care of the bill? Please? We'll meet you downstairs."

There was a moment of confusion. Eve, rising, still stared past him at the table where the Brazilian, the Haitian, and the man with the scarred lip sat. Mildred looked completely bewildered, yet wanting to help. Then dependable Jeff Legg came to the rescue with a solemn nod.

"Of course," Jeff said. "Run along, the two of you."

Mark reached for Eve's hand while she still stared past him at the other table. For a moment he thought she might suddenly refuse to leave—might have become a victim of the very telepathy she had saved him from. But with a shake of her head, as though to dislodge something that was trying to claw its way inside, she freed herself.

Hurrying her through the restaurant, still without yielding to the command to look toward the three at the table, he rushed her down the gloomy stairway to crowded Princess Street. And there, with the sunlight bouncing off the pavement and the holiday crowd of shoppers milling by, the agony in his head subsided as though he had swallowed a fast-acting painkiller.

He looked a question at Eve and she nodded, clinging to his hand. "I'm all right," was the mental message he received.

Thank God, he thought. But they've found me. And they know I'm at Shepstowe. Now what do I do?

Should he tell Goodwin?

He thought about it on the ride back to the Great House, over the mountain road he had walked that night alone. The road seemed even more sinister now. This despite the fact that the afternoon sunlight transformed it into a golden river, with shadows of leaves dancing on it as a cooling breeze shook the roadside trees.

Dependable Jeff Legg drove. Mildred, beside him, gaily chattered about her day in town.

Yes, Mark decided, he would probably have to tell Goodwin.

On the way to the city he had shared the front seat with Jeff. Now he rode in back with Eve. His hand sought hers, and he was pleased when she did not draw away from the contact. Yet it was no ordinary ride for her. He knew her well enough now to observe, by looking at her face, that she was still very tense. So concerned was he about it that he neglected to reply when Mildred spoke to him.

Mildred turned to look at him. "Is everything all right, Peter? The road isn't making you carsick, is it?"

"No. I was just thinking."

"It makes me wobbly at times. These curves, and the way Jeff rips around them. The height, too, sometimes."

The road *was* on the edge of space at the moment. Mark looked down and saw a thread of river flashing through boulders far below—the same stream in which Eve and he had gone swimming at the pools. He had seen a tree near the pools that would do nicely for a Christmas tree, he suddenly remembered. He would have to go for it, or send McCoy.

But would he be at Shepstowe for Christmas? When told about the three in the restaurant, would Goodwin permit it? And again, *should* he mention the trip to Kingston when Goodwin came tomorrow?

At home, when the Leggs had departed, Mark sat at his typewriter and asked Eve what she thought.

"I think you ought to speak to him," she replied.

"But how, exactly? I mean, just what am I to tell him? What did *you* feel in that restaurant?"

She thought about it before attempting to answer, then took her time at the machine, choosing her words with care. "I first felt something like a discomfort in my head. Or a kind of pressure. Then it became a voice pounding at my mind, commanding me to look at those men." Her hands hovered above the keys for a few seconds while she frowned. "But, of course, I was already looking straight at them, so I knew I must have intercepted a command meant for you."

He nodded.

"*Did* you feel you were receiving such a command? To turn around and look at them?" she asked.

"Good God, yes!"

"Of course," she wrote, "you already know I'm one of the sensitive ones when it comes to ESP and telepathy. Just as you are, though you haven't had any reason to work on it as I have. Mark"—she paused to look up at him, and he saw anxiety in her frown—"isn't it likely that my being so sensitive could add to the danger you're in? Even though I was able to help you in the restaurant?"

She was right, he supposed. The Disciples just might get to him through her.

"I ought to leave here," Eve wrote. "For your sake I ought to go home."

It was ironic. A little while ago he had suggested she leave because *she* might be in danger. "No!" he said aloud, fiercely shaking his head.

"But if I stay—"

"No!"

"Should *you* stay here?" she asked. "The Haitian must have suspected who you are—I mean he must have thought you were Vin—or those men wouldn't have commanded you to turn around so they could get a better look at you."

Yes, he thought, the black man in the restaurant had seen him here at Shepstowe. But if he left here, where would he go?

He put the question to Eve.

"We might move to my house in Trinity," she wrote, but almost at once rejected that idea. "No. That's only a few miles down the road, and the whole district would talk about it. You know how our country people gossip. What about Kingston?"

He didn't want to return to Kingston. During his brief stay at the guest house there he had learned to dislike that hot, noisy city with a passion. "No, not Kingston," he wrote. "To play it really safe, I suppose I'd have to leave the island—leave you—and I won't do that, either."

She studied his face for a moment. Then she wrote, "Perhaps we could stay here but work out a plan as your brother suggested. I mean a plan in detail, so we can be ready at once if we have to be. Doing it that way would at least lessen the tension. What do you think?"

"Let's do it."

"Right now?"

He hesitated, then shook his head. "No. We're tired, both of us, and tired people don't think straight. Nothing's going to happen here tonight."

"Mark, we can't be sure."

"In the morning," he insisted. After all, if the men in the restaurant thought they had him trapped here in the old Great House, why should they be in a hurry to pounce? "Good night, my darling," he typed. "In spite of everything it was a beautiful day, thanks to you."

22

In the morning they discussed the situation more fully but accomplished less than Mark had hoped for. The isolated location of the Shepstowe Great House presented insoluble problems without a car.

If members of the group Vin had warned about were suddenly to show up here, the mountains appeared to offer his only means of escape. He would simply have to take to the coffee-field tracks or the longer, more dangerous track up the river, and hope to avoid capture.

"But don't be discouraged," he found himself writing when their search for options appeared to have run into a dead end. "We'll be working on it and will surely think of something in time. Now, what about Goodwin? Do you still think we ought to tell him what happened in town? Or even that we went to town?"

"I don't know, Mark. I thought so yesterday, but now I'm not so sure."

"You don't completely trust him, do you?"

"From the beginning I've had uneasy feelings about him."

"I think I've been aware of it, and I'm not sure I trust him, either. Let's play it by ear."

The golden-haired man arrived soon after lunch and walked from his car whistling, with a carton of groceries balanced on his head. The tune he whistled was a Jamaican folk song, "Linstead Market"—"Carry me ackee, go-a Linstead Market, not a quattie worth sell"—and when he dropped the carton on the drawing room table, he grinned.

"Offer me a drink, my friend. The day is hotter than Dutch love, you may have noticed, and I had a lovely flat tire on the climb from Richmond Vale. Had to change it myself, too. Not a soul around. Would you have a rum and ginger?"

Mark mixed him one.

"I splurged on you this week," Goodwin said brightly. "Got to thinking that if I were buried out here the way you are, I would be subject to cravings. So I marched up and down the aisles of the supermarket with an eagle eye, and I have brought you"—with exaggerated gestures he lifted the items one by one from the box—"some delicious canned ham, a jar of lambs' tongues, a can of lichees from Hong Kong where they make all those flashlights that don't work—"

At that moment Eve came into the room, to carry the food supplies down to the kitchen as she always did when Goodwin paid a visit. The man from Kingston greeted her with a limp wave of his hand. She responded with a smile and quickly disappeared.

"Sit down," Mark said, turning Goodwin toward a chair. An idea had come to him when he realized the man was a little drunk. Perhaps he could discover

Goodwin's reaction to the Kingston trip without actually telling him anything. "I've something to ask you."

The golden-haired man plucked his glass from the table, settled himself, and thrust his long legs out. "Proceed."

"I've a request to make, and you put your finger on the reason for it when you spoke of my being subject to cravings here. The Leggs want Eve and me to go to town with them to do some Christmas shopping. Would you object?"

"My God," Goodwin said harshly. "Are you out of your mind?"

"It seems harmless enough. Just the four of us, a day in town, lunch in some restaurant that will be crowded with shoppers."

"Until you *think* about it. Which, obviously, you haven't. Are you completely forgetting how much effort was expended to get you here unfollowed?"

"I'm not forgetting anything, nor am I likely to. *I* was the one who walked out here from town at night, remember, not you or Graham. The point is," Mark went on, his voice still under control, "I'm a little tired of being cooped up here."

"You have the whole district to move around in. Kingston is out of bounds. Definitely."

Mark leaned against the table and gazed at him. "Are you trying to tell me something?"

"Like what?"

"That I may have been followed to Jamaica from the States, after all? That Mexico City and Mérida were just a waste of time?"

Goodwin shrugged. "I'm not saying that. On the other hand, the people who are after you are pros,

Donner. We don't take anything in this game for granted."

"The people who are after my brother, I suppose you meant to say."

"What? Oh yes—of course." Reaching for his drink, Goodwin sipped it, then scowled again. "And while we're on the subject of indiscretions, if I may use that word, let me say you're doing another unwise thing in allowing Eve Vernon to live in this house." His glance flicked to the door through which Eve had disappeared.

Mark had trouble remaining calm now. "How do you know she's living in the house?"

"It's my job to notice things, such as the way you two have been acting lately. It's my job to check up on things I notice—like by leaving my car on the road the last time I left here and walking back to do some professional snooping. Do you mind telling me *why* she's in the house?"

Mark said in a barely controlled voice, "Because I want her here."

"Obviously. But why do you want her here?"

"Not for the reason you're probably thinking of. The boy who used to work in the garden with McCoy tried to break into her cottage and molest her. I had to fire him."

"I see." Goodwin slowly nodded. "Well, that's a good enough reason, I suppose."

"It is to me. You can't run my entire life, you know."

The man from Kingston finished his drink and stood up. His face had softened. There even seemed to be a touch of sadness in it as he shook his head. "Believe me," he said, "I wish I didn't have to run any part of it. You're a nice guy, God help you. I wish I'd never laid eyes on you."

When the growl of the car had died away, Mark went to the typewriter and tried to recall, for Eve, exactly what Goodwin had said. On reading it over he thought it was fairly accurate. Eve studied it for some time before commenting.

"We haven't learned anything, have we?" she wrote. "I felt we might when I saw he'd been drinking."

"He wasn't drunk enough to be careless."

"And have you noticed," she wrote, "that he still hasn't given you an inkling of what you are supposed to be hiding from? Aside from generalities, I mean. Your brother has, but not Goodwin."

It was too bad, Mark told himself, that friend Goodwin had not had a whole lot more to drink. Then the session might have been really interesting.

23

Mark worked on a letter to brother Vin and watched a hummingbird at the same time. It was the morning after Goodwin's visit.

The bird was a doctorbird, a tiny, iridescent creature with a brilliant coral bill and long twin tails.

The letter told of his encounter with the Haitian who had wanted water for a car that wasn't hot and—in much more detail—what had happened in the Kingston restaurant.

The bird hovered just outside a window of the drawing room, tapping the glass with its bill now and then, apparently curious about what he was doing. In the garden one day a doctorbird impelled by the same curiosity had flown up to tap a packet of flower seeds in his hand.

Suddenly this one flew too hard against the glass and fell stunned to the sill. Mark opened the window and picked it up. In the palm of his hand it lay unmoving with its head upraised, returning his gaze.

Eve came down the driveway with a basket in her hand. He was surprised. He had not seen her leave the house; had thought she was downstairs in the kitchen. He watched her with pleasure. It always delighted him to watch her walk. She did so as though there were a layer of something soft between her feet and the earth.

The bird stirred in his hand and he returned it to the windowsill, lowering the window so it would not fly into the room and find itself in a prison. Then he went downstairs.

Eve had some eggs and a live chicken in the basket, the fowl's legs tied together with cord. He was puzzled. Usually she bought chickens from a woman who came to the house, and would not buy them live because she hated having to kill them. She bought eggs from one of the Mango Gut women, too, when Goodwin forgot to bring them.

"Where did you go?" he asked on her slate.

"Rainy Ridge."

She had been gone a good while, then. Had he not been working on the letter, he would have missed her.

"You haven't shopped there before," he wrote.

"The women didn't come. They hadn't anything to sell this week, I expect." She seemed unwilling to be drawn into a dialogue, and with mock indignation pushed him aside when he sought one. "If you want lunch today, go away," she wrote. "Shoo!"

He climbed the stairs and returned to his letter, with a glance at the window to see if the hummingbird had flown away. It hadn't. It was still there, looking at him through the glass. The market business troubled him, but he was anxious to finish the letter and get it to the post office.

"The third man in the restaurant," he wrote, concluding his account of what had taken place there, "was one I haven't seen before. He was from the Middle East, without a doubt. He wore a dark gray suit and was shorter than the other two—say about five-six. His hair was black. He had a black beard. And he had a scar that curled along his lower lip. If the other two are Disciples, he is probably one, too, don't you think? Perhaps the scar will tell you something. Not many men have scarred lips, surely. I'll be anxiously waiting to find out what you think about this."

He read the letter over. Hearing a car coming down the driveway, he hurriedly sealed the envelope before going to the door. His caller was Jeff Legg.

"Morning. Mind if I come in for a minute?"

Mark opened the door wider.

Lowering himself onto a chair, Jeff glanced about the room. "Is Eve here?"

"In the kitchen."

"M'm. I wasn't going to trouble you with this until I had to. But I heard she was in the village buying eggs and a chicken this morning, and when I asked how come, I was told the women who usually deliver here won't come anymore. It occurred to me she needs to be careful."

Mark stood with his back to the table, waiting.

"I haven't got the whole of it yet," Jeff went on. "But you seem to have done something to bring the local people down on you."

"I went looking at graves."

"That's part of it, I gather. But why at night?"

Curbing his impatience, Mark told how he had torn his clothes and bloodied his hands. "I suppose I did give the woman a bad scare, letting her catch me red-handed, so to speak."

No smile appeared on Jeff's leathery face. "More than a bad scare, I can tell you. You gave her something to talk about, and they do love to do that. The trouble is, they were already talking. That walk of yours from Kingston at night."

"So I'm a freak?"

"I wish it were only that. Freaks they know all about. That fellow they call Iron. Another loony, called Duppy John, who walks around his yard naked. Oh, they know that sort. In a community like Mango Gut, where they're practically all cousins or worse, they've got a full collection. But they don't have people who walk the country roads at night and come out of graveyards with blood on their hands."

"Don't tell me they're afraid of me."

"How many have spoken to you since you frightened the woman?"

"Well—"

"How many have crossed over to the other side of the road when they saw you coming?" Jeff rubbed his jaw. "There's something else, too. I shouldn't mention it because even Milly and I have noticed it, and we think it's damned wonderful—but it's hurting you all the same."

Mark's frown asked the question for him.

"The way you and Eve communicate. Somebody's been telling these people you *talk* to each other."

Mark remembered his exchange of words with McCoy's granddaughter. Had he actually told the child he was able to talk with Eve? He was not sure.

"Merlinda," he said, and explained.

"The point is," Jeff said, "they *can't* communicate with her and they know it. So you're different on that score, too."

"I see."

"Do you, really? I wonder. These are superstitious people, Peter. Ignorant. They're born believing the damnedest mess of nonsense you can imagine, and go on believing it, most of them, until they die. No ordinary person walks alone at night; duppies might snatch him. No one prowls in a burying ground at night; he could disappear into the earth. No one can talk to a girl like Eve Vernon; it's not possible. But you're able to do these things. You have powers. In short, old boy, you're someone to be feared."

"Is Eve in this, too?" Mark asked unhappily.

"She's in it, too." Jeff pushed himself to his feet at last. "What I don't fully understand is how it got around so fast. It shouldn't have. They talk a lot, but it usually takes a team of mules to get them moving on something. I know; I have to work with them. There's someone behind all this, pushing it. Some person with a grudge against you, maybe, or an imagined one. I think so, anyway."

Reaching out, he laid a hand on Mark's shoulder. "Take care. And look after Eve. They're only scared now, but after a time some fellow may build up his courage with white rum or ganja and decide to become a hero."

There was something Mark felt he ought to know. "You mentioned ganja before. Do they actually use it here?"

"Some do. There's a law against growing it, of course, but up here in the mountains the government has to use helicopters to spot the plantings. Don't get reckless if you learn something. Let me handle it."

"All right, I will." Mark reached for the letter on the table. "Are you going by the post office?" It would save him a walk if Jeff would post the letter, and for some reason he now felt too tired for such an effort.

"No problem." Taking the letter, the coffee-works manager departed.

Mark remembered the doctorbird and wondered what had happened to it. He walked across the room to see if it was still on the sill.

It was, but it no longer looked in at him. On raising the window, he was saddened to discover the bird was dead.

Thinking of what Jeff Legg had said about Eve, he went down to the kitchen in search of her and asked her to come upstairs with him. On the typewriter he told her what Jeff had said, then asked what she thought of it.

"I'm not really afraid," she wrote. "They are not bad people, Mark. Only uneducated. It's a dreadful pity, isn't it, that so much needless misery is caused by ignorance?"

Then, after a long pause at the machine, she wrote more slowly and deliberately, "But that isn't the worst of it, I think. There is hope for the merely ignorant ones, and we are trying hard to improve our schools here in Jamaica. The really evil ones are those who use the little people for their own ends. That's what frightens me most: not the ignorance itself, but the heartless schemers who take advantage of it. All over the world it's happening, isn't it?—wicked, clever men manipulating the stupid ones, stirring up senseless hatreds in a savage quest for power."

Reading what she had written, Mark felt a deep inner warmth as he gently touched her face with his fingertips.

24

There was but one sensible thing to do, Mark decided. While waiting for Vin's next letter he must maintain the sharpest kind of vigil, of course. At the same time he should try to live as normal a life as possible. Anything else would be intolerable.

Meanwhile, Christmas was coming.

Cautioning Eve to be everlastingly alert for strangers, he took McCoy with him to the pools one morning to find a suitable tree.

Rain had fallen during the night. The track up the river was muddy, and the forest dripped. It was cold, too. The temperature at night might soon be in the fifties, Eve had warned. McCoy had already begun to lay in a supply of wood for the fireplace.

At the place where Eve and he had heard the wild pig, Mark called a halt. They had walked a long way in silence. The time was right for a cautious attempt to obtain some information.

"I haven't seen your little granddaughter in quite a while, Zekiel."

"Squire?"

"She isn't ill, is she?"

"No, squire."

"She used to spend a lot of time with Miss Eve in the kitchen. Talked to me a lot, too."

"They is fickle, the little ones." McCoy was not a man who grinned often, and looked foolish when he did so. "She want to stay home now, makin' up games to play with her dolly."

"Oh?" Mark remembered his purchase in Kingston. "She has a doll?"

"I did make her one, squire."

"Well, I'm glad to know she's not mad at me. I thought I might have done something."

"No, sah. You don't done nuttin'."

Nor am I learning anything, either, Mark thought.

206

He tried again when they reached the pools. After a brief swim to wash off the sweat of the journey, he put his clothes back on and said, "There's something troubling me, Zekiel."

McCoy had not gone in the water. He sat on the ledge where Eve and Mark had eaten lunch. "Sah?"

"Merlinda asked me one day why Miss Eve never talked to her. I tried to explain."

"Yes, sah?"

"I don't think I was very successful. The child seemed to think Miss Eve *can* talk to me and hear me when *I* talk. That isn't so, of course, as I'm sure you know. We communicate by writing to each other."

McCoy seemed uncomfortable. He took up a dry stick and frowned at it while breaking small pieces off and tossing them into the pool. "Yes, squire. I know."

"You mean you know the child misunderstood me?"

"Not that, squire. But I know how you and Miss Eve manage."

"I just wouldn't want Merlinda to get any strange ideas," Mark said carefully.

"No, squire."

There were other leading questions he might ask, Mark supposed. Why, for instance, did McCoy still come faithfully to work every day when the women of the district would not call at the house to sell things? And how *had* the story got around that Eve and he "talked" to each other, if not from the child or McCoy himself? Such questions were not likely to help the situation, though. They might even drive the man from evasiveness into total silence.

"Come on," Mark said. "Let's find that tree."

They walked upstream to the sawyers' cabin. In front of it Mark picked up an empty cigarette box that had not been there before.

He handed it to McCoy and watched the man's face as he said, "Iron was here hunting pigs, you suppose?"

McCoy only shrugged. "Plenty people smoke Albanys. Every shop have them. I smoke them myself." He fumbled a box from his shirt pocket, though he had not to Mark's knowledge used a cigarette all morning. "I shouldn't think Iron would be lookin' pigs this low down, anyhow. More likely some sawyers was here, sah."

Mark went into the cabin but found no sign that the place had been used since his visit with Eve. "Just how do your sawyers operate?" he asked on coming out.

It was a long story the way Zekiel told it—so long that Mark suspected it was being dragged out intentionally to keep him from asking more questions. The sawyers worked in pairs. First they set up a camp, or used one like this that was already in existence. The trees they selected were first felled with machetes. Then for each clump of trees they constructed a platform onto which they rolled the fallen trees one at a time after limbing them. Finally, with one man on the platform and the other under it, they cut the trees into boards with a long, two-handed saw.

"Often they stay in the bush a week or more," Mc-

Coy added, "using boys to head the boards out when they cut." Turning in the cabin doorway, he pointed to the steep slope on the other side of the stream. "The sawyers that was up here last did leave a big bulletwood on the cliff up there, sah. You can see it?"

Mark thought he saw a limbed tree lying in the brush of the upper slope, and nodded.

"Sometimes it difficult to build a platform in the right place after a tree is felled," McCoy explained. "So they will leave it until the easier ones are looked after. This cigarette pack most likely was dropped here by sawyers come back to see if that tree was worth the extra trouble to get it out."

"If you say so, Zekiel." Mark had a feeling he was being lied to. Yet almost anyone could have come this way, he supposed. For instance, the yellow passion fruit that Eve occasionally bought from higglers—"golden apples," the people called them—grew abundantly on tree-climbing vines here. And according to Jeff Legg, a man wanting cedar or juniper poles for a new house usually managed to "t'ief" them from the cooperative's property. To buy them would be to invite ridicule from neighbors.

The tree Mark wanted for Christmas, a pretty, bright green cupressus, grew just behind the cabin. There were no others like it in the vicinity, so far as he could see. He pointed it out to McCoy, wondering aloud how it had got there.

"Likely a bird did bring the seed, squire."

"It seems a shame to cut it down. I'm not sure, after all—"

"We can take just the top part. It won't dead. In

fact, it will grow a new top or even two of them for next year."

"Good."

With a few deft strokes of his machete McCoy removed the wanted portion, then tied the branches with lianas for easier carrying. He swung the load to his shoulder. It seemed almost an afterthought when he fumbled the box of cigarettes from his shirt pocket and placed one between his lips.

"I beg you a light, squire. I don't have a match."

They walked home in silence. When they reached the meadow across the road from the Shepstowe drive, Mark called a halt. It would not do for Eve to see the tree yet, he explained. She must see it for the first time Christmas morning. "Where can we hide it, Zekiel?"

McCoy was weary. The tree was no light burden; the journey had been long. In bewilderment he returned Mark's gaze for a few seconds, then shook his head. The gesture was a kind of scolding, the way he sometimes scolded his granddaughter when she did a foolish thing.

"Now, look at that. We come all this long way from the river, and you only just remember."

"We can hide it somewhere here in the meadow, can't we?"

"No, squire. You has trees in America maybe that can last that long without water, but not this tree. This tree would dry up. It must leave in the river where it can stay fresh."

Feeling stupid, Mark looked the length of the meadow and sighed. "Well, if you insist—"

"Is no need you tiring youself, squire," McCoy said mildly. "I will carry it back."

* * *

Mark found Eve in the kitchen and handed her a paper bag filled with passion fruit.

"So this is what you went for," she wrote. "And you don't even like them very much!"

"You like them," he replied.

Delighted, she kissed the tips of her fingers and touched them to his mouth.

25

The two callers were resplendent in white. White shirts, white trousers, even white shoes. Both were Chinese. Mark watched from a window as they marched down the driveway. Eve had seen them coming while hanging out some laundry and had hurried back into the house to warn him.

As they drew near, he recognized one as the proprietor of the "Chinaman's shop" in Rainy Ridge. The other he was sure he had not seen before.

Turning to Eve, who watched at his side, he saw an expression of alarm on her face as the callers approached. But he himself was only amused. After all, the shopkeeper had promised—or was it threatened?—to pay him a visit.

Leading Eve to the table, where he had been working on his book, he quickly wrote, "It's all right, I'm sure. Yee said he'd come to call." It seemed a good idea to put his manuscript and the note out of sight, however, so he carried them to his bedroom.

By the time he returned, the two men were marching up the veranda steps. He met them in the doorway and was greeted with a stabbed-out hand and the remembered toothy smile.

"Good affernoon, Misser Burke!"

"Good afternoon to you."

"I keep promise, come pay you a visit. This my friend, Ling Gan." Yee rattled the words off with such speed that Mark felt machine-gunned.

"Please come in."

They made themselves at home on the red divan, sitting with their backs stiff, hands on white trouser knees, mouths smiling. Eve had disappeared— hardly generous of her to leave him alone at such a time, Mark thought, but of course she was only a servant when strangers were present.

"This gentleman from New York," the shopkeeper said. His head bobbed as it had when he stood behind his counter, backed by shelves of dusty merchandise. "He good friend my son in school there. Come Jamaica on vacation. Come see me."

Ling Gan smiled and nodded. Younger than Yee, but still rather old to be a friend of Yee's son perhaps, he was slender to the point of being frail, with hair that looked as though it had been sprayed with black enamel. "Most fascinating country, Jamaica. And this house. Mr. Yee tells me it is one of the old estate Great Houses. Most interesting. I hope I do not intrude." He had a high, soft voice that sounded like soprano crooning.

"Not at all. It *is* an interesting old house."

"And have you been here long?"

"Not yet. I expect to stay for some time, however."

"I tell him you write books," Yee said, beaming. "Maybe you even writing about this place, yes?"

"I've thought about it."

"I very sad about your books. This gentleman ask if I read any yet and I have to say no. I try Sangster's bookshop in Kingston, ask for books by Peter Burke. They big bookshop but don't have them."

"I'm sorry. But, of course, not all American books are stocked by Jamaican bookshops." Mark waved airily toward the shelf over the fireplace. "And I can't lend you any, I'm afraid. I have only one copy of each here, as you see." That's another score against you, Graham, he thought. If I'm a writer, why don't the bookstores have my books?

Yee and his son's friend rose from the divan and crossed the room to peer at the volumes over the fireplace, as though it were a gesture of politeness expected of them. The younger man, reaching for a volume, apparently thought that might *not* be so polite, and turned his head.

"May I, Mr. Burke?"

"Be my guest."

The man seemed puzzled. "Your guest?"

"Go right ahead."

"Ah yes. Thank you." Both of them reached for books. Opening them, they turned pages and looked at each other and nodded. Then they put the books back and returned to the divan.

"You must find it lonely here, Mr. Burke," the man from New York said.

"Serene is a better word, I think."

"Ah yes, of course. For your writing."

"I could never live in your New York. Too much go-go."

His callers' faces went blank.

"Too much rushing about. Too frantic," Mark amended. "I'm a quiet man."

The faces came to life again, beaming with comprehension. Then the New Yorker looked at Yee, and Yee stood up.

"We like walk about if all right," the shopkeeper said. "See gardens and such. Ling Gan never see Great House before. You don't mind, please?"

"Not at all. Sorry I can't give you a guided tour, but I've rather a lot to do."

"You are very kind," said the man from New York. "I hope we may meet again."

They shook Mark's hand and departed.

He watched them for a time, moving about the house from window to window so they would not be aware of his surveillance. With the shopkeeper in the lead, jabbing out a hand to point now and then, they walked the paths of the place, circled the old carriage house, looked at the garden. He lost them when they went to the rear of the house, and last saw them ascending the driveway.

When Eve reappeared, he carried his typewriter to the drawing room table and motioned her to sit at his side. "You've never been to New York, have you?" he wrote. "Certainly you never lived there."

She shook her head.

"Do you know what the expression 'go-go' means? If I were to say, for instance, 'New York is too much go-go for my liking'?"

"I think so. You would mean it's too fast or too frenzied. That you dislike crowds and hustle and noise."

"Good. Now, if you wanted my permission to look at those books there"—he nodded toward the shelf—"and I said 'Be my guest,' what would that mean to you?"

"That I *had* permission, of course. What is this all about, Mark?"

He hesitated. It could be nothing, really, and he did not want to alarm her over nothing. After all, even in New York there must be some Chinese who lived completely as Chinese, shunning the mainstream. Still . . .

"I thought our friends seemed a bit inquisitive," he wrote, "but maybe they were just being extra polite. I don't imagine we'll see them again."

But if Yee's friend Ling Gan was not from New York, where was he from? And did the Rainy Ridge shopkeeper know that, or was he, too, being fooled?

26

The night before Christmas, Mark walked with Eve to the top of the driveway and down the road a little distance, not quite to the coffee works. The road was deserted except for a large white owl that flew from the meadow to glide along ahead of them.

This was another thing the peasants might hold against him if they knew, he mused. According to McCoy, the white owl was an omen of evil. If one circled your house at night, someone in the family would die before morning.

Eve retired when they returned, but the lights were brighter than usual—someone at the factory must have cleaned the turbine—and Mark went downstairs to build a stand for the Christmas tree. He had acquired a few old tools from the factory and had found some suitable small boards in the garage.

The stand finished, he carried it upstairs and went to bed, setting his alarm for five-thirty. At quarter to six McCoy showed up as arranged, and they went to the river together.

Mark had not been in the meadow at that hour before. It was just turning milky with daylight, and he was greeted by a symphony of bird calls that delighted him.

The tree, thanks to McCoy's foresight, was as fresh and green as though only just cut, and when the gardener lifted it from the water, Mark held it upright on a rock to admire it.

"Merry Christmas, Zekiel."

"The same to you, squire."

"You must come and see this later on." He had a gift for McCoy: a pipe he had bought in Kingston. "Bring Merlinda."

"If I is able to, squire. But this will be a busy day at home. I do thank you, though."

Mark himself carried the tree to the house—his privilege, he insisted—but McCoy helped set it up. They moved about the drawing room quietly, McCoy barefoot, Mark in his socks, because Mark was convinced now that Eve could hear certain vibrations. Sometimes when he walked about the house at night, wrestling with his problems, she was aware of it.

With the tree up he gave McCoy the pipe and a gift of money, and received in return a dignified "Thank you, squire."

"Don't forget, now. Come back later on with Merlinda."

"If I can, sah." Lifting a hand to his nonexistent hat brim, a gesture dispensed with of late, McCoy departed.

Mark had just finished hanging the last of the ornaments bought in town when Eve opened her door.

She saw the tree from her doorway and stood motionless, gazing at it. She wore a new dress this morning. Soft, pale yellow, it made her look like a young girl. Perhaps she had bought it when shopping with Mildred that day, while he was telling Jeff of his feelings for her. Her eyes as she gazed at the tree were bright with pleasure. She came slowly into the room and stood beside him.

It was no time for talk. Taking her hand, Mark led her to the tree and closed her fingers around the box from the Swiss Store, wrapped in Christmas paper now and hanging from the tree like an ornament. When she had removed it, he stepped back to watch her open it. He was tense with excitement.

She lifted the lid and looked at the circle of gold on its bed of velvet. It seemed to him she would never move but would go on standing there, a statue in pale yellow, gazing at the gift until the end of time. He could hear his heart beating, the room was so still.

Then she raised her head to look at the shelf of books, and he knew she remembered.

It was, of course, in one of the books Mildred Legg had lent him, not in one he was supposed to have written. But Mildred's, too, were there above the fireplace. Eve went to them and took down the governor's journal, and with her back to him turned its pages until she found the remembered passage. When she had reread it, she replaced the book and turned to face him.

There were tears in her eyes.

Mark had not moved. During her reading of the governor's journal he had silently echoed the words in the book, but he had not moved. He said the words aloud now—"My love, like this circle, shall have no ending"—and still did not move. Not even when Eve went to her room.

She had her slate when she returned to him at the tree. She wrote on it and held it out to him, gazing at his face. "And I love you the same way," she had written. "Even if we fail, I will at least have had you for a time, and have it to remember, my darling."

He put the slate on the floor because there was nowhere else to put it without moving away from her. He took her hands and drew her into his arms and kissed her. Her lips were timid. No mouth before his had ever touched them in just that way, he was certain. After a moment he put his face against hers and simply stood there, holding her.

When he let her go at last, she fastened the golden circle to her dress and shyly smiled at him.

218

* * *

Eve, too, had bought a gift in Kingston that day. After breakfast she gave it to him: a box fashioned of the island's prettiest wood, blue mahoe, to hold his manuscript papers. It was handsomely made, and she must have spent a good amount of time searching for it.

To demonstrate his gratitude he promptly put the pages of his new book into it and made a ceremony of throwing away the greenish black chunk of serpentine stone with which he had always anchored them to the table when working with the door open.

In the afternoon Jeff and Mildred Legg came. At once they noticed the circle of gold on Eve's dress and delighted her by nodding their solemn approval. Turning to Mark, Mildred asked the obvious question with her eyes.

"We love each other," Mark said.

"And?"

"I can't say more than that. As I told Jeff in town, this was a very special gift. She knew its meaning. I wasn't sure she would accept it. By the way, can I buy a slate in Rainy Ridge?"

"A slate?"

"The kind Eve uses. What she wrote when I gave her the pin can't be wiped off like a comment on the weather, you know. It's the first love letter I've ever received."

"Of course you can't wipe it off!"

"Are you planning on marriage?" Jeff asked.

Mark's upraised hands said, Hold on a minute. "Of

course, but we haven't got that far yet. Lord, man, this only happened a minute ago. I'm still in shock."

"I hope you know you're a very lucky man," Mildred said.

"Believe me, I do."

Eve had been out of the room during this exchange. She returned now with a tray of soft drinks and cookies. As she put the tray on the table, Mark went to her and wrote on the pad he had substituted for her slate, "They're talking about us, darling. They approve."

She turned to look at the Leggs, and Mildred beckoned. "Bring that pad here, will you, Peter?"

Handing it to her, he stood at Eve's side, as though the two of them faced a judge. On the pad Mildred wrote, "You have our love and blessings, both of you. May you be as happy as Jeff and I are."

"Amen," Jeff said.

"You must tell her everything, Peter," Mildred said. "All about yourself. What to expect when you take her away from here. Everything."

"I intend to."

"Much more than you've told us. We really know very little about you. You're not at all a talker."

"She'll know everything. I promise." He had to smile as he added, "She already knows more than you and Jeff do, you know. We didn't arrive at all this without talking."

"'Talking.' I like the way you say that."

Jeff frowned but did not comment. Was he thinking of McCoy's granddaughter? At that moment a car came careening down the driveway into the yard, skidding to a halt just short of crashing into

220

the carriage house. Goodwin, the man from Kingston, flung its door open and shouted, "Merry Christmas, everybody!"

This time the golden-haired man was really drunk. On his way to the veranda Goodwin walked with exaggerated care as though walking a guideline. Climbing the steps, he had trouble judging the height of the risers and twice fell back. In the doorway he seized Mark's hand and pumped it. "Deck the halls," he said, vacantly grinning. "Ol' Goodwin's here with Christmas cheer. How's that, huh?"

"Come in and meet my guests." It was not what Mark would have liked to say, but a blunt "Behave yourself, I have company" might have embarrassed Jeff and Mildred.

"Uh?"

Bearing down hard on the man's hand in warning, Mark drew him inside. Jeff shook hands, saying, "How are you, Mr. Goodwin?" They had not met, Mark knew, since Goodwin rented Shepstowe for him. He wondered how he was to explain the man's presence today, and welcomed the chance to think while Jeff introduced Mildred. Some sort of explanation seemed necessary.

Goodwin seemed to think so, too, and tried to fill the gap. "Been hoping to persuade ol' Peter here to write some government stuff for us. That's what I'm here for. Haven't had much luck, but I keep working on it. Who reads novels anymore, huh? There's no future in that, I keep telling him." He began to sway again, and stopped himself by moving his feet farther apart. "Everywhere *I* go, people just watch TV."

"You should try libraries instead of lounges,"

Mark advised, smiling. "Better for the ulcers, too." It seemed safer to joke than show annoyance.

"*Touché*," Goodwin said. "Look, Peter, I have some things in my car. Champagne. A Christmas pudding straight from merry old England, it says on the can. Oops, pardon me—the tin. I thought you'd be alone out here and bored to tears, so I—"

"Later."

"Okay, later." He walked to one of the overstuffed chairs and fell into it. "Sorry," he said to Jeff and Mildred. "Guess I was bored, too."

Eve, Mark noticed, had disappeared. He wondered whether she would return presently, pretending to be only his housekeeper, and whether, if she did, Jeff and Mildred would notice the difference. Goodwin knew she lived in the house, of course, but no more than that. He wished to heaven Goodwin would leave. Perhaps if he gave the man a stiff drink he might pass out.

But Goodwin was not even close to passing out. He suddenly swung forward in his chair and began talking to Jeff.

"That's just how it is," he said. "I been tellin' Peter here he should quit writin' novels and work for the gov'ment. Wha' ya think about that, huh?"

Jeff seemed to be groping for an answer when Eve came back into the room. She had removed the pin from her dress, Mark saw, and was wearing an apron. She had McCoy's little granddaughter by the hand.

Goodwin stopped talking and flapped a hand in salute. When she acknowledged the greeting with a smile, he turned back to Jeff.

"What was I sayin'? Oh. About workin' for the gov'ment. It has drawbacks, o' course. You take me, f'rinstance. Half the time when I'm told to do things, I don' have the foggiest notion why. Would you believe that?"

"Excuse me a moment." Mark went into his bedroom for the doll he had bought. Eve had tied the box with red Christmas ribbon. He handed it to her and she gave it to Merlinda. The Leggs watched, ignoring Goodwin, so Goodwin swiveled his head around to watch, too.

"Open it," Mark told the child. "It's for you."

She ran a finger over the ribbon and looked at him in wonder. "Is for my hair, this?"

"If you like. But see what's inside."

Merlinda worked the ribbon off with care and solemnly handed it to Eve for safekeeping. Removing the lid from the box, she handed that to Mark. Placing the box on the polished wood floor, she knelt over it and opened the wings of tissue paper with mischievous slowness, pausing after each tug to look up and laugh her sound of bells.

Mark laughed, too. Goodwin's drunkenness no longer seemed important. His hand touched Eve's and she smiled. Jeff and Mildred Legg came to stand beside them.

"Well, go ahead, Merlinda," Mark encouraged. "What are you waiting for?"

The child peered at the last layer of paper and suddenly plunged both hands into the box. Doll and crumpled paper came out together. As the wrapping fell to the floor, she rose slowly to her feet, holding the doll out in front of her with both hands.

"Is for *me?*"

"For you," Mark said.

She hugged the doll, putting its face against hers and rocking herself back and forth. After a moment she looked up at Mark and made a sighing sound. "I can leave it here with you?"

"Leave it *here?* Why?"

"I not supposed to come here. If I take it home, I'll get whupped."

"I see." Mark looked at Jeff Legg and saw an angry scowl. He, too, felt angry as he took the doll from the child's hands and returned it to its box. There was no way he could answer the question on Eve's face.

"Wha's the trouble?" Goodwin asked from his chair.

"Yes, you may leave it here," Mark said to Merlinda. "We'll keep it nice and new for you until your grandfather says you may come here again." The longing in the child's eyes filled him with bitterness, and he wished fiercely that he could be alone with Eve to talk this over. "You'd better run along now," he said. "Take some of these." He filled her hands with cookies. "You can eat them on the way home and no one will know."

The child gazed at her feet as she walked slowly into the hall. Not until she turned for a last look at the box did Eve realize she was leaving. Then with a questioning glance at Mark, who could only nod, Eve went after her and they disappeared down the hall together.

"Now, what was all that about?" Goodwin demanded.

Mark was suddenly tired, suddenly fed up. "Oh, go to hell!"

Goodwin seemed to stiffen a little, as though jerked from his slouch. Then to Mark's surprise he grinned. "You know something?" he said. "I think you've got something there." Struggling to his feet, he walked unsteadily across the room and pushed his clenched hand gently against Mark's chest. "Uh-huh, Peter Burke old boy, you've got something. I'll go home, anyway. I can do that for you, at least."

Stumbling to the door, he departed, but was back again in a moment with the champagne and tin of Christmas pudding. Handing them to Mark, he turned himself around to face Jeff and Mildred.

"You know what this man needs? He needs to get mad more often. Not at me. Christ, I'm just a two-bit errand boy. But that's what he needs—to get goddamn good and mad and stay that way. So long, all of you." He flapped a hand in farewell. "This time I'm gone."

"I hope he's able to make it home," Jeff said as the car growled up the drive.

Mildred said, "I think we'd better go, too, Jeff, when Eve comes back. Peter looks exhausted."

"Forgive me," Mark said.

"For Goodwin?" Jeff retorted. "You're not his keeper."

"Thanks."

"And we're happy about you and Eve," Mildred said, touching her lips to his cheek. "We really are. It's all so very wonderful."

Eve came back into the room then, and after saying good-bye to her, too, they left.

225

27

O n the morning of the twenty-seventh, Eve wrote on her pad, "We don't expect rains like this in December. The big rains are usually over by now."

A radio announcer had just said much the same thing, though the sound of the rain all but drowned him out. Some kind of front, it seemed, had perversely decided to stop dead over the island. Conditions were not expected to change for several days.

The rain drummed on the Shepstowe roof and filled the house with dampness. It dribbled down the drawing room windows, fogging their insides so that Mark, when Eve offered her pad, simply stepped to a window and used his finger on a misted pane.

"At least we won't have callers," he wrote.

She nodded. Since Christmas Day they had been left alone and had spent most of their time just "talking" to each other. Right now the big table was covered with pages of dialogue done on the typewriter.

As honestly as he knew how, Mark had tried to tell her the sort of life she was likely to face as a teacher's wife in the States. And with the same frankness, she had warned of the frustrations he was sure to encounter when married to a woman who could neither hear nor speak.

They would both learn some sort of sign language, they had agreed. Eve could learn lipreading, too. She had been able to read her father's lips a little. "From you I get something, too. Not much yet, but it will come."

And, of course, they would continue practicing "talking" to each other with their minds. "After all," Eve wrote, "we're both a bit special in that department."

They would be married in Jamaica when the Graham-Goodwin business was settled. Then they would leave. Meanwhile, only Jeff and Mildred would know. And before the wedding Jeff and Mildred would have to know more, of course. The truth about Mark and the reason for the masquerade, for instance. The sooner all that could be straightened out, the better.

The rain fell. Eve busied herself at the table, gathering up the pages of talk. Surprised to hear a car in the driveway, Mark stepped onto the veranda.

It was Jeff. The rain ran from his hat brim in a cascade as he splashed along the walk. On the veranda he removed the hat and slapped it against his leg before stepping inside. To Eve he raised a hand and nodded. To Mark he said, "Brace yourself. I bring trouble."

It was not Jeff's way to speak of trouble without a smile to lighten the blow. Mark felt a tightening inside him as the man sat. Seating himself, he stared and waited.

"I don't fancy this," Jeff said grimly. "It's got me

boiling mad, so I'll come straight to the point and get it over with." He leaned forward, his hands gripping his knees. "I just stopped at the factory. We've that important big rush order to fill and should be working, rain or no, but we're not. There were only three women in the place, and they were waiting to hand me an ultimatum."

Mark continued to stare in silence.

"I'm to turn you out of here," Jeff said, "or the women won't come to work."

Stunned, Mark turned to look for Eve. She had disappeared. Probably she had gone to the kitchen to start some coffee for them, expecting him to talk to Jeff for some time about her and himself. "Why?" he asked helplessly.

"Someone saw the little girl leave here Christmas Day. She fell ill that night. She's sick right now. They're blaming you for it. You've poisoned her or put an obeah spell on her—some crazy thing like that."

Mark stood up and paced the length of the room, turning at the fireplace. He supposed he was white. "They can't believe that!"

"They can believe anything, damn their ignorance. I've been arguing with those three women for the past hour, trying to find out what's behind all this. It was a waste of breath."

Mark walked back from the fireplace and said, "What can I do?"

"It's not what *you* can do, but what can *I* do? What in God's name *can* I do?" Jeff plucked a post office telegram from his shirt pocket and slapped the arm of his chair with it. "I've three days to get this coffee to the wharf, they tell me now. It has to be sorted and barreled. If the weather were halfway decent I could send a truck down the road and round up enough new people, maybe. But nobody new is going to turn out in this weather."

Eve had come back into the room. "Wait a minute," Mark said, and went to his typewriter and wrote, "Jeff says Merlinda is ill. Could anything have happened to her here?"

She gave herself time to think before answering, then wrote, "She was in the kitchen Christmas Day when I went down. I suppose she could have been there for some time."

"She might have eaten something there?"

"Perhaps. What's wrong with her?"

He turned to Jeff. "Did the women say what's wrong with Merlinda?"

"I told you. You've put a spell on her."

"No details?"

"They're not concerned with details. If she'd broken her leg on the way home, you'd be to blame for it."

"Jeff doesn't know," Mark typed. "I suppose if she was in the kitchen awhile, she might have found something and eaten it. She used to make herself right at home there."

"From the fridge maybe," Eve replied. "There's nothing much else she could reach. But I can't think what from the fridge, either."

Mark went back to Jeff. "Can you get your order out without working today? They won't come today, anyway, will they? Even if you agree to put me out."

"I haven't said anything about putting you out, have I? Damn it, man, what do you take me for?"

"You'll have to put me out. You've a coffee works to run. Give me the rest of today, Jeff."

Jeff Legg said in a voice of controlled rage, "I'll give you until I'm fired. To hell with them." He looked at Eve and his eyes smoldered. "They want her out, too. *That* girl. Damn their evil minds!"

"Can you come back this evening?" Mark asked.

"What are you thinking of doing?"

"I don't know. Go down there and see the child, I suppose. I don't know what I can do. It depends on what they do."

Jeff stood up. "All right, I guess. Be careful. I'll come around later." At the door, jamming his sodden hat on his head, he scowled at the rain and said, "And this. The weather has to be filthy, too, of course."

Soaked by the rain, Mark walked down the path that led to the cluster of houses in Mango Gut. Water ran from the red clay banks and formed ankle-deep pools among the boulders. He strode through the pools rather than slow his progress by seeking ways around them.

He passed the place where the woman had shone her flashlight on him when he stumbled from the graveyard with his hands bloody. He came to the house he knew was McCoy's, and halted.

The yard was fenced with bamboo and there was a gate fastened with a loop of rusty wire. He stood at the gate, in the rain, and called McCoy's name. When he repeated the summons, the door opened and McCoy appeared in the opening.

"I want to talk to you, Zekiel." The yard was large, the house well back from the fence, and Mark had to shout to be heard above the rain. "May I come in?"

McCoy walked out of the house. When the full force of the rain struck him, he halted. "Wait, squire." Disappearing for a moment, he came out again with a burlap bag draped like a cowl over his head and shoulders. He came to the gate. "Yes, squire?"

"Merlinda is sick, I'm told."

McCoy only nodded.

"How is she sick, Zekiel? What's the trouble?"

"I is not familiar with these things, squire. I can't say."

"She must be complaining about *something*, man—a stomachache or a hurt somewhere. What does she say?"

McCoy gazed down at his big-knuckled hands on the gate. "She is just sick, it seem like."

"Have you had the doctor in? Or the nurse?" Help was available, Mark knew, at a government clinic in Rainy Ridge.

"No, sah."

"Why not?"

"Sah, my woman is lookin' after the child."

"Let me in, Zekiel," Mark said. "I want to see her. If she needs the doctor, I want to get him."

McCoy spread his hands apart on the gate then, but not to open it. He spread them to prevent Mark from pushing it open. "No, squire. No, sah." He shook his head violently now. "My woman say I must not allow you in."

"Let me in, Zekiel."

"No, squire! She say no!"

Mark stood his ground, not trying to force the gate open but not retreating, either. "And suppose I say that if you don't, you won't have a job tomorrow. I'm saying that, Zekiel. I mean it. I came down here in the rain to see this child, to help her if she needs help, and if you don't stop this nonsense and let me see her, I'm done with you." It seemed a silly threat, since he would be through at Shepstowe if he failed now. But he could think of no other way to shake the man.

McCoy remained unshaken. "Me can't help it, sah. If the job gone, it gone."

"And if the child *is* seriously ill and *should* have a doctor? If she should *die*, man? What will you say then? 'If she gone, she gone'?"

"Squire, please. Go away. Me begging you, please go away!"

"You won't let me in? You're determined?"

Like a monk at prayer McCoy bowed his cowled head again and stubbornly shook it. Defeated, Mark let go the gate and turned away.

He walked the path slowly now, indifferent to the rain, almost unaware of it, and not eager to complete the return journey to the Great House. What was he to do? For Jeff's sake Eve and he would have to leave, probably tomorrow. At another time they might have had a few days' grace, but with a critical coffee order pressing him, Jeff had no choice, did he?

Eve would go home, Mark supposed. He would go to Goodwin in Kingston, and probably would be ordered to hide out in some little-known guest house such as the one he had stayed in briefly before. It didn't matter, really, what happened to him. Not now. All that really mattered was for Eve to be safe, secure, away from all this. But what would he do without her?

"Obeah man, go 'way!" The cry came at him in a child's hysterical shriek from a tangle of bushes beside the path. Something whistled past his head in the rain. He stopped and turned.

"Go 'way!" It was a boy's voice, frightened and show-off bold at the same time. This time the hurled stone did not miss but struck the side of Mark's head and caused a bright flash of pain. The blow spun him and he fell to his knees in a pool of water.

He heard his assailants—there were several—racing away through the brush as he knelt there with bowed head, waiting for the first rush of pain to subside. Children, he was sure. The stampede of their flight died away, and only the drumming of the rain was left.

His head throbbed. When he touched it, a swelling had already begun above his right eye. A little lower, and a stone thrown with that much force would have taken the eye itself.

He pushed himself weakly to his feet and went stumbling up the path.

Eve must have been on the veranda, waiting for him. Even before he reached the steps she came running, to steady him on his feet when he would have fallen again. The pain kept coming in waves. He was only dimly aware that she led him into the house to the divan in the drawing room, and bandaged his head.

28

Someone else had challenged the peasant stolidity of Mango Gut that afternoon.

Leaving Shepstowe, Jeff Legg headed for home but stopped at a shop in Rainy Ridge to buy bread. As he got back into his car he recalled with a frown the night Peter Burke had walked from Kingston.

Peter's fortitude in undertaking that nighttime hike had always impressed him.

"What's wrong with you, Legg?" he asked himself. "If that sweet, troubled guy cares enough to go tramping down to the Gut in search of information, what right have you to quit and go home at this point?" As a kind of postscript his mind added, "What must Eve be thinking of you, walking out on them like this? You're supposed to be a friend of theirs."

No, he could not go home.

Beyond the village a small side road, seldom used by anything on wheels, wound its way around a mountain shoulder to Mango Gut. He took that.

Always a bad road, it was nearly impassable now because of the rain. If you'd had any sense, Legg, he thought angrily, you'd have gone back to the Great House and walked down with Peter. But the distance was less than a mile. Eventually he got there.

With the rain slanting against the windshield he sat for a few minutes, trying to work out a plan of action. Mango Gut people knew him well enough. The men kept the co-op's tracks and fields clean and ran the factory machinery. The women picked coffee, worked in the sorting room, and fertilized the trees after men with mules transported the heavy bags of fertilizer to the fields.

My people, he thought. This wasn't their idea. Someone put them up to it.

Right now it was only the women he had to think about. Once the coffee was sorted he could find a few men somewhere to help him barrel it. He himself could drive the co-op's big truck to the wharf. So, then, the women . . .

Outside of the three he had already talked to at the factory, the most influential was probably Trevor Taylor's woman, the one they called Miss Carlene. Yes. That would be the logical place to start. He headed for her home, sloshing through pools of muddy water as he trudged up the village road—a mere footpath, not for vehicles—in a downpour he was now heartily sick of.

The handsome brown woman who opened Taylor's door appeared to be startled, but quickly found her voice and invited him in.

Jeff entered, removed his hat, and thanked her when she urged him to "Sit, sah." A glance around the room showed him they were alone. On an afternoon such as this her two children were probably in the adjoining bedroom, asleep. Her man might be anywhere.

Though it had only the two rooms, the house was a little better than most. Its wooden floor was bare, but the heavily varnished furniture had surely come from one of the big stores in Kingston, and there were curtains at the windows.

"Good evening, Carlene," he said. "How are you?"

"Me fine, Busha. How is you?"

"Not so good today. Troubled." He rubbed his jaw and frowned at her. "Those three women who came to the factory to talk for all of you . . . Do you know what they said to me?"

Returning his gaze without flinching, she moved her head slowly up and down. "Me know, Busha. We did discuss it long time here in the village first."

"They told me you won't come to work again until I've sent Mr. Burke away."

"That is what we did decide, sah."

"Why? What's wrong with him?"

"Busha, me sure you don't have to ask that. You know."

He shook his head. "I don't know. I've heard talk, but I don't *know* anything. You and I have always got on well, Carlene. We've even solved problems at the factory together by talking about them. Suppose you tell me now what I'm supposed to know about Mr. Burke."

The way she looked away from him, yet apparently didn't quite know where else to look, told him he might have put her on the defensive, if nothing else. "Him did walk here from Kings Town at night." Some of them still pronounced the name of the capital that way.

"Why shouldn't he? He's a writer of books. In the book he came here to write—about Jamaica and our people—a man has to walk from Kingston to Rainy

Ridge at night. Would you want him to describe such a journey without having done it? Without knowing what it's like to be on that road at night with the dogs running out of their yards to bark at him and all?"

Again she hesitated. They *were* reasonable most of the time, Jeff reminded himself. Maybe he had got through to her. But she was shaking her head again.

"No, Busha. Is not only the walk from the city. Him did come from the buryin' ground in the dark with blood all over him."

"So you think he was meddling with the people buried there." Jeff let his breath out with almost a roar. "What nonsense! He went to the graves because he's doing a book about Shepstowe, and some of Shepstowe's people are there. It was not very bright of him to go down at dusk and have to find his way back in the dark, I grant you, but he's a stranger here; he didn't know. And he certainly didn't know he'd get caught in wait-a-bit and cut his hands on the barbed-wire fence. It was just an accident."

"Yes, Busha." The reply was almost too low-pitched to be audible.

"Then why are you hounding the man?" he demanded angrily.

"Is not only the walking at night from Kings Town, Busha. Or the buryin' ground. Him did give a poison to little Merlinda McCoy."

"Who told you that?"

"Everyone talkin' 'bout it, Busha."

"Just because the little girl went up to Shepstowe House Christmas Day? For the love of God, Carlene, be reasonable. The child could have eaten some bad food anywhere. It doesn't have to be obeah that made her ill." Jeff leaned forward on his chair. "That *is* what you're saying, isn't it? That obeah made her ill."

This time her silence lasted so long he thought he might have shaken her. But in the end she said, "Busha, is too many things to be just happenstance. A man like you would not understand."

"So I'm to get rid of him or you and the others won't work." He could taste the bitterness in his voice as he stood up.

She neither answered nor nodded. She simply rose to her feet and stared at him.

Controlling his anger with an effort, Jeff said so quietly that now *his* voice was almost inaudible, "All right, Carlene. I'll get to the bottom of this somehow, and when I do you'll see me again. Maybe even this evening."

"Me sorry, Busha."

"Are you? If you are, why don't you tell me who started all this talk about Mr. Burke?"

She seemed genuinely bewildered. "Who what, sah?"

"Who started it!"

"But, Busha, nobody did start it. Don't you understand? All of we saw something was wrong about that man, right from the day he came here."

"Carlene, I said who *started* it? There was an obeah sign on the Great House door the very first time Mr. Burke climbed the veranda steps and went to open it. Who put it there? Nobody knew then—nobody in this district, at least—that he had walked here from Kingston."

He had hit home, he saw. This time she was really shaken. He waited, hoping he had at last hit pay dirt. But—"Me don't know 'bout any obeah sign on any door, sah," she said at last. "Me never hear 'bout that."

And maybe she hadn't, he reasoned. For *he* had told no one about the lizard on the door, and was pretty sure Peter hadn't, either. And Eve, of course, couldn't have. Maybe—just maybe—the only other person who knew about the lizard was the one behind the whole ugly business.

He said good night, knowing he had at least planted a seed of doubt in the woman's mind and she would be half expecting him to return. Now began a dreary dredging for information in some of the other Mango Gut homes.

In one after another, his feet more muddy in each, his old felt hat more sodden, his clothes more clammy, he sat and asked questions. It was the women he tried to talk to, even when men were present. The men, anyway, did not seem to know much about what was going on. Many did not even know their women had declared a boycott of the factory. But from the women he was able to extract no more information than he had obtained from Carlene.

Peter Burke was an obeah man, period. Why? Because he had walked from the city alone and unafraid at night. Because he had come from a burying ground at night with blood on him. Because the granddaughter of Zekiel McCoy was even now ill after visiting the Great House.

"Who told you this?" he asked again and again.

"Everyone know it, sah."

"But who told *everyone?*"

"Sah?"

And then at last he found a woman who answered that question differently.

"Well, sah, it be Roselda Weeks told *me* about the poisoning, and her did go all about, telling everybody, it seem. And me not so sure we should believe everything that woman say, because of her brother."

"What do you mean, because of her brother?" All at once Jeff was alive again, after being almost too weary to care anymore.

"Well, sah, the writer man at the Great House did cause Iron to leave home, no? And Miss Roselda hate him for that. So it seem to me she could be saying lies about him to get even."

It occurred to Jeff then that there was a question he should have been asking all along, but hadn't. "By the way, just who was the woman who saw Mr. Burke coming from the burying ground?"

"The same Roselda Weeks, sah."

From there he went directly to the house of McCoy and found all three of them present: McCoy, Roselda, and the child. The child was in bed, asleep.

End of the line.

"All right, Roselda, I want the truth. And I mean to get it, woman, or you go before the magistrate in Morant Bay tomorrow! I'm a justice of the peace, remember, and I'm tired, wet, and furious. Don't you dare lie to me!"

It was probably the fury of that initial statement that decided her. Everyone in Mango Gut knew Busha to be a mild man. He seldom raised his voice. He nearly always had a smile, even when pointing out a fault or an omission at the factory or telling them they were handling their yard coffee in such a way that the co-op's quality was falling off. Busha angry? Fire in his eyes? It was unthinkable.

But he was enraged now. He was a wholly different man, trembling from head to foot. And the questions he hurled at McCoy's woman were as loud and forceful as shots from a rifle.

"You're the one, aren't you?"

"Uh? Wha', sah?"

"You're the one! It's you, all along, been telling the people Mr. Burke is an obeah man so they will drive him out of here."

"Sah, me don' know what—"

"Oh, stop it! I've been all over this damned village talking to people, and every shred of evidence points to you. You got mad with Burke when he fired your rotten brother, as he had every right to. Then by pure chance you were the one Burke stumbled into when he came from the graveyard with that innocent blood on his hands, and you made the most of that. Oh God, did you make the most of it!" He swung on McCoy. "Zekiel, did Burke come here tonight?"

McCoy stared at his woman. She was a pretty creature, years younger than he. Undoubtedly he enjoyed sleeping with her and did not want to lose her. But after gazing at her in silence for a moment, obviously stunned, he mumbled, "What, Busha?"

"Did Mr. Burke come here tonight?"

"Yes, sah, him was here. Him lef' long time ago."

"What did you say to him?"

"Busha—me never did let him come in."

"You what?"

"Me never did 'low him in, sah."

Jeff rose to his feet and stood glaring. As he swung on the woman, his eyes were probably as red, he thought, as those of the duppies they were so much afraid of.

"Roselda, I want to tell you something. Are you listening?"

"Y-y-yes, Busha," she breathed.

What he told her then was that if she did not go with him at once to all the houses in the village where he had already asked questions without getting any answers, she would find herself deep in the worst kind of trouble. And so, of course, she went. And people listened. And at long last, exhausted, Jeff was finished.

But it was now too late for him to go to the Great House as he had promised. He was too wet, too cold, too sick of the whole dreary business. My people, he thought. Yet they had meant no harm. Except, of course, McCoy's Roselda.

One thing still troubled him, though. He had asked one question even Roselda had not been able to answer.

"Who put that lizard on the Great House door, Roselda? You?"

"A lizard, Busha?"

"Damn it, don't play any more games with me, woman. There was a lizard on the door when Mr. Burke first arrived at the house."

"Busha, me don' business with no lizards! Me 'fraid of them things!"

"And you don't know who put it there?"

"No, Busha."

She had not been angry with Peter at that time, had she? So she could be telling the truth. In any case, the lizard had been put there by someone who practiced obeah, and she was certainly not one of those. The whole purpose of her campaign against Peter had been to make people think *he* was one.

It was something to think about. Premature complacency at this point might prove to be dangerous.

29

Jeff Legg had not come. Mark lay on the red divan in the drawing room, his bandaged head on a pillow. Close enough to be touched if he needed her, Eve sat on a chair beside him, gazing into space.

It was not like Jeff to fail to keep his word. But the hands of Mark's watch were moving up to ten o'clock.

He reached for Eve's hand and she quickly looked at him. He only smiled to reassure her. She knew he had failed at McCoy's house. She would go home tomorrow, she had said. It would be lonely there without him, but she had lived alone before. And surely it would not be for long.

As for him, she had argued that he need not go to

Kingston. True, it would not be wise for him to stay with her; people would talk, as she had pointed out before. But there was a small guest house in the hills near her home. Or the Leggs might insist that he stay with them.

"We have done nothing wrong!" she had written almost fiercely. "Why should we be afraid?"

He looked at his watch again. Ten o'clock. Eve's writing pad lay on the floor between them, and he reached for it. "You should go to bed," he wrote. "You must be tired."

She was more than tired, of course. She was emotionally spent. At first, seeing the ugly bruise on his head, she had wanted to go for a doctor, though to do so would have meant walking to Rainy Ridge in the rain.

Reading his message, she shook her head.

"Please," he insisted. "Jeff must have run into some trouble, but he'll come. Otherwise he would have sent word."

"Half an hour more," Eve wrote.

He did not press the point. If she went to her room and Jeff did come, he would only have to wake her. She would never forgive him if he didn't. Besides, the old house was damp and gloomy tonight, and rain was still falling. The lights were little more than a glow, with leaves and forest trash no doubt clogging the intake at the river and the long, open gutter that fed the turbine.

Mark dozed. On waking, he heard a car.

He had been lying there with his shoes off. As he sat up to put them on, he glanced at Eve. She was asleep in her chair now. He leaned over to tie his laces, and his head began to throb. He did not care. At last, after an endless evening of waiting, he would learn something.

But when he opened the heavy double doors to the veranda, the car noise puzzled him.

The machine was not coming down the driveway. It was still on the road above. Jeff seemed to be turning it there—no easy feat on an unpaved road so narrow, with a ditch on one side and the sharp drop to the Great House yard on the other. Still, the driveway itself would be a river now, perhaps too risky in the dark.

The car's muttering ceased, leaving only the sound of the rain. He stepped to the veranda railing to watch for the beam of Jeff's flashlight. No man in his right mind would attempt to walk that slippery slope tonight without a light.

Minutes passed. The drive remained dark.

Something was wrong, apparently. In trying to turn the car, had Jeff mired it in the roadside ditch up there? Mark went back into the house for his own flashlight, left in readiness on the drawing room table in case the electricity failed altogether. It refused to work when he thumbed the switch. Something always seemed to happen to flashlights here, he thought resignedly. He had bought this one in Kingston, the day of that frightening experience in the restaurant.

He left it on the table. Then, remembering the effort Eve had expended on his bandage, he went to the hall for her plastic raincoat, which had a hood that would keep the bandage dry.

The path from the veranda to the carriage house

was a stream now. His shoes filled with water the moment he stepped into it. The rain made his head pound. At the end of the path, pausing to adjust the raincoat hood and get his breath, he looked anxiously at the top of the drive again.

Something moved up there. Good. Jeff was coming down. He would not have to go up.

But was it Jeff?

It was not. At least, it was not Jeff alone. There were two figures—no, three—descending the inundated drive in the dark, without flashlights. Why without flashlights? Everyone in a country district such as this carried a light of some sort at night, even if only a bottle of kerosene with a rag wick. And none of the three was tall enough, anyway, to be Jeff.

He had been going to call out when he thought it was the coffee-works manager, but now was silent. Taking a backward step, he put a high part of the driveway hedge between himself and the intruders; otherwise they might see him standing there, even in the rain, before he could identify them.

Frightened now as he recalled his brother's letters and the three men in the Kingston restaurant—not to mention the Rainy Ridge shopkeeper and the man from New York who didn't know what "Be my guest" meant—Mark stood motionless, watchfully waiting.

Three of them. Three men from a car parked up there on the road, *already turned around so it could be driven away quickly*. They had thought he would not hear the car, perhaps. Strangers would not be aware that sounds carried so far in this place. They wore dark coats. Raincoats, perhaps, but *dark*. And dark hats.

Just short of the upper end of the hedge they stopped, as if at a signal or at a point agreed on. For a moment the three moved closer together and became a single black stain on the wet murk of the night. He thought he saw a dark-sleeved arm stab out, a pale hand pointing to the rear of the house, to the sides, to the path where he stood with pounding head and quickening pulse, his fear a living, swelling thing that threatened to devour his will and leave him helpless. Then the single large blob broke apart into three smaller ones, and the three moved away in different directions. Only one of them continued on down the drive.

Mark bent himself low and retraced his steps to the veranda, one slow stride at a time until the Great House bulked high beside him. Feeling himself safe then, he raced up the steps and into the house, where he sped to Eve and roughly shook her awake.

"Danger!" he scribbled on her pad. "Come quick!"

Thrusting the pad into his raincoat pocket, he took her hand and pulled her into the hall, snatching a raincoat for her from the hall closet as he passed it.

They ran on down the hall, down the stairs to the kitchen and through that to the labyrinth of small rooms beyond. There were no lights here, not even dim ones. Had he attempted such a flight during his first few days at Shepstowe he would have run into dead-end passageways, but he knew the way now, even in darkness. They were on the little path to Eve's former quarters before the man assigned to that part of the yard could have reached it from the driveway.

He ran with Eve along the path. At the cottage she stopped, thinking he meant to hide there, but with a shake of his head he pulled her on. This was the way Iron had fled when caught at her window. But where the brother of McCoy's woman had gone plunging down the slope toward Mango Gut, Mark turned and climbed.

The rain was an ally now. Its ceaseless mutter on brush and boulders, its loud drumming on the Great House roof—these sounds absorbed the smaller ones made by Eve and himself as they worked their way up the hillside. Near the top of the yard he looked back, clutching a small tree with one hand and holding Eve steady with the other. Something moved below them on the path to the kitchen, he thought. He could not be sure.

He climbed the last few feet to the track the Mango Gut people used on their way to the factory, and drew Eve up to him. They could not go to the Gut; no one there would shelter them. Swiftly he led her in the opposite direction, first to the road at the top of the Shepstowe drive, then across that into the meadow. There they were like the wild pigs, he thought as he bored his way through clumps of brush, pausing every few steps to be sure Eve was close behind him.

Somewhere near the far side of the flat, by a tall tamarind tree on a rise of ground, he stopped for the rest they now desperately needed. His head was full of pain and, worse, seemed to be under assault by another kind of torment as well. Remembering his sensations in the restaurant, when he had felt himself being commanded to turn and look at the men at the other table, he thought he understood what was happening.

Someone was telling him not to run; there was no need to run; there was no danger. Someone or something had reached into his mind, even through the pain of the stoning, and was whispering over and over, "Come back, Donner, come back. Nothing at the house will hurt you. You are being childish."

Mind control. The mind control Vin had warned about. *Don't listen!*

"Think of the girl, Donner," the voice persisted. "She must believe you mad, forcing her to flee from a warm and comfortable house in such weather. And for no reason, except that your mind has played some stupid trick on you. Come back and be safe."

Come back, he thought. Not *go* back to the house, but *come* back. So they were there. The message was from there, and the house was the last place he must turn to.

He looked at Eve. In their flight through the roughest part of the meadow she had suffered less than he had, he saw with relief. Thorns had raked his face and torn his hands again; she had escaped the worst of it by keeping close to him. But something else was wrong.

Clinging to him with one hand, shivering, she was pointing back the way they had come and trying to tell him something. As it had so often lately, his mind picked up the message.

"Mark, we shouldn't be doing this. It's so cold, and we're so wet, and you're hurt. Really, Mark, there's no danger. Let's stop being foolish and go back."

"No!" he told her, or his mind did. "No, no!"

Again she tugged at him, trying to make him change his mind. Failing, she suddenly let go his

arm and even succeeded in taking a step toward the
road before he could pull her down again.

"Eve, no," he said again without voicing the words
aloud. Then, knowing there was no other way, he
snatched the pad and pencil from his raincoat
pocket and wrote, "Remember the restaurant, what
they did to us there. And Vin's letter. We can't go
back!" Could she read it without a flashlight?

She managed to and subsided, staring at him with
eyes full of fear. Suddenly she clapped both hands to
her head, as though to shield her mind from alien
thoughts being driven into it. She was more suscep-
tible to this kind of thing than he was, he remembered, and the torment in *his* head was now so acute
he wanted to scream. Full of compassion for her, he
put his arms around her and held her close.

He thought then that he could see the car. It was
hard to be certain at this distance, but there seemed
to be something dark on the road, not far from the
top of the Shepstowe drive. It had to be there somewhere, of course; it would be waiting to speed the
three men away when their mission at the Great
House was accomplished.

Leaning forward, he parted the bushes in front of
him and began a vigil, even while the voice in his
head—more than one voice now—continued to tell
him he had no reason to be afraid.

The men searching for him, now probably prowling through the house itself, must be members of the
organization Vin had written about. No local people
would have a car. Three men. Four, if one had stayed
with the car. Who were they? The three from the restaurant? The man the Rainy Ridge shopkeeper had
brought to the Great House?

He thought about it. Then came the bitterness, the fury, as he realized that if he was right about what was happening, Graham or Goodwin could so easily have warned him.

Why hadn't they?

Suddenly he heard the soft thud of car doors closing, followed by the crunching of tires on the road's loose surface. There was no sound of an engine's being started, but the car-shape was in motion now, coasting down the grade toward the coffee works and Rainy Ridge. When the crunching of the tires had almost died away, he saw a pale glow as the machine's headlights came on far down the road. Then the mutter of an engine became faintly audible.

He waited. It could be a ruse: the car seemingly gone, one or two men left behind to trap him when he showed himself. There might even be someone in the house. In any case, it meant nothing. Eve and he could not go back there, no matter what the voices were telling them.

Was Eve still hearing the voices, as he was? He looked into her face. Her eyes were closed, her lips turned inward and trembling. In the curve of his arm she huddled against him.

Yes—no doubt of it—she *was* still hearing the voices. But now she knew what they meant.

And he? Well, his life at Shepstowe Great House was over and done with, obviously. The people who thought he was Vin Donner had hunted him down and would not rest until they had him.

But somewhere on this side of the meadow was the track leading from the factory to the river, and at the factory Eve and he might be safe for a few hours. Long enough, at least, to think things out.

If the mind-control people would let them.

30

In the coffee-works yard a light glowed above the powerhouse door, another above the door of the cooper's shed. The other buildings were merely black stains on the night's dripping darkness. There would be a watchman somewhere, but the fellow was that in name only; at this hour he would be sleeping.

Leaving Eve at the edge of the compound, Mark tramped through a sea of mud to the powerhouse. The door had no lock. Guided by the lone light above its entrance, he made his way to a box of tools inside, knowing its location from having cleaned the turbine at times. From it he took a heavy screwdriver. Returning to the doorway, he beckoned Eve to him, then led her to the cooper's shed.

That door was padlocked, but the lock was old and rusty; a twist of the screwdriver opened it. When they were in, he drew the door shut and fumbled for the switch that controlled the inside lights. Four went on when he thumbed it. Quickly he loosened three of the bulbs. Eve and he must discuss what had happened now, and what to do about it, and would need that much light to read and write by.

But no more than that, lest it show through cracks in the walls.

Wet through and exhausted, they sank together onto a bench.

The place was a mixture of smells. A sharp, clean odor of fresh-cut wood. A pungent reek of manure from a mound of burlap sacks in a corner. The unmistakable odor of rat droppings. The smell of dampness.

Rain drummed steadily on the metal roof and found its way through a hole to fall *tunk-tink-tunk* onto a board.

Rising, Mark went exploring and found some clean sacks which he carried to the bench to make a bed for Eve. But by pointing to his bandage and emphatically shaking her head, she sought to make him lie down instead.

Refusing, he took the pad and wrote, "I can't stay here. For the time being I'd better go to the sawyers' hut at the pools. They won't look for me there."

Eve gazed at him in sadness, as though at a small child struggling to explain a bad dream that had caused him to wake up crying. "Really, Mark," she wrote, "you're not making sense. We should go back to the house."

So they *are* manipulators of minds, Mark thought. And they've left their thoughts in your mind, my darling, even though we've managed to elude the men themselves.

"Who do *you* think those men were?" he asked.

"Just friends."

"What friends?"

She hesitated, then wrote defiantly, "I don't know,

but they were coming to see *me*. I do have friends, you know."

How long, dear God, would it last? When would she begin to think for herself again?

Almost too tired to make the effort, he took the pad from her and forced himself to write, this time choosing his words with the utmost care. He reminded her of Vin's warnings and all that had happened to give them substance. "Don't you realize you are only thinking what they want you to think? You know you're extrasensitive. And don't you realize that if we hadn't been expecting Jeff tonight, they would have taken me by surprise and it would now be all over for me?"

He had got through to her, he saw with relief. A look of near panic had driven the defiance from her face.

Suddenly she was in his arms, trembling against him.

He held her that way until the trembling ceased, then took up the pad again. "I ought to go," he wrote. "I'm sorry, darling."

"To the pools?"

He nodded.

"You will need food and a change of clothing. I'll bring them."

He shook his head and warned her she must not go back to the house. They might be there waiting and would force her to tell where he was—or, even more likely, to lead them to him. Nor must she come to him at the hut. They would be watching the district and might follow her.

"Wait here until Jeff comes in the morning, then

tell him everything. Who I really am, why I came here, the whole story. Tell him about Vin's letters. Jeff can telegraph Goodwin at the embassy and send me food by someone he trusts."

Sorrowfully she nodded. "How is your head?"

"Don't fret about me. Where will you go? Home?"

"I don't know. I'll think about it."

It would be best for her to go home, he advised. If she remained in the district, his pursuers might suspect she was still in contact with him.

"They can't know I've been anything more than your housekeeper," she protested.

"They know you fled with me tonight. That should tell them something. Besides, they searched the house tonight; be sure of it. They will know you have been using the big bedroom. And they may have found some of our conversations that I saved." Using a kind of shorthand now because his fingers were numb with cold, Mark begged her again to go home after she had seen Jeff. He would find some way to let her know what he was doing.

"What if Goodwin wants you to leave Jamaica?" she wrote.

"I'll come for you first. Darling, be careful. If you feel them working on your mind again, fight it."

There seemed to be nothing more to say. Holding her hands for a moment, he studied her face, aware that her own gaze was fixed on his bandage and she was afraid for him. Her mouth was cold when he kissed her. When he turned to go, she went with him to the door.

Again the rain beat down on him.

He walked slowly, knowing he had far to go and

was already tired. On reaching the meadow he stood motionless in the brush for a time, looking across at the road. Nothing was there. Nothing, at least, that he could see. Should he risk going to the road to look down at the Great House? No. Anyone left behind to trap him would expect just that. Through the dark and the rain he went on again, to the river.

So much had happened in the last few hours, he thought as he rested before attempting the hazardous descent to the fording. Jeff's visit with news of the coffee workers' ultimatum. The stone throwing in the Gut. Now this.

He was so tired. And suddenly so very lonely. And now very much afraid.

31

Arriving at the factory yard at 8 A.M., Jeff Legg leaned back in his pickup and by deep breathing sought to ease the ache in his chest. He was stiff and sore this morning. Too much walking in the rain yesterday. Perhaps even too much fury after his confrontation with McCoy's woman. He was a man not used to being angry. It affected him physically.

The rain, worse luck, was still pounding down, and the factory buildings were gray cubes in a world of mist. The yard was a lake. If this weather kept up much longer, the whole district would be a sea of mud, with the bay road under water below Seaforth and the mountain road to Kingston blocked by landslides.

How, then, would he get the coffee to the wharf even if the women turned up to sort it?

The women *would* come, he felt. One after another had solemnly promised to when he walked Roselda Weeks through the Gut last evening, forcing her at every house to confess her part in the persecution of Peter.

Well, he would get the coffee sorted, and the problem of transporting it to Kingston would have to wait its turn. What he had to do now was start the women working, then drive on up to the Great House to tell Peter what had happened and apologize for not having returned last night. Peter must be wondering what kind of friend he was.

Lowering himself from the pickup, Jeff turned toward the powerhouse to clean the turbine. When the women did come, they would need all the light they could get in the sorting room on such a gloomy morning.

The door of the cooper's shed suddenly creaked open and Eve Vernon came running to him through the wet.

He caught her as she stumbled. Holding her by the arms, he looked at her in amazement. Then he walked her quickly to his office.

Seated there, Eve handed him a pad of paper from her raincoat pocket. Pages and pages were covered with her small, neat handwriting. When he took up a pencil and asked what she was doing here at such an hour, she motioned him to read what she had written.

He read swiftly at first, then slowly, then more slowly still. He read the whole thing a second time and even then was not able to absorb it all. Peter Burke was not Peter Burke but a man named Mark Donner? Was not a writer but a schoolteacher with a twin brother who worked in some mysterious capacity for the American government? Was hiding out from some terrorist crowd called the Disciples because they were after his brother, Vincent?

None of this, for God's sake, could possibly have anything to do with obeah signs at the Great House, or broken gutters, or the campaign by McCoy's woman to avenge the firing of her half-wit brother. What was it all about?

He finished reading and sat for a moment without moving, to give his mind a chance to stop whirling. Milly would have to help with this; it was too much for him to handle by himself.

Taking up a pencil again, he wrote simply, "All right, Eve. Let me just open up the factory, then we'll go down to my place and talk to Milly." The coffee was already in the sorting room and the women would need no instructions when they arrived; last night he had told all of them how important it was to get this order out on time. But, he thought, he had better alert the watchman, wherever he was, in case the people hunting Mark Donner came prowling around.

On the way down the road to his house, with Eve on the seat beside him, he did some more thinking.

There was something else he should do right away, he decided. On handing the pages of writing to his wife, he said, "I'm going up to Shepstowe for a look around, Milly. Be back soon. Read this while I'm gone, and you'll understand."

Strange, he thought as he drove back up the road, past the factory to the Great House. All the time he had been trying to get to the bottom of that other business yesterday, Peter Burke—Mark Donner— had been facing a greater peril. Yet his failure to call back at the Great House as promised was all that had saved the two of them. Had he shown up there, talked awhile, and gone home, they would most likely have been asleep when the intruders arrived.

Milly would have words for that. "Everything's best that happens."

He walked through the house. Nothing in the upstairs rooms appeared to have been disturbed, but each room had been visited, beyond a doubt. The polished juniper floors were marked everywhere with sneaker prints.

Downstairs in the kitchen he found an empty carton, one of the many brought by Goodwin, and began to fill it with things Mark Donner would need. Then he had second thoughts. Eve's kitchen shelves were like those in a supermarket, everything in neat array. If the intruders came again, they might notice the difference and put two and two together—supplies missing, their quarry must be hiding somewhere in the neighborhood. Annoyed with himself for having so nearly made what could have been a serious blunder, Jeff replaced the items he had taken and put the box back where he had found it.

Donner would need clothes, too, Eve had written. All right, but not from here. The closets, too, might have been checked. *Must* have been checked—by anyone clever enough to have tracked him here to Shepstowe from the States, by way of Mexico City, Mérida, and Kingston.

He made sure some of the lights were on then. Lights might help to discourage prowlers. Finally, on leaving, he locked the doors.

The factory yard was empty when he passed it, but, of course, in weather like this the women would not be standing around chatting as they usually did of a morning. At home he found an empty carton in his garage, carried it to Milly's kitchen, and talked to her about Eve's long letter while she packed it. "Were you as bowled over as I was?" he asked.

"I can hardly believe it, Jeff." She stopped for a few seconds to look at him. "I mean I *do* believe it, of course—Peter wouldn't be lying—but for something like this to happen here—"

"Peter wouldn't lie, you say. That was almost my first reaction when I read what Eve had written. Why are we so sure? I wonder."

"Because we know him. And how he feels about Eve."

"And because you trust your woman's intuition, m'm?"

"Partly, I suppose. It tells me he wouldn't lie to Eve, even if he would to us. He loves her, Jeff. They love each other."

He nodded, feeling she was right. Then, "Hey, take it easy, woman," he admonished when she would have stuffed into the carton everything but the kitchen stove. "Somebody has to carry that."

"Get some blankets and some of your clothes for him," Mildred ordered. "And your rifle."

"Milly, I doubt if he's ever had a firearm in his hands."

"Take it. And some ammunition. He needs something to protect himself with."

She had put Eve to bed, she told him. The girl was exhausted. "She thinks she ought to go home, but I'm not having any of that, I can tell you. She stays right here with us until this is over." Finished with the box, she turned to frown at him. "Jeff, this gives me the creeps. Imagine a man facing such trouble and danger just because of something his brother is doing."

Jeff only nodded. When he came back with clothes and the gun, Mildred said, "Have you sent a telegram to Goodwin yet?"

"I will, on the way back up."

"What will you say?"

"What Peter said to say. It's in Eve's letter. 'Come at once, urgent.' Isn't that it?"

Mildred took the letter from her apron pocket and found the passage. "Yes, that's it. And Mark was told not to sign his name."

"I'd better sign mine. Otherwise Goodwin may waste a lot of time looking for Mark at Shepstowe."

"Don't you wonder where Goodwin fits into all this, Jeff?"

"Well, that's in the letter, too, more or less. There are those Argus people in the States who arranged for Mark to come here. Goodwin is their man in Jamaica."

"I just hope he's sober."

Jeff's reply was unusually ominous for him. "He'd damn well better be, or I'll make him wish he were."

He put the carton and gun into the pickup then and drove back up to the factory, stopping at the post office to send the telegram. You could send a telegram from any post office in the island. This one would be phoned to Morant Bay, then sent to Kingston by teletype. There was no letup in the rain, and the factory yard was still deserted. When he walked into the sorting room, though, he found all but a few of the tables occupied. The women gazed at him in silence, waiting for him to speak.

Usually he joked with them a little at the start of the day, but this morning he only frowned at the empty tables. The woman in charge said, "All would be here, Busha, except it raining so hard. The rain giving some of us plenty troubles at home."

"Do the best you can."

"We will surely do that, sah."

Confronting the rain again, he lowered his head and made for the office, wondering which of the factory crew he should send upriver to the pools. Several were trustworthy enough, but the Jamaican countryfellow who wasn't fond of talking just didn't exist. As he approached the office a figure detached itself from a wall and stepped toward him, lifting a hand to a nonexistent hat brim in salute.

After what had happened last night in the man's house, Jeff was surprised. "Yes, McCoy?"

"Busha, it seem Mr. Burke is not at the Great House this morning. It seem nobody is there."

"What do you want him for?"

McCoy gazed at his shoes. "Don't ask me that,

Busha, after last night. I must set things right with that man."

"All right, Zekiel. Come inside." Jeff entered the office and McCoy followed him. "Close the door. Sit down."

Still gazing at his shoes, McCoy sank onto a chair.

"So you want to do something to right the wrong. Is that it, Zekiel?"

"Yes, Busha."

"Can I trust you? Really trust you?"

"Yes, Busha. Yes, sah!"

"I'm not so sure. You knew bloody well your woman was behind all that obeah talk. You knew she was out to get even with Mr. Burke for firing her brother. Why didn't you do something about it?"

McCoy shook his head, looking pathetically eager to make amends. "Busha, that don't true. I did know she have bad feelings for Mr. Burke, but not how she the one spreading the obeah talk. No, sah, not that. Not till you come last night and make her admit it. Is God's truth me telling you."

"All right. There is a way you can help."

McCoy waited in silence.

"I'll tell you where he is," Jeff went on. "And I'll tell you something else. It isn't our people he has run away from. Before I left the Gut last night every living soul there knew the truth—you know how I walked your woman around and made her talk—and Mr. Burke had nothing more to fear from there. The fact is, he left Shepstowe for a different reason altogether."

McCoy looked puzzled.

"Mr. Burke is a good man," Jeff said. "I expect I don't have to tell you that."

"No, sah, you don't. I know it well."

"But some wicked men are out to get him. I expect you've seen them a time or two if you'll think about it. You *have* noticed strangers in the district, haven't you?"

McCoy thought about it. "Well, I did see a strange Chinaman in Mr. Yee's shop a time or two. Nobody else I can think of."

"They're here. Three others, at least, maybe more. I don't suppose they've been moving around too much. They won't want to attract attention."

"Yes, sah."

"And never mind why they want him," Jeff warned. "Don't start getting curious, Zekiel. It's enough for you to know they do want him, and you're not to repeat even that. Do you hear? Not one word."

Wide-eyed, McCoy nodded.

"All right, then. With that understood, you can help. Mr. Burke is at the sawyers' cabin up there by the pools. You know the place; you went there with him for the Christmas tree. I want you to carry some things to him."

Turning to the desk, Jeff took up pen and paper and composed a note to Mark. "Eve has told me everything. Am sending food and clothing with McCoy. Also a rifle and some ammunition. If you don't know how to use the gun, he will show you.

"Have sent word to Goodwin and will come up to you when I've seen him. Don't worry about Eve, she is safe at my place, and well." He paused, then added, "She sends her love," and signed it. Then he added a postscript.

"I've instructed McCoy to tell you what happened when I confronted his woman in the Gut last night. Make sure he does so. It was because of what I got into down there that I didn't make it back to the Great House as promised. Sorry about that, old boy, but when you've heard the story I think you'll understand."

When he had sealed the envelope, he thrust it into McCoy's shirt pocket. "Give him that, and tell him what happened at your house last night. You understand?"

"How you did talk to Roselda, sah? And got her to go around the village with you afterwards?"

"Yes, and be *sure* you tell him. He has enough to worry about without thinking the obeah business is still hanging over him. And take him the rifle and the carton from my pickup."

"Yes, Busha."

"Come to me when you get back. I want to know how he's getting along up there."

"I will do that."

"One thing more, Zekiel. Keep off the road with those things. Go through the meadow, and make sure no one sees you."

"Yes, Busha."

And if you let me down, Jeff added mentally as the man touched his imaginary hat brim and walked out, be sure neither you nor your woman will ever work at this place again. Not for one minute. No matter how desperate I am for help.

32

By midmorning all but two of the factory women had turned up for work.

The sorting room was quiet, though, as Jeff walked through it. The usual chatter was missing. Now and then a worker looked up from her tray to speak to a neighbor, but voices were subdued. The injustice of yesterday's ultimatum hung like a pollution in the air. Some, perhaps, were even wondering how they would feel had they actually succeeded in driving Peter Burke from the Great House.

Yes, they were subdued now, Jeff thought bitterly. Their consciences troubled them. But next week or next month the same stupidity could erupt in another colossal wrong, and some other innocent victim could be crucified. Ignorance was a curse.

Milly talked about it at times, angry with him because he usually shrugged it off. "You think because this is only a small part of a small country, it doesn't matter," she had said once. "But the world is millions of small places like this, Jeff. Can't you see?"

He saw now.

In the afternoon Goodwin drove into the yard. Hatless in the rain, his face a thundercloud under the close-cropped yellow hair, he looked about with a show of impatience until Jeff beckoned to him from the office doorway. He came over the threshold stamping mud from his shoes.

"What the hell happened? Do you know what that road from town is *like* in this filthy weather? I had to *shovel* my way through one mud slide!"

Jeff gestured him to a chair. "Sit. There's nothing you can do in a rush." The fellow really had pushed on the way from Kingston, he saw. The palms of his hands were red from fighting the wheel.

While he told the story, his caller fixed him with a suspicious stare. The distrust was still in evidence when he finished.

"So you know the whole thing." Goodwin's voice seemed barely under control.

"I know what Eve Vernon told me. What Donner told her."

"Where is he?"

"For the time being I'll just keep that to myself, if you don't mind. It seems to me you've given him trouble enough."

The man's face would have resembled concrete except for the red flush that took possession of it. "Damn it, Legg, we're trying to help him!"

"Are you? I think if I'd wanted to help a man in his position I'd have come clean with him. I'd have told him what he was up against, not tugged him about like a monkey on a string." Jeff's face had hardened, too. "Anyway, it's up to him whether he wants to see any more of you or not."

"Is he hiding around here?"

"I can get a message to him."

"The men who tried to take him at the Great House—are they still here? My God, Legg, don't play games! You don't know what you're sticking your head into. This man's life is in danger!"

"Seems to me it was more in danger when you kept him guessing," Jeff retorted. "No, I don't know where those men are, though I suspect they're still in the district somewhere. I don't even know *who* they are. Do you?"

"Where's the girl?"

"*Do* you?"

Goodwin exhaled noisily. "If I did, I wouldn't tell you. Damn it, man, I *can't* tell you. I'm not running this show; I just follow orders. Is the girl with Donner?"

"No, she's not. She isn't anywhere you can talk to her, either."

"Now, see here, Legg—"

"No, *you* see here." Rising, Jeff leaned against the desk with his hands turned backward gripping the edge of its old, scarred top. His hands, his face, too, looked equally old and scarred, seasoned by years of physical work and problem solving. "Until a few hours ago," he said, "the people of this district were giving Mark a rough time through ignorance, and I was thinking what a damned vicious thing ignorance is. But what you people have done to him is even nastier, it strikes me. You've got intelligence. With you this didn't just happen; you planned it. You're a hell of a lot more guilty, it seems to me, than our peasants could ever be."

Goodwin surprised him by taking the denunciation calmly. In a voice suddenly soft, almost pleading, the golden-haired man said, "Haven't you got your villains mixed up a bit? It's the Disciples he's running from, not us."

"All right, it's the Disciples."

"In trying to protect him we may have done some things that don't sit well with you, but we *have* been trying. At least agree to take him a message. Will you do that?"

"Yes, I'll do that."

"Tell him to stay in hiding, then. Tell him I'll be in touch with Graham for instructions and will be out here again as soon as I'm told what he's to do. My hunch is that Graham will want him out of Jamaica fast. Just how we'll get him out without leaving a trail they can follow, I don't know."

"I'll tell him."

Goodwin offered his hand and seemed grateful when Jeff accepted it. "You know, I don't blame you for thinking me a heel, in a way. He's one hell of a nice guy. Why all this has to be happening to such a man is beyond me."

Nodding in agreement, Jeff stood in the doorway, watching the man from Kingston trudge through the sea of mud to his car.

At four o'clock McCoy returned, plodding on shoes half filled with water. The river had given him trouble, he reported. "Busha, I will never know how that man reached up there in the dark. That river nearly drowned me, and I know it well."

He had found Mark asleep in the hut, on a mattress of burlap scraps made from the two beds left by the sawyers. "He look like he dead, sah, but after a little food he seem to feel some better. We did clean up the place, and then I did chop some branches to make him a real nice bed. By the time I leave, he is well content."

"You gave him my message?"

"Yes, sah."

"And told him about Roselda being the one behind the obeah business?"

"Of course, sah." McCoy looked hurt.

"All right." Jeff laid a hand of friendship on the man's shoulder. "Go on home now, Zekiel, and don't say a word about this to anyone. Not to a living soul, you hear?—least of all to your woman. I'll be the one to go up there tomorrow. I want to talk to him. But you can do something else to help if you want to. Do you want to?"

"Yes, Busha."

"It's important for us to know if there are still strangers in the district. Not just in Rainy Ridge or Mango Gut, mind you, but anywhere close by. If there are, Mr. Burke is in danger. Can you find out, do you think?"

"Sah, if any strangers is about, I can know. Trust me."

"Good."

McCoy hesitated. "Busha, I did see the swelling on Mr. Burke's head where the stone did lick him down. That was a wicked thing to do. I should find out who done it?"

"A child did it, he said."

"So he did tell me. But I should find out which child?"

"Do you think it will happen again?"

McCoy wagged his head. "They know now they was wrong about him."

"Then why don't we just forget it, Zekiel? Our Mr. Burke is not a vengeful man, I'm sure."

33

During the night the rain stopped, but the river remained high and the forest still dripped. Jeff arrived at the pools feeling older than the sum of his years, and sat to rest.

He had seen the stream higher at times, but not often. Not once had he lost the sound of it, even where the track ran high above the inaccessible gorges through which it plunged. Here the sound was different: not a muffled thunder, but a slithering voice, a snake on glass, as the flow sped flawlessly past with scarcely a ripple. The pools themselves were under it, invisible now.

As he rested, gazing upstream, he saw Mark at the water's edge with a bucket. Out of curiosity he watched for a moment.

Mark was no woodsman. When he knelt to scoop up water, the current all but pulled the bucket from his grasp and toppled him off balance. He caught himself by clutching at a branch, then tried to stand before his feet were properly braced and had to grab the branch a second time. He had not brought the rifle to the stream with him, either, Jeff observed with a frown of disapproval.

When Mark was safely away from the stream's edge—to startle him there might be disastrous—Jeff stood up and called to him. He turned with a look of alarm that swiftly became an expression of delight. Enthusiastically he waved, then did not move again until Jeff reached him.

They shook hands and went to the cabin.

"Brought you a letter from Eve," Jeff said at the doorway. "She spent most of last evening writing it." He took the envelope from his shirt pocket and was pleased when the other all but snatched it. "I'll just have a look around outside while you read it. A man should be alone with a love letter."

"Thank you."

The place was quite decent, Jeff saw. McCoy no doubt was responsible for the leveling of the brush and small trees around the building. That was machete work and done with a conscience. The two men together had probably gathered the bundles of fresh grass for the roof. Eve had said the door was half off its hinges, but it was back in place now with hinges ingeniously fashioned of the vine called tree rope.

When Mark called to him to come in, he saw that the interior, too, was respectable. The two old beds mentioned by Eve had been replaced with one good one—a woodsman's couch of boughs and saplings that appeared to be both solid and comfortable. The table was adequate. The chair beside it was a piece of juniper trunk left behind by the sawyers, apparently. The rifle leaned in one corner and a twig broom in another.

Mark seemed amused by the inspection. "Do I get my merit badge?"

"Well, it's no north coast hotel, but it will do for a short stay, I imagine."

"Actually I can't claim much credit. McCoy not only did most of the work, he showed me how to do what I did." Seating himself on the bed, Mark waved his caller to the chair. "Did Goodwin come?"

"He came. I was a bit rough with him, I'm afraid."

"Why?"

"For what he and those others have done to you. I bore down so hard he had to remind me it was the Disciples who are out to get you, not his people."

"I've had to remind myself at times. What does he want me to do?"

"Lie low here until he's had a talk with Graham. By phone, I suppose he means, though I have no idea how these chaps work."

Mark realized he hadn't much knowledge of how they worked, either. "I see. But I may not follow his instructions again. Before, I had only myself to think of. *My* future, which wasn't all that important. Now there's Eve."

"I shouldn't think she's in any danger."

"I mean I might lose her."

Jeff went to the door and stood there for a moment, gazing down the river. "You certainly have solitude here. Does it get you down?"

"I don't mind being alone."

"Walked about, have you?"

"Not far. I did go up the river yesterday after Mc-Coy left. There's a spectacular place above here where three separate streams fall from a height to form this one. Two are waterfalls and one is a sort of chute or water slide, in a deep cleft, some eighty feet high and maybe thirty wide. It's a thing to see."

"It's called Three River Mouth."

"I heard something up there that gave me a scare," Mark said. "Tell me, do wild pigs scream?"

Jeff went back to his chair. "Scream?"

"That's about the only way I can describe it. It seemed to come from the heavy bush up there near the top of the slide: a series of screams, really hair-raising. It lasted maybe two or three minutes, then sort of faded out."

"Could have been a pig. A wounded one. I don't know what else." Remembering the not-bright brother of McCoy's woman, Jeff became alarmed. "You haven't seen any hunters, have you?"

"No one." But, stepping to the table, Mark picked up a red and white cigarette box and said, "I found this on the floor, though, when I got here."

Jeff took it from him, scowling.

"Actually," Mark remembered aloud, "there was one here when I came with Zekiel for the Christmas tree. I asked him if Iron might have been here and he just shrugged and said plenty of people smoke Albanys. Are they Jamaican?"

"English, I believe." Jeff did not smoke cigarettes. "Made here under license or something." He handed the box back. "You know, of course, that McCoy's woman is the one who turned the people against you. I told McCoy to tell you."

274

"He told me. He also said it was you who made her admit it, for which I haven't thanked you."

"Did he tell you why she did it?"

"Because I fired Iron and caused him to leave home. Or, rather, caused McCoy to throw him out."

Jeff nodded. "We have a word for her kind in Jamaica's country parts. 'Ginnals,' they're called—a corruption of the word 'general,' I suppose—and every village seems to have one. They're smart enough to know the others aren't quite as smart as they are and can be used."

"I see."

"A lot of what happened was grist for that woman's mill." Jeff shook his head in disgust. "Your walking out from town that night. The graveyard business. Merlinda's babble about your being able to talk to Eve. Even the way she used the little girl's tummyache."

"That's all that was wrong? A tummyache?" Fond of the child in spite of everything, Mark was relieved.

"She wasn't sick," Jeff growled. "Just had the gollywobbles from eating a lot of penny candy she didn't even get from you. The shopkeeper gave it to her." He hiked his shoulders in a shrug. "Of course, you left yourself wide open when you *admitted* in Henderson's shop that you'd walked out from town. When Roselda turned on you she was able to tell people she heard you admit it—in front of witnesses, to boot."

"So she was the one who questioned me in the shop that day."

"She was the one. Roselda Weeks. And as luck would have it, the one you ran into when you came out of the graveyard. And I'm not at all easy about that brother of hers, Mark. If he's prowling about up here—" Abruptly rising, Jeff began to pace. "Look. When you went down to the river for water a while ago, you didn't even have your gun. If he'd been nearby, he might have jumped you. You can't afford to take such chances."

"But I've seen no one."

"You heard a hog screaming. Caught in a trap, maybe. I don't like it. I don't like the idea of—" Aware that he might be doing more harm than good, Jeff stopped. After all, Mark had to remain here and there were nights to be got through. The hours of darkness in a place like this must be frightening to a man not used to them.

This thought led to another. "Why don't I send McCoy up here to stay with you?" Jeff asked.

Mark smiled. "He might not consider it a privilege."

"He'd come. He wants to help you. On the other hand"—Jeff scowled in confusion—"I've got him on the prowl, so to speak, tracking down the chaps who are after you. He's probably of more value doing that. I could send someone else, though."

"I'll be all right. I've got the gun."

"Ever use one?"

Mark's smile was apologetic. "I practiced with it yesterday, with McCoy's help. I can manage."

"You fired it?"

"No, no. We couldn't risk that, the way the sound would carry up here. I went through all the motions, though."

Jeff glanced at the weapon leaning in the corner—a

four-shot Browning BAR, semiautomatic. Not new, but it would do the job if Mark had to defend himself. "Well, all right. I'll send McCoy up tomorrow with a fresh lot of supplies. Anything special you want?"

"Can you wait five minutes?"

"Of course."

"Just let me write a note to Eve. I've already written her, but I'd like to add a few lines to answer what she wrote."

Jeff went out again, glancing at the sky as he strolled down to the stream's edge. The rain was finished, the last of the overcast thinning out to reveal patches of blue. Mark would like that. The forest would seem less sinister. On the other hand, a pig hunter would like it, too. In better weather he'd be able to move around more.

"Take care of yourself, old boy," he said when Mark handed him the letter. "Quite a few of us have become pretty fond of you."

34

The Leggs' two English bull terriers roamed the grounds by day but were confined after dark to a screened front veranda where they served as watchdogs. At nine o'clock that evening they barked a warning that someone was approaching along the woodsy driveway from the road.

In the drawing room Mildred looked up from a book and said, "Jeff?"

Jeff had been sitting there staring into space, thinking about Mark Donner in the cabin at the pools. "All right," he said, and went out, silencing the dogs with a quiet command.

Bathed in moonlight, the yard glistened as though layered with frost. A pair of nutmeg trees near the veranda seemed sprayed with white paint. Through the eerie brilliance Zekiel McCoy came trudging along the drive, casting a bulky shadow.

Jeff went out to meet him.

"There is strangers around, Busha." McCoy used a low voice, as though fearful of being overheard. "The Chinaman I did mention before is staying at Yee's house in the village. Victor Henderson did talk with two others in Hegley this afternoon."

"In Hegley?" That village was five miles away, across the river from Mango Gut. There was a driving road up the valley on that side, but none from here. People from here had to use footpaths and a fording.

"They did ask Victor plenty questions about Mr. Burke," McCoy said. "They is friends of his and anxious to find him, they said, 'specially now that he seem to be in some kind of trouble. They will pay well for information, they said."

"What was Henderson doing over there in Hegley?" The man was a sawyer, a decent sort, a son of the Mango Gut shopkeeper.

"He did go to sell a goat, sah."

"Did these fellows question anyone else?"

"It seem so. They was there most of the afternoon."

"What do they look like?"

"Well, Busha, according to Victor one of them is a black man and the other just barely brown, and neither one is Jamaican. He said that if he had to guess where they was from, he would say the black one might be from Haiti and the other from Cuba. But it would be just a guess."

"And Victor reported this to you?" Jeff scowled again. "How did he know you're interested in them? You must have told him."

McCoy gazed at his shoes. "Busha, is a big job watching the whole entirely district. I did have to tell two or three that I know we can trust."

Jeff sighed and shook his head. The man was right, he supposed. No matter how great the risk, there was probably no other way to handle this. "You haven't told anyone where Mr. Burke *is*, I hope. If you've done that, Zekiel—"

"Oh no, sah! I wouldn't do that!"

"All right, but for God's sake be careful. If these fellows are offering to pay for information—well, you know what can happen. And the third one is at Yee's, you say?"

"Yes, sah."

And all three are just waiting, Jeff thought, for the careless word, the telltale move that will lead them to their quarry. They're bloodhounds sniffing for a scent.

"All right, Zekiel. I went up to see Mr. Burke today. You did a good job helping him. I want you to make a quick trip up there at daybreak with some things for him. I'll have them ready at the factory. Then keep your eye on our strangers again. Incidentally"—he laid a hand on McCoy's shoulder—"you can tell Victor Henderson and any others you've recruited that Mr. Burke, too, will pay for information. We can play that game."

Mildred was on the veranda when Jeff turned back to the house. "I heard," she said. "Jeff, I can't believe Mr. Yee is mixed up in this. That man must be using him somehow."

"When Yee brought the visiting Chinaman to the Great House, he introduced him as a friend of his son in New York." It was one of the things Eve had left out of her first hurried account but jotted down since coming to stay with them. "But Mark didn't buy it."

"Didn't what?"

"Believe it. There, you see? I said, 'Didn't buy it,' because I've just picked the phrase up from a book I'm reading. Something of the same sort happened at the Great House, according to Eve. The Chinaman asked if he might look at Mark's books. Mark said, 'Be my guest,' and the fellow didn't know what he meant. But Mark felt a New Yorker *would* have known."

Mildred nodded. "I don't suppose it makes much difference, does it? The others had already followed Mark from Mexico and seen him that day in the restaurant."

Jeff put an arm around her and led her inside. "I had an idea today, coming back from the cabin. Do you suppose our dogs would stay up there with him?

They'd warn him if anyone came snooping around. Be company for him, too."

She shook her head. "If you left them there, they'd be back here in an hour."

"I suppose."

"They'd bark at all sorts of things up there, too. It might even *bring* someone snooping."

Jeff turned his head to glance into the adjoining room. Eve Vernon sat there at a table, alone in her world of silence—as alone, he thought with a twinge of sadness, as Mark was in the cabin at the pools.

She was reading, for the third or fourth time, the letter he had brought from there.

35

"Good Christ!" Goodwin exclaimed with fervor. "I can't imagine any man walking this at night in a downpour!"

Jeff said quietly, "He did it. Believe me."

"And I thought he was the timid type. Brother." The golden-haired man stopped and looked down, then drew back with a shudder.

The track was high above the river here. Backed by an almost vertical wall of black rock, it overhung a gorge from the green and misty depths of which the stream sent up a muted roar.

This was not the first time the trail had sapped the color from Goodwin's face. It was not to be the last, either. When Mark greeted them at the cabin, the Argus man gazed at him with new respect and said, "Mister, anyone looking for you here would need to be a mountain goat."

Mark smiled. "If you think that track is a bad one, look over there." He pointed to the almost vertical slope across the river from the cabin clearing. "See it?"

Goodwin wagged his head.

"See that big tree the sawyers left high up on the slope?"

"Well, yes. I think."

"Look below it. That brown streak is a track."

"More likely a wild-pig run," Jeff said.

"It was that once, McCoy says, but the sawyers improved it. Now it goes on up to Three River Mouth, and you should see what McCoy has done for me there."

Jeff gave him a quizzical look.

"If anyone came up the river I'd be trapped here, he insisted," Mark went on with enthusiasm. "But it seems there's another old track up there by which I can get out to Hegley if I have to. McCoy built a bridge across the slide for me, so I can reach it. Like to see it, would you?"

"Later," Goodwin said. "I came to talk." With a dour glance at the wild country above the cabin clearing, he walked inside and sat down.

Jeff handed Mark a letter. "From Eve."

"Thanks, Jeff. How is she?"

"Lonesome, as I'm sure you are. Otherwise fine."

Mark glanced hungrily at the envelope before putting it into his pocket, then walked into the cabin. Jeff followed. The man from Kingston, seated there, at once began talking.

"I've been in touch with Graham by phone," Goodwin said. "I've got your instructions. You'll be leaving here in three days."

Still standing, Mark gazed at him in silence.

"You're to come out Friday night," Goodwin continued, "quitting this place in time to reach the coffee works by four A.M. at the latest. I'll be there waiting. I want to get you out of the district while it's still dark. I'm taking you to Montego Bay."

Mark still stared.

"That's all you need to know for now," Goodwin said. "But I can tell you this: You're going to South America."

"That's what you think," Mark said quietly.

"What?"

"I'm going nowhere."

An expression of astonishment reddened Goodwin's face; then outrage took over. His hands gripped his knees as he leaned forward on the section of juniper log that served for a chair. "Now, see here, Donner—"

"No, *you* see here. I'm not leaving this cabin until *I* decide to."

"Damn it, man, don't be insane! You know you're in deadly danger!"

"I also know I have friends," Mark said in the same quiet voice. "Jeff, here. Certain others. On the run again I would have no one. I'm tired of running."

Goodwin had not anticipated this and had to think about it. He got up and walked to the door, looked out for a moment, turned himself, and glared. He took in a deep breath. With his hands on his hips he said at last, loudly, "You can't mean this, Donner. My God, man, use your head. If those fellows get on to where you are and come after you, Legg here won't be able to protect you. Nor will I." His gaze shifted from Mark's granite face to the rifle in the corner. "And if you're thinking *that* thing will do you any good in a showdown—"

"I wasn't thinking that."

"Sure, you might get one of them. But they're not stupid enough to come at you one at a time."

Mark said, "I've told you. I don't plan to shoot anyone."

"You plan to sit here, then? Until they find you?"

"I intend to look after myself in my own way. How I do it is none of your business. Go back and call Graham. Tell him I've rebelled, revolted, or however you want to put it, and you've washed your hands of me." Mark was actually smiling now—the smile of one who had deeply pondered a problem, arrived at a solution that satisfied him, and made a commitment to it. The smile hid a dark, seething anger, however, which had been growing in him ever since his escape with Eve from entrapment at the Great House. "I'm sorry if this is going to make a lot of trouble for you, Goodwin, but I've had my share of trouble thanks to your Argus crowd. Let it be your turn now."

In reply Goodwin smiled, too, but twistedly and with a touch of triumph. "And what will you do for money? Have you thought about that?"

"I'll manage. The rent here is quite reasonable."

"Damn it, you know what I mean!" Goodwin's face had begun to look badly sunburned. "What about when you leave here? *If* you leave."

"I'll work on that. The point is, Goodwin, I'm mad as hell about the way you've used me. Maybe you had to do it to protect my brother, but I had a right to know what I was running from. For not being honest about that, I'll never forgive you and your people."

"My God," Goodwin said.

Mark shrugged and turned to Jeff. "Want to see my bridge?"

Jeff nodded.

"You, Goodwin? It's quite a thing, really."

"Thanks, but I'll stay here and try not to go crazy."

"I think he's annoyed with me," Mark said as he and Jeff crossed the cabin clearing. "Did he really expect me to be the mechanical rabbit in a second dog race, do you suppose?"

"He did, I'm sure."

"And did you?"

"No." Jeff shook his head. "I don't think so."

"Thanks."

To reach the track to Three River Mouth they had to cross the stream. Wading through swift, knee-deep water strewn with boulders, Mark reached the other bank well ahead of his companion and turned to watch Jeff struggle after him.

His stay at the cabin had toughened him, he realized with a touch of satisfaction. Before, he would have hesitated even to tackle so swift a stream, and now Jeff, catching up, was gazing at him in astonishment. To hell with Goodwin and the Disciples. Eve would be proud of him.

Having been to Three River Mouth with McCoy, he continued to lead the way as they climbed the steep slope to the track he had pointed out from the cabin yard. When they stopped to rest on reaching it, he turned to point higher.

"I sat on that fallen tree up there a while ago and forgot all my problems for a while."

"Oh?"

"I'd gone up out of curiosity, because Zekiel said it was a valuable tree, a bulletwood, the sawyers had felled and were probably planning to come back for. I sat on it to rest and while I was just sitting there, feeling proud of myself for climbing up there, a couple of baby mongooses came out of nowhere and started to play. Have you ever seen baby mongooses at play?"

Jeff smiled. "A time or two, I think."

"Cute as kittens. And fearless. They romped all over my feet."

Jeff smiled again. With anyone else he might have pointed out that mongooses had been brought to Jamaica to kill rats in the cane fields, and became a pest because they seemed to prefer birds to rats. A love affair with a couple of baby forest creatures would do Mark Donner no harm. "How long did you watch them?"

"Oh, fifteen minutes. Twenty. I had some of those

peanuts you sent up by McCoy, and at the end they were taking them from my hand."

"Now, that *is* something. I'll have to tell Eve." And Eve would be delighted, Jeff thought. Few people were able to make friends with Brother Mongoose.

High above the stream they continued along the cliffside path that had once been a pig run. The cabin clearing disappeared. The sun blazed down on them. The air quivered with a humming of insects. After a while Jeff heard water smashing against rocks, and the new sound slowly increased in volume until suddenly he rounded a bend and faced its source.

He halted. Once before, but at least six years ago, he had visited this remote spot while hunting a reported planting of ganja on the Shepstowe property. He had never forgotten its awesome splendor. The river gorge ended in a vast, sky-reaching bowl of forest green, gashed vertically in three places. The gash on his left housed a ladder of flashing cascades. Down the center slit, which was too sheer-sided to admit any sunlight, wriggled a smaller stream that resembled a thread of quicksilver. The right-hand cleft held not a fall, but a water *slide*.

It took a man's breath away with its wild beauty, that nearest section of Three River Mouth. A monstrous fingernail seemed to have gouged the mountain from top to bottom there, scratching away trees, brush, and soil in a cleft several yards deep and some thirty feet wide. Down the glass-slick core of stone in the cleft sped a flow of water so swift, so smooth, it seemed not to flow at all until at the bottom, with a sound of thunder, it exploded among boulders and filled the air with spray.

Halfway up the mountain a rude bridge of planks and tree rope, like a strand of spiderweb, spanned the slide from a stand of tall junipers on one side to a giant bulletwood on the other. A handrail of tree rope looked even flimsier than the bridge itself.

Jeff stared up at it. "McCoy built that?" he asked in awe.

Mark nodded. "My way out if I need one. I'm to go up on this side through the junipers, cross the bridge, and pick up an old track. In case anyone's too close behind me for comfort, he left a machete at the cabin for me so I can cut the contraption loose after crossing it."

"He built this *alone?* You must have helped him."

"Well, yes, I did. And a fellow named Henderson came with him, too. We all worked on it."

Still stunned by what he was seeing, Jeff stood there wide-eyed. "How in God's name did you get the bridge across there?"

"We built it at the top, using boards the sawyers left up there. Then we lowered it on tree ropes and went down to make it fast. I say 'we' but of course Zekiel and Henderson did most of it. They also provided the know-how."

Proud of his part in the project, and grinning like a schoolboy, Mark went on to explain that McCoy and Henderson had cleared the old track on the far side of the slide, and by using it he could reach a track to Hegley. "So you see I can get out of here if I have to."

"And you'd have the nerve to *use* that bridge?"

"I've already been back and forth over it several times. We had to try it out, didn't we? Anyway"—the grin lingered—"I've done quite a few things lately that I never dreamed I'd have the nerve to do."

When they returned to the cabin, Goodwin began his argument again, armed this time with new persuasions he had thought up during their absence. Mark remained obdurate.

"Well," Jeff said, "we'd better be going. Is there anything you want me to say to Eve?"

Mark produced a letter for her. "But wait a minute, will you? Let me look at hers in case there's something I should answer." Tearing open Eve's letter, he quickly read it. "No. There's nothing that won't keep."

"Take care of yourself, old boy," Jeff said.

Goodwin said nothing, nor did he offer to shake hands on leaving. Our Man in Jamaica was definitely angry, Mark thought. More than that, he appeared to be badly frightened as well.

Even before the two men were out of sight, Mark began a slow rereading of Eve's letter.

My darling,

I wonder if you know how much I love you. Ever since you asked me to marry you, my life has been completely topsy-turvy. No, I don't mean that. It isn't topsy-turvy at all; it is just wonderful. I never dreamed I would ever feel this way.

Of course, there is another side to the coin. Being away from you like this I suffer torments of loneliness. Mildred and Jeff are understanding and kind, but it still isn't the same as being in the same house with you, talking to you the way we do in so many different ways.

Most of all I think I miss the way we used to sit quietly together in the Shepstowe drawing room of an evening, you working or reading, I mending or reading or whatever, and every few minutes we would feel something that made us look at each other. Am I being silly?

The Leggs are fond of you, darling. We talk to one another by writing, and I know they are by what they say about you. About us, perhaps I should say, for they link our names together as if they just automatically think of us that way.

I am going to ask Jeff to bring your typewriter from the Great House so I can communicate with them more easily. And so I can write to you more easily, too, of course. But really I must begin to learn how to read lips. Believe me, if I can get my hands on a book about lipreading, I'll soon surprise you. Perhaps the Tom Redcam Library in Kingston has one.

And do you know something, my darling? I remember my father telling me once that deaf people can learn to talk. I don't know just how, but it has something to do with letting them hear words through some kind of instrument that makes sounds audible through vibrations. Or maybe the word I'm thinking of is "electronics." We must look into it, for if I can read lips and then learn to talk, I won't be very different from other people, will I?

Those men who came to the Great House are still in the district, Jeff says. For a time I was afraid they would try to reach into my mind again, perhaps to find out from me where you are. I'm sure your brother is right about their being adept at some terrible form of mind control. But so far I have felt nothing.

Jeff thinks we can outwit them if we are patient. Sooner or later they will leave, he says, believing you have given them the slip. I pray it will be soon. I want so much to be with you again. Last evening I begged Jeff to let me go to you if only for a few hours, pointing out that I had been to the pools before and knew the way. But he said it would be too dangerous.

Take care of yourself, my love. Know that I love you with all my heart and am with you in my thoughts always.

Your Eve

36

In the Leggs' drawing room Mildred read a book she had borrowed from the small library in Morant Bay, where she had gone that afternoon to find something for Eve on how to read lips. There hadn't been a book on lipreading.

Jeff had the day's *Gleaner*, picked up at a shop in

Rainy Ridge on his way home from the coffee works, and after glancing at a headline about labor troubles on a sugar estate, he turned to a column by his favorite writer.

One of the finest newspapers in the West Indies, Jamaica's *Gleaner* had had a number of distinguished columnists over the years, and Matthew Grid—if that was his name—was one of the best. You could rely on him to tell you honestly what was going on in the island, and to fit the bits and pieces of the world's news together and explain what was happening out there, too.

Today the column was not about union disputes on Jamaican sugar estates, as Jeff thought it would be. It was not about Jamaica at all. Even for this unpredictable writer it was unusual.

I may pay with my life in some hideous fashion for writing this, but I must warn you, my readers, while there is time.

There is a mad monster loose in our unhappy world. His name is Aram Sel and he is the insane ruler of a Middle Eastern country called Siricus. There, I have said it. Dare you print it, Mr. Editor? If so, may God protect us from this creature's wrath.

Other madmen before him have exercised awesome power in this imperfect world, of course. I could name half a dozen quite easily, and so, I am sure, could most of you, my readers. Our problem with this one is that he has a compatriot, one Khargi—actually a cousin, I believe—who happens to possess the mental powers of the Devil. Working together, madman Aram Sel and Devil

Khargi may soon rule the world unless some country powerful and bold enough musters up the courage to eliminate them. This is perhaps too much to hope for, since Siricus supplies much-needed oil to those countries.

On the world news wires supplied to this newspaper over the past six months have appeared many items concerning this grisly pair. Oh, their names were not used in most instances, but never mind: their trademark was evident. Not necessarily in this order we have read of the following ghastly acts most probably committed by Aram Sel/Khargi's disciples. (Yes, that is what they call themselves: the Disciples. But there are many more than twelve of them.)

1. The poisoning of food and medicines on store shelves in London caused the agonizing death of more than 80 persons, including small children.

2. The poisoning of the water supply of the capital of a small country whose ruler dared to call Aram Sel a murderer resulted in the death of nearly 400, with many more still dying.

3. The destruction with explosives of a dam in a mountainous Asian country unleashed a raging flood upon unsuspecting villagers below and resulted in the death by drowning of more than 800. Many more are still missing. Property damage was staggering.

4. A bus in Norway carrying children to a Sunday school picnic plunged into a ravine after running over a land mine. All but three of its young passengers were killed.

5. One of India's renowned holy men, the guru Babananda, was made to destroy himself and his temple-school—a crime we can lay at Aram Sel's

door without any question because the guru told us even in death who was responsible.

I could go on and on. The list grows almost daily. Probably half the other acts of terrorism perpetrated upon civilized nations in the recent past were the work of Khargi's Disciples. Airplane hijackings, airport bombings, the seizure of a cruise ship in our own peaceful West Indian waters, the slaughter of innocents by masked machine gunners in supermarkets, the blowing up of trains, planes, embassies . . . if these monsters possessed nuclear weapons they would use those, too. Never doubt it.

The point is, my friends, they soon *may* possess such weapons if they are not stopped. A great evil is loose upon our planet, raging across it like a wind of war. We had better do something to halt it, and we had better do that something *now* before we run out of time.

"Milly," Jeff Legg said.

His wife looked up from her book.

"Milly, read this." He handed her the paper.

The only sound in the house while she read it was the tap-tapping of Mark's typewriter, being used by Eve at the dining room table. She was writing to her man at the cabin again, Jeff guessed.

Milly lowered the newspaper and looked at him, white as a sheet. "Oh my God, Jeff," she said.

He only nodded.

"Jeff," she said, "you'll have to take this to him!"

"I will. Though I don't believe it will surprise him much. He has a pretty good idea of what's going on."

In the other room Eve had stopped typing and

risen from her chair. Now she came to Jeff and held a sheet of paper out to him.

He'd been wrong; it was not a letter to Mark. What she had written was, "Would it be all right for me to go up to the village, do you think?"

Puzzled, he glanced at the clock atop the bookcase. The village, at quarter past eight in the evening?

Plucking a pencil from his shirt pocket, he scribbled on the same sheet of paper, "What on earth for?"

She took the pen from his fingers and replied, "I want something from the shop."

Something was wrong here, Jeff thought apprehensively. She knew she shouldn't be seen in the village.

"What shop, and what is it you want, Eve? I can get it for you."

Now *she* seemed puzzled by her behavior. Holding the sheet of paper in both hands, she stared wide-eyed at what they both had written, and suddenly began to tremble. Crumpling the paper into a ball, she let it fall to the carpet and, whirling, ran wildly through the dining room to her bedroom, where she slammed the door behind her.

Jeff turned to Milly and found her frowning at him. "Now, what was that all about?" she asked.

He retrieved the crumpled paper, smoothed it out, and handed it to her. She read it. "Jeff, you don't suppose—"

"I think you'd better talk to her."

"But they can't possibly know she is that close to him—can they?"

"We don't know what they know. We only know

what she's told us. About what happened in the restaurant that day, and how they got to her in the meadow when she and Mark escaped from the house." He stood up, knowing he was alarmed and, yes, frightened. He had never really understood what Eve said about the men who were after Mark. Until lately he would have frowned at the notion that one man's mind could control another's.

"See what you can find out, will you, Milly?"

Milly departed, leaving him alone with his anxiety. While waiting he paced the floor, switched the radio on, turned it off again, and strode to the dining room sideboard where he poured himself half a glass of rum—he, Jeff Legg, who almost never drank anything hard after dinner.

Glass in hand he walked out onto the veranda where the two bull terriers eyed him as though they sensed something wrong. There he peered out through the screen at the dark, silent yard.

It would not have surprised him at all to see something shadowy and sinister gliding toward him through the trees.

Milly was gone half an hour. Returning, she handed him sheets of paper covered with scribbling, and nudged him toward a chair.

"Read *that*," she said, and stood there gazing at him while he did so. When he finished, his hands were shaking.

The questions Milly had asked Eve were the ones he would have asked, though perhaps he would have phrased them differently, sticking more to the tune without the woman-to-woman accompaniment. No matter. Pieced together, the fragmented replies told him all he needed to know.

Something had happened to Eve while she was at the typewriter writing to Mark Donner. Something had happened to her mind—a mere whisper at first, then a kind of scratching, then a feeling that some large insect had bored through her skull and was doing things to her brain.

She had suddenly become obsessed with the idea that she must go up to the village and buy some cigarettes for Mark. He was out of cigarettes, he wanted some, he was relying on her to take him some. And she must buy them at the shop of the Chinaman, Mr. Yee. There were other small shops in Rainy Ridge, but she must go to Yee's.

It was like a command. Go to Yee's shop and buy cigarettes for Mark Donner and take them to him. Now. At once. Without fail!

Jeff looked at Mildred. "Mark doesn't smoke, you know."

"*I* know, but maybe they don't."

"His brother," Jeff suggested. "The brother they think they've run to earth here. Maybe he smokes."

"Yes, maybe Vin does."

"But Eve couldn't see what was being done to her? Even knowing Mark doesn't smoke?"

"Until she came and asked you if she could go," Milly said. "Do you see what she's written here? It was the way you answered her, the look in your eyes, that made her realize what was happening."

Needing time to get his thoughts together, Jeff peered at the scribblings again. "All right, we know what we're up against, at least. They've guessed she and Mark are friends. Maybe they found something at the Great House. They suspect she knows where he is. They'll be working on her. What should we do about it?"

"I think I ought to visit my sister in Sav-la-Mar and take Eve with me," Milly said. Savanna-la-Mar, in the western part of the island, was miles distant from this easternmost parish. "I've been promising Kim a visit, and now's the time for it." Still standing there before him, she jammed her fists against her hips. "Those men can't hang around here forever, Jeff. They'll have to give up sometime."

Would they? Jeff wondered dourly. The truth was, or seemed to be, that the men hunting Mark Donner were hard to convince. The one at Yee's house in the village had been joined by the bearded, scar-lipped Middle Eastern type from the restaurant; Jeff had seen both of them in the Chinaman's yard when driving home from the coffee works. And the other two appeared to be methodically working the Hegley side of the river, claiming to be friends of "Mr. Burke, the writer" and offering to pay anyone who would lead them to him.

But, of course, the four had not been in Jamaica such a long time, really. Not when you stopped to realize they must have followed Mark for weeks before coming here. They were not likely to pack up and go just yet.

So, yes, Milly ought to visit her sister in Sav-la-Mar and take Eve with her. It was no longer safe for Eve to stay here.

On the veranda the dogs were barking. Jeff went out and found McCoy in the yard. Fumbling a small square of stiff paper from his shirt pocket, the man handed it over.

"Busha, those two in Hegley did give this to Victor Henderson today, to prove they is true friends of Mr. Burke."

Jeff held it to the veranda light and saw that it was a photograph of Mark, a head-and-shoulders picture that might have been taken for a college yearbook. "Have they been giving out a lot of these?"

"This the only one I see personal, sah. But not everybody they talk to reports to me."

Jeff frowned long and hard at the photo. "I don't like this, Zekiel. Sooner or later someone from that side of the river, with no idea of what's going on, will go hunting pigs or pigeons up there at the pools and see Mr. Burke and lead these fellows to him."

"I is afraid of that, too, Busha."

"We can't just wait for things to go wrong. We've got to do something. But what can we do?"

They could, of course, move Mark out of there. But where would they find another hiding place half as good? The cabin was so ideal with the stream at hand and McCoy's fantastic "escape bridge" across the water slide if flight became necessary. And even though it was remote, either he or McCoy had managed to get up there every day.

"Busha, you will be going there tomorrow?"

"No. I've a big shipment of coffee to get out. Why?"

"It don't matter. Mr. Burke did ask me to bring him some nails, but he in no hurry, I expect. It better I go to Hegley and see what I can learn about this picture."

"I think so, Zekiel. Yes. Go to Hegley."

Raising a hand to the hat that was not there, Mc-Coy departed.

Inside, Jeff handed the photograph to Eve, scribbling on her pad to explain how it had come into his possession. Her face glowed as she studied the picture. It was the first one of Mark she had ever seen, he guessed.

But her glow faded after a moment, and a frown took its place. Rising, she carried the photo to a lamp to study it in better light, then violently shook her head and ran to her typewriter.

Puzzled, Jeff stood over her as she typed rapidly, "This is not Mark!"

He took up the photo and peered at it again.

"It is not!" she wrote. "It may look like him, but I *know*. It must be his brother."

Mildred came into the room at that moment and Jeff beckoned to her. Showing her the picture, he told how he had got it. Like Eve she held it close to a lamp to examine it. "She's right, Jeff. This is not Mark. Look at the eyes."

"It looks like Mark to me."

"It isn't. Any woman would know."

Jeff walked frowning to a chair and sat, aware of something in all this that was eluding him. Something that might be important. It continued to escape his understanding, though his mind labored back over all he knew, all Eve had told them, about Mark Donner's reason for coming to Jamaica and hiding out at Shepstowe.

The clatter of the typewriter disturbed him and he looked up. Eve's lips were pressed tight in concentration as she bent over the keys. Mildred stood beside her, reading the words as they appeared.

Mildred motioned to Jeff. He got up and went to her.

"This is monstrous," Eve had written. "It is obvious now that from the very beginning the man in Washington, Mr. Graham, has been lying to Mark." She had forcefully underlined the word "lying."

"Think about it!" the message continued. "He said Mark's brother, Vincent, was involved in secret work for the government and was in some terrible danger. Because they were twins and Mark could so easily be mistaken for Vincent, the danger might focus on Mark. So it was necessary for Mark, for his own safety, to leave home, leave the country, come here to Jamaica under an assumed name, and stay quiet in the old Shepstowe Great House until the danger was past or his brother's work was finished. And now think."

Still typing, Eve again backspaced to underline a word, this time "think." Then, trembling with emotion, she continued:

"To lessen the danger to Mark—to make him look less like his brother—he was to grow a beard. It was one of the reasons he had to stay so long in Mexico, perhaps the only reason—to grow a beard. And it was all a lie! Don't you see it was a lie? Because Mark's brother, Vincent, *had* a beard. He has one in this picture, which must have been taken before all this started."

Pausing, she looked up at the two who stood there beside her, waiting for more. Her face was almost empty of color, Jeff saw, so great was her anger or fear or whatever the emotion was that was tearing at her. And he, too, was beginning to feel an emotion that was close to being a physical thing, causing him to clench his teeth so tightly they ached from the pressure.

"What they did," Eve was pounding out in a fury, "was to make Mark look even MORE like his brother, EXACTLY like his brother"—she had shifted from underlining to capitals, as being faster and perhaps even more emphatic—"and there can be only one reason for it. They WANTED those people to pursue him.

"Don't you see?" she continued, biting her lip now. "They arranged the whole thing so Mark would be the hare in a dreadful game of hare and hounds, and if you ask me I think they probably betrayed him as well, making certain the Disciples would find out enough to follow him here. I don't mean they actually pinpointed Shepstowe as Mark's hiding place. They couldn't do that or the game would be over too soon. But I feel sure they must be responsible for the Disciples coming to Jamaica. Because, don't you see, Graham and his monsters WANTED those people to stay on Mark's trail, so Vin would be free to do whatever he's doing."

Again Eve looked up at Mildred and Jeff, her face glistening now with perspiration. "And now they want Mark to run again," she wrote. "Not because they care what happens to him, but to give his brother still more time. They don't want Mark to be CAUGHT, of course—you can see that, can't you? Followed, yes, they want him followed, but not caught because then the Disciples will discover he is not the man they are after. So Mark is supposed to keep on running, and he has refused to, and that's why Goodwin is so angry, isn't it? If Mark won't run

anymore, the whole monstrous scheme will col-
lapse."

Exhaling heavily, Eve leaned back, let her hands
drop to her sides, and again looked up at them,
awaiting their reaction. Jeff rubbed the leather of his
jaw and slowly shook his head. "My God," he said—
not to Milly, certainly not to the deaf girl at the
typewriter; just to vent his feelings.

Taking the paper to a chair, he sat for a time
studying it, then returned to the table and picked up
the photograph and studied that. There was a difference, he decided, and Mildred was right: it was in
the eyes. Those of the man in the photo were too res-
olute. Mark Donner was a gentler man.

Jeff reached for the pad. "You may be right, Eve,"
he wrote. "But I don't see how Mark can benefit
from knowing the truth now. Do you?"

She gazed into space for a moment, thinking, then
slowly shook her head. "I suppose not," she typed.
"Of course, he wouldn't feel Vincent was privy to all
this. Graham didn't even tell Vin where Mark had
been sent to; Vin had to find out for himself. Still,
you're right, I'm sure. To tell Mark about this now
would only add to his anguish. I believe we ought to
wait."

Only one thing could help Mark Donner now, Jeff
thought. That would be for his pursuers to be convinced somehow that he had escaped them and *was*
on the run again. If they believed that, they would
leave the district and at least waste some time trying
to pick up his trail.

But in the end—what? Did everything depend on

what brother Vincent might be able to accomplish in the States?

There was one other thing. He had been thinking about it ever since Eve had asked if she might go up to the village to buy some cigarettes. Waiting until Eve had gone to her room—just in case she might be able to read something from his lips—he put his hands on his wife's arms and turned Milly toward him.

"I'll be sleeping on the veranda tonight," he said gravely. "With the dogs."

"Why, Jeff?"

"Those people got to Eve once, about the cigarettes. If they try again to get her out of here, I want to be where I can stop her."

37

McCoy awoke in the dark. Without disturbing the woman beside him or the child asleep in the corner, he got out of bed and walked barefoot into the adjoining room. His clothes were there, and his shoes. He put them on and went outside, shivering in the nighttime chill.

Opening the gate which he had refused to open for Mark when the little girl was supposed to be ill, he walked up the dark path to a large mango tree where Victor Henderson awaited him.

Tall, sturdy, about McCoy's age, Henderson greeted him with a nod and handed him a small, flat bottle of white rum. McCoy drank and passed the bottle back.

"You ready, Victor?"

"I ready, Zekiel."

"We must have to take an oath on this, you know. Say after me now: I do swear by the Holy Bible—"

"I do swear by the Holy Bible—"

"That no matter what happen—"

"That no matter what happen—"

"I will never tell a soul—"

"I will never tell a soul—"

"What we do this day—"

"What we do this day—"

"So help me God."

"So help me God."

"All right. Remember to give me time enough now, Victor. Walk those two real slow, and take them the long way 'round. Plenty can happen to make me late at the bridge, and if you get there too soon and have to wait, they bound to be suspicious."

"Me understand. And Zekiel?"

"Uh?"

"You is sure Busha not walkin' up there this mornin'? Him mustn't know 'bout this!"

"Busha not goin' there this morning. I did ask him straight out." McCoy thrust out his hand. "All right, Victor. I gone."

They touched hands. Then McCoy hurried up the track to the wire fence where Mark had startled his woman when coming from the graves. After crawling through the fence, he climbed the slope to the Great House yard. It was the shortest way for one like himself who was used to darkness and rough going.

Without even a glance at the house he hurried up the driveway to the road and down the road past the coffee works, dark now except for lights at the cooper's shed and the powerhouse. Without turning his head even there, he continued on down to Rainy Ridge.

Except for a solitary dog sniffing at some garbage in front of the Chinaman's shop, the village slept at this hour. The dog fled with its tail between its legs as McCoy approached. Passing the shop, the Jamaican went quietly along a narrow lane beside it to a house in back. There he curled his heavy lips and made a hissing sound.

"Pssst!"

A slender, dark shape came quickly around a corner of the building, followed by a shorter, not so slender one. The first was the Chinese who, with the owner of the shop, had called upon Mark Donner at the Great House. The other was the bearded, scarlipped man Mark had seen in the Kingston restaurant.

"Two of you?" McCoy asked with a frown.

The Chinese shook his head. "Only one. But it will be this man, not I."

"What for you changing you plan?"

"Mr. Yee says the walk up the river would be difficult for me. My feet give me trouble. So this man will go with you in my place."

McCoy gave the second man a searching look and did not much like what he saw. Chinese people he was used to. Men with heavy black beards and scarred lips, no.

"Mr. McCoy," the Chinese said, "you will be paid the same for your services. What difference can it make to you?"

McCoy could not define the difference, but felt it. Still, he could not back down now without endangering Victor Henderson. "Well, all right," he grudgingly conceded.

"Thank you."

McCoy frowned at the bearded one. "You is ready?"

The man nodded.

"Come, then. Don't make no noise. Like how I did tell you friend here, most people thinks you is looking for Mr. Burke to do him some kind of harm. If they sees us, they will likely give us trouble."

Scar-lip only shrugged. When McCoy turned and walked out to the road, he followed in silence.

The dog was again sniffing at garbage in front of Yee's shop. Again it fled with its tail curled down and under.

At the coffee works McCoy turned up the driveway. Behind him Scar-lip hesitated, then halted. McCoy turned back.

"We must have to go through the yard here to get to the track. Is the shortest way. Besides, I must pick up a machete. I did forget to bring my one from home."

He had not forgotten, of course. Would he forget the very thing he needed most this morning? But he

307

had not wanted to have one in his hand when the Chinese first laid eyes on him, lest the man be suspicious.

"Is there no watchman here?"

"He asleep."

"Well, all right," Scar-lip said with a shrug.

McCoy led him to the powerhouse, where Busha kept a machete at all times to use in cleaning leaves from the turbine. Feeling better with the weapon in his hand, he then led his companion across the dark of the yard and turned along the track that wound through the meadow to the river.

At the river he allowed the man to rest a little. Daylight was still not near and they would have to descend to the fording in the dark. Leaning against a tree, McCoy scowled at his companion and said, "Mek me ask you once again—is you truly a friend of Mr. Burke?"

"Of course."

"I got to be certain. Mr. Burke a good man. I would not want no harm to come to him."

"He is a very good man but sick here." Scar-lip tapped his temple with a forefinger. "It makes him do strange things at times, like running away from Shepstowe when there was no need to."

"Well, if you sure. I just hope I is not making trouble for him by taking you there."

"On the contrary, you will be helping him. Believe me."

Facing the descent to the stream, the bearded man did not show the trepidation McCoy had expected. A bad sign, for it could make things harder later. McCoy went down the cliff first and turned to watch him, hoping he would fall. He did not fall.

Again, while crossing the stream in the dark, McCoy hoped for an accident. The stones were slippery and all but invisible. The river rushed around and over them with a roar that shattered the forest stillness. But Scar-lip did not slip.

"How far is this place?" the bearded one demanded on reaching the other side.

"Like how I did warn the Chinaman, it plenty far."

The man made sounds of displeasure. But later when the first haze of daylight filtered through the forest gloom, he seemed less annoyed and even urged McCoy to set a faster pace.

Good, McCoy thought. If I can weary him some, the job will be easier.

They neared the place where a cliff towered greenish black on one side and a sheer drop yawned on the other. High above the river, the track made an abrupt turn there and was but a yard wide.

McCoy had slyly lengthened his stride and was well in the lead. He rounded the bend before the man behind him reached it. Hidden from view, he flattened himself against the wall and swung his machete up for the single slashing stroke that would either kill Scar-lip outright or send him hurtling with a half-severed head into the wild white water below.

But the crunch of approaching footfalls suddenly ceased. There came a puzzling silence, disturbed only by the muffled roar of the river. And then a voice.

"Is this where you plan to kill me, McCoy?"

McCoy sucked in a breath.

"Sorry," the voice continued, "but I do not choose to die here. Or anywhere else. Put down your machete, please."

Step out and strike at him! McCoy silently screamed at himself. *Him is on the ledge; there is no way him can escape! Do it, man, do it!* But something had happened to his will. He could not move except to obey the command. Like a robot being manipulated by one he could not even see, he lowered his right hand and let the weapon fall. Its heavy metal blade made a clanging sound on the stone.

"Now kneel," the voice said.

McCoy knelt, not knowing why he had to. Never before had he felt he must do something just because someone told him to. It was as though a huge, powerful hand had him by the throat and was forcing him down, filling his head with pain. Never before had he felt such pain—not even that long-ago day when he fell from the top of a breadfruit tree and ended up in the Princess Margaret Hospital with a fractured skull.

Kneeling there, he heard footsteps again. The bearded man came around the bend of the track and halted before him, gazing down at him. Not afraid of me, McCoy thought. Not afraid of me at all.

"So you thought to kill me," the man said. "Amusing. You, a stupid peasant, daring to think you could destroy Khargi. Why?" And McCoy felt the grip on his mind ease a little so he could reply.

"You is not a friend of Mr. Burke," McCoy mumbled. "You is out to harm him."

"Interesting." Coming a step closer, the man who called himself Khargi reached down and picked up the machete. "And do you know something, my Jamaican friend? With your peasant mind you almost *succeeded* in killing me."

310

McCoy only stared. His head was full of hammers again, as if he had stupidly swallowed a big gulp of overproof white rum straight from the bottle.

Holding the machete in his right hand now, Khargi tested the edge of its blade with his left thumb and made a face. "M'm," he said. "This is like a razor, isn't it? You would have taken my head off. Was that your intent?"

McCoy remained silent.

"Answer, please. I am curious. Did you mean to behead me?"

"Or knock you off the track," McCoy mumbled.

"The reason I have to ask—your mind didn't tell me just how you were planning to dispose of me. Only that you meant to do it. And the reason you nearly succeeded, my peasant friend, is that you did not begin to think about it until we were approaching this place."

"You—was reading my mind?"

"What there was of it to read. Actually, at Mr. Yee's house in the village you were thinking of a dog, wondering who its owner was. And at the coffee works, when you took up the machete, your only concern was whether someone named Busha would think it had been stolen."

McCoy's stare became one of amazement. It was all true what this man was saying!

"Then at the river crossing," Khargi continued calmly, "your thoughts were of me but not yet of killing me. You were hoping first that I might fall from the cliff and injure myself, and then that I might slip on the stones and fall into the stream."

He smiled. "But then as you neared this place and

311

quickened your pace to get ahead of me, your mind betrayed you. It began thinking about *how* you would murder me—how you would hold the machete, how you would strike with it in such a way that I would fall from the track, either dead or mortally wounded, into the river down there. Am I not correct?"

McCoy slowly nodded.

"And now what should I do with you, do you think? Kill *you* to even the score?"

"If you likes." McCoy heard the words and wondered about them. Were they his, or had they been put into his head by his tormentor? Still on his knees, he gazed at the machete in the other's hand and felt a film of sweat break out on his face.

A couple of years ago a man in Mango Gut, out of his mind from smoking ganja, had run amuck with a machete and chopped a neighbor, all but severing the man's head from his body. McCoy had wondered then how the victim felt when it happened. Now he wondered how *he* would feel if executed that way by the man standing before him.

The sweat dribbled down his face and he felt his tongue swelling to fill his mouth. But there was nothing he could do to help himself. He could not even rise. The thing controlling his mind would not let him.

38

Eve Vernon opened her eyes and looked at the clock on the table beside her bed. Her room at the Leggs' was dark, but the luminous hands of the clock told her daylight would soon come.

She sat up, listening. The house was still. Her head was not equally still, though. A voice inside it was commanding her to do something.

"Get up. Get dressed. You are to go to Mr. Yee's shop for cigarettes and take them to Donner. He wants them. He must have them. Do you hear? You are to go to Mr. Yee's shop for cigarettes and take them to Donner wherever he is. Now. But first write a note for the Leggs and leave it in your bedroom where they will find it. Tell them you do not wish to make trouble for them any longer and are going home. Write it now on your pad of paper. Do this!"

The voice was not loud. In fact it seemed to be no louder than the droning of an insect. But as it droned on, repeating the same commands over and over, it became hypnotic.

Sliding silently out of bed, Eve exchanged her nightgown for the pale blue blouse and tan skirt on the chair near the bed. She reached under the chair for her sneakers and put those on. Then on her pad, which she had used in talking to Mildred before retiring, she wrote what she had been told to write.

"Dear Milly and Jeff, I have caused you enough trouble and feel I must leave. Please don't be angry. I will just go to my own place in Trinity until all this is over. When I think of how I almost went up to Rainy Ridge last night, I am too frightened to stay here, anyway. With love, Eve."

They would think she had walked home from here. It was only a few miles. Everybody in rural Jamaica walked, all the time.

The house had a back door off the kitchen. She went that way. And knowing the dogs would be on the veranda, sensitive to any sound of footsteps, she avoided the driveway and reached the road by going through Jeff's acre of Blue Mountain coffee trees.

Dawn was just breaking when she reached Rainy Ridge, but the door of the Chinaman's shop was open and a lantern over the counter was lit. Mr. Yee always opened his doors at an early hour to catch the farmer folk on their way to work far-off grounds. When she walked in, he stood behind the counter and showed his oversized teeth in his usual smile of welcome.

"Ah, good morning, Miss Vernon." As if she could hear! "What I can do for you so early?"

She handed him a slip of paper on which she had written, "Two packs of Albanys, please."

He put them on the counter.

Nodding her thanks, she paid him and put the cigarettes in a pocket of her skirt, then hurried out and turned up the road toward the coffee works.

Yee yanked open a door behind his counter, crossed the cluttered stockroom beyond, and opened a second door leading out to his yard. Having crossed the yard to his house in a dozen long strides, he yanked open a door there.

"She came!" he hissed.

Appearing from an inner room, the man who had worn white when calling on Mark at the Great House was now dressed all in black. "Which way did she go?"

Yee told him.

The man shoved Yee aside and rushed out.

Returning to his shop, Yee pondered the puzzling sequence of happenings. First, he had been told to expect a visit from Miss Vernon last evening, not this morning. His two guests had told him that—first his son's Chinese friend from New York, and then the bearded, scar-lipped man who had joined that one yesterday afternoon.

Miss Vernon would come, they had said, to buy cigarettes for her friend Peter Burke, and would take them to Burke at the place where he was hiding. That, no doubt, was somewhere not too distant.

At that time the two men would be waiting at the house to follow Miss Vernon. And for this special service Yee would be well paid, just as he was being paid to provide his guests with a room in his house until this affair was finished. Not that he would have demanded payment for such a service—after all, the New York stranger was a friend of his son's, and the bearded man was a friend of *his*. Also, he had his own secret reason for wanting Mr. Burke removed from Shepstowe.

But Miss Vernon had not come last evening, and the two men had been greatly annoyed. He had overheard the bearded one saying that now they would have to rely on a backup plan involving stupid Jamaican peasants. And being on the alert because of this, he had in fact seen a Mango Gut man, Zekiel McCoy, come a while ago in the dark and talk to the two, and then go off with the bearded one.

It was a little too much for an honorable Chinese shopkeeper, Yee decided. But if it ended with Mr. Burke's being banished from Shepstowe, he would be well satisfied.

As the shopkeeper took a tin of lichees off one of the shelves for his breakfast, Eve Vernon trudged along the track from the meadow to the river, mechanically placing one foot in front of the other as though drugged.

Her destination was the cabin at the pools.

Not far behind, picking up scattered fragments of her confused thoughts, trudged the "New Yorker" who had not known what "Be my guest" meant when calling on Mark at the Great House.

To keep from being bored with this simplest of assignments, he reviewed in his mind the sequence of events that had brought him to Jamaica.

1. A fellow Disciple named Kalim had been caught by Khargi's number one target, Vincent Donner, while trying to poison food at a restaurant in Mexico City. Kalim escaped but criminally failed to destroy Donner and was subsequently punished. He still lived, but as a vegetable.

2. Vincent Donner left Mexico but soon returned—a foolish move—and other Disciples working there spotted him. Convinced that Argus was about to establish a headquarters outside the United States, in case their U.S. base was discovered, Khargi ordered two Disciples, the defector priest from Brazil and the voodoo priest from Haiti, to trail him. They did so to Jamaica, where he again did a foolish thing, making such a scene at Kingston airport about leaving the island that anyone with sense would know he had *not* left.

3. Convinced that Donner had walked from the airport to some secret destination, so as to leave no trail that could be picked up and followed, the two Disciples had studied a map of the eastern end of the island, marked off all likely sites for the setting up of a headquarters, and begun to check them out.

In Rainy Ridge they were told that an American writer had recently taken up residence at Shepstowe Great House. Something? Perhaps. The Haitian stopped at the house on the pretext of having lost his way. Was the man Donner? He could be. Someone with more authority would have to decide. Meanwhile, the former priest, seeking information, had talked to the proprietor of a Chinese shop in the village and learned among other things that he was uncommonly proud of having a son at a New York art school.

Enter Ling Gan, now trailing a stupid woman through a mountain meadow.

He, Ling Gan, had never seen New York, but had been summoned by Khargi from training in Siricus to appear in Jamaica as a New York friend of Mr. Yee's son, about whom he was supplied with detailed information. Yee believed the lie and made him welcome. Now the Disciples had a convenient base, and with all preparations complete, Khargi himself arrived for the kill, or rather the capture. For Donner must now be taken alive; it would not do to kill him. His organization, Argus, had become dangerous. He must be forced to identify all in it so they, too, could be eliminated before the strikes against the U.S. began.

Also, Donner must be taken by Khargi. It was a point of pride with the Great One.

I could have taken him myself the day I called on him with Yee, Ling Gan thought sadly. But no, I am too insignificant. So when we did go for him he was on guard, and he escaped.

Now again I am nothing as I follow this woman to his hiding place, because the timing has gone wrong and Khargi will get there first.

39

Jeff Legg awoke on his veranda and walked into the house, followed by his two bull terriers. Mildred was in the kitchen making breakfast. Yawning, he stretched both arms over his head.

"Stiff?" Mildred said.

"A little, but I slept some. Is she all right?"

"Her door is still closed. Poor thing, I'm not going to wake her. Let her sleep it off."

Jeff ate his breakfast and drove up to the coffee works. As he neared the Chinaman's shop in the village he saw its proprietor slouching in the doorway. Grinning a toothy grin, Yee lifted a limp hand in salute as the pickup passed.

The first hour at the coffee works was uneventful. The workers had promised to come early and most of them did. But while crossing the yard to the cooper's shed about an hour after his arrival, Jeff saw a car climb past the factory drive on its way to the Great House.

Now, who would be going there at this hour? he wondered. Someone looking for Mark Donner? Or Eve? Someone just interested in old Jamaican Great Houses? There'd been a few of those. Tourists, mainly. But not this early in the morning.

Anyway, as custodian of the house he was covered. With the place empty and locked up now, he had tacked a note on the door: "For information, see Mr. Legg at the coffee works." Anyone interested would look for him here.

He was back in his office when the same car pulled into the yard and its driver got out. Peering through the office window, Jeff scowled at what he saw. Mark Donner? Here? In a car? What was going on?

He hurried outside, all but colliding with his caller. They stopped only inches apart, both staring. Jeff spoke first.

"You've got to be Vin Donner."

"I am. And you're Jeff Legg."

They shook hands.

Jeff had to agree with Milly and Eve: there was a difference in the eyes. But he saw precious little else by which Mark and his brother could be told apart.

"Thanks for the note on the Great House door," Vin said. "But if it hadn't been there or you hadn't been here, I'd still have found you. Mark's written about you fondly in his letters. I'm sure everyone knows you."

"How did you get here?" Jeff was really puzzled about that. "There's no plane in from Miami at this—"

"One of our Argus pilots flew me here. Phoned ahead for an embassy man to meet me with an unmarked car."

"Does your man Goodwin know?"

A look of long-felt anger changed the shape of Vin Donner's face. "No, and I don't intend him to." Even Vin's voice had changed. "He's not 'my man,' Jeff. He's Graham's man, and I want no part of the bastard. Let's just say I'm here—an Argus plane brought me here—but I still have a score to settle with those sons in Washington."

Jeff decided he liked the man, and nodded approval. "We'd better go inside. Workers may see you out here and think you're Mark."

They went into the office, but Vin was obviously too impatient to sit. Pacing, he said, "Where is he, Jeff? Is he safe?"

"He's at a sawyers' cabin in the bush. And, yes, we think he's safe enough. For now, anyway. But you'll want to go to him, of course. Damn." Jeff was thinking of the coffee order. "Maybe I can have one of my men . . . No, no, I can't do that to Mark. I'll take you myself." He reached into a desk drawer for paper and an envelope. "Just let me write my wife a note, so she'll know."

With Vin watching he quickly scribbled, "Mark's brother is here, Milly. I've got to take him to the cabin, so if I'm late home, don't fret." Sealing the envelope, he stepped to the door. "Be right back," he said to Vin. "Better put your car behind the office here, where it won't be seen from the road."

Soon afterward a young factory hand named Manny went trotting down the coffee-works drive on his way to deliver Jeff's note to Mildred.

And soon after that, Jeff departed with Vin Donner for the cabin at the pools.

At the Leggs' house, Mildred came from Eve's room with a frown on her face. In one hand was the pad on which Eve had written her letter of farewell.

Tearing the page off, Mildred stood at the kitchen counter and began a note to Jeff. Then she remembered having heard the yard boy whistling a moment ago. It was he who would have to carry the note *to* Jeff, so she walked out on the veranda to look for him.

He was raking up red and gold almond leaves at the end of the yard.

"Bobbsie! Come here, will you, please?"

He trotted over with the rake on his shoulder.

"Don't go away, now, Bobbsie. I want you to carry a message to Busha at the coffee works."

"Yes, ma'am."

She went back to finish the message, then read it over. "Jeff, dear, I just went into Eve's room to see if she was all right, and she isn't here. To leave during the night without disturbing the dogs, she must have

321

gone out the back way. She left this note I'm sending you. I don't suppose there is anything much to worry about, but thought you should know."

When she carried the sealed envelope to the veranda, the yard boy was waiting. But Jeff's messenger from the factory was coming along the drive just then and saw her. "Wait, ma'am!" he called, waving another white envelope. "Me have a letter from Busha!"

She read Jeff's note. "Well," she said, "it seems this is a morning for sending messages back and forth, isn't it? All right, Manny. I've already written to Busha but just let me add something in answer to this." With the pen she was still holding she wrote on her own envelope, "Yours rec'd and noted. Here's one from me. Be careful."

Handing her envelope to the coffee-works man, she said, "Now hurry back with this, won't you, Manny. See if you can catch him."

But when Manny arrived back at the factory, Jeff Legg and Vin Donner were already long gone.

40

Brandishing McCoy's machete, the bearded man with the scarred lip gazed down at McCoy, kneeling before him.

"We have an interesting situation here, my

friend," he said. "Had Mr. Burke's Miss Vernon done what she was told to do last evening, you would not now be here in your present predicament. Actually you were only our backup plan. We hoped to use the woman as a guide."

He shrugged. "However, for some reason Miss Vernon did not obey my instructions. So if it will give you any solace, you can blame her for what is to happen to you."

Reaching out, he touched McCoy on the head. "Look at me, please, and answer a few questions before I decide what to do with you. First, what about my two associates? If you remember, you said we would be meeting them. You do remember, don't you?"

"Yes, sah," McCoy mumbled.

"Good. Sometimes the mind goes totally blank when pressured. Had you planned to kill them, too?"

Facing execution, McCoy was too frightened to find his voice.

"Come, come!" Khargi did not have unlimited patience, it seemed. "I can cause you to think about it and read your thoughts, but why should I expend that much effort? Tell me!"

"Tell you what, sah?"

"About the two from Hegley! Your friend Henderson was to guide them up that side of the river."

There was a slight easing of the terrible pain in McCoy's head, permitting his mind to function better. "Yes, sah, that right."

"You told me we would meet them near our destination. But you were lying because you really meant to kill me here. What *was* your plan for my associates?"

"Victor was to lead them to the bridge at Three River Mouth."

"And?"

"After I did take care of you here, I was to go up there on this side and wait for them. When I did hear them coming, I was to give him a signal to let him know I ready."

"Really?" A smile crawled in Khargi's beard. Perhaps he had little respect for Jamaican plotters and considered their efforts childish. "What kind of signal?"

McCoy pursed his lips and whistled a flute note that soared high and clear above the muted roar of the stream.

"And what is that?"

"A solitaire bird, sah."

"I see. And with it you were to inform Henderson, on the far side of the bridge, that you were in position on this side, waiting. Then what?"

"He was to lead them two across the bridge."

"Which is high above the gorge there?"

"Yes, sah."

"And something was to happen to my friends while they were crossing it?"

McCoy licked his lips to stop their quivering. The more he confessed, the more certain he was to be killed. He ought not to be talking at all. But when this man with the crawly smile commanded you to do something, you did it.

"Well, sah . . . when they halfway across, Victor was to run the rest of the way to where me waiting. Then I—then—" *Don't say it*, McCoy warned himself.

"Then you what?"

"I was to chop the rope that hold the bridge up."

"Sending my people to their death in the gorge below?"

"Yes, sah."

"Get up," Khargi ordered.

McCoy wagged his head. "No, sah. Go ahead 'n' kill me. Get it over with."

"I wish to join my friends at the bridge, McCoy. And if we waste any more time here, we may be late getting there."

"Uh?"

"Get up! Take me there!"

Bewildered, but feeling like a man granted a stay of execution while standing on the scaffold, McCoy pushed himself erect. With a mumbled "All right" he went trudging up the track.

Khargi followed a few yards behind and was implacably there with the machete every time the Jamaican turned his head to look back. But the weapon was not the real threat, McCoy knew. That lay in the man's eyes, or in something behind them.

It was not total control such as had been used on him before, though. Perhaps that required more effort than Khargi now wished to put forth. He could still wonder, for instance, why he did not turn and challenge the man. After all, he was physically bigger and more powerful; it should be easy for him to overcome such an adversary, machete or no. But while he could think about it, another part of his mind would not let him put the thought into action. He had been told to guide the man to Three River Mouth. So be it.

They came to the pools and McCoy held his breath lest the man look into the shadows upstream and see the cabin. It did not happen. They crossed the stream at the pools and began climbing. Maybe here Scar-lip would have to concentrate so hard on where to put his feet, he would become vulnerable. But that did not happen, either.

A little farther on, though, from a brief stretch of high-up track where the sawyers had cleared away parts of the slope, the cabin was in full view. There was nothing McCoy could do about it; Khargi had only to look down.

But, thank God, the yard was empty and the place looked long abandoned.

Khargi did see it. He did say, "What is that down there?" But, ready for the question, McCoy was able to mumble in reply, "It nuttin', sah, just a old sawyers' shelter, like how you can see they was cutting trees here." And the reply was accepted.

Even a man with this one's awesome powers could become careless for a moment, it seemed.

They went on through the silence. On along the track, with McCoy knowing he was about to be killed and only wondering how. On to the place where the three waterfalls met at the bottom of the great curving cliff to form the single stream they had been following. A muffled thunder forced McCoy to shout as he raised an arm to point. "There the bridge is. Up there."

"Take me to it."

McCoy toiled up the track he had created when building the bridge with Peter Burke, again hoping the climb would be too much for his companion. But again the fellow was surprisingly strong and agile, and stayed close behind.

I could turn and tackle him, McCoy thought. Both

of us would go crashing down to the river, maybe, but at least I wouldn't die alone. The thought fled from his mind at once, though, and its flight left his mind a blank.

Both were out of breath when they reached the bridge at last, but Khargi no more so than the Jamaican. With a hand on the vertical strand of rope that held this end of the span in place, McCoy looked down. The sheet of water gliding down the cliffside, its edge almost within reach, exploded into spray among the boulders of the streambed below. The height had not affected him when he was building the bridge. It terrified him now.

"Sound your signal," Khargi instructed.

The flutelike call of the solitaire trilled from McCoy's lips. He and Victor Henderson had chosen that particular call because it was high enough, pure enough, to be heard above the thunder of falling water.

There was no answer.

"Them don't come as yet, sah."

Khargi shrugged. "So we wait."

41

Mark finished his bath and stood at the edge of the pool, waist-deep in cold, clear water. His mirror from the cabin, a small one in a cheap white plastic frame, was propped against a stone on the rock shelf in front of him. With razor and scissors he patiently trimmed the beard he had been forced to grow.

He was not fond of the beard. From the very beginning it had bothered him. The first thing I do when this nightmare ends—if it ever does end—will be to get rid of the damned thing, he promised himself.

Climbing out of the pool, he dried himself, picked up his things, and walked to the cabin. Sunlight gilded the clearing now, warming him in spirit and melting away some of his fears. Not all of them, of course. There was still a nagging anxiety, for instance, that Eve might reveal his whereabouts to the Disciples. Not for a moment had he been able to forget how determinedly she had urged him to return to the Great House the night they were nearly trapped there.

Would the Disciples find out she was staying with Jeff and Mildred? If they did, would they be able to work on her mind again?

Entering the cabin, he took his time getting dressed—why hurry when he had the whole day ahead of him and was going nowhere, anyway?— then went to the table and took stock of what supplies he had left. Before bathing he had searched the river for crayfish but, finding only two, had put them back into the water. For breakfast now he had a choice of canned corned beef or what was left of a box of pancake mix. The two remaining eggs would do for lunch and supper. In addition he had some yellow raspberries he had gathered and a loaf of hard-dough bread.

McCoy would come today with more food, though. The man had become a real friend.

Going out to his stone fireplace at the side of the cabin, Mark got a fire started, then returned to mix the pancake batter. *Was* there a possibility the Disciples would be able to force Eve to disclose his whereabouts? The thought was like one of the pesky deerflies that infested the clearing, everlastingly darting at him. Unlike the deerflies, it couldn't be slapped dead.

As he ate breakfast he thought of what Eve had written about evil. Not precisely about the evil of the Disciples, as described in the letters from Vin, but evil in general.

That of ignorance, for instance. The Mango Gut kind of ignorance, exemplified by the peasants' willingness—almost eagerness—to follow the leadership of McCoy's woman. That kind was primitive and frightening, and so often led to violent injustice.

"But the evil of intelligent men is worse," Eve had written. Such as the Disciples, who were not only *more* learned than most but had elected evil as a way of life.

As a teacher he could see a distant hope of uplifting the merely ignorant. But he saw no hope at all of curbing the wickedness of learned men who actually worshipped evil.

A cry from the direction of the river broke into his morbid thoughts, causing him to jerk his head up. It came again, hoarse with pain or terror. Lurching to his feet, he ran to the door.

At the door he paused, remembering Jeff Legg's rifle. It should have been leaning in its usual corner, but was not. Damn. This morning at daybreak he had climbed the cliff across the river to pick raspberries and in hope of seeing the baby mongooses at the felled tree again. He had taken the weapon with him and must have left it there.

Nothing could be done about it now. Telling himself he ought to have his head examined, he hurried out into the clearing. Hearing a groaning noise, he went warily toward it, peering through the undergrowth as he advanced.

A man knelt there near the edge of the stream.

At Mark's approach he looked up in apparent terror, struggled to rise, fell back. His right knee was caught in the jaws of a trap. Blood darkened the torn leg of his trousers.

He was the pig hunter, Iron, the brother of McCoy's woman.

Mark continued his cautious advance until the youth cringed as though expecting a blow. "No." Mark shook his head. "Don't move. Be still."

The trap was ancient and rusty. It was a pig trap, he supposed. To spread its ugly jaws required all his strength, and when he let it go after removing it from the boy's leg, it snapped shut with a finality that made him wince. Tossing it aside, he said harshly, "Can you walk?"

Iron cringed again.

"Come on, try it." Mark took him under the arms and lifted him. "You can't stay here and bleed to death."

With his help the youth was able to hobble to the cabin, where Mark lowered him onto the bed and examined him. Fear still filled the watching eyes as he eased away the bloody pant leg.

"I'll have to wash this." There was water in a bucket under the table; he reached for it. "What were you doing out there with a trap, anyway? Who were you setting it for?"

No answer.

Mark dipped a towel in water and cleaned the mangled knee. It was beginning to swell. The trap's rusty jaws had bitten through the skin and flesh to touch bone. Perhaps the bone itself was cracked. He should have heated the water, he supposed, but that would have taken so much time. In any case, McCoy would be here soon.

He went to an otherwise empty carton and took out a bottle of rum Jeff had sent. Wanting to be at his best if suddenly faced with an emergency, he had not opened it. Twisting the cap off now, he handed the bottle to the boy and watched him drink until it was a third empty. Then he took it from Iron's hand and put it on the table.

With strips cut from a towel he did his best to bandage the knee. "I suppose the trap was meant for me."

Iron said nothing, but his eyes were beginning to lose their animal fear. As he watched Mark's struggle to stop the flow of blood, his face filled with bewilderment.

"Why?" Mark demanded. "Because I stopped you from molesting Miss Eve?"

Still no answer.

"You should be glad I stopped you. If you'd succeeded with her, you would be in serious trouble now, probably in prison. I saved you from that. Hunting wild pigs may not be an easy way to live, but it's better than hard labor in jail."

"He say I must kill you," Iron said suddenly.

"What are you talking about? Who said?"

"The Chinaman."

"What Chinaman?"

"The shopkeeper. Mr. Yee."

Mark stopped working on the leg and frowned at him. "The fellow in Rainy Ridge?"

The youth nodded.

"You've been taking orders from *him*? I don't understand."

Iron hesitated, then slowly, almost regretfully, said, "My sister work for him, sah."

"Your sister? Zekiel's woman?"

"Yes, sah."

"I still don't understand." Did Zekiel's woman work at Yee's shop? It was possible, of course. Even in a shop that small the man probably had to have help at times. But was that the kind of "work" Iron was talking about?

Suddenly the youth said, "Mr. Yee did see Merlinda come from the Great House on Christmas Day, Marse Burke. He did tell my sister we must make people know she is sick from poison you did give her. What she have is a bellyache from candy *he* did give her hisself!"

Mark took in a breath. When told about the candy, he had assumed it was the Mango Gut shopkeeper who had given it to Merlinda. Jeff had thought so, too, no doubt. This made a difference.

"Why, Iron? Why was Mr. Yee using your sister against me? Why does he want me out of Shepstowe?"

The boy on the bed would not answer.

"But he did tell you to kill me?" Mark persisted. "He sent you here to do that?"

"Him and the other one."

"The other Chinese, you mean? The one staying at Yee's house?"

"Not him. The man from Kingston."

"What are you talking about, Iron? What the *hell* are you talking about?"

Iron moved his shoulders in what could have been a shrug. "Him with the yellow hair. He say I must kill you because I have to live in the bush now like the pigs them live, and it all your fault. He did talk to me in Hegley, in him car."

Mark was too stunned to think of a reply.

"I tell him I is expecting to look for you soon, anyway, because the Chinaman tell me to, and he say I must do it right away. He tell me you is here at the cabin."

Numb with shock, Mark thought: *Goodwin? But why?* And could Iron be believed? "What else did this man tell you?"

"He say you have a gun and I must take care. Is better I catch you in a trap. Then it will look like how it was an accident."

"So *two* people have instructed you to kill me? But why, man, why?"

Again Iron shrugged. "I don't know 'bout the yellow-hair man, sah. But Mr. Yee want you dead because him have a big planting of ganja on the Shepstowe property above here."

"What?"

"It true. I see it lots of times when I go hunting pig up there. A big, big planting. And I know for a fact

333

him already been paid for most of it but have to get it harvested now and trucked out of here. And with you at the Great House, exploring around like how you do, him can't do that."

Ganja and Goodwin, Mark thought. My God. Was Our Man in Jamaica involved with Yee in a marijuana operation? No, no, he took his orders from Graham in Washington, and there couldn't possibly be a connection.

Unable to think straight, he got up to close the cabin door, then walked back to the bed. "How do you feel?"

"You goin' turn me in to the police, Marse Burke?"

Mark gazed down at him. "I don't know. What about Miss Eve? Were you told to kill her, too?"

"Huh?"

"Miss Eve! Did the Chinaman or the man with yellow hair tell you to get rid of her, too?" Mark's voice had acquired an edge.

Iron wagged his head. "Oh no, sah. I see her just a while ago and she not in no trouble. She fine."

"You've seen her this morning? Where?"

"Down below here on the river track. And I don't never go near her, I swear." Raising himself on an elbow, the boy suddenly seemed terrified again. "*Is* you goin' tell the police 'bout me, sah?"

"No," Mark said, turning away. This was the greater evil that Eve had written about, wasn't it? The schemers using the ignorant little people for their own wicked ends.

"You don't mad at me, Marse Burke?"

"I'm not mad at you. When Zekiel gets here, he can carry you out to a doctor. Look, Iron—I've got to leave you now." Mark was already at the door. "I have to find Miss Eve!"

42

Ling Gan was bored and disgusted. Following a stupid woman along a West Indian mountain trail that seemed to have no ending was not his idea of excitement. Was this to be his reward for having given up a life of adventure in China to join the great Khargi's band of terrorists?

From the very start of this project he had loathed his assigned role in it. He, a master of the martial arts, must pretend to be a friend of the son of an ignorant Jamaican Chinese? And must go with Yee to call on Vincent Donner at the Great House, while forbidden by Khargi to make any move there, even if certain the man was Donner?

It was humiliating. And now *this* insulting assignment.

For half an eternity he had skulked along behind this deaf-and-dumb woman who was unwittingly leading him to Donner's hideout. For what? Khargi and the others were far ahead of him and would make their move before he ever got there. He would have no part in the action.

Didn't they know, damn them, that he could kill a man with a single chop of one hand?

Still, he had better be less morose and more careful. The trail had turned away from the river now, to curl through deep green shade under close-together tall trees. The woman he followed had vanished!

Ling Gan lengthened his stride.

Suddenly from the hidden trail ahead came a sound of someone falling. Then silence. Then stumbling footfalls and a sound of falling again.

Ling Gan halted. A frown fastened on his face. When he moved again he went forward one slow step at a time, making no more noise than he would have made back in China when closing in on a victim to be slain and robbed. His hands led the way, slowly curling and uncurling in front of him.

The path bent to the left. He followed it. Then he halted a second time.

No more than twenty feet from him, the woman sat on a fallen tree at the track's edge, leaning forward to massage her right ankle. She must have turned it—a thing all too easy to do here. But she did not appear to be badly hurt.

Very well, wait. There was no hurry. As he had told himself before, Khargi and the others would have all the excitement, anyway. "Stay here at Yee's," Khargi had instructed. "If the girl does come, follow her. Just as a precaution, you understand, in case I meet with some trouble." So all right, he would wait with patience until the woman resumed her journey, then follow her again. Maybe as a reward his next assignment would be less tedious.

But wait. What was happening here? Was he to have a little excitement, after all?

He was hearing footsteps in this quiet place, and neither he nor the woman was making them. Someone was approaching from the direction in which the woman had been leading him. Suddenly a hurrying figure lurched into view just beyond where she sat.

She lifted her head. She saw the man and eagerly waved. The man came running to her side.

Ling Gan was seized by the same elation he had so often enjoyed in China when an intended victim came in sight. For the man was the very one he and the others had been sent here to capture, question, and kill! Khargi had not got to him first, after all!

Leaning over the woman, Donner took her face in his hands and looked at her. Probably with joy at having found her, since she was surely more than his housekeeper. He sank onto the log beside her and held her in his arms.

In a moment he produced a pad of paper and began writing. It was their way of talking. They would have a conversation. It would take some time.

Time enough.

In motion again, Ling Gan slipped like a shadow into a clump of trees to his left, where the shade was dense enough to have concealed an elephant. Stealth was second nature to him. Gliding from tree to tree, he worked his way swiftly through the forest until he was behind the two on the log.

They were still talking to each other by writing on the pad, totally preoccupied with their exchange of words. Excellent. He could, of course, resort to the mind control taught him at Khargi's base in Siricus. He could command them to rise and come to him, or simply to sit there without moving until he reached them. But he preferred his own methods.

Silently he ghosted forward, both hands outstretched and fingers twitching. He would not use the chop; Khargi would be furious if he killed the man or even badly hurt him. It must be a clean, quick capture of both man and woman, a grip on the throat that would render each unconscious for a time while leaving them unharmed for Khargi to deal with later.

While stealing up on them he silently counted off the distance between their necks and his hands. Six feet, five feet, four . . .

Suddenly for no apparent reason the man came violently to life and bore the woman to the ground with him in a headlong dive from the log.

In the deep green shadows beyond them a gun spoke, then spoke again, shattering the silence with twin claps of thunder.

Ling Gan halted in his tracks with a look of astonishment on his face. Before falling backward he tried feebly to touch the twin holes in his forehead, but failed.

He was dead before the blown-out back of his head hit the ground.

With the automatic still in his right hand, Vin Donner ran to the fallen man and looked down at him to make certain he was dead. Then he turned and with the aid of Jeff Legg, who had followed him from the shadows, helped Mark and Eve to their feet.

"You all right, Zinger?"

"I got your message," Mark said.

The brothers suddenly stepped closer and wrapped their arms around each other while Eve and Jeff looked on.

"In case you don't know," Mark said to Jeff Legg, "he sent me a message as you two approached. 'Don't look, but there's someone behind you,' he said. 'Grab Eve and dive for the ground.'" Mark turned to Eve, who had limped back to the log and was seated there. "Did you hear Vin's message?" he asked her. Not in writing this time. Mind to mind.

The shooting of Ling Gan seemed to have cleared her mind of other things, and she nodded.

Turning, Mark frowned at his brother. "Vin, why are you *here?*"

"Your letter describing the three in the restaurant, old buddy. The bearded one with the scar is Khargi."

"You mean—"

"Himself, in the flesh. We were waiting for him to turn up at the farmhouse so we could move in. But why the hell wait, I asked myself, when thanks to you we knew where to find him."

Jeff Legg had picked up the pad on which Mark and Eve had been conversing. On it he wrote, "Eve, were you taking cigarettes to Mark?"

She nodded.

Jeff turned to the others. "I think I know what's been happening here. They got to Eve and persuaded her to go to the Chinaman's shop for cigarettes and take them to Mark. Vin, do you smoke?"

"Until I learn how to quit."

"They think Mark is you. Hence the cigarettes. And this fellow here"—Jeff looked dourly at the dead man—"was to have followed her, so they'd know Mark's hiding place."

"And now?" Vin said.

"They're bound to try again. Why don't you three

stay up at the cabin until you can figure out your next move?"

Vin nodded.

"I'll go back to the factory and take care of that coffee order," Jeff said. "What's to be done with the Chinaman here?"

Vin answered that without hesitation. "He's a Devil's Disciple, one of the slimiest gang of killers that ever crawled out of hell. Leave him here for the maggots."

"Should I take Eve back with me, do you think?" Jeff asked. He looked at Eve and wrote the question on the pad for her.

She emphatically shook her head.

"I thought so." Jeff reached out to pat her hand. "Well, then, I'm gone. See you all later."

Everything would work out for the best, Mark told himself while kneeling with his back to Eve so she could lock her arms about his neck. Clamping his arms around her legs, he stood up with her, and with a nod to his brother began the walk back to the cabin.

At the cabin Iron would surely be no threat now, and Zekiel McCoy would soon be showing up with food. Zekiel could carry Iron back out. Eve's ankle would quickly mend. Yes, everything would work out.

On reaching the edge of the cabin clearing he was tired, though. Halting to get his breath, he called out to let Iron know they were coming, so the youth would not be frightened on hearing footsteps.

There was no answer.

He called again. The door was open, he saw.

Trudging on, he entered the cabin and found it unoccupied.

43

At the bridge, the bearded man with the scarred lip addressed himself to Zekiel McCoy. "How will you know when they get here? In the presence of my two friends, your partner will not be stupid enough to signal you with a bird call."

"We will hear them arrive over there."

"Above all this noise from the water?"

"Victor will know what to do, sah."

They sat to wait, McCoy close to the end of the bridge, Khargi a few feet away. Only one plank wide, the span seemed almost too fragile to support a man's weight as McCoy looked along it to the far side. It had been well constructed, though. The overlapped planks were held together with windings of tree rope as well as nails. And there was the handrail of the same vine tightly stretched between trees on either side, for a man to cling to in case he got nervous or frightened looking down.

Anyway, it had been well tested. Even the writer man, Mr. Burke, had walked it.

McCoy glanced at the man beside him. So close he

was! So easy to get the best of. *If I could just pull myself together and give him a little nudge, he would fall the whole way. The whole entirely way. Why can't I do it?*

Above the noise of the waterfalls came the sound of a boulder crashing down the cliffside.

"Them is here," McCoy said.

Scar-lip frowned, evidently suspicious. "How do you know?"

"Victor did kick that loose to tell me."

"Answer him, then."

McCoy made the call of the solitaire, then glued his gaze to the far end of the bridge and waited. In a few moments three men appeared there, with Victor Henderson in the lead.

McCoy wondered vaguely about the man beside him, thinking that if Victor Henderson saw him he would know the plan had gone awry. Never mind that the fellow was Scar-lip when he was supposed to be Mr. Yee's Chinese friend—he should be dead at this point, not standing here. McCoy alone should be here, and even he should be where Victor's pair would not see him when Victor led them to the middle of the span before racing across to safety.

How would Victor act with so much to think about all at once? He was a sawyer, and sawyers had to be quick and strong. Intelligent, too, for no stupid man would be able to fell a forest tree and roll it onto a platform to cut it into boards.

What Victor might do, knowing the plan had gone wrong—he just might turn on the two he was guiding and knock them off the cliff before they ever set foot on the bridge. It would be riskier, of course, than using the bridge the way they had planned, but it could work.

Do it, Victor, McCoy thought. Do it, man!

But Henderson was doing no such thing. In the act of walking out onto the bridge he had stopped as though confronted by a wall, and now he stood there staring.

Behind McCoy, Khargi had risen to his feet. "Henderson!" he said softly—too softly, surely, for Victor to hear. "Stay where you are. Let the others come first."

Henderson did not move except to raise his arms and press the palms of his hands against his head. McCoy could guess what had happened. More than the command had reached him across the slide. The pain had hit him, too. The terrible pain that made a man so helpless.

Apparently it was not necessary for the three strangers to do any yelling at one another. They could talk some other way, with their minds or feelings. One of them nudged Henderson aside. Then both of them stepped out onto the bridge and began to cross it.

It frightened them, even so, McCoy noted with some surprise. You could tell. Halting every few steps, they looked first at the cables of tree rope as if expecting them to break, then down at the gliding water and the explosion of spray far below. You could almost hear them asking each other, "Can this be safe?"

They were so afraid, they perhaps made the bridge less safe by staying too close together as they crossed it. This was a possibility he and Victor had considered long before, but in reverse, so to speak.

"What will we do, Victor, if them come across that bridge one at a time?"

"Well, Zekiel, I will be the first across in any case, so we can just let one come over after me and drop the bridge under the second one." Henderson's shrug indicated he did not believe it was much of a problem. "When the one who is over see the bridge go down, he is bound to be stupid with fright and easy to push off the cliff there."

But the men from Hegley had safely completed their crossing and were being embraced now by Scar-lip on McCoy's side of the span.

"You were supposed to die here," Khargi informed them, smiling. Yes, smiling.

They looked at McCoy with amusement. One was black, most likely Haitian, the other maybe from Cuba or Latin America. "We knew," the Haitian said. "Our guide began thinking about it when we were halfway here."

"And thought about nothing much else," the other said. "They are such children, these people." His gaze fell on McCoy. "And this one?"

"Also a child." Khargi shrugged. "But we have no need for them now. I know where Donner is."

"Ah?"

"We passed a cabin and he was quite desperately hoping our man might not step out where I would see him." The smile crawled under the beard again. "I can take us there."

"And these two?"

"Let me." Stepping forward, Khargi looked along

the bridge at Victor Henderson, who still stood immobilized on the other side. "You, Henderson!" he called. "Do you hear me?"

The Jamaican moved his head.

"Come to the middle of the bridge."

With no will to resist, the sawyer stepped out on the bridge and began walking. In the center of the span, directly above the swiftest flow of water, he halted.

"Wait there," Khargi ordered, then turned to McCoy. "Now you, McCoy. Walk out there and stand beside him."

They were going to cut the bridge cable, McCoy thought, just as he himself had planned to. As soon as he reached Victor's side, the machete would flash against the rope and this end of the bridge would fall, dropping the two of them onto the rocks below. But though he knew what they intended, there was nothing he could do about it.

His mouth had gone dry. For some reason that was beyond his understanding, he suddenly thought of his little granddaughter, Merlinda—how she liked to climb up on his lap and go to sleep there as if she were a kitten. Tears filled his eyes, blurring his vision. But slowly, as if they had a will of their own, his feet carried him out along the bridge to Henderson's side.

"Let go the railing, both of you," Scar-lip ordered.

They did so.

Turning to the tree to which the rope railing was fastened, Khargi swung his machete. The rope dropped from the bridge and was trapped for a moment in the fall of water. Then it whipped itself free and writhed like a wounded snake for a moment before deciding to hang motionless on the far side.

The bridge itself would hang that way, McCoy thought, when Khargi cut the cable.

He looked down, then at Henderson. With the handrail gone, there was nothing now for them to hang on to, to steady themselves as they stood there. They were two men on a narrow catwalk eighty-odd feet above the fury at the base of the cliff, with the gliding water behind them and only empty space in front.

Worse than that, McCoy was aware of something in his head—a pressure, a pounding, a *command*—that said he must stand there where he was, he and Victor, without moving, forever.

For all time. Forever!

At the end of the bridge Khargi turned to his two companions. "When fatigue overcomes them, they will fall from there," he said. "But perhaps, given our talents, we can devise a more entertaining way."

"Entertaining?" the Haitian said.

"It occurs to me that after we have finished our business with Donner, we might permit these two to have an illusion. They will be fatigued by then, and we can persuade them they are also thirsty. We might let them imagine themselves in Rainy Ridge, standing together in front of Yee's shop."

The other two looked at him expectantly.

"As I say, we can make them thirsty. And, of course, Yee sells beer. So we can allow them to think their ordeal has ended and they are free to step into his shop for a Red Stripe."

The man Mark Donner had met on the train to

Mérida laughed outright, slapping his thigh with a beefy hand. The slender Haitian only grinned and said with a chuckle, "I would like to watch them take that first happy step, if we can spare the time to come back here. It will be a tale to tell."

"Indeed it will," Khargi said. "A tale to tell in Florida, before we direct our talents at the United States."

44

Eve slept on the cabin's only bed. Vin Donner occupied the sawed section of tree trunk that served for a chair. Mark sat on the floor, legs outthrust and his back against a wall.

"How long have you had the beard, Vin?" During a rather long period of silence Mark had been staring with half-closed, angry eyes at his brother's face.

"Long time. I grew it in college."

"I thought so. I didn't have one, you know, when Graham first called on me. I was to grow one in Mexico City so I'd look *less* like you. They knew we hadn't kept in touch, and I wouldn't know."

It was Vin's turn to stare. "That's what he told you?"

"That's what he told me. 'If I'm to hide out in a Jamaican Great House,' I asked him, 'why must I spend time in Mexico?' 'To grow a beard,' he said, 'so you won't look so much like your brother.'"

"Where'd you stay in Mexico City? I mean what hotel?"

"A small one called the Guarida, off Cinco de Mayo."

"Not a block from the restaurant where I tangled with a Disciple named Kalim." Vin slowly nodded. "That's why you were sent to Mexico City, old buddy. To grow a beard and to be seen by Disciples working there."

"One of them was on the train I took to Mérida."

"And followed you to Jamaica." Vin got to his feet and began to pace. "You know now, of course, that they could have taken you in Mexico. I mean if they'd wanted you to cut your throat or step in front of a speeding car on the Reforma, you'd have done it. They held off on Khargi's orders. He wants me for himself."

"So I've been used. Just as I've thought."

"To lead them away from me while I set up our counterforce in Florida. Yes, you've been used. Without my knowledge. They told *me* they had to protect you because the Disciples were certain to zero in on you." Vin stopped pacing and swung around, his face flushed with anger. "That was how the Disciples worked, Graham said. Wanting someone who was hard to find, they'd dig deep into his background, family and all, to pick up some clue to his whereabouts. So they were certain to check you out and they'd think you were me doing the schoolteacher thing for a cover."

"If they went that deep into your background, they'd learn you had a twin brother," Mark protested.

"But not a twin who still looked so much like me.

Family records wouldn't tell them that, old boy. That schoolteacher just had to be me. Or so Graham insisted, and I guess I believed him." He shrugged. "As you know, he's a convincing bastard."

Mark rose from his seat on the floor and walked over to look at Eve on the bed. To dull the pain of her sprained ankle he had given her a generous drink of the rum McCoy had brought. Perhaps too generous a drink. She slept soundly.

He sat again, this time on the seat Vin had vacated.

"Do you suppose they somehow managed to keep the Disciples on my trail, Vin? I mean, did they just *hope* Khargi's people would spot me in Mexico, or did they supply some clues?"

"I'm sure they supplied clues," Vin said darkly. "But what clues or how they did it I wouldn't know. This was handled from Washington. I was in Florida watching the Disciples' farmhouse headquarters."

"How did *you* find out I was in Jamaica? You said in your first letter they tried to keep it from you."

Vin shrugged as though it were not important. "They sent us a man from the Washington office and I talked to him."

"And he told you?"

"Mark, old buddy, they put me in charge of Argus field work because I had certain qualifications. I told you that in a letter, didn't I? Since we were kids shooting thoughts back and forth to each other, I've worked like hell on the talent Mom willed to us. All I had to do was take the new man to lunch."

Mark looked at him.

"Funny," Vin said. "They gave me the job because I had those powers. I guess it didn't occur to them that if I got suspicious I'd use them to find out the truth about you. And you know something?"

Mark waited.

"All I wanted to know, really, was where Graham had sent you. Finding out you hadn't been told the why of it was a surprise to me. That's when I got mad."

"That was in your letter, too."

"I was tempted to phone Graham and blast him for it. I mean really blast the bastard. Then I thought no, the son of a bitch just might fire me and I'd be throwing away my last chance to help you. So I wrote to you instead."

"And?"

"And of course your reply really shook me. That route they made you take—why through *Mexico* to Jamaica? Why not direct?"

"When this is over, will you still work for Graham?"

"When this is over, I intend to pay Mr. Winston Graham a visit he won't ever forget. But it isn't over yet." Vin had been pacing again. Again he stopped. "I didn't come here just to make sure you were okay, buddy. That's a big part of it, but I also came for Khargi. Without him I could be in big trouble for persuading an Argus pilot to fly me here." Vin took in a breath that swelled his chest. "And I have to find Khargi before he finds me, buddy. Or us. But how do I go about it?"

"Be patient. McCoy is due with some food. He may know something."

"Who's McCoy?"

"He worked for me at the Great House. Don't worry. He'll be here."

But brother Vin was not that patient. Walking to the door, he paused there only long enough to turn his head and say, "Well, all right. I'll just look around while we're waiting." Then he stepped outside and was gone.

Mark looked at Eve and saw that her eyes were open. Taking up her pad, he sat on the bed and asked her in writing how she felt.

"I'll be all right," she wrote in reply. "I love you."

For ten minutes or so he just sat there holding her hand and wanting to be close to her. Then, wondering what his brother might be up to outside, he went to the cabin door to look out and found himself face-to-face with Goodwin.

45

Cold with shock, Mark faced the golden-haired man in the doorway. From the looks of him, Goodwin must have stumbled while wading the stream. He was wet to the waist. The legs of his pants dripped water.

He had a small, flat-looking gun in one hand, and his face wore a scowl that seemed molded of pale clay.

Mark walked backward to the bed and sank down beside Eve, reaching for her hand. He was numb. He could feel himself shaking. He could think of nothing to do.

Goodwin leaned in the doorway, scowling the pale clay scowl.

"I hate your guts for this," Goodwin said. His tongue slurred the words. Obviously he had been drinking again, though the hand holding the weapon was steady enough. "If you'd done what you were told to do, goddamn it, I wouldn't have to be here."

Mark waited, seeking something helpful to say.

"All you had to do was clear out of here," Goodwin said. "Go to South America."

"So they would follow me and leave Vin free to do his job?"

"You finally figured it out. Christ."

"I don't suppose I've got everything straight yet, but I know enough, I think. Iron was here, telling me you sent him to kill me."

"So the clod came, did he?" Water from Goodwin's shoes had formed a puddle on the floor and he stepped out of it, rubbing the back of his free hand against his mouth.

"There's something you don't know, Goodwin. My brother is here."

"What?"

"Vin is here. Not just in Jamaica, but here at the cabin. Now, do you still want to murder me?"

"My God," Goodwin said.

"I suppose you were told to kill me, or have me killed, because I refused to go on playing your game of hare and hounds. That's it, isn't it? If the Disciples took me, they'd find out I'm not Vin. So you planned to dispose of me in the bush here, in such a way they'd never find me. Then they'd think I'd eluded them and would continue looking for me, leaving Vin free to function. That *is* it, isn't it?"

"Jesus," Goodwin said. "What's Vin here for?"

"Khargi is here."

"What?"

"Your people haven't been too smart, Goodwin. They set me up so the Disciples would think me Vin and follow me here. That would leave Vin to concentrate on the Florida farmhouse, ready to take the place when Khargi turned up there. But Khargi won't be making any move in the States until Vin is disposed of, and he wants to do the disposing himself. In person."

Goodwin looked bewildered. Perhaps he *had* drunk too much, and with this unexpected twist of events the liquor was taking effect. But he was not letting his guard down. The gun still stared at Mark.

"There's more," Mark said. Anything to maintain a stalemate until Vin returned. "The Chinaman in Rainy Ridge, Mr. Yee, is growing ganja up here."

"What?"

"Those tools in the corner there are not the kind sawyers use; they're for farming. Or wouldn't you know?" He had not known, himself, he thought wryly, the day Eve and he first saw them. But Eve had sensed something wrong here and gone to the tools to examine them. He should have asked her about it when they returned to the house, but had attributed her change of mood to some wrong move *he* must have made.

Anyway, the purpose of the farming tools had become obvious after his talk with Iron about the ganja growing.

"To hell with that," Goodwin said thickly. "It doesn't concern me."

"Yee is not one of your hirelings?"

"Are you crazy? If anything, he's one of theirs. But I don't believe that, either. I think he took in that other guy just because they're both the same breed."

Mark turned his head to look at Eve. She had heard nothing, of course, but could see the gun in Goodwin's hand aimed at the man she loved, and perhaps sensed the tension in their talk. Her eyes were wide. Her face wore a tension of its own.

"You don't know what to do now, do you?" Mark said. "You didn't want to kill me, anyway. You haven't liked this job from the beginning."

Goodwin's reply was a snarl. "Somebody has to do these things, for Christ's sake!"

"You're wrong. If nobody did them, we wouldn't—"

"Will you *wake up*, you dumb bastard?" In his anger the yellow-haired man took a lurching step forward. "Don't you know what these bloody Disciples have been *doing* all over the world?"

"What have they been doing?" That should buy a little more time, but where, oh God, was Vin? Why didn't he come?

"Listen to me!" Goodwin was livid now. "Khargi's people have been slaughtering innocents as if they were cattle. In England, India, Italy, France, even in a couple of no-account countries that did nothing but call Aram Sel a murderer—Jesus Christ, man, it's been total carnage. Because Sel is crazy, he's mad, he's a total weirdo with an insane grudge because civilization has blackballed him from the club. Don't you *see*, for God's sake? He has to be stopped, no matter how we do it!"

The man was right, of course. If what Vin had been saying was true—and of course, it *was* true—then all the talk in the world wouldn't help, would it? And the Argus people were justified in doing almost anything they could to put an end to it.

Mark looked at the man from Kingston with new understanding, almost forgiveness. Goodwin, really drunk now with emotion, had sucked in a deep, noisy breath and begun shaking. His whole body was shaking.

Would he use the gun, even knowing Vin was here somewhere? He was capable of it. Perhaps he had already forgotten Vin was here. He was even capable of killing Eve.

What to do? *If I get up off the bed and try to take the gun away from him, I'm sure to fail. But if I don't even try . . .*

Mark turned his head to look at Eve one more time, and as he did so, realized there was now someone in the cabin doorway. Behind the man with the gun was—no, not Vin, but the boy called Iron, slowly rising from a crouch with a massive chunk of firewood upraised in two powerful hands.

Mark watched, fascinated, as the boy took a forward step on bare feet and brought the length of wood down on the back of Goodwin's head. He saw the wood shatter into two pieces and felt himself wince as one piece flew halfway across the cabin.

Falling forward onto his knees, the Argus man sprawled full length on the floor.

Iron limped forward and stood gazing down at him. The bandage on the injured leg was still in place, dark with blood now, but obviously the wound had not disabled him. He wasn't called Iron for nothing. "I did hear him coming through the bush, sah," he said. "We is even now, you and me?" He picked up Goodwin's gun and handed it to Mark.

"Yes, we're even, Iron. Thank you."

"I glad. You know why I come back?"

"Why did you come back?"

"'Cause I did forget to tell you it was me put that lizard on you door and done them other things at Shepstowe. Mr. Yee did pay me to do them." Turning, he peered at the man on the floor. "You goin' kill him now?"

All through the long talk with Goodwin, Mark had been cold and trembling. The trembling had stopped now. His little conversation with Iron had drawn him back out of the nightmare. Gazing at the boy, he shook his head.

"But he was goin' kill you!" Iron protested.

"Maybe. That's what he came for. But I'm not sure he would have done it."

Goodwin, moaning in pain, pushed himself up to a sitting position and looked at them both. "For God's sake give me a drink," he begged.

Mark handed him the rum bottle. He tipped it to his mouth, drank, then closed his eyes and let the liquor take effect. When he opened them, he looked at Mark and said, "Well, what now?"

"Iron wants me to kill you."

"I heard him."

"All I want, Goodwin, is to walk out of here with Eve and marry her and go home—back to teaching school in Connecticut. Do you think I could do those things if I killed you? Even if Iron buried you up here somewhere, the way you planned to dispose of me?"

"So you're letting me go." Struggling to his feet, Goodwin swayed from the effects of the blow and the rum. "Christ, you're crazier than Iron here; you know that?"

"I didn't say I was letting you go. Iron, is there some rope around here?"

"I can find some tree rope, sah."

"Will it hold him?"

"Like how it would hold a hog, squire."

"Get some, please. And you, Goodwin"—Mark gestured with the gun—"sit down. Sit, damn it, and shut up before I lose my head."

Staring at him, the Argus man saw something in Mark's face that made him decide to obey very quickly.

They waited. In a few minutes Iron returned with a length of the tough brown vine called tree rope.

"Tie him so you can walk him out of here," Mark instructed. "I want you to take him to Mr. Legg at the coffee works. I'll give you a note. Goodwin, turn around."

Goodwin sullenly obeyed.

While Iron was binding the man's wrists, Mark reached for Eve's pad. Shifting the gun to his left hand, he wrote, "Jeff, this man Goodwin came to the cabin to kill me. We can't keep him here—too risky.

Please hold him until Vin and I are able to come out and deal with him." Tearing off the sheet of paper, he handed it to Iron.

Iron thrust it into a ragged pants pocket and said, "For Busha. Yes, sah."

"Don't let this man give you any trouble, Iron. If he tries to, knock him cold and carry him. Understand?"

"Yes, sah. Me purely understand!"

"And Goodwin, if you do make trouble for him, I hope he knocks your brains out." Mark's voice had become sandpaper. "When I think of what you and your people have done to me—and to Eve, damn you—I wouldn't shed a tear if he killed you."

Goodwin's head drooped, but he stayed silent.

Mark still held the gun. Feeling a sudden warmth in the fingers of his other hand, he looked down and saw that Eve had taken that hand in both of hers and was pressing it to her face. Had her mind picked up his words to Goodwin? He had a feeling it had, and that she was proud of him.

"I can go now, sah?" Iron said.

"Yes. But remember, be careful. He'll turn on you if you let him."

"I should take the rifle Marse Legg did lend you?"

Oh Lord, Mark thought, the rifle. It was still up there by the felled tree, above the track to Three River Mouth, where he had left it while watching the mongooses. Again he had neglected to go after it.

"Iron, I don't have the rifle. Not here."

The boy shrugged. "Is no problem. I did carry a live hog home from here once. This man not goin' give me a hard time."

"I'll see you later with a reward, then."

"With what, sah?"

"I'll be paying you for this, Iron. Paying you well."

"Sah, you already paid me well, fixing me up when the trap catch me, and not turning me in to the police." Bending to pick up a piece of the club he had already used on the Argus man, Iron gave Goodwin a shove that sent him stumbling out the doorway. Then with a solemn wave of farewell the boy went limping out after him.

46

Mark stood in the cabin doorway and watched the two men depart. Had he done the right thing in trusting Iron to take Goodwin to the factory? He thought he had. It would get both of them out of here at a time when he and Vin ought to sit down and talk about what to do next.

Because they must do more than stay here in hiding. Sooner or later the Disciples would find out about the cabin. Especially if one of them was Khargi.

He watched Goodwin and Iron go down along the stream's edge to the pools, where they disappeared with the Argus man plodding like a zombie and the

Jamaican only a yard behind. I could have given the boy Goodwin's gun, Mark thought, but at once realized it would have been a dangerous move. Iron was still not bright, despite his demonstration of gratitude. With such a weapon in his hand he just might decide, after all, that Goodwin deserved to be killed.

The cabin clearing seemed a peaceful place again. For a while Mark stood in the doorway, letting the silence soothe his nerves. Then he went back to sit beside Eve on the bed.

"How do you feel?" he asked her on the pad.

"Much better. Shall we talk about what just happened, or should I try to walk?"

"Can you walk, do you think?"

"I believe so. Help me up."

He lifted her to her feet and was helping her to walk about the cabin, delighted to discover she had recovered so quickly, when Vin reappeared. Looking tired, his brother sank onto the tree section that served as a chair.

"This place is a trap, old buddy. We've got to get the hell out of here."

Mark led Eve back to the bed. "As soon as McCoy comes. We'll need help with Eve for a hike that long."

Vin saw the automatic on the foot of the bed and leaned forward to reach for it. "Where'd you get this?"

"Goodwin was here."

"What?"

Mark filled him in on Goodwin's visit, the reason for it, and its outcome. The silence seemed to last a long time. Then Vin said in a voice of controlled but savage fury, "The bastards. So after setting you up as bait, those desk heroes in Washington would have had you killed to make Khargi's people think you'd given them the slip."

He glared at the weapon as though longing to use it on the men he was talking about. Then from his pocket he took out the weapon he had killed the Chinese with. "We need something better than these if they come for us here, old buddy. Didn't you say Legg lent you a rifle?"

Mark nodded.

"Where is it?"

"Across the river, up on the cliff."

"What?"

"I'm sorry. I'm a schoolteacher, remember? I carried it with me when I went up for berries." Never mind the mongooses, Mark thought; Vin wouldn't understand. "Then I forgot it when I came down." He glanced at the door. "I can go for it now if you think I should."

"Go for it. If Khargi and those others find out we're here and come for us, we'll need something more than these short-range flyswatters."

Mark penciled a note on Eve's pad, telling her where he was going, and walked out of the cabin. The clearing still seemed too peaceful for what was happening here. The gentle warmth in the air, the ever-changing voice of the stream—none of what had taken place here, or was now taking place, seemed real. So why was he suddenly as tense again as when he had first confronted Goodwin in the cabin doorway?

At the clearing's edge he looked down toward the

pools, where Goodwin and Iron had disappeared, then up at the track that stretched like a scar across the side of the gorge in front of him. One part of his mind remembered baby mongooses at play—tiny ferretlike clowns as lively as kittens. Another part recalled the physical effort of climbing up there to get to them.

Should he go down to the pools and follow the track up from there? It would be easier because the ascent was much more gradual. But it would take too long. Vin wanted the rifle now.

Wading the boulder-strewn stream, with its swift water at times swirling about his knees, he reached the opposite bank and began the climb. There was a difference between now and the last time, though. He hadn't been this tense or afraid before, hadn't known one of the men seeking him was the infamous Khargi. His objective had been simply the gathering of food and the pleasure of watching young wild animals at play.

There was no track here, of course. The track to Three River Mouth began at the pools. Here you faced the cliff itself, irregular, crumbly in places, jaggedly sharp in others. You climbed by grabbing at scraggly small trees or bushes that literally grew out of rock. You zigzagged along switchbacks that could have been taken for wild-pig runs had they been more level. Nothing to equate with climbing the side of a tall building, of course, or schoolteacher Mark Donner would not be attempting it. Still, when you paused and looked down on the rocky streambed, you knew what a fall could mean.

On reaching the track that ran to Three River

Mouth he paused for another such downward look and saw Eve standing outside the cabin, watching him. Brother Vin stood just behind her in the doorway. He waved. They waved back.

Now the worst of the climb was behind him. Above the track the mountainside had been cleared of brush by the sawyers who had felled the tree that was his destination. And, yes, the rifle was where he had so thoughtlessly left it, leaning against the far end of the limbed log.

Winded, he sat on the log to rest for a moment, and as before, it moved slightly. No doubt if the sawyers returned for it, they would simply build a platform just below here and roll the log down onto it. He remembered it had stirred a little when he first sat on it to watch the mongooses, and thinking it might roll on down the slope, he had quickly jumped up. But the movement had been a false alarm.

Just give me a minute to get my breath, Vin old boy, he thought. Then I'll get the gun and start back down.

At the cabin, Vin and Eve had gone back inside, Eve to sit on the bed, Vin to pace. They couldn't stay here, Vin told himself again. If attacked, how would they get out?

The sawyers must have built the cabin here for two reasons. One, it was close to the stream and they would need water. Two, the site was already a natural forest clearing; they wouldn't have to create one. But, being men used to a rough life in the bush, they hadn't bothered to cut a track from the pools up this side of the stream. They had simply waded up here through the shallows.

And that, for God's sake, was how he and Mark and Eve would have to get out if discovered by the Disciples. Not up the cliff the way Mark had just gone; to attempt that in a hurry would be suicidal. They would have to go downstream to the pools and pick up the track to the coffee works, which Khargi and his people would already have zeroed in on.

Got to get out, Vin thought. Just as soon as Mark comes with the rifle. Got to leave at once. If we get trapped here, we're fish in a tank.

For some reason his head was hurting. Still pacing, he raised a hand to rub the furrows above his eyes caused by a sudden expression of alarm. Into his mind, wiping away what he had been thinking about, flashed a scene from the past.

He was in a Mexico City police station, confronting a Disciple he had just picked up at a restaurant where the bastard had tried to poison food at a salad bar. At last we've got one of the creeps, he was thinking. At last we've nailed one we can put the screws to, to find out who the rest of them are and how they operate. But the man was staring at him in a special way, and his head was aching.

"Turn around, Donner," the man was saying. His name was Kalim, wasn't it? Yes. Kalim. "Turn around and pick up the lieutenant's gun." He meant the Mexican at the desk there. And then he said—perhaps not aloud, but he said it and Vin's mind received it—"When I am gone, you will give me five minutes to be safely out of the building, and then you will use that weapon on yourself, Mr. Donner. *On yourself.* Do you understand?"

Somehow he had found a way not to obey, hadn't he? But the torment that had built up inside his head that day in Mexico was back now. His eyes felt like red-hot coals. There was a chain-saw whine in his ears. His whole head felt about to explode.

"Come out of the cabin, Donner," a voice was telling him. "Come out of the cabin, Argus man. Let me have a look at you."

Stricken, Vin turned to Eve with his arms outstretched. If only she could hear! If only he could get through to her and tell her what was happening!

But she seemed to know. Seated there on the bed, she was rigid now and staring at the doorway, seemingly ready to spring to her feet. *Was* she aware of the command? Mark had said he was able to converse with her mentally at times. They had been working on it.

"Come out, Donner. Let me have a look at you before I decide what to do with you. You are very special to me, Argus man." The voice in his head was louder now. It was a siren on a police car speeding toward him. When it got close enough, the pressure would crack his skull and splash his brains over the cabin walls.

But he had certain powers himself, didn't he? Of course he did. That was why he had escaped in Mexico. It was why the Chief had chosen him for this job in the first place.

Use your talent, Donner, for Christ's sake. Fight back!

He had stopped pacing moments ago when the agony first hit him. Now he stumbled to the bed and sank down on it beside Eve, closing his eyes and pressing both hands to the sides of his head. In a struggle for mind control such as this, the thing to do first was to block the enemy's intrusion into your thoughts with a counterthrust. It was like being locked in a physical shoving match, calling on every ounce of your strength to stop being forced back, then to gain control and make your adversary retreat.

"Goddamn you, Khargi, get out of my head!"

"It won't work, Donner. Come out and face me."

"Get out of my head, you murdering bastard!"

"You're wasting my time, Donner. What makes you think you can resist me when you were barely able to resist one of my pupils in that Mexican police station?" The voice was all derision now. A total sneer. "Stop being childish, Donner. Come out where I can see you and gloat a little."

Vin felt himself shaking. It had begun with his hands and traveled up his arms. Now his whole body was shaking; even his feet performed a weird kind of shuffle on the cabin's dirt floor. Try as he would to block the voice in his head, it would not be denied. It was agony even to think thoughts of his own as he called on the last whimper of his will to continue the struggle.

He became aware then that Eve was watching him. Her eyes wide with understanding, she had reached out to clasp his left hand in both of hers, as though to add her strength to what remained of his. But it was not working. Khargi was right. If he had almost failed in Mexico with a mere pupil, how could he hope to succeed here against the grand master?

In despair he stopped staring at the doorway and

turned to Eve. "I can't handle it," he moaned, forgetting she could not hear. "He knows I can't and he's just prolonging it for his own pleasure. Oh God, Eve—where's Mark with that rifle? Why doesn't he come?"

The answer could not come from Eve, of course. But as if he had screamed the words through a megaphone, a reply did come at once from his tormentor.

"For my own pleasure, Donner? Why not? But it's time to end our little game now, isn't it? I am looking down on you from the track to Three River Mouth, Argus man. Come out and face me while I decide on the most suitable way to handle you."

Donner rose like a sleepwalker from the bed and shuffled to the doorway. It was true. Over the river, up on the track that snaked across the cliff, three men stood side by side in bright sunlight gazing down at him. They were not close enough for him to make out many details, but he could see that only one of them, the one in the middle, wore a beard.

Hearing a movement behind him, he turned his head. Eve was there, pushing him aside so she could get past him. As she stepped through the doorway she touched his hand. Then she stood squarely in front of him, blocking his exit from the cabin as she looked up at the three figures on the track.

Or was she looking above the three Disciples at a fourth figure higher up on the cliff?

47

Mark was sitting on the felled tree, ready to go to the other end of it for the rifle and begin his return to the cabin, when the three men came into view on the track below. They came single file from the direction of Three River Mouth.

They were the three who had sought to identify him in the Kingston restaurant, the three Eve had saved him from turning to face. In the lead was the black man from Haiti, next the bearded one he now knew was the mastermind of all the Disciples, Khargi, and then the former priest from South America.

Fearing they would look up and see him, he flattened himself behind the log. And again the log threatened to roll as he pressed himself against it.

Did the three men know Eve and Vin were in the cabin? Perhaps not, and perhaps they would not think it worth their while to investigate. Descending the cliff from there would not be easy.

What had they been doing up at Three River Mouth, anyway? Had they come up the other side of the mountain and across the bridge, by the route McCoy had planned for him to use if trapped here?

He watched them. They had halted now and were standing close together—touching, actually—as they looked down on the cabin clearing. Please, dear God, don't let Eve or Vin come out of the cabin right now! Let these monsters think the place deserted!

But if they thought the cabin deserted, why were they standing there so long? Why so motionless? Why were the Haitian and the Brazilian now looking at Khargi while Khargi alone stared down at the cabin?

"Move on, damn you!" Mark silently begged. "Don't stand there forever! Move!" Flat on the ground behind the felled and limbed tree, he was trying so hard not to slide down on the tree that his whole body ached. If he were to start it rolling now, even if it rolled only a few inches, the men below might hear and look up. To make an awkward situation worse, his right foot had apparently disturbed a nest of the ferocious little ants Jamaicans called "pity-me-likkle," meaning "it's too bad we're not bigger so we could eat you alive."

The little horrors were swarming up his leg, biting as they marched. It was like being jabbed with hot needles.

And *still* the three men had not moved. Did they know Vin was there in the cabin? Was Khargi commanding him mentally to come out?

Suddenly he saw a movement in the cabin doorway and, yes, Vin was standing there. Just standing there in the opening, looking up at the three on the track. Like a statue, or a man mesmerized. Helpless.

So Khargi *had* been using his telepathic powers. Those fabled powers that even the Russians were said to envy.

The rifle, Mark thought. If I can reach it without drawing their attention.

To get to it he would have to crawl the whole length of the log, which must be all of sixty feet long. And if he happened to lean against it while crawling, he might start it rolling.

But what else could he do? The rifle was the only answer. It held enough shots if he could make them count. But could he, firing it for the first time ever?

He drew his legs up to begin the crawl, one of them so afire with ant bites now that he wanted to turn on the beasts and slap them dead. Then he saw another movement in the cabin doorway.

Brother Vin had been pushed aside. Eve stepped into the yard and planted herself in front of him.

Looking up at the men on the track, she clamped her hands on her hips in an attitude of defiance. That she couldn't talk did not matter. Her stance alone was a challenge that clearly said, "What do you want, you men? What are you doing here?"

But the real message, the mental message, was for Mark.

"Mark, you must save your brother! Shoot them!"

Never before had he received a thought from her so sharply. It was cleaner than speech itself. The words rang in his head as though formed of crystal. "Mark, you must save your brother! Shoot them!"

But the Disciples had received it, too. As one, they turned to look up at him. He would never reach the rifle.

A shooting star stabbed his head and exploded in his brain. *You! Stay where you are!* But one burst of agony was not enough. Not with Eve and Vin down there depending on him for their lives.

The tree. Up to now it had been a thing that might betray his presence. Now suddenly it was a weapon.

With the torment swelling in his head, he twisted his body around on the slope and got his feet against the log, his knees high, his hands gripping the ground to give him leverage. He sucked in a breath. Sent up a prayer. Pushed both legs out straight with every ounce of force he could muster.

It was almost too easy. The tree had been wanting to roll from the beginning. Now the thrust sent it thundering down the slope like a gigantic rolling pin. And with all their mental powers, the three men in its path were as helpless to stop it as three of the pity-me-likkles biting Mark's leg.

They tried to leap clear. Khargi himself even tried to leap *up* so the implacable projectile would pass under him. It didn't work. The tree sent Khargi flying even higher while crushing the other two into heaps of blood and bone. It rolled on down to the stream and fell with a crash among the boulders.

Khargi floated down after it like a wounded buzzard, to land on it facedown and lie there with his arms and legs draped over it. And was still lying there unconscious when Vin Donner reached him from the cabin and Mark from the cliff.

They touched hands over Khargi's limp form. "You know something, old buddy?" Vin said. "We owe you, Eve and I. The whole world owes you. But I've got something for this bastard. Wait."

He went to the cabin for his jacket. From one of its pockets he took a book of paper matches. One "match" that he carefully removed was a thin vial of colorless liquid. Another was a small hypodermic syringe.

He filled the syringe and shot the liquid into Khargi's arm. Khargi felt nothing; the tree had done its job. The serum would keep him unconscious, incapable of using the envied mind, Vin said, for at least forty-eight hours.

"And there's more here if we need it. We'll just take him to Washington, drugged, on the Argus plane waiting here at the airport." He stepped back, still scowling down at the man draped over the tree in the stream. "And believe me, buddy, before we're through with this bastard we'll know the names of all his people, where they are, and what they're up to, even though without him I don't think there'll be much of an organization left. And we'll have enough on Aram Sel to turn the world against *him*, no matter if he's swimming in his bloody oil. Yes, by God, there are drugs to make even a Khargi talk."

The words were those of a tormented man still shaken by what had been done to him, Mark realized. Getting them out of his torn mind was a kind of therapy. More followed, but Mark had stopped listening.

He had Eve in his arms now, both of them still knee-deep in the stream where brother Vin, wiser than before, had just made sure that what had happened in Mexico City would not happen again.

Once more this special little part of the Blue Mountains of Jamaica seemed beautiful and blessed.

Standing on the flimsy footbridge at Three River Mouth, with the water gliding down behind him to crash among the rocks below, Zekiel McCoy suddenly because aware that his mind was his own again and was telling him something.

Was telling him—hallelujah!—that he was no longer under any compulsion to continue standing there.

He felt as though his brain had been freed from the grip of a ganja binge and his body from a ghastly paralysis. Turning, he peered at his co-conspirator, Victor Henderson, and saw a hallelujah kind of expression on Victor's face as well.

"You, too?"

Henderson looked down and shuddered. "But we still out here on this thing without a handrail to hang on to, and God help us if we don't careful. Come on now, Zekiel, but come real slow."

At the cabin clearing they found Mark and Vin Donner discussing how to dispose of two dead Disciples and transport a live one out of the wilderness. McCoy solved the problem with typical peasant directness.

"Victor and me can bury those two." He pointed to the crushed bodies on the cliff track, which he and Henderson had stopped to examine en route to the cabin. "Him"—pointing to the drugged man at the stream's edge—"we can easy carry out for you."

"While you're at it," Vin said, "there's a dead Chinese down the line who probably ought to be buried, too. We can take care of him on our way out."

"What about Goodwin?" Mark asked.

Vin gave it some thought, then shrugged. "Well, he was really only following orders, wasn't he, so the quarrel there is with Graham or the Chief. And even that will have to wait, now that we've got Khargi and can move on the situation in Florida. I think I'll enlist brother Goodwin to help with our embassy people and the government here in getting Khargi out of Jamaica. He should be eager to cooperate."

Mark turned for a last look at the cabin where, despite everything, he had spent enough serene moments to have some happy memories. The one that came most readily to mind was his reading of Eve's love letter.

When they began the walk out half an hour later, he held on to her hand and realized she was writing him another, this time with her mind.

48

The Christmas tree still stood in the Great House drawing room. The Leggs were there. Eve wore on her yellow dress the golden circle Mark had bought for her in Kingston.

My love, like this circle, shall have no ending.

She wore it proudly, along with a band of gold on the third finger of her left hand. Mark drew her into his arms and gently kissed her, then put his face against hers and simply stood there holding her.

They had been married only a short time before in the Morant Bay church attended by the Leggs.

Jeff Legg said with a smile, "It's all settled about Shepstowe, then, is it? You'll be staying until your year's leave from teaching is up?"

"We'll be staying," Mark said. Eve and he had discussed the matter at length, and it was her belief as well as his that they should finish the year at the Great House.

Goodwin, back in Jamaica and attending the wedding, had brought a message from Vin. "At that farmhouse in Florida," Goodwin said, "they took a page right out of the Disciples' own book. First they painted the name and logo of a well-known TV repair company on a van loaded with explosives. Then your brother drove the thing right up alongside the house and broke the hundred-yard-dash record getting clear while one of his men blew it up by remote control. End of farmhouse and every son-of-Khargi in it. You should be proud."

"I am proud."

"Oh, and he said to tell you one thing more. After he's rearranged a few teeth in Washington he'll be quitting Argus and returning to California for a job in Silicon Valley. And he wishes Eve and you a long, loving life."

Mark nodded.

As for Yee and his ganja growing, the shop in Rainy Ridge was closed now and its proprietor was in jail awaiting trial. It had been, the police said, one of the biggest operations of its kind in Jamaica's long history of ganja production—more than enough reason for Yee to have attempted murder to protect it.

And it would be a long time, Mark felt, before the people of the district allowed themselves to be used again in such a way. Some of them, even McCoy's Roselda, had already come to the Great House to say they were ashamed.

"Well, then," Mildred Legg said, "we'll run along home now, Mark. Let me have that pad of paper for a minute, will you?"

He handed it to her with a smile of anticipation, then stood before her with Eve at his side and watched her write on it. When she had finished, she turned the pad so they could read what she had written.

"You have our love and blessings, both of you. May you always be the kind of people you are."

"Amen," Jeff said.

About the Author

Hugh B. Cave's more than twenty years in the Caribbean, studying the islands, their people, and their diverse cultures, have influenced much of his fiction, especially his *vodun* novels, which chillingly combine fact and fiction to produce true horror.

Cave has published four highly-praised non-fiction books about the islands of Jamaica and Haiti. In addition, he has written over 350 short stories and many novels, including *The Cross on the Drum, The Evil, Shades of Evil, The Nebulon Horror,* and *Legion of the Dead*. In 1977 Cave won the World Fantasy Award for *Murgunstrumm and Others*.

Cave and his wife, Peggy, for many years residents of Sebastian, Florida, moved early in 1988 to Oak Harbor, Washington.

THE BEST IN HORROR